Vamped: The Turning

by

Chris Holmes

A Paranormalice Press Book
1201 Scottsdale Drive
Ormond Beach, FL 32174

www.paranormalicepress.com

Vamped: The Turning

Chapter 1

The Black Swan—an event or occurrence that deviates beyond what is normally expected of a situation and is extremely difficult to predict.

A narrow panel in the door, eye-height, slid open. I held up the printed ticket I had purchased online. Unseen eyes studied it and, I assumed, studied me as well. Though I couldn't discern the eyes through the dark narrow slit, I felt their intense scrutiny. A slow chill crept down my back and the slip of paper trembled in my hand. The panel closed. I pushed my eyeglasses up on my nose.

I waited.

A series of clicks, the sound of a heavy bolt sliding, and then the thick steel door opened inward. A broad-shouldered man with a shaven head grunted as he motioned me inside. He snatched the ticket, stamped a small black swan on the back of my left hand, and jerked his thumb in the direction of a dim corridor. With the interior as dark as the moonless night outside, my eyes adjusted quickly, and I followed a path of tiny recessed blue lights along the floor.

The hallway opened into a large room that thrummed with

people—talking, drinking, smoking, and dancing. Smoke hovered overhead like hazy gray ghosts trapped in the cramped realm between the patrons' heads and low ceiling. Blasts of air-conditioning chilled the space and intermingled the odors of perfume, alcohol, and cigarettes.

I headed for the oval-shaped bar that dominated the center of the room. To my right, past the dance floor, the band played on an elevated stage, their name, *Night Train,* scrawled in black script across the base drumhead. Lorelei, the undisputed queen of vampire rockers, buoyed my hopes. She was the reason I had driven over an hour to the secret club. Her wild platinum hair matched her pearly complexion and she moved to the music with the stealthy grace of a panther in a black leather halter and skin-tight pants.

Unlike Lorelei, the crowd gyrating to the heavy metal music disappointed me. They wore Goth-style clothing and most sported ink-black hair streaked with red, purple, or blue. Their pale faces and black-outlined eyes expressed little interest in me as I walked past. Dressed in a black T-shirt and skinny-legged jeans, with my naturally pale completion and thin build—or to use my father's favorite adjective, puny build—I blended in with the clientele.

My heart sank a bit more as I climbed onto a blue vinyl bar stool flecked with glitter. A female bartender in a lacy bodice poured a frothy red beverage from a stainless-steel shaker into two tall glasses. She garnished the drinks with cherries and sank a black straw into each glass. Laminated tent cards lined the bar top and advertised specialty drinks with ridiculous names—Bloody Magpies, Draquiris, Fanghattans, and Sanguintinis.

I ordered a bottled apple ale. Another barmaid, her eyelids caked with shimmery purple, set the bottle down with a smile as fake as her eyelashes.

"Something wrong?" she asked.

Shaking my head no, I pushed a ten dollar bill across the lacquered bar top. Inwardly, the masquerade sickened me. The Black Swan was purported to be a haven where real vampires gathered, or so their website claimed. Yet, as I scanned the room surrounded by costumed wannabes, my expectations deflated. This place looked no different than the numerous other vampire clubs I'd visited.

I swiveled around on the stool and drank my ale, impressed by the size of the club. Its entrance, hidden below street level, belied the square footage inside. The space equaled about half of the huge building above, and as expected on a Saturday night, the industrial park outside appeared deserted from the road, unless of course, you knew where to look.

Steps away from me, patrons danced while Night Train's amplifiers rattled the pock-marked acoustic tiles above my head. Bursts of flames shot from the border of the stage in unison with ear-splitting shrieks of electric guitars. The song ended in a barrage of bashing cymbals, then a red velvet curtain dropped over the stage. The band took a break.

The members, four males and Lorelei, exited from a dark stairway to the left of the stage and converged around the bar. She settled on the stool next to mine. Her shocking, silvery-white hair stood out among the mass of mostly raven-haired men and women. It shone blue, red, and green as the lights above the bar flickered through their colored repertoire. I tried not to stare at her breasts, perfect pale globes barely reined in by her low-cut top.

The bartender pulled a decanter from underneath the bar and poured a dark crimson liquid into a wine glass. Lorelei clasped the glass with two hands and drank without stopping to take a breath. She tilted the stem upward until the last drop drizzled into her mouth. A red, viscous coating tinted the inside of the glass.

As she swallowed, the movement in her slender, paper-white neck mesmerized me. Her gaze turned to me as she set the empty glass on the bar, her electric blue eyes as startling as the rest of her. Perhaps a trick of the strobe lights, her pupils swelled, covering her irises in a moist black. Thin, spidery veins of black bled into the whites of her eyes. I blinked. The brilliant blue irises and whites had returned. She ran her forefinger around the inside of the glass and then stared at me as she sucked the red liquid clinging to her fingertip.

"Why are you here?" Her voice, barely a whisper and her warm breath tickled my ear even though she sat two feet away. A coppery scent wafted beneath my nostrils.

"I want to be transformed."

Her laughter exploded inside my head like particles of glass cascading onto a sheet of tin. She flicked her hand and dismissed me. "You and everyone else."

"No." Urgency welled inside me. I had to convince her. "No. I'm not like them. I'm a true believer. I'm ready to join the Night Flock."

"You are naive." She swept back her long mane of hair and stood. The male band members gathered around her forming a protective entourage of leather-clad muscle. They walked toward the short flight of stairs leading up to the stage.

I leaped to my feet, raced after her and pushed through a slice of space between two of the male musicians. As my fingers grasped her slim wrist, I was shocked by the chilly firmness of her flesh.

Strong hands immediately gripped my shoulders and arms.

Lorelei whirled and faced me, eyes ablaze. Her snarl revealed pointed teeth.

"Please," I said. "You have the power to transform me. I want it. I need it."

She waved and the men released me. My bones felt as fragile as a sparrow's in her grasp as she plucked my hand from her wrist. "This is our last set. Stick around." Her full smile showed dazzling white teeth with elongated canines, but whether it held mirth or malevolence, I couldn't quite tell.

An instant later, she stood with the four men on the stage, their ascent up the stairs a blur and her voice still echoing in my ears. As the band warmed up with random keyboard riffs and guitar chords, a mass of black-garbed bodies drifted from the bar and surrounding tables and gathered on the dance floor in front of the stage. Their anticipation jelled into a palpable presence.

I ordered another ale. Taking advantage of the crowd's exodus, I moved to an abandoned table next to the stage. Though I didn't much care for it, heavy metal music embodied the soul of these clubs. Loud, raucous, edgy—it created an audio backdrop of lust, rage, and violence, the same sentiment the patrons attempted to project, though not always achieved, with their sinister make-up and dress.

I sat on the edge of my chair watching Lorelei, my pulse racing

4

from the memory of her touch. More impressive in person than in her online photos, her icy eyes, white face and hair gave off a ghostly aura beneath the bright stage lights. She swung the microphone stand one-handed and belted out lyrics in an impossible range from a deep, throaty growl that made my scalp crawl to stark, piercing screams that pained my ear drums.

Halfway through their set, a tap on my shoulder jolted me from the scene on stage. With the music booming, a young woman mouthed something and motioned to an empty chair at my table.

I nodded automatically. Was she asking to sit with me or just wanted to sit near the stage? She hadn't looked at me the way girls usually did, with a mixture of annoyance and disgust, the same way they might look at ants crawling in their potato salad at a picnic.

Something about her demeanor distracted me. She wasn't a beauty. Neat and clean, my mother's words, came to mind. She had shoulder-length, light brown hair and a tan complexion, both unusual in this setting. Her white tank top and faded blue jeans didn't fit in either. Her eyes sparkled when she looked at me, though I couldn't tell in the dark club if they were blue or green. The fleeting thought she might be interested in me passed as she turned her chair to face the stage. She sat with her back to me. No drink. No purse. Just sat with shoulders squared, back straight, and watched the band.

Even as Lorelei fascinated me, a dull ache grew in my temples. The constant, driving drumbeat interspersed with raging electric guitar and keyboard solos wore on my nerves. Jets of freezing air from ceiling vents billowed cigarette smoke into my face. I removed my glasses and rubbed my eyes. My fingers, cold and wet from holding the sweating bottle of ale, soothed the irritation. Disappointment churned with the alcohol in my gut. A lightweight, two drinks were my limit. Besides Lorelei, this club offered nothing I hadn't seen a hundred times before. I should go—to hell with the one hundred and seventy-five dollars I'd paid for admission.

As I stood to leave, the music stopped. The lights went out and submerged the band and the crowded room in velvety blackness. A drumbeat began, a slow, steady thump-thump that mimicked a heartbeat.

The rowdy patrons hushed, save for the barely audible sound of their collective breathing. The darkness ebbed and swelled, as if it too, breathed. I sank back into my chair, my heartbeat matching the deep bass beat of the drum. Something was about to happen, but what? Anticipation held me in a state of rapture. Lorelei had said to stick around.

A lone blue spotlight shone down on stage and bathed Lorelei in its spectral glow. Her body undulated like a snake, a boneless creature with pale arms extended and long, spidery fingers that probed the darkness above the crowd.

"Who shall it be tonight?" The microphone amplified her throaty whisper. It reverberated around the silent room.

Gasps and then shouts rose from the crowd. "Me!" "No, me!" The random shouts blended together until they rose into a cacophony of screams.

My heart beat faster as the drummer quickened his pace and the scene at the foot of stage turned riotous. The crowd surged forward, dark silhouettes jostled against each other, spike-haired heads bobbed, hands stretched upward grasping at air in frantic but futile attempts to touch Lorelei.

"Silence!"

Lorelei's thundering command halted the pandemonium. "I see you all. See who you really are. Posers. Charlatans. Fakes. I will not allow mundane scum to drink my pure blood."

I jolted upright in my chair. Drink her blood? The website hadn't lied. Lorelei planned to transform someone. Right here, right now.

"There is only one among you tonight who is ready. One who is strong and worthy of my gift."

The pounding in my chest vibrated upward into my throat. Me. She was talking about me. She told me to stay. My mind reeled. The gravity of how my life was about to change both stunned and thrilled me.

A deathly quiet blanketed the room, broken only by the soft shuffle of feet as they backed away from the stage and Lorelei's fierce glare. A spotlight flashed on and scanned the crowd. The white beam sliced through the blackness and swept back and forth across the room, faster and faster. Its strobing effect made me dizzy. I forced myself to look away. The drumbeat sped up, the sound harder, louder, faster—thump-thump, thump-thump. My heartbeat synced to it, thundering in my ears.

The roving spotlight stopped. I looked up. Light blinded me.

"You, are the only one here who is worthy." Lorelei pointed to me. "Rise."

I jumped to my feet, light-headed. I squinted through the harsh glare reflecting off my lenses. Lorelei had seen my need. She knew how much I wanted this, deserved this. My impulsive move of grabbing her arm had paid off in a way I could hardly fathom. I sucked in a gasp of smoky air. Fear and desire washed over me. My scalp and fingers tingled, alternating between icy, then fiery waves. Tonight, my life as a vampire would begin and even better, the misery of my human existence would end. My tears magnified the glare of the spotlight.

"What is your name?" Lorelei asked.

Rapid breaths had dried my throat, my tongue stuck to the roof of my mouth. I croaked out, "Tim." Simultaneously, a vibrant female voice rang out, "Jane." The woman sitting at my table stood and walked toward the stage.

No. No! It's me. Lorelei pointed at me. Spoke to me. Words screamed in my head as I watched Lorelei beckon Jane toward the stage. Two of the male musicians reached down, grasped Jane's outstretched arms and lifted her up onto the platform. Jane stood, tall and confident, next to Lorelei. Stood where I should be standing.

My shaking legs could no longer hold me. I collapsed in my chair. The drumbeat slowed, still steady but softer. An ethereal lilt of keyboard notes joined in. My entire body shook as waves of nausea swelled in my gut, then crashed in a sea of bile at the back of my throat. Get up. Jump on the stage. Take my place next to Lorelei. Fear of vomiting or passing out paralyzed me. Numb, I sat, my fingers gripping the seat of my chair as I swallowed back the bitter-tasting acid. Shock and anger dueled in my brain.

The two guitarists pushed an ornate, high-backed chair—throne-like—to center stage. Jane settled into it. She gazed out over the murmuring throng standing watch at the foot of the stage.

One of the guitarists brandished a long, thin sword. He swiveled it in the air letting the blue light play off the gleaming metal. Lorelei stood next to the throne and took Jane's hand. They stretched their arms outward, hands clasped, fingers interlaced. In a lightning fast, silvery blur, the blade swiped across their arms. Dark lines immediately formed on their skin. Under the blue light, the liquid welling from the slashes appeared black.

Lorelei leaned forward and licked Jane's arm. Her tongue caressed the skin, a delicate gesture like a cat lapping milk. Then, her mouth widened, glossy red lips enveloped the bleeding wound. My breath caught in my chest. Lorelei's fervor intensified. She clutched the arm with both hands and her head moved up and down in frenzied blood-sucking. A lioness feasting on bloody meat. Jane's eyes squeezed shut, her face twisted with pain or maybe ecstasy. Lorelei pushed the arm away. Tongue lingering on her bloody lips, she pressed her bleeding arm to Jane's mouth.

Jane sucked the dark pool oozing from the wound. The eerie organ music swelled and faded as she drank. Lorelei's body swayed in rhythm to the sensual melody. My breath came fast and shallow and I moved with her as did the pulsating mass of silhouettes in front of the stage. Voyeurs, all of us. Time hung suspended as the lurid scene on stage filled my senses, the faint wet sounds, the metallic scent. Sweat formed under my arms and ran down the center of my back. My shirt stuck to my damp skin. I squirmed in my chair embarrassed by the hardness growing inside the painfully snug crotch of my jeans.

Lorelei shook her head, her tousled white hair falling across eyes that glittered with lavender light. "Enough!" She pushed Jane's mouth away and withdrew her arm. The dark gash on Lorelei's arm faded to smooth, alabaster skin.

The guitarist stepped from the shadows, this time twirling a strip of filmy white gauze instead of a sword. He knelt on one knee beside the chair and wrapped Jane's wound.

Hypnotized by a spectacle I had only read about until tonight, my anger and nausea dissipated, replaced by awe, lust, and envy. My desire to be transformed renewed. It overwhelmed me.

Jane sat in the chair, eyes closed, and her expression peaceful yet triumphant—smug even—her arms resting on the plush red velvet cushions of the chair's arms. The two guitarists picked up their instruments and the tickle of guitar strings filtered seamlessly into the haunting melody. Lorelei gripped a hand-held mic and sang unidentifiable words in a whisper-soft voice. A demonic lullaby that both soothed and unnerved me. The dark ballad ended in an elongated sigh which Lorelei issued as she slowly bowed from the waist, the ends of her hair grazing the stage floor. The drum beat continued slower, softer, then faded, until it too, stopped.

Jane opened her eyes and stood. The two women embraced as the heavy velvet curtain fell. I stood, craning my neck to peer beneath the curtain. The crowd dwindled. People ambled across the shiny floor, murmuring, whispering as they drifted toward the exit.

The overhead lights in the club flicked on. I turned, squinting in the harsh light as the last of the patrons wandered down the narrow corridor and out the doors. Behind me, bartenders washed glasses, straightened bottles on shelves and wiped down the bar top, their routine no different than closing time in any night club.

I hurried to the bar.

The barmaid glanced up at me. "Last call was an hour ago."

"I don't want a drink. When will she be back?"

"Who?"

"Lorelei—Night Train—when are they playing here again?"

"Next Saturday night's their last gig here before they go on tour."

I spun around and raced toward the stage. The barmaid yelled, "Hey, you can't go back there."

The curtain obscured the stage. I veered left to the side entrance, took the flight of steps two at a time and burst through a doorway and onto the stage.

Lorelei and Jane stood talking. I ran toward them. One of the men stepped into my path and blocked me with his bulk. His hands clamped my shoulders and shoved. I flew backward. The back of my head slammed against a speaker and my eyeglasses clattered on the wooden floor. The blurry legion of giants standing over me could have been four, or maybe eight.

"Stop." Lorelei's voice.

The hulks separated. She stood over me. "You again. What do you want?"

"T-To be transformed." I rolled up onto my knees and felt on the floor for my glasses. Once I became a vampire, I wouldn't need damned eyeglasses. I stood up, fumbling to fit the thick black frames onto my face. "You told me to stick around, remember? I thought you had chosen me, not her." I nodded in Jane's direction. "I've studied. I'm ready. Strong."

The men broke into laughter. One gripped my shirt collar and yanked me toward the doorway.

With my feet unable to touch solid ground in his steely grasp, I twisted my torso around and reached out to Lorelei. "Please! Please Lorelei, I'm begging you."

"Seth, wait," she said. He stopped dragging me and stood, his fingers a tight vise on my upper arm. Lorelei's frigid eyes bore into mine. "I doubt you are ready. Or worthy."

"But—"

"Shush." She turned and opened a battered old trunk behind the speaker. "Complete these six tasks in the next seven days. If you succeed, return here next Saturday night and I shall give you what you desire."

She handed me a piece of yellowed parchment paper, the numbers one through six hand-written in black ink down the left side.

"What tasks? The paper's blank."

"Press your finger on the first number and instructions will appear. The next will not appear until you have completed the one prior. The difficulty rises as you progress down the list." Her cold hand encircled my throat, sharp fingernails pressed against my skin. "If you fail to complete all six, do not dare return here. Ever." She released my throat and slapped my face with the back of her hand.

Blood smeared my fingertips when I touched my stinging cheek. Lorelei licked the treacherous-looking ring on her right middle finger. Like an inverted spider, a ring of pointy prongs caged a round, ruby-red stone. She nodded to Seth.

Seth shoved me through the doorway to the platform at the top of the stairs. As I started down, his heavy boot struck me square in the ass. Tumbling down the steps, I landed face-down on the shiny floor. The thick velvet curtain muffled their laughter.

"Let me help you."

I straightened my glasses and looked up. Jane crouched beside me, her teal-colored eyes burning with an inner light. Her sandy hair now shone like polished gold and framed her radiant face. My hopes were confirmed. She was no longer plain. She had been transformed.

"I don't need your help."

She sighed and stood. Her footsteps echoed in the empty club as she strode across the dance floor, turned, and then disappeared down the corridor toward the exit.

My butt, knees, and arms ached as I climbed to my feet. I tucked the parchment inside my jacket and limped to the exit.

"Ya shouldn'a run backstage." The huge, bald guy's ham-sized fist impacted half of my face. Sucker punched, I barely had time to scoop up my fallen glasses before he heaved me out the door. My outstretched hands saved my face from kissing the concrete stairs outside. Locks clicked behind me.

Salty-tasting blood oozed from the split in my lower lip and tears blurred my throbbing left eye.

I grasped the railing and climbed up the steps to the parking lot behind the warehouse. Below me, a plain black awning hid the entrance to the Black Swan. Only the faint blue light emanating from twin iron sconces gave any indication of what lay beyond the door.

Tonight wasn't the first beating I'd endured, but it would be the last. From elementary school through college, I had drawn bullies like a chunk of bloody chum in the sea drew sharks. But now I knew why. My entire life had propelled me toward this—my pending transformation. I smiled in spite of the pain. In fact, I couldn't stop grinning as I staggered to my car in the deserted parking lot.

"In seven days, I'll be a vampire."

Chapter 2

The gem cannot be polished without friction, nor man perfected without trials. —Chinese proverb

The drive from the club in Santa Verde to my home in suburban Spring Meadows should have taken over an hour, but in my haste to get started on the tasks I made the trip in under fifty minutes. That included the time I'd wasted fumbling with the security code buttons at the entrance of the gated community. Thankfully, I finally nailed the code on my third try. Three incorrect entries would have summoned the security company, and worse, their call would have awakened my parents.

My Camry, the only moving vehicle in the development, cruised along the winding, tree-lined streets past million-dollar-plus homes, while luxurious vehicles sat idle in massive driveways or tucked inside garages larger than most people's houses. I killed my headlights as I turned into my parents' drive. Their sprawling Spanish-style stucco house stood dark, save for the front path lights which Mom had left on for me. The dashboard clock read 3:07. My parents had been asleep for at least five hours.

I unlocked the door, crept through the enormous open kitchen and then down the tiled hallway past my brother, Steven's, empty room. I slipped into my room, grateful my parents' master suite was situated on the other side of the house. Waking my father was the last thing I needed. He'd be up soon enough, heading out to the clubhouse gym for his morning workout. Thankfully, he'd given up on dragging me with him years ago. Unlike his super fit, ex-military body, no matter how many weights I attempted to lift, my scrawny physique never changed. At least Dad had his first-born and namesake, Steven, to be proud of. After two medal-winning tours in Iraq, ol' Steve-o decided to make the Marines his career, just like Dad. Steve junior now trained recruits in San Diego. I loved my big brother, but living in his hard-bodied, heroic shadow sucked.

On some level my father accepted—maybe even approved of—

the late hours I kept on weekends. It offered him evidence that I had some sort of social life, though once he caught me wearing black eyeliner and demanded to know if I were gay. So much for don't ask, don't tell. His stony gaze and tight-clamped jaw revealed how much he feared an affirmative answer. I stammered something about a costume party. He grunted and looked relieved, but not convinced. I'm not sure which would freak him out more: If I were gay, or if he discovered I frequented vampire clubs.

After shrugging off my jacket and kicking off my tennis shoes, I flicked on the bathroom light, pulled a towel from a hook, rolled it and then placed it at the bottom of my door before turning on the overhead bedroom light. Even though I was twenty-five, Mom was known to prowl the house checking to see if I had come home safely. I didn't need her questions now, only time to assess my injuries and then come up with a plausible lie to explain them.

The quick glimpse of my face in the mirror wasn't pretty. I returned to the bathroom and inspected the damage. Purple and black ringed my left eye, and the red, puffy lid drooped downward obscuring my vision. My lower lip had swollen to twice its normal size, the split accented by a crust of dried blood. Deep purple bruises from Lorelei's goons stained the skin on my upper arms. All in all, I had been beaten up worse before.

I gathered ice cubes from the freezer of my small refrigerator— a gift from my parents for my college dorm room—scooped them into a washcloth and pressed it against my throbbing eye. Worry of how I'd explain my injuries to my doting mother lingered, but my excitement to inspect the parchment Lorelei had given me took precedence.

Moving my laptop aside, I plopped the icy rag on the end of the desk, then smoothed the parchment paper flat and pressed my finger on the number one. As Lorelei promised, words appeared, one letter at a time.

1. *What do you wish to become after your transformation?*

I grinned up at my collection of vampire posters hanging on the wall. This is a no-brainer. "A sexy, hard body with a six pack and bulging biceps." Hell, why not? Male or female, vampires were always hot-looking. "I want women to lust after me. To get laid every night. I want guys to fear me. And if any of them are stupid enough to pick a fight, I'll kick *their* asses for a change." *Kicking ass and taking names*, one of my father's favorite phrases popped into my mind. "Nobody will ever screw with me again. Plus, I'll live forever." I think. Well, at least for a really long time. "I'll stay young and strong my entire life. I'll do whatever I want, whenever I—" Words emerged on the page next to the number two. I had completed the first task!

2. *Choose three words to describe your ideal transformed state.* Write them below, in your own blood.

_____   _____   _____

"Shit." Only three? And write them in blood? I stood and paced my room. "Don't panic. You can do this. You *have* to do this." One step at a time. First, I needed to condense everything I wanted to become into three words. I rummaged in my desk drawer and pulled out my notebook. I flipped through my video game notes searching for a blank page. I had given up my dream of being a video game designer to appease my father. As soon as I had graduated college, he demanded I find a job and utilize the computer programming skills I'd learned. *Make your own money, provide for yourself, be a man.* Translation, he'd paid for my education, now get a job and get the hell out of his house.

I had wanted to wait and find a job in the gaming industry, but he said that was a stupid idea—a waste of my brain power. To shut him up, I took an IT position at an insurance company. The job paid well, but bored me to tears. I spent my days rebooting technology-challenged employees' computers and updating the company's interactive client software. Ironically, I only used the advanced coding skills I'd learned in college while developing my video game in my free time after work.

Vampire Warriors would have been a kick-ass game. I'd created the first ten levels and had a detailed outline for the next ten. From designing each character to world building with an amateur program hacked from the internet, I had all the rudimentary animations stored on my laptop. Given time and professional gaming software, I knew *Warriors* could rival the best-selling games in fantasy, role-play, and action adventure genres. But that dream would have to wait. First

14

things first.

I pressed the start-up button on my laptop. Lorcan, the brooding vampire hero from my game, stared back at me with dark eyes and long, wavy hair from my homemade desktop wallpaper. Tall and muscular, he stood decked out in full battle gear. The long black leather cape fluttering around him hung from the spiked epaulettes that graced his broad shoulders. His name meant fierce, dark, and silent. I'd hard-coded everything I ever longed to be into Lorcan's character. Perhaps I'd take his name as my vampire name. Shit, why not? Anything's better than Timothy.

I scribbled *FIERCE, DARK,* and *SILENT* on a blank notebook page. "Silent? What the hell does that mean anyway—a mute? Crap." I scratched through silent. Then I scratched out dark.

"Okay, fierce is good. Two more." I tapped the pen on the paper. My left eye hurt, and I could barely see through the swollen slit of an opening. The washcloth lay balled up on my desk in a puddle of melted ice. I pressed the cold, wet rag against my eye. Water dribbled down my cheek and stung my cut lip. My body ached. Part of me longed to crawl into bed and smother my pain in the sweet oblivion of sleep, but the tasks had to be completed. Lorelei said they'd get more difficult as the list progressed and here I sat, stumped on number two. I scribbled two more adjectives.

POWERFUL. RESPECTED.

I stared at the words. Were fierce and powerful the same? Maybe, but fierce sounded cooler—dangerous, sexier. Should I cross out powerful and write sexy instead?

A new thought wormed into my overtired brain. Were there right and wrong answers? Would I be graded, or worse, would Lorelei laugh at me for wanting to be sexy? Maybe it was too lofty a goal considering where I stood now on the attractiveness scale—a solid zero.

Yet, Lorelei was sexy. Hell, her smoking hot body left sexy in the dust. And she was fierce and respected. She may have had her thugs beat me up, but in the end, she understood my need for transformation. She offered me a once in a lifetime chance. I had to go for it.

FIERCE. RESPECTED. SEXY.

15

I underlined the words and then put down the pen. Done. Now I needed to write them in my blood on the parchment. "Shit."

I walked to my bathroom and scanned the medicine cabinet for something sharp and a disinfectant. I took a bottle of alcohol and a box of Q-tips from the shelf but found nothing sharp except for a couple of plastic disposable razors. I used them on the fine hairs that sprouted on my upper lip every few days. Sadly, I had no real need for a razor. "That too will change. I'm gonna be a fierce, sexy and *hairy* mother by next Saturday night."

I went back to my desk and searched the drawers. An X-Acto knife and—hello—yes!—my old Rapidograph pen. The bits of crystallized black ink inside the plastic cartridge wiped out easily with an alcohol-soaked cotton swab. Now, I needed to fill it with blood. After wiping alcohol on the blade and my left middle finger, I poked the point of the triangular blade into the fleshy pad. "Ow! Damn, that hurt." I squeezed until my fingertip turned bright red yet only managed to coax one drop of blood from the wound. Pressing my fingertip over the small round opening of the pen cartridge, the blood dribbled down the side of the clear tube and seemed to disappear in the bottom. I needed a lot more drops.

Finally, after pricking all five fingers on my left hand and three on my right, I managed to fill a quarter of the cartridge with blood. Screwing the pen back together, I printed the words in tiny letters to conserve blood. The *X* and *Y* in sexy looked pinkish and more scratched into the parchment than inked in blood.

I pressed my unbloodied right forefinger tip on the number three. Letters began to appear.

"Yes!" Two down, four to go. Not knowing how difficult the tasks might be, I wanted to get as many done as soon as I could and leave myself time to complete all six. So far, they proved easy enough.

My computer screen showed the time as 4:16. Exhaustion blurred the vision in my good eye and my bruised body ached from head to toe. I waited. Perhaps because I was so tired, the letters formed even slower. I decided I'd read number three, then lie down and think about it before falling asleep. I'd have the answer ready when I woke tomorrow morning—or afternoon at this rate.

While I waited, I studied the familiar faces that watched over me from my movie posters. All the actors who portrayed famous vampires hung on my wall in order of my favorites. My father considered my collection weird, but harmless. Mom said their eyes creeped her out and followed her around the room when she came in and changed the sheets on my bed.

Bela Lugosi, Christopher Lee, and Frank Langella in their movie roles as *Dracula* were taped across the top row of the wall. All three exuded the mixture of fierceness and sexiness I hoped to emulate. Below them, Jack Palance and Gary Oldman, fangs glistening, gave monstrous scowls. Another row of smaller posters showed Klaus Kinski and Max Schreck as the ancient but ever-creepy Nosferatu; Jonathan Frid, the melancholy Barnabus; and last but not least, Brad Pitt and Tom Cruise as the sensitive Louie and brazen, over-the-top vampire, Lestat. Their hypnotic eyes encouraged me.

Finally, the letters stopped forming. I rubbed my bleary right eye and adjusted my glasses to read the words.

"Oh, c'mon. No. This has got to be a freaking joke."

3. *Drink the blood of a virgin.*

How could I possibly drink a virgin's blood? What the hell was I supposed to do, walk up to a woman, ask her if she's a virgin and if she says yes, then what—bite her or jab her with a pin and suck her blood? I pictured myself getting cursed at, slapped, kicked in the nuts and then probably arrested. My father would refuse to post bail for his perverted son. Mom would cry and bring me granola bars and clean underwear at prison visitations.

It's not fair. The first two questions I'd completed on my own, as it should be. This is my dream, my quest, it shouldn't involve other people.

I picked up the washcloth, wiped the dried blood from my tender fingertips then walked to the bathroom door and tossed it into the sink. I missed, and the wet rag hit the tile floor with a slap.

Returning to my desk, I shut down my laptop. Task three stared up at me from the parchment.

"Dammit. It's impossible." Yet, if I didn't complete all of the tasks, Lorelei wouldn't transform me. My vision of a spectacular new life was evaporating before it even began. I pressed my finger

17

on number four and waited. Nothing. The damned parchment wouldn't allow me to cheat. Task three had to be completed before I could move on.

Fierce, respected, sexy, the bloody words mocked me from the paper. "Might as well have written, puny, loser, failure."

Frustration turned to anger and tore at my gut. I am a failure. Always have been, always will be. I slammed my fist on the desk. The X-Acto rolled off the edge and onto the floor. Too tired and disgusted to bother picking it up, I trudged toward my bed. A thin trickle of red ran down the side of my right palm.

"Great. Now that I don't need blood, I'm bleeding like a pig." I turned back to the desk but remembered I'd discarded the washcloth, so I licked away the blood oozing from the paper-thin cut.

Movement on the parchment—letters began to appear next to number four.

I sat down hard in my desk chair. "Crap."

I'm a virgin. Even alone in my room, I couldn't dare to say the words out loud. Twenty-five years old and never been laid. It hadn't occurred to me to drink my own blood. How freaking humiliating. If Lorelei asked me how I accomplished this task, I'd lie. I'd rather tell her I bit a ten-year-old girl in a schoolyard than admit I'd never had actual intercourse with a woman.

I took a deep breath and shoved my humiliation aside. With task three done, I was halfway to my goal and still had six whole days to complete the remaining three. With my ego now as bruised as my body, I vowed my virgin status would be the first thing I'd change after my transformation. Once a vampire, I'd become a chick magnet and have banging-hot women stuck to me like Velcro.

The letters stopped forming next to number four on the parchment. The wicked smile from my imagined future sexual exploits morphed into open-mouthed horror as I read task number four.

4. *Drink the blood of your mortal enemy.*

"What the hell?"

You're your own worst enemy, Tim, another of my father's gems of wisdom came to mind. I sucked on the cut on my palm, then pressed my finger on number five and waited. Nothing. I blew out a weary breath. "Shit. Not this time, Dad." Exhausted, I tucked the parchment inside my desk drawer, turned off the light, and collapsed onto my bed.

Who was my mortal enemy? Did I even have one? I racked my brain to come up with a name. I had to have one or I wouldn't be able to complete the tasks.

Through the window next to my bed the predawn sky cast a weak yellow-gray light on the facing wall. The top row of Draculas returned my gaze—my role models, heroes. "Who is *my* Van Helsing?" I searched their faces for inspiration but came up blank.

Even if I managed to somehow complete number four, what about five and six? How difficult will those tasks be?

But I'm halfway there, I can't give up.

I won't give up.

With eyes closed, I whispered a promise to the silent gallery on the wall. "I *will* complete all six tasks. I *will* be transformed."

Chapter 3

Beware of no man more than of yourself; we carry our worst enemies within us. —Charles Spurgeon

Sunlight streaming through my windows woke me after eleven o'clock. The question of who is my mortal enemy plagued me while I showered.

My stomach growled, but I heard voices murmuring in the kitchen. I couldn't avoid my parents all week. Besides, I needed to tell them I'd be moving out on Friday. Once transformed, living in my parents' house would no longer be an option. My brain welcomed a reprieve from pondering potential enemies and I shifted my focus to the matters of quitting my job and moving. Though mundane, they were steps forward and necessary for my new vampire lifestyle.

A new job in the video game industry would provide a believable excuse. I fired up my laptop and checked the Create-A-Vision website, a hugely successful game developer headquartered in Azure Springs, not far from L.A. I read up on their stats before facing my parental inquiry board.

Dishes rattled and my parents' voices echoed through the vast open-plan house. I steeled myself as I rounded the corner and entered the kitchen.

". . . about fifteen min—" My mom jumped from her chair and rushed toward me. "You're hurt! Oh my God. Steven, look."

My father glanced up from his stool at the breakfast bar where he sat reading the newspaper. "What the hell happened to you?"

Mom, ever the retired nurse, fussed around me touching my cheeks and peering at my eye.

"I'm fine, Mom. Looks worse than it is."

"I'll drive you to the emergency room."

"That's overkill for a black eye, don't you think?" my father grumbled. He folded the paper, sharpening each crease with his fingers before he laid it on the counter. "Slap a raw steak on it. It'll be fine."

"His lip is cut, too. What happened, Tim? Who did this?"

"Just, um, a little scuffle at a nightclub last night."

"What was the fight about?" Mom asked.

"Probably a woman. Always is." Dad said.

The proverbial light bulb flicked on in my mind. "Um, yeah. It was."

My father's eyebrows rose. "So, who got the girl?"

"Oh, Steven, please," Mom said.

A white lie might earn me valuable points with my father. "I did, I think."

"Way to go." On his feet now, he set his reading glasses down on the counter and patted my back. "But, what do you mean you *think*?"

"Well, I have a date with her next Saturday night." I pulled away from my mother's solicitous pats and shrugged. "I'll see how it goes."

"You won this woman in a fight?" Mom asked. "How barbaric."

"I didn't win her, Mom. A group of creepy-looking guys were following her around the club. I wanted to talk to her. And one thing led to another." It wasn't really a lie.

"A group? So, more than one beat you up?" Mom shook her head, still hovering around me. "That's not fair."

"Bar fights usually aren't, Mindy." Dad's steely fingers gripped my shoulder. "You did the right thing, standing up for the young woman." To my surprise he walked to the refrigerator and returned holding a plastic-wrapped steak. "Here, open this up and hold it against your eye."

"Thanks, Dad."

"No." Mom snatched the meat from my hand. "That's a myth. Raw meat will cause an infection if bacteria gets into a cut." She returned the steak to the refrigerator drawer, then filled a plastic bag with ice cubes and twist-tied it closed. "You'll need ice for the first two days to constrict the blood vessels and reduce swelling. After that, warm compresses will help the blood circulate under the eye and alleviate the bruising." She poured a tall glass of orange juice and set it on the bar. "Vitamin C helps healing."

Dad checked his watch and nodded to Mom. "We should get going."

"We have a few minutes. Allison and Bob booked the court for noon."

Their blinding-white matching outfits meant it was tennis today, not golf. I pulled a box of Cheerios from the cabinet and opened the refrigerator door. Cartons of kefir, rice, and almond milks lined the top shelf. Despite Mom's noble efforts to improve our diets, Dad still had his cache of red meat and I had a shelf filled with sugary cereals.

"Behind the rice milk," Mom said.

I ducked down and retrieved the carton of whole fat cow's milk.

She and Dad fiddled with their canvas tote bags and tennis rackets.

"I'm moving out the end of this week." I dropped the bomb, knowing they had to leave in five minutes. "I have a new job. It's too far away to commute."

Mom's racket clattered on the tile floor. Dad turned and frowned at me.

"It's with a big video game developer, Create-A-Vision in Azure Springs."

"Tim, what—when did you decide this?" Mom steadied herself by gripping the counter.

My lies flowed as freely as the milk I poured into the bowl of crunchy oat rings. "I applied online and then met with the Creative Director last evening. I snagged the job."

"How will you live? If you're just starting out, you can't afford an apartment." Mom nudged Dad. "You'll need money for housing, utilities, car insurance, gas, and food."

Dad rolled his eyes. "You're quitting a well-paying job with benefits for this pie-in-the-sky video game nonsense?"

I swallowed a mouthful of cereal without chewing it all the way. "Starting pay is ninety thousand a year, Dad. More than twice what I'm making now. Plus benefits. The video game industry is one of the few job markets that have grown about nine percent annually in spite of the economy." I glanced at Mom. The worry on her face erased my smug smile. "The company is helping me to relocate. I'll be fine."

Mom stepped to the other side of the breakfast island and nodded for Dad to join her. Ridiculous, but ever since I was a kid, they thought the four-foot tall granite slab somehow radiated a sound-negating aura in the open space above it, despite the fact I sat two feet away from them on the other side.

"Steven, talk to him. Please."

Dad raised his hands. "If he wants to throw away a good job to chase after this crazy obsession of his, so be it. He knows how I feel about it." He picked up his bag and racket. "We're going to be late." He started toward the front door and then stopped. "Tim, if you move out and take this job, you will be on your own. Make it or break it, son, understood?"

He didn't wait for my reply.

Mom kissed my cheek as she hurried past. "If things don't work out, you know you can always come back home. We'll talk more about it later."

I let out a long sigh as the front door closed behind them. To Mom, I would always be the premature baby who grew into the thin, sickly kid. Her late bloomer who required constant nurturing.

Mom's father died while she was pregnant with me. In her third trimester, hormonal fluctuations overrode common sense and she decided to name me after her deceased dad, Timothy Clarence. While I thought the name Timothy had been a curse during my school years, to have used my middle name would have equated to social suicide. My middle initial still remained a well-guarded secret.

Middle name aside, while the gods bestowed blue-eyed, Adonis-like looks and Herculean strength on my older brother, my genetic joker card was drawn from Mom's family deck. And I was dealt a royal flush—pale skin, wispy body, and piss-poor eyesight to boot. While my petite mother pulled off her porcelain complexion and brown eyes that sparkled beneath contact lenses with grace, her family traits weren't as complimentary on males.

But my mom only acknowledged the positive in me, what little there was, and bragged how I had my dad's height and my grandfather's mental genius. An entrepreneur and stock market player, Grandpa died a multimillionaire and left his only child, my mother, an incredibly wealthy woman. I often wondered how her immense wealth co-existed with my father's pride. Though he succeeded at everything he did, his military pension could never provide them with this house or lush lifestyle.

Maybe Mom was right. My intellect drove me to search the internet for knowledge. It's where I discovered modern day vampires existed. And now, here I am, three tasks away from obliterating all of my genetic flaws and changing my life forever. I set the empty cereal bowl into the dishwasher, picked up the ice bag and strolled to my room, snickering at the possibility that one, or possibly all, of my immediate family members might qualify as my mortal enemy.

I stretched out on my bed and stared up at Bela Lugosi's image. "C'mon, Count, help me. I need a name." I closed my good eye and held the ice bag over the injured one. Think, dammit. Think.

Bullies.

My eyes jerked open. I bolted upright. "Who said that?" I peered up at Bela. He glared back.

I must have nodded off for a second and my subconscious had solved the problem.

"Bullies." I sneaked a sideward glance at Bela. Did the corners of his mouth just flinch? Nah.

Hurrying to my desk, I wrote names on a notebook page. Billy—don't remember his last name. I was five years old. He shoved me into a tower of wooden blocks I had proudly constructed. I cried. Billy pelted me with the fallen blocks while the rest of the kids in kindergarten class stood by and laughed. That scene set the stage for my entire life. Ian Hunter, first grade, every recess he slammed a dodge ball into my face. Ray Peppitone, second grade, tripped me in the hallway. What the hell was so funny about a kid falling and dropping his books? Whatever it was, the same theme continued into high school, along with body slams into lockers, cafeteria trays slapped from my hands and general daily ridicule. Gym class

24

conveniently provided equipment to assist the bullies: ropes, balls, bats. It was always deemed an accident. I visited the ER or doctor's office at least once a month for cuts, sprains, and two minor concussions. Around third grade, some dim bulb christened me Tiny Tim. The name stuck all through elementary school with a few creative variations, Timid Timmy and the ever so clever, Tim-o-flea.

Dad's attempts to teach me to fight proved fruitless—and painful—I ducked into his fist instead of away from it. Was that my first black eye? Maybe, definitely my first pair of broken eyeglasses. Then Mom took over. She told me, "Use your brains not your fists, Tim. You have a superior intellect."

I think her advice finally clicked in my junior year in high school when I tutored several of the popular jocks. The rich ones paid me cash, and the not-so-rich paid by simply not picking on me. Looking back on it, junior year wasn't such a bad year.

But senior year . . . Chris Bagwell. The pen tip scratched the letters of his name into the paper.

"Sick, sadistic sonofabitch." My fingernails dug into my left palm. Unclenching my fist, I forced a deep breath. Just looking at his name written on the pad made my heart race and my stomach twist.

On a whim I pulled out the parchment and pressed my finger over the number four. "My mortal enemy is Chris Bagwell."

The words on the parchment flashed red, then returned to black.

The revelation of finally identifying my mortal enemy brought little satisfaction. Instead it brought anxiety and fear. A lot of fear. Sweat beaded on my forehead and a wave of nausea twirled the Cheerios in my gut. Milk lapped at the back of my throat.

Senior year had started out good—hell, for me, fantastic. I tutored six or seven popular jocks. Most acknowledged me with a nod as we passed in the hall and I always had a wad of extra cash. A growth spurt over that past summer made the nickname Tiny Tim obsolete. Even those dimwits couldn't call a six-foot-four kid, Tiny. And there was Leslie. The first girl I ever asked out. The first girl I kissed. Her soft lips tasted sweet and fruity like her peach-colored lip gloss. She wasn't a beauty, but she was damn cute, long strawberry-blonde hair and a rocking body, though she was painfully

25

shy and hid her boobs under baggy hoodies and her sea-green eyes behind gold wire-framed glasses.

I'd asked her to the prom, and she stunned me when she answered yes. Mom took me to rent a tux. Dad said I could drive his new Camry that night. Life moved in slow motion that entire blissful week, like a montage of happy scenes in a corny old movie where people smiled, and sappy music played in the background.

It was three weeks before prom, four before graduation, when Chris Bagwell showed up in my school. I had no clue where he came from—a late transfer student or more likely a demon spat up from hell. He just appeared one day, strutting down the halls. He flashed white teeth, smoothed his sun-streaked hair and winked his sky-blue eyes at all the girls. He wore the latest style clothes on his tanned, pro-body-builder body.

All the girls had a crush on him, even Leslie. He quickly ingratiated himself by hosting a pre-graduation party on a Saturday night when his parents were out of town. All seniors were invited.

Leslie wanted to go, so of course, I agreed to take her. If she had asked me to take her to Mars, I would have stolen a spaceship to oblige her. She was my official girlfriend of two weeks and the hope of groping under her baggy clothes gave me a constant half hard-on each day and wet dreams at night.

Chris' parents lived in a mansion on a hill with sprawling grounds and an Olympic-sized swimming pool. Parties made me nervous enough and I refused to bring a swimsuit. My pasty-white torso and legs weren't making their debut in front of my senior class. If I ever got lucky with Leslie, it would be in a dark room or the shadowy back seat of a car.

She and I stood by the pool, holding bottles of hard lemonade and nodding our heads to the music blasting from the awesome sound system. For once in my life I was one of the cool kids, hanging out at an unsupervised party, drinking alcohol—and with a date no less. Life couldn't get any better. Then, an instant later, I was in the pool pushing my head above water, coughing, sputtering, my glasses gone and eyes stinging from chlorine. A muscular tan arm reached down to me. "Hey, sorry, man." Chris crouched at the side of the pool and dragged me from the water like a wet cat.

"Didn't mean to bump into you, man." His brows knitted in concern above clear blue eyes. "C'mon over to the cabana. There's swim trunks and robes. You can hang your clothes up to dry."

Leslie's cheeks pinked when she looked at me. She shrugged and then stared down at her feet.

I'd embarrassed her through no fault of my own.

I followed Chris for a few strides and then stopped. "My glasses." I scanned the pool in a futile attempt to see anything besides a field of blurry, blue water.

Again, concern flooded his face. He cupped his hands around his mouth and called out to the crowd loitering about the patio. "Hey! Keep an eye out in the pool for Tim's glasses."

The same arm that saved me, slapped me on the back. "No worries, buddy. They'll turn up."

With water gushing from my Nikes, I followed Chris around the corner of the house. He pointed to a cedar wood structure with glistening glass sliding doors. "Go change."

I entered and pulled a blue and white striped curtain across the glass doors. Light from the setting sun filtered through a sunroof and washed the wooden walls, floor and exposed ceiling beams in pale orange. An open shower stood in one corner, rattan chairs and table in another. A pile of clear plastic dry cleaner bags lay on the floor, but I didn't see any robes or swim trunks. The room was freezing cold. I didn't see a thermostat, either.

"Chris?" I slid open the door. He grinned at me from where he sat on the railing. "Um, there's no robes in here."

"Oh, sorry, bro. Strip off those wet clothes. I'll go get you a pair of my sweats."

My teeth chattered so hard I thought they'd break as I peeled off my soggy shoes and clothes. I found a white hand towel in the bathroom. It only covered my front and left my wet ass exposed. I fumbled one-handed to spread my wet clothes over the rattan chair backs while holding the towel like a terry-cloth fig leaf. Chris Bagwell's sweats would no doubt hang like a baggy sack on my scrawny body and the pants would be high-waters since I was much taller. I'd look like an idiot at the first cool party I ever attended, and Leslie would be even more ashamed to admit she was with me.

The slider door opened. Chris and three other guys barreled into the room. One of them charged, grabbed me around my waist and tackled me. My head banged on the wood floor. Another ripped the tiny hand towel from my hand.

Plastic rustled and feet kicked at my back, butt and legs. I rolled across the floor. They wrapped the plastic around me. I kicked, flailed my arms and finally screamed for help, convinced they intended to smother me in plastic. Chris's fist whammed into my jaw. Their faces swirled in my poor vision, then blackness.

Icy liquid splashed my face. Something was wrong, I felt weird. Laughter assaulted my ears and I struggled to draw a breath. Something constricted my upper chest. Disorientated, I opened my eyes and squinted into a bright light. A crowd of kids gathered around me. Rope dug into my armpits, wrapped once around my chest and then over my head where it was tied to a wooden beam. I bent my neck forward and saw myself hanging from a ceiling beam, arms pressed to my sides, buck naked with the exception of clear plastic wrapped from my ankles to my neck and secured with duct tape. I wished they had covered my face. Suffocation would have been a mercy.

Chris Bagwell's voice boomed, "Hey look everybody, it's *Slim Tim*!" He jerked a bottle in the air and another wave of cold beer stung my eyes. Then he shoved a Slim Jim beef jerky stick into my mouth. It lodged between my back molars and the roof of my mouth and stuck there. It wouldn't budge and I gagged when I tried to shove it with my dry tongue. Laughter drowned out the choking sounds. Hands holding cell phones rose all around me.

I swiped tears from my eyes and gritted my teeth. "You bastard. You ruined everything." I lost my clothes, my glasses, and Leslie that night. I never went to the prom and refused to attend my graduation and accept the four honor awards I'd earned, which caused a huge fight with my parents.

The Slim Tim moniker stuck. Kids from my high school who attended the same college I did not only remembered it but recited it every day when we passed in the halls. I have no idea how many phones held—still hold—that humiliating image, or how many times it crisscrossed the World Wide Web.

I never saw Chris Bagwell after that night. Or Leslie, except as she scurried down the hall and away from me the last day of school.

A drunk girl and two guys I didn't know showed pity and cut me down after the crowd of gawkers had thinned. The girl draped an orange and blue school rain poncho over me, and I ran to my car clutching the thin material around me. Strips of duct tape and shreds of plastic clung to my skin. I drove home squinting through the windshield and nearly ran off the road twice, and then I waited until after ten when my parents were asleep before I sneaked into the house.

Three months later, I scoured my college freshman roster but wasn't surprised when I didn't find his name. Chris wasn't the academic type.

So where could the miserable prick be now?

My fingers flew over the keyboard as I typed his name and town into a Google search field.

A millisecond later, a thumbnail of his smirking face appeared next to a listing in the search results. Of course, the asshole had a Facebook page.

His profile was public. I scrolled through scores of drunken posts, vulgar jokes, and borderline pornographic pictures of women. Then I clicked on his personal info. No college or relationship status listed, but Chris worked at a Thrifty Lube in Sago Palm Park, a twenty-minute drive away. I remembered hearing how his father had made a ton of money in the automotive industry. That was it, his old man owned a national chain of thirty-minute oil change shops. Chris' title was Crew Manager.

I opened a new tab and pulled up the store location on Google maps, zooming in and then switching over to street view. A shiny blue and glass store front stood on a corner lot adorned with rows of well-manicured sago palms.

With no plan in mind, I jammed my bare feet into my tennis shoes and shoved my car keys and wallet into my back pocket. How could I make Chris bleed? Dark thoughts involving Mom's kitchen knives slithered around my brain. Plunge a blade into his gut? Slit his throat?

No. I sat down at my desk. Even though hatred for Chris seared though my veins, I wasn't a fighter and certainly not a murderer. Besides, I didn't have to kill the dickwad. All I needed was a drop or two of his blood. After I became a vampire, I'd visit Thrifty Lube and kick his ass for old time's sake.

A silver glint on the floor caught my eye. I leaned down and picked up my X-Acto knife. "Razor sharp, but it's not illegal to carry a craft knife." An idea sparked. Drive in for an oil change. Ask him to check something under the hood—I'll use the X-Acto to point out an imaginary loose hose, then—oops—slice his arm. *Sorry, Bro,* just an accident. I'd pull a tissue from my pocket and wipe off the blood. Then I'd just drive away and swallow the bloody tissue later. Mission accomplished.

I shut down my laptop and headed outside to my car. The plan was brilliant in its simplicity. Task four would be completed and I'd be home in time for dinner. Then on to task five after dessert.

"Superior intellect is gonna kick your dumb ass, Chris." I grinned and started up my car.

Chapter 4

We often give our enemies the means for our own destruction.
—Aesop

My sweaty palms slipped on the steering wheel causing the car to swerve as I turned onto Triangle Palm Boulevard, the four-lane thoroughfare in downtown Sago Palm Park. I tightened my grip and eased the car into the left lane of traffic. Traffic flowed on either side of the grassy meridian lined with the town's namesake palm trees and interspersed with colorful patches of wildflowers.

The knot in my stomach tightened and my heartbeat vibrated in my dry throat. According to the GPS on my phone, the Thrifty Lube should be four blocks west, on the left-hand side. Chris Bagwell, my mortal enemy, waited there, minutes away. My simple plan suddenly felt too simple. What if he recognized me? What if he beat the living bejesus out of me before I had the chance to cut his arm? As crew manager, would he order his employees to strip me naked and cinch me up in the doorway of the shop?

My gleeful confidence quickly deteriorated into heart-pounding panic. A horn beeped behind me and my foot hit the gas pedal. The light had turned green. I closed the wide gap between me and the red car ahead. I peered through the driver's side window as we approached the next traffic light. The Thrifty Lube stood on the far corner. The light turned red and I jammed on the brake. The tires screeched as my car jerked to a stop inches from the red car's bumper. Shit.

Calm down. When the light signaled green, I cruised forward. The shop looked closed. Had dumbass Chris managed to ruin his father's business, too? I pulled into the left turn lane, made a U-turn and then switched into the right lane to make the turn into the entrance.

Thrifty Lube's driveway had three wide lanes that led to the side of the building and three large work bays. The bay doors were all shut tight. I steered to the front of the building and stopped. White letters printed on the glass door showed the hours, seven a.m. to eight p.m., Monday through Saturday. Closed Sunday.

I banged my hands on the steering wheel. "Shit. I'm an asshole." Today was Sunday.

As I sat there staring at the front door, a blue and white box truck pulled in, drove past me and rounded the corner of the building. I inched my car forward until I could see around the corner. A black Jaguar sat in the corner of the lot, partially obscured by the truck.

The truck parked and a man with a clipboard jumped out. He banged on a side door.

The door swung outward and Chris Bagwell strutted outside. He looked the same as he did eight years ago, except his upper body appeared even more bulked up than I'd remembered. His bulging biceps forced his forearms to hang away from his trim waistline. The skin-tight blue golf shirt he wore with Thrifty Lube printed on back fit like one of the Incredible Hulk's shirts did after his transformation. I could see the outline of his back muscles even at this distance.

Chris propped the door open while the man opened the back of the truck and pulled down a hand truck. The two checked the clipboard and pointed at stacks of boxes inside the truck.

I shifted into reverse and rolled my car back out of sight in front of the store. I slipped from the car and pressed my face against the front glass doors. It was dark inside. Chris must be here alone. A plastic holder mounted to the outside of the door held business cards. I took one and glanced at it as I sprinted around my car and slid into the driver's seat. Maybe I could use the card as a prop to get close to him. Of course, he might wave me away and tell me to come back tomorrow. He's probably only here today to accept the delivery.

I needed a new plan and needed it fast. My mind raced to invent one. I'd wait until the delivery guy left, then pull up before Chris entered the building and ask for directions. As soon as he came close to my window, I'd jab his arm with the X-Acto knife and blot the blood with a tissue. Then I'd floor the gas and drive like hell. But what if he decked me before I could capture his blood on the tissue?

Shit, tissues! Opening the glove box, I rummaged through my

CDs, ear buds and loose change. No tissues. Damn it. I'm an idiot. But there was a roll of paper towels in the trunk. Dad's car cleaning supplies came with the Camry when he gave it to me after my graduation.

My hands shook and I couldn't think clearly. Backing the car up, I pulled into the road. I only had a short window of opportunity and I couldn't afford to screw up. I needed a better plan, fast.

I cruised down the road a half a block and pulled into a strip mall. Though Sunday, it was crowded with foot traffic for a sidewalk sale. Racks of clothing and tables of items littered the walkway in front of the shops. I found a space and parked.

At least Chris was alone. No buddies to help him and no witnesses. I had to get some of his blood but didn't want to be recognized or beaten to a pulp in the process. A disguise! Why didn't I think of this back at my house?

Stands of colorful wool hats in the midst of the sidewalk merchandise caught my attention. The pull-on caps had rows of long, fake hair braids attached to them.

A perfect disguise. Hopping from the car, I jogged to the store. An elderly Asian woman with beady, dark eyes sat on a low stool surveying the shoppers meandering about.

I pulled a hot pink wool cap with a ring of long blonde braids from the rack.

"How much?" I asked.

She stood, the action making only a minor difference in her height. "Sale. Twenty dollar."

I laid the wig on top of a table full of over-sized bejeweled sunglasses and slid my wallet from my back pocket. "Crap." I fingered a worn ten-dollar bill and several ones. I hadn't thought to withdraw cash from an ATM either.

"We take credit card." She pointed to the platinum card in a clear plastic sleeve in my wallet.

I looked around. Both she and her store front looked sketchy, but Chris could leave at any minute. She snatched the card from my fingers and stepped into a dim open doorway to the shop.

"Wait!" I tried on a pair of rhinestone encrusted sunglasses large enough to cover my own glasses. "These, too. And, hold on a minute." Behind the display of hat-wigs I spied another rack of long dresses with a sign, *one size fits most.* They were tie-dyed in multiple bright colors, had some sort of built-in bra and tied at the back of the waist. It should fit.

I grabbed one and tossed it next to the wig and glasses. "That's it."

She squinted at me for a moment, then scuttled off into the store. While I waited, I mentally rehearsed a plan. Chris wouldn't recognize me in this get up. He'd think I was a tall, ugly girl. Maybe a Freudian move on my part, but if he believed I was a girl, he wouldn't kick my ass.

The old woman finally returned with my card and receipt.

"Sign paper," she said.

While I scrawled my signature, she stuffed my purchases into a plastic bag.

I turned for my car and stopped. "Hey, my card?"

She grunted something and flipped it at me, then sat down on the stool with a sigh.

The delivery truck was still parked at Chris' business when I drove past. Five minutes later, I stood in the lot of a closed office building next door to the Thrifty Lube wearing the long dress, wig, and sunglasses. The puffy foam breasts should distract Chris just long enough until I moved close enough to strike. Why couldn't it be dark out? I tied the sash tight around my waist. My tennis shoes and hairy shins protruded below the fluttery skirt, but I didn't have time for shoe shopping and needed footwear I could run in.

I had parked my car in a space near a garden bed of Sago palms that separated the two properties and obscured it from view from the Thrifty Lube lot. I didn't need Chris reporting my license plate. Armed with a paper towel and my X-Acto knife, I ducked under the palm fronds and sprinted across the Thrifty Lube lot to the back of the building.

The back door of the truck rolled and slammed shut with a metallic bang. The engine started and the truck beeped steadily as it backed up along the side of the building and then turned onto the road. I peeked around the corner. The door still stood propped open and Chris sauntered around the lot holding a cell phone to his ear.

34

My heart drummed in my chest and despite a steady breeze, the cheap, itchy dress clung to my sweaty body. Chris slid the phone into his jeans pocket and pulled a pack of cigarettes from his shirt pocket. He lit one and stood by the open door, facing the street with his back to me. With each drag he took, I tried to convince myself to run around the corner and confront him, but fear had frozen my legs.

Drawing in a deep breath, I started to make my move just as a black, low-rider Chevy pulled around the front corner of the building. I ducked and flattened my side against the cool bricks. Loud music with heavy thumps of base blasted from the car. Easing my head forward, I peered around the corner. The driver handed Chris a large package wrapped in white plastic. He carried it to his Jag, popped open the trunk and laid it inside. He leaned over the open trunk, fiddling with the plastic. Then he slammed the trunk, approached the car and handed the driver an envelope. The car immediately backed up and then sped off down the road. Chris walked to the open side door. He was going inside. I had to make my move now.

"Excuse me." My voice cracked as I forced it several octaves higher.

Chris spun around and then smiled. His hands rested on his hips and his chest puffed up even bigger as he posed.

His smile faded to a frown as I sauntered closer and his gaze traveled down my body to my black Nikes and hairy shins. He shifted his feet. "What do you want?"

"Um, directions." Close enough now to smell him, a mixture of sweat and sickening woodsy cologne drifted past my nostrils in the wind. My legs quaked and for a split second I feared my knees might give out.

His cheesy smile gone, he now eyed me with a disgusted scowl. "Directions to where?"

Where? Shit, I didn't know any place in this town. No matter, I took one more step, reached out and raked the small knife blade across his perfectly tanned forearm.

"Hey! What the fuck?" He jumped back just as I reached out to blot the blood with the crumpled paper towel I clutched in my hand.

35

With some distance between us, he stared down at his bleeding arm. A perfect thin red line oozing multiple rivulets of blood. His mouth fell open at the sight.

Seizing the moment, I lunged at him, my gaze fixated on the bloody prize running down his forearm. Forgetting to change my voice I said, "I just need your blood."

"Blood? Get away from me, you fucking freak!" He swerved sideways and shoved me.

I staggered backward but managed to regain my balance by grasping onto his bloody arm. I swiped the paper towel across the cut. A swatch of the thirsty white towel turned bright red. Success!

His fist hit my jaw and the force spun me around. I crashed against the open door and fell on my side, dropping both the knife and the bloody paper towel. So much for not punching a girl.

"Get outta here you crazy he-she, or whatever you are." He kicked my hip and I rolled onto my stomach banging my head on the bottom of the open door.

Dazed and ears ringing, I lay on the asphalt. Something red and white tumbled past my face. I pushed up onto my knees and then stood, dizzy but upright, and chased after the bloody crumpled paper towel as the wind propelled it across the parking lot. The rubber toe of my tennis shoe snagged in the front hem of the dress. I tripped and my knees smashed down onto the asphalt

The curb of a garden bed stopped the paper towel's roll. The lightweight ball twirled in the breeze and lifted slightly as if teasing me to catch it. If it hopped the curb, the street and traffic lay only feet away.

Chris' footsteps stomped behind me. I crawled on scraped knees and lunged for the towel. My fingertips grazed the paper just as a gust of wind lifted it over the curb. It tumbled across the flower bed, the sidewalk, and then flew into the road right under the rear tires of a passing car. "No!"

"Freak." Chris' cut arm dangled at his side taunting me. He held his cell phone in his other hand. A siren sounded close by.

Still on my knees, I turned toward him. "Please. I just need a little bit of your blood."

Climbing to my feet, I jogged toward Chris and smacked right into the front end of a white car that pulled in between us.

The nose of a police cruiser blocked my path. Both doors flew open and two cops jumped out.

"Hold it!" One shouted. The driver unclipped his gun holster.

I froze for a second before full-blown panic shot though my body. Heart pounding, I darted around the police car, zigzagged past Chris, and raced around the back of the building. I ran full-out across the parking lot and dove headfirst into the thicket of palms. I crawled out the other side, feet from my parked car.

Palm fronds rustled and the younger of the two cops emerged, training a red laser dot on my padded chest. I doubted the cheap foam breasts would absorb the shock. The cruiser, lights flashing, and siren wailing, raced into the lot and screeched to a stop behind me.

"I said, *hold it.*" The taser cop walked toward me. Dark aviator-style sunglasses hid his eyes, but the tone of his voice made me freeze and raise my hands above my head.

"Put your hands on the hood of the car."

I did as he commanded. The cop from the car came up behind me and patted me down. Then he grabbed my arms and pulled them behind my back. Cold metal encircled my wrists accompanied by a loud snap. He spun me around and studied me with eye slits so narrow, I couldn't see their color. He was about my dad's age, but had a paunch hanging over his belt. "Sit down on the curb. What's your name?"

I sat, my mind numb. I couldn't tell them my real name. My eyes scanned the stores across the boulevard and focused on a huge red and white banner advertising twenty percent off lamps. "Tiffany."

The younger cop snorted and put away his taser.

"So, you working the block, Tiffany?" Squinty Eyes asked.

"Um, no . . . no, sir. I mean, officer."

"Looks like you got on your Sunday best. You propositioned the owner of the Thrifty Lube?"

"What?" The meaning of his words trickled into my stunned brain. "No. No! I'm not a prostitute."

Sunglasses joined in, "He says you assaulted him, cut his arm. My guess is, he turned you down. And you got pissed, is that right?"

Squinty Eyes leaned over me, "Where's the knife?" He nodded at the thicket of palms. "You ditch it in the flower bed?"

"No. That's not what happened."

"Then tell us what did happen." Squinty Eyes bent and searched along the flower bed.

A childhood of watching crime shows with my dad and older brother flashed by my eyes. "I-I want a lawyer."

The two cops looked at each other.

Sunglasses smiled. "You're not under arrest."

Chris crashed through the flower bed in a rustle of palm leaves. "You gonna arrest this freak?"

"Are you pressing charges?" Squinty Eyes asked.

Chris shrugged. "Can't you just arrest him—her . . . it?"

"We didn't witness any crime. Just Tiffany here running away," the cop said. He cocked his head and stared at Chris. "Frankly, you looked more like the aggressor chasing him."

Chris hesitated and took a step backward. "I was only defending myself from this freak. I won't press charges. Just get her—him outta here, all right?" He turned and stomped back through the flower bed toward Thrifty Lube.

"Stand up, Tiffany."

"I-I didn't do anything." My voice quivered and my stomach roiled.

As the cop jerked me to my feet, I gagged on a column of rising bile. I pitched forward and vomited on the asphalt. The yellowish liquid splashed the shiny black toes of Squinty Eyes' shoes.

"Oh, for Christ sake. Shit, I just polished them this morning." He shook his feet. "Lou, put him in the car."

Sunglasses shrugged.

"Just do it. Smells like booze to me."

Squinty Eyes stalked to the driver's side and took out a plastic water bottle. He poured it over his shoes.

The younger cop took my arm and led me to the patrol car.

"Please, just let me go. I'm not drunk. I'll never come back here again. I swear."

"You shouldn't have barfed on Mike's shoes. Pissed him off." He pushed down on the top of my head as I folded into the backseat

38

of the squad car.

The ride to the police station and the jaunt through processing was a surreal blur. They took my hat, wig, and sunglasses before photographing me. I finally gave them my real name after they convinced me I'd be in more trouble if I didn't. The female cop who fingerprinted me led me down a long hallway to a door with a wire-reinforced glass panel. A stocky, bald-headed cop opened the door, removed my handcuffs and then pushed me toward a large cell on the right. Steel bars formed the front wall and pale-green painted cement blocks formed the other three. Long vinyl benches lined the block walls. A disheveled old man slept on one. Two guys about my age sat across from him and stared at me. Once inside, the heavy barred door clanged shut. The cell smelled of stale alcohol and urine. In one corner, behind a short clear Plexiglas panel stood a stainless-steel toilet and tiny wall sink.

"Take a seat, Nancy," the desk cop said.

I turned and gripped the bars. "What happens now? What am I charged with?"

The two young men behind me snickered.

The cop waved a paper. "Public intoxication. First appearance is at ten tomorrow morning."

"But I wasn't intoxicated. What's first appearance?"

The cop settled back at his desk. "You go in front of a judge. He sets your arraignment date and maybe bail, or if you're real lucky, he cuts you loose." He studied a laptop in front of him.

One of the young men walked over and stood in front of me. His bare arms, thin but muscular, were covered in tattoos and crossed in front of his chest. "*Nina fea.*" He reached over and squeezed one of the foam breasts protruding from my chest. He turned laughing to his friend. "*Falso.*"

"Knock it off," the desk cop growled.

The two smirked and whispered vulgar comments in a mixture of Spanish and English.

I huddled in the corner on the bench next to the bars until they grew bored with taunting me. The sleeping man rolled off the bench onto the tile floor and awoke yelling curse words. Holding onto the bench he climbed to his feet and staggered to the toilet. A strong

39

odor of urine filled the cell.

When he finished, he stumbled back to the bench and sat fumbling with his pant's zipper.

"Hule mal! Mal!" The quieter of the two Latino men jumped up and flushed the toilet with his foot.

"What the hell are you?" The drunk stared and pointed a shaky finger at me.

I looked down at my feet below the hem of the tie-dyed dress. I wished they had taken the damn dress and given me a jumpsuit, but maybe they only did that on television. My clothes, keys, wallet, and cell phone were all in my car. I couldn't remember if I'd locked it. Probably not, since I'd planned a quick getaway. Now, my car and everything inside it could be stolen.

Worse, I had failed to get Chris' blood. I had the bloody paper towel in my hand, and I dropped it. How could I complete the fourth task now? Even if I had a plan, there was nothing I could do about it locked in jail. Time ticked away, taking my dream of becoming a vampire along with it.

The drunk guy was on his feet now, holding onto the bars and inching his way across the cell.

"You a ugly woman or a man?" he slurred.

Before he lumbered any closer, I stood and walked to the other side of the cell. Something sharp poked my chest and I turned away from the three and reached into the foam cleavage expecting to rip out a tag. Instead I pulled out the Thrifty Lube business card. I'd forgotten I had tucked it in the dress as a possible plan B. Looking at it sparked a desperate idea. I skirted around the drunk and called out to the desk cop. "Do I get a phone call?"

The cop pointed to a pay phone on the wall inside the cell. "You got money?"

I looked down at the ridiculous pocket-less dress. "No."

"Hey, *Chica-Chico*, I give you a quarter for a phone call." The tattooed guy stood and grabbed his crotch while his friend doubled over laughing on the bench.

"Please, officer, is there a non-pay phone I can use?"

"Yeah, yeah. Just a minute." He turned back to his laptop and tapped the keyboard.

I perched on the edge of the bench next to the bars. The drunk had fallen into my former spot on the bench across the way and slumped over on his side, mouth open and snoring.

Finally, the cop rose and unlocked the cell. I stepped out and he motioned to a battered beige push-button phone on the corner of his desk.

After studying the business card a moment, I pushed the buttons for the emergency cell phone number. Was it even possible to have an oil change emergency? Whatever, maybe they did other types of automotive repair. My heart raced as the phone rang, once, twice—

.

"Thrifty Lube automotive emergency, this is Chris. How may I help you?"

My words fired out in a rush. "This is the guy who got arrested at your store today."

"What the fuck—?"

"I need you to lock up my car and, uh . . . drive it to the courthouse tomorrow at ten."

"Screw you. Why the hell should I?"

I turned away from the desk cop, my voice a hoarse whisper. "'Cause I saw your friends in the black low rider. I know what's in your Jaguar's trunk. Do what I say, or I'll tell them everything."

"Fucking asshole. Where are you? You calling from a police station?"

"Yes I am." I drew in a deep breath. The receiver shook in my hand. "Listen Chris, you owe me. You wrecked my senior year. Hell—my whole life. I-I still have nightmares—"

"What the hell are you talking about? Who are you?"

Hot tears stung the inside of my eyelids. "S-Slim Tim."

Silence.

"Your pool party senior year. The cabana. The plastic. You strung me up."

"No shit, Slim Tim, huh? Yeah, I remember."

The desk cop tapped his fingers on the desk. "Wrap it up, Nancy."

"I have to go. It's a 2006 white Camry in the lot next to yours. My keys are in it."

41

"Why'd you cut me?"

If I told him I wanted to be transformed into a vampire, he'd most likely hang up. "To join an exclusive video game club. I needed a few drops of my mortal enemy's blood."

"Freaking geek." Laughter. "So, *I'm* your mortal enemy, huh?"

The satisfaction in Chris' tone gave me an idea. I'd play to the asshole's ego.

"Yes, you most certainly are."

The desk cop was on his feet now, motioning for me to hang up.

"I mean what I said, Chris. I swear I'll tell them. Bring my car to the courthouse. Ten o'clock."

I hung up the phone just as the cop gripped my arm and led me back into the cell. Given the two thugs eying me and the drunk snoring, sleep wasn't going to happen. Not to mention my mind wouldn't stop whirling. First, the image of Lorelei's brilliant blue eyes peering into mine as she promised to transform me if I completed all six tasks and then Chris' face, a reddened mask of rage looming over me. Yet, I called him. What had I done? I couldn't trust Chris. He'd steal my car, hide his drugs, and deny everything. They'd believe him. He owned a business in town, while I had wandered into town in a dress and puked on a cop's shoes. I'd be left stranded in Sago Palm Park, forced to call my parents and attempt to explain what happened. Or worse, put in a real jail. I pictured my dad's face and my empty stomach twisted. Earlier, as they booked me, my stomach growled with hunger, a bowl of Cheerios the only food I'd eaten today. But now the foul smells inside the cell squelched my appetite. And I needed to piss— wearing a dress in an open toilet in front of the two Latino guys. I hunched down on the bench and tried to convince myself I didn't have to pee. Maybe they'd fall asleep like the drunk and then I could sneak over to the toilet.

Black metal armor covered my chest. Lightweight, the burnished metal scales molded to my torso like a second skin and allowed full movement. A long leathery cape blew in the wind behind me as I stared down the gang of Latino men. With lightning speed, I gripped their leader by the neck and raised him in the air. He made a

gurgling noise. His feet kicked wildly. One-handed, I flung him into the other four men who stood wide-eyed and open-mouthed. The scent of their collective fear filled the air. Then, a wiry man with two full sleeves of tattoos charged at me. He brandished a long shiny knife.

I waited until the instant he lunged, spun and whipped the knife from his hands with my cape. I grasped his arm, twisting it backward until it made a popping sound. He screamed and crumpled to the ground. The remaining three dragged him and their leader to their feet. They all ran down the alleyway, turned the corner, and disappeared from sight.

Lorelei's long delicate fingers traced the bulging muscles of my biceps, still pumped from battle. "You are so fierce." She pressed her body against me. "And so sexy." Her head snuggled against my chest as she gazed up at me, her electric blue eyes shining with desire. I stroked her silken blonde hair.

I awoke with a start, disorientated and heart racing.

The drunk had sidled up next to me on the bench. His head lay cradled in my lap. My fingers tangled in his greasy, matted hair. I wormed my way from beneath the odorous weight of the old man's head and stood. The chill in the room attacked my full bladder. Across the cell, the two Latino men stretched out head to head, asleep on the long bench. I tip-toed past them to the toilet. Fumbling with the long skirt, I balled it up in one hand while I positioned myself over the steel bowl. My stream hitting the water sounded like a fire hose and echoed through the silent cell. I feared I might overflow the tiny stainless bowl. Overwhelmed by the simple pleasure of finally relieving myself, I closed my eyes and took a deep breath.

"*Yo, María; el macho.*"

I dropped the skirt to cover myself and squirmed to reposition my underwear.

"*Maricon.*" His friend chimed in.

The two men stood on the other side of the low Plexiglass partition, arms folded across their chests.

I flushed the toilet and rinsed my hands in the sink. Not seeing any paper towels, I wiped my wet hands on my skirt as I hurried toward the bench.

The men blocked my path.

I conjured what I could recall of my high school Spanish. "*Perdón.*"

They laughed.

"*Por favor,*" I avoided looking directly in their eyes.

"What's going on in there?" The welcome interruption came from the desk cop, a different officer than the stocky older man from earlier. This man was young, fit, and black with a deep voice that commanded respect.

The two Latino men parted, and I rushed past. The wiseass with the tattooed arms stuck his foot out. I went sprawling across the cell in a wave of tie-dyed material.

"Hey! You two. Sit your asses down. Now!" the cop shouted.

Tattoo guy shrugged and said in perfect English. "He tripped on his skirt." They snickered as I climbed to my feet and sat on the bench across from them, away from the sleeping drunk.

"You all right?" the cop asked.

"Yes, Officer. Thank you."

He shook his head and then returned to his desk and picked up a paperback book. After a few more whispered comments, the two men settled onto their backs and closed their eyes. I sat upright and leaned my head back against the cold block wall.

Clanging metal woke me from a fitful doze. I took off my glasses and rubbed my eyes. The stocky, older day cop was back, handing out sandwiches wrapped in white paper and small juice cartons.

Famished, I devoured the thin cheese sandwich in three bites and then opened the juice. The drunk plopped down next to me smelling riper than he had the night before.

"You gonna drink that?"

I stood, walked to the bars at the front of the cell and chugged down the pint-sized drink.

Not long after, we were lined up, cuffed by one hand to each other and led down the hallway to a heavy steel exit door. I was first, connected to the drunk and then the two Latino men brought up the rear. Two cops directed us into the back of a windowless van where we sat hunched together on a long bench seat.

The pageantry and effort involved to cuff and load us into the van hardly seemed worth the two-minute drive. As we exited the van, I realized we were at the courthouse across the street from the police station. We were led into a windowless, wood-paneled room with nothing but rows of plastic chairs. As we settled into the front row of seats, a court officer and a harried-looking, middle-aged woman conferred over papers. The woman clapped her hands to get our attention and then explained the procedure in a monotone voice. We would be taken into a courtroom before a magistrate and prosecutor to have the charges against us read. Bail would be set and if we couldn't afford it, we'd be taken to the county jail to await arraignment.

My head pounded and my throat felt like sandpaper. After waiting for what seemed like an eternity we were herded into the courtroom and told to sit on yet another wooden bench, this one polished oak. An officer made his way down the line and unlocked the cuffs that bound us together. I scooted across the bench to get away from the drunk, though his stench had no boundaries.

"Timothy C. Gardener?" the clerk called out.

"Y-Yes," I croaked.

A court officer poked me in the shoulder. "Stand up."

I stood on shaking legs.

The same harried woman approached the tall bench and handed papers to the gray-haired judge. He adjusted his glasses as he scanned the papers, then looked down and studied me with grim beady eyes. Deep jowl lines framed his down-turned lips.

I am so screwed.

The woman spoke fast and too low for me to hear. The judge nodded, a nearly imperceptible motion. His gavel hit the wood so hard that I jumped, stunned but not oblivious to my former cell mates snickering on the bench behind me.

"Case dismissed with prejudice. Next."

I stood gaping up at the judge. He lowered his glasses and glared. "You're free to go. So, go."

An officer gripped my arm and led me across the room to another door. He handed me a paper. "Get it stamped and signed at the desk." The door closed behind me. Ahead in the small office, a

45

chubby black woman waved me forward. I approached the desk. She snatched the paper from my hand.

"I'm free to leave?"

"That's right. Must be your lucky day." She stamped the paper, scrawled her signature at the bottom and handed it back to me. She motioned to another door with a red and white exit sign above it. "Hold on a minute."

I froze. Was it a mistake? A wild thought of bursting through the door and running for freedom gripped me. I took a deep breath and turned to face her.

"Take that paper across the road to the police station to claim your personal items. And take this, too." She held out a pamphlet and smiled. "A list of free social services. Maybe they can help you, honey."

"Uh-ok, thanks."

I slipped out of the room into a long hallway which led to the front lobby of the building. A security guard frowned at me as I walked through the exit lane. Ten more steps across the glossy marble floor and I pushed open the front door to freedom. The glare of the sun on my glasses blinded me as I stood at the top of a wide stone staircase.

Crumpling the papers in my hand, I tossed them into a trash can. My only personal effects were the stupid hat-wig and the rhinestone sunglasses, neither of which I ever wanted to see again.

I ran down the steps clutching my skirt so as not to trip, keenly aware of the stares from people walking up the stairs. When I reached the sidewalk, I shaded my eyes and searched the street. Traffic moved up and down the wide four-lane road. No-parking signs lined the street in front of the courthouse. My white Camry was nowhere in sight.

"Who am I kidding? Chris won't show." I had no money for a cab or bus, nor any idea which direction to walk to get back to my car. If my car was even where I had left it.

I approached a young woman pushing a baby stroller. "Excuse me?"

She pursed her lips, gripped the stroller handle and sprinted past me.

Two men in suits started up the courthouse steps.

"Hey, excuse me! Can you tell me how to get to Triangle Palm Boulevard?"

The older of the two men lowered his sunglasses and studied me. "You walking?"

"Yes."

He scratched his head and thought. "Guess the best way is to go six blocks east on Alameda." He pointed. "That's this road here. Go right when you get to . . . uh, Mason Drive, I think. Another seven or eight blocks south and it runs right into Triangle Palm."

The younger man spoke up. "No, I think it's Grove, not Mason."

A horn blared and we all turned. Chris Bagwell waved from the driver's seat of my Camry idling at the curb.

"Oh, never mind. Thanks." I hurried to the car and leaned in the passenger window.

"Hurry up and get in. This is a no parking zone."

The car started rolling as I slid into the seat. I slammed the door on my dress.

"So, I kept my end. Did you keep your big freaking mouth shut?"

"Yeah." I pulled the seat belt over my shoulder and fastened it. "Um, thanks for coming."

Chris scowled at me, then grinned. "I recognize you now, without the hat and wig. Slim Tim."

"Yeah." My wallet and cell phone lay on the console, the phone plugged into the car charger.

Chris grinned at me and a chill ran down my back. "Charged up your phone for you, bro."

"Thanks." I shifted in my seat and pulled my skirt down over my knees, except for the part that was stuck in the car door.

"Where are you going?" I asked.

"Back to work."

"Thrifty Lube?"

"Yup."

We drove in silence. I stared straight ahead out the window. After about ten minutes, Chris pulled into the driveway of Thrifty Lube. He cruised past the three open bays and parked at the back of the building.

47

"Now, you're going to do me a favor." He reached into his shirt pocket. "Hold this." I automatically put out my hand. He placed a small glass vial of pale blue liquid in my palm. Before I could ask what it was, he aimed his cell phone and took a picture.

"What is this?"

"Steroids. You know, bro, you could definitely use some. You got any money?"

"About ten bucks, but I don't want—"

"You'd need ten times that." He snatched the vial from my open hand and pocketed it.

"So, uh, that's what was in your trunk?"

"Yup. And now I have a picture of you holding a vial. My insurance policy."

"Look, I wasn't really going to turn you in. I'd never been in jail before. I was desperate."

He grinned but the humor stopped below his cold blue eyes. "I figured I owed you one after the cabana thing. It was funny as shit, though. You should of seen yourself hanging up like a—"

"I did. Over and over on Facebook, Instagram, and various cell phones." Anger flooded over me and bolstered my courage. "So, can I get a few drops of your blood?" I braced myself for his reaction.

Chris only laughed. "So, what is this freak club you want to join?"

"A video game club."

"How would anyone know it's my blood? You could cut yourself or buy a bloody raw steak at the supermarket."

I thought a moment. Chris was unpredictable. I had to play this right. "You're absolutely right, they wouldn't know." I sighed and then paused to add drama to my lie. "But I would know. I-It's an honor thing. I wanted to face my mortal enemy. Take a drop or two of your blood. You know, like when a hunter eats the heart of his kill. A symbolic gesture of respect. A way to gain some of your power."

"No shit?" Chris cocked his head and studied me through squinted eyes. "That's really deep, dude. My blood means that much to you?"

"Yes. Yes, it does."

"It took balls for someone like you to try to take me on. I respect that." He leaned forward and pulled a knife from his back jeans pocket. He pressed a button and a long shiny blade shot out with a click. My heart skipped a beat. Was he actually going to cut himself? Or cut me?

I slowly reached through the opening between the front seats and tore a paper towel from the roll lying on the back seat. "Just a small cut, a few drops is all I need."

Without a word, Chris nicked his forearm with the point of the blade. Blood oozed from the cut. He took the paper towel and held it against the wound. A bright red stain formed on the towel.

He held the bloody towel out to me. "This is what you wanted?"

"Yes." My mouth turned bone dry and my hand trembled as I took the towel from him. I possessed my mortal enemy's blood! Superior intellect had prevailed. I played the big dumb asshole and he fell for it. If only I had thought of this yesterday.

"So, we're done now?" he asked. "And I won't ever see you back here again, right?'

His goofy, lopsided grin bothered me. It didn't match his tone or his icy eyes. I nodded. "Yeah. We're good. Thanks." Staring down at the bloody prize clutched in my fist, I never saw his arm move until it slammed into my throat and pinned my neck against the headrest.

"No, we're *not good*, bro." Leaning over me, his breath reeked of stale tobacco and onions. Purple veins bulged in his temples and his upper lip curled above his bleached white teeth. He pressed the cold steel blade against my cheek, his eyes narrow slits. "Nobody threatens me, you little freak. I have a picture of you holding illegal drugs. Maybe I hid some in your car, too." He rapped my nose with the side of the blade. "I went through your phone and your wallet. I know where you live and where you work." He paused and snickered. "I know people who'd break into your house at night and slit everybody's throats for twenty bucks. Hell, I know one guy who'd do it just for fun."

His arm pushed harder into my windpipe. My fingers clawed his arm in a futile attempt to pull it away, but his tensed muscles felt like steel cables. I tried to swallow but my Adam's apple wedged against his elbow. His face grew dim and my lungs burned for a breath of air.

"I think this time, I'm going string you up and cut you from here," he poked the tip of the blade under my chin, "all the way down to your girly little balls and then watch you bleed out like a fucking chicken."

I tried to form words, but only managed a gasp.

Chris withdrew his arm and flicked the knife closed. He slid out of the car and slammed the door.

Gulping in air, I scrambled over the console. The thin material of dress ripped, leaving a ragged swatch sticking in the passenger door. I fumbled to grab the key and started the car. The long skirt tangled between my legs and soaked in the fresh urine from my wet underwear.

"Hold it." Chris reached through the window and gripped my arm. I froze as he reached around to his back pocket. His mouth twisted into a sick grin. "I wasn't gonna do it, bro, but you know, I have to."

"No, please—"

He tossed a coupon for a free oil change in my lap. "It's good business. There's a Thrifty Lube three miles from your house. In and out in thirty minutes. Swifty, thrifty, and hassle-free, plus you get a thirty-day guarantee." He saluted, turned and sauntered off toward the bay doors.

As much as I wanted to floor the gas pedal to get as far away from Chris the roid-rage psychopath, I forced myself to drive the speed limit until I found a rest stop. I parked away from the other vehicles, peeled off my wet underwear and pulled on my jeans. Then I yanked the damn dress over my head and put on my T-shirt. Balling up the dress, I got out of the car and flung it and my soaked briefs into a trash can. I ripped the piece of tie-dyed fabric from the passenger door that waved at me like a flag and tossed it as well.

I drew in a deep breath, tore off the blood-stained portion of the paper towel and stuffed it into my mouth. Chris had not only scared the piss out of me, but apparently all of my saliva as well. I hurried to a water fountain, gulped in a mouthful of cool water and then swallowed the soggy ball of blood-drenched paper.

"I did it. I tasted the blood of my mortal enemy."

Exhilarated and exhausted, I sped home to check the next task on the parchment.

Chapter 5

Do one thing every day that scares you. —Eleanor Roosevelt

My father waxed his ride-on lawn mower as I pulled into the driveway. I'd never seen anyone wash and wax their mower after each use—except for my dad.

A pattern of laser-perfect mower marks etched across the sprawling lawn. An aerial view of our freshly mowed yard would rival the perfection of crop circles created by extraterrestrials. Sometimes I wondered if the aliens were inspired by our lawn.

"Your boss, Todd, called." He didn't look up from his polishing as I stepped out of my car.

Crap. It was Monday. I had planned to go into the office this morning and give Todd my resignation.

"Oh, okay." I shuffled toward the front path. My brain fired on the minimal amount of cells needed to move my legs and propel my weary body toward my bed.

He straightened up and stared at me, the chamois clenched in his hand. "Okay? You just blew off your job without the simple courtesy of giving the man any notice and all you have to say is, 'okay'?"

I stopped. "I'll call Todd and explain, Dad."

"Where the hell were you last night?" He asked.

"I-uh, was at a meeting for my new job."

"A business meeting that lasted all night?"

"It went later than expected. I-I slept in my car. It was too late to drive all the way back from Azure Springs."

He checked his watch. "Tim, it's sixteen-forty-five hours."

That's dad, forever stuck in military time. As my tired mind did the calculations, a spark fired off. "Shit, it's a quarter to five already?"

"Yes." He sighed and shook his head. "Look, Tim, you're a grown man. You'll have to live with your decisions. For the record, I think you're making a big mistake. And if this is the lifestyle you choose to lead, abandoning all responsibility, well, perhaps it's best you're moving out."

He turned back to the mower and buffed the shiny green hood.

Oh. Today was Monday. Crap. Every Sunday for years, my chore was the futile attempt to cut the lawn to my father's exacting expectations. "I'm sorry Dad, I forgot about mowing the yard yesterday." The last two days blended into a chaotic haze in my mind. Even more pressing than the grass, was the fact I had lost two whole days and only completed the one task. Now, less than four days remained for the two remaining unknown tasks. If each took two days I would barely make the Saturday deadline. If they took longer, I would fail.

He waved the cloth in front of my face. "Did you hear me?"

"Uh, no. I'm sorry. What?"

"For Christ's sake, Tim. I said you can wash my SUV. I didn't get to it today because I had to do your job and mow the grass." He sat on the mower and started up the engine. The sun glinted off the shiny paint as he steered it into the garage.

Wash his vehicle? Shit. I was so tired I could barely stay upright. Plus, I needed to get to the parchment and find out the next task.

"What's that on your car?" Dad had returned to the driveway and pointed at my car.

My heart jumped. I spun around and studied the Camry expecting to see a plastic bag of illegal steroids duct-taped to the fender.

Dad strode to the car. Fear motivated my legs as I hurried behind him. "What? What do you see?"

"Put some elbow grease into it and you can buff this out." His finger touched a tiny scratch near the driver's door handle. The man had the eyesight of a bionic eagle.

The breath I had been holding rushed from my mouth. "Oh, right." Chris Bagwell wouldn't waste his steroids to stash in my car. He probably bluffed to scare me. I hoped.

"Let me call Todd and change my clothes. Then I'll wash your Escalade." If I touched the parchment, at least I could start thinking about the fifth task while washing the SUV.

"The Camry needs washing, too. Looks like you've gone mudding in the damn thing."

My father exaggerated. The white car had a light coat of dust on the hood. But since it used to be his, he expected me to keep the car up to his standards. "Yes, sir." No point in arguing.

The cool, quiet house beckoned me to curl up in my bed and sleep. I plodded through the kitchen and turned into the hallway to go to my room when my mother called out. "Tim, wait."

I couldn't catch a break. My mother padded toward me in her yoga slippers. Her thin mat faced the north on the tile floor of the glass-enclosed sunroom. Soft strains of sitar music swirled in the air.

"Your supervisor called this morning. He said you never came into the office." She picked up the notepad on the counter next to the telephone. "Todd Grayson."

"I know. Dad already told me."

"Tim, you should have gone in and spoken to him. People take other jobs, but you should never burn bridges in the business world. You may need Todd as a reference someday."

"I *said* I already got a speech from Dad about it." I paused and took a deep breath. Taking my anger out on my mom was wrong. I focused on removing the edge from my voice. "I'm going to call Todd right now. Before five." I glanced up at the clock, four fifty-six.

"Fine."

The hurt in her voice cut me. She turned and headed back to the sunroom. I felt like crap for speaking so sharply to her.

Once inside my room, I pressed the button on my cell for Todd and slid the parchment from my desk drawer. I pressed my fingertip on the number five while the phone rang.

"IT, this is Todd."

"Hey, Todd, it's Tim."

"Tim, is everything okay? It's not like you not to show up or call."

"Yeah. Um, look, Todd, the thing is, I found another job. I meant to come in and talk to you in person this morning, but I had a meeting at the new company and time just got away from me."

"Wow. Geez, Tim, we're going to miss you."

I sank down onto my desk chair. The sincere sadness in his voice surprised me. "I'll, um, miss you guys, too."

"What's the job?"

"Video game designer at Create-A-Vision, over in Azure Springs."

"Whoo hoo!" Todd's yelp hurt my eardrum. "That's awesome, buddy. Congratulations, you deserve it."

"Uh, thank you, I appreciate that. And I apologize for not—"

"Are you kidding? I'd blow this place off in a heartbeat for a job at Create-A-Vision."

Todd, an avid video game player, was the only person I had shared my game idea with. He loved the concept and had volunteered to beta test the game if I ever finished it.

"Listen, Tim. I'm sure the rest of the team would want to take you out to say goodbye and celebrate your new job. How about this Saturday night? The Orange Tree Grille?"

Saturday night I planned to be on stage at the Black Swan drinking Lorelei's blood. "Sorry, man. I can't. Tight schedule. I'll be packing and moving this weekend."

"Oh, right. Well, then maybe another night?"

"Sure. I'll give you call." I said, distracted. The word *Name* had finally formed on the parchment.

"Yes, call me. And I'll have HR mail your check out." He paused and then sighed. "Well, good luck, Tim. Keep in touch, okay?"

The sadness returned to his voice. Until this moment I'd never considered him more than my boss. "I'll definitely keep in touch. Thanks for everything, Todd." I pressed the End button and peered down at the parchment. A faint mark appeared next to *Name*, but I couldn't tell if it was an X or a Y. Why was it taking so damn long to form the words?

A loud rap on my door made me jump. "You're losing daylight. Those vehicles aren't going to wash themselves."

"Be right out, Dad." Shit and double shit. I wanted to see what task five was and then take a nap. The scant sleep I'd had in the jail cell had left my mind foggy and my body sore. Instead, I pulled off my jeans and put on a pair of old sweatpants. Checking the parchment one more time and finding no further progress, I headed outside to wash the vehicles.

As usual, Dad came outside and inspected my work. I tried my best to polish his Escalade, but the black color showed every swipe of the chamois. I rushed through washing the Camry, at least as much as I could force my weary arms to hurry.

He grunted, took the cloth from me and rubbed a spot on the hood of his vehicle. "Sun's going down. Too difficult to see now. Guess it'll have to do."

Every chore I did, from mowing grass to taking out the trash to washing the car, ended with the same "guess it'll have to do" assessment from my father.

I put the car washing supplies on their designated shelf in the garage and trudged back to my room. *Name Your G* was all that had appeared on the paper so far. It had to be a set up. As I progressed down the list of tasks, the words lagged in slower and slower, causing me to lose precious time. The Saturday night deadline added pressure to my growing anxiety of what task five might entail. Task four had landed me in jail and then nearly got my throat cut by a psychopath. What if I couldn't complete the last two tasks? The entire ordeal with Chris Bagwell would be for nothing.

"Tim?" My mom called from outside my bedroom door.

I hurried and opened the door, still feeling guilty for snapping at her earlier.

"Dinner will be ready in ten minutes."

The savory aromas from the kitchen drifted in the open door. My stomach responded with a low rumble. "Great. Thanks, Mom."

She smiled at me. "Tim, I'm happy you're going to realize your dream of designing video games."

"I appreciate that. And I'm sorry I was short with you before. I'm just tired. Long day and lots of stress getting everything ready in time." None of it was a lie.

Her smile widened and she reached up and hugged me. "I know,

Sweetie. You do look tired. Get cleaned up for dinner. Your body needs fuel and then rest."

I changed my shirt and splashed water on my face before checking the parchment again. It read, *Name Your Greates.* Must be *Greatest*, but greatest what? At this rate I'd lose what few hours remained of Tuesday before I even discovered what the task was. For the moment, hunger overrode my frustration and I headed to the kitchen.

My parents stopped talking as I entered the room and joined them at the table. Mom, ever the peacekeeper, kept up a monologue of small talk. She told us tomorrow's weather forecast, that her favorite rose bush had finally bloomed, and our next-door neighbors were having their roof replaced. Dad grunted and nodded as he ate, scowling at me through the entire meal. I scarfed down a full plate of grilled salmon, wild rice, and fresh green beans and then accepted a second large helping of rice from Mom.

Dad excused himself and settled on the sofa in the family room. Gunshots and screeching brakes emanated from the sound system of the colossal television screen.

I helped mom clear the table and then she chased me out of the kitchen and told me to get some rest. Grateful for the escape, I hurried back to my room and peered down at the parchment.

Name Your Greatest Fear.

I let out a sigh of relief and stretched out on my bed. I could handle this. Hell, fear ruled my daily life ever since I could remember. My most pressing one at the moment was the fear of failing to complete these tasks. I dragged myself up from the bed and held my finger on the number five. "I fear not completing all six tasks." Nothing, the words didn't flash red as they had on the prior task. I tried another, "Getting my ass kicked by a bully." No reaction on the parchment. I'd had my ass kicked so many times, I'd probably earned immunity from that fear.

I picked up my notepad and pen and returned to the bed. I fell face down into the soft pillows and then rolled onto my back.

This task wasn't so difficult. I'd make a list of my fears and then read them aloud one at a time until one of them made the words on the parchment flash red.

I wrote *airplanes*. The one flight I had taken as a little kid scared the crap out of me. We'd encountered turbulence that rocked and jolted the plane for hours, though my father informed me the entire incident lasted less than three minutes.

I scrawled more items on the list. Fear of being rejected by a girl. Worse, fear of remaining a virgin until I died. That went hand in hand with fear of being seen naked and laughed at by a girl. I feared public embarrassment in general. And gym class, but at least that horror was behind me.

And I didn't like small, enclosed spaces. I might be claustrophobic. Dogs scared me. A dog had chased me once. A small yappy thing that had broken loose from its leash and charged into our yard. It barked, snarled, and nipped at my ankles until Mom chased it away with a broom.

Spiders, I both feared and loathed them. The sneaky way they crept across ceilings, hid in dark corners, their sticky webs—all of it gave me the creeps. A shiver ran down my back. Only last week there had been a large Calisoga spider in my room. A fancy name for a false tarantula, it was slightly smaller than but just as hideous as the real deal. I'd yelled for my mom to bring bug spray, but my father came instead, sans the spray. Disgusted by my cowardice, he snatched my nineteen seventy-two *Tomb of Dracula* first edition comic book and used it to smack the spider. I had scored the classic comic for a mere one hundred and sixty dollar bid in an online auction. Collectors valued it at over five hundred dollars in its mint condition, which, thanks to the spider guts, was now debatable. After my dad stalked off, it took all the nerve I could muster to slide the book inside a plastic trash liner—the crumpled remains of the eight-legged menace glued to the cover with its own oozing guts. The soiled magazine still lay untouched on the floor in my closet. I'd told myself I'd deal with it later.

Going to the dentist scared me silly. Literally. Poor old Doctor Phillips had to administer enough gas to knock me out cold even for cleanings. I giggled all the way home in the back seat of the car.

My Dad's temper. Not that he ever hit me or even threatened to hit me. He didn't have to; the look of disappointment on his face always sent me into a nervous sweat.

Wasps, bees, and snakes made me anxious. I feared getting stung or bitten. I wasn't really afraid of cats but avoided them due to allergies. The thought of encountering a rat frightened me, though I'd never seen one in real life, only on television.

Then there were heights in general, amusement park rides specifically. Any rides that soared really high, or spun around fast, terrified me. In seventh grade, I puked from the top of the Ferris wheel at a school carnival. My high-wire vomiting act earned me six months of teasing from my classmates. It would have been longer if they'd known I'd peed my pants, too.

Public speaking. I played sick and stayed home whenever we had to stand in front of the class in high school and give an oral report. That fell under public humiliation. Of course, Chris Bagwell's stunt topped that category.

And I feared death. I didn't want to die or ever think about my parents dying.

Crap. I stared at the growing list. It would be easier to write down what I didn't fear. I gazed up at Bela Lugosi and sighed. "I'm a total wuss." His intense stare shamed me, and I rolled on my side to avoid his scrutiny. Here I am attempting to be transformed into a member of the Night Flock and I had already filled two pages with my petty fears. Maybe I wasn't worthy.

I awoke with a start to the sound of clanging metal. My eyes flew open expecting to see the iron bars of a jail cell surrounding me, but instead they took in the blurred image of my bedroom.

I rubbed my eyes to clear them and then felt around in the rumpled sheets for my glasses. Thankfully they were still intact, and I slid them onto my face and sat up. The notepad lay on the floor. I scooped it up, stood and stretched. Again, a loud metallic noise. Parting the window curtains, I peered out at workmen raising a tall ladder to the neighbors' roof. Though well-kept, the house was older and one of the few three-story homes in the neighborhood. Metal screeched against metal as the men pushed the extension ladder to its full height and then leaned it against the house.

I checked my cell phone for the time. Shit, eleven fifty-three. With half the day gone, a surge of panic sent me hurrying to the parchment. I pressed my finger to the number five on the parchment and read from my list.

"Airplanes." Nothing. "Rejected by girls." No reaction.

A soft knock sounded on my door. "Tim?"

I padded to the door and opened it.

"Just making sure you're okay." Mom said. "It's noon. Your father and I going out for lunch with the Millers, then over to the golf course."

"Okay. Have fun."

She gently touched under my eye. "The swelling is gone, just some discoloration. Remember to put a warm cloth on it." Her eyes glistened and she gave me a weak smile. "Are you sure you're all right?"

"I'm fine. Just lots to do. You know, pack and all."

She nodded and bit her lower lip. "I made a quiche. Your favorite, spinach and feta cheese. It's cooling on the counter."

"Thanks, Mom." I started to close the door as she turned, then swung it open and called, "Love you, Mom."

"Love you, too." She smiled and walked down the hallway.

Back at the parchment, I sat at my desk and read from my list, but the words on the paper didn't react.

"Claustrophobia. Dogs. Spiders." The letters flashed blood red.

"Yes!" I completed task five. One more to go. I held my finger on the number six. Once the letters began appearing, I could enjoy a piece of Mom's warm homemade quiche while the words of the final task filled in at a snail's pace. I was almost back on schedule.

Words appeared rapidly under the number five task, not six.

Name ALL of your fears.

"Okay, okay." I huffed, held my finger on the number five and continued reciting the humiliating list. The letters flashed red again when I read fear of heights. I continued until I reached the last item, but the only two that had caused a reaction were spiders and heights.

"There. Are you satisfied?" I asked the parchment. "Now, for the last task." I held my finger on the number six. Words appeared above my finger, still beneath the number five.

You must conquer your fears of spiders and heights.

"What?" Holy shit. Conquer two fears that had plagued me my

60

entire life in only three days? Plus, there was the unknown sixth task to deal with, too.

"Okay. I'll start with . . . spiders?" As if to dramatize my fear, the words on the parchment gleamed red then faded to black. My scalp quivered and a wave of imaginary segmented legs scuttled down my back accompanied by a tingling chill of dread. I stared at my closed closet door. "Crap."

Now or never, I couldn't put it off any longer.

I opened my closet door. There it was, the benign-looking white plastic bag on the floor just as I had left it. I kicked aside a flip flop and some dirty socks partially covering it and then used the other flip flop to nudge the bag from the closet.

The thin plastic lay flat over most of the surface except for the misshapen lump dead center on the cover. "Damn, that was a big spider."

What if it were pregnant when Dad squashed it? Would I open the bag and unleash a horde of baby tarantula wannabes? I shivered as I pictured hundreds of spiders scurrying across the floor, up the walls and scuttling up my legs and back. And I had no defense. I ran into my bathroom and pulled sheets of toilet paper from the roll. The handful of white fluff looked too insignificant for the chore. Balling up the tissue I tossed it into the trash can.

Plan B. I hurried to the kitchen to arm myself with paper towels. They'd be thicker, sturdier. Two or three sheets should do the job. But just in case, I removed the entire roll from the holder and tucked it under my arm. From the cabinet under the kitchen sink, I snatched up the can of bug spray. Armed, I returned to my room.

Crouching down, I grasped the bottom edge of the bag and slowly pulled. The bright red banner and yellow title of the comic slid out first. I yanked the bag from the rest of the book and stepped back.

"Oh, man." I hadn't looked closely at the magazine the night my dad smashed it against the hairy arachnid. Even after a week of drying inside the closet, the sight sent a wave of chills through me. The head and legs were intact, though the rear legs crumpled at odd angles which made it worse. Its fat rounded abdomen formed an elongated hairy smear twice the size in death as it had been in life.

Its eyes, a series of shiny black dots, peered up at me between two hooked fang-like appendages. I backed away from the comic book until my butt bumped into my computer desk.

"It's dead. It can't hurt me." I wasn't convinced.

I sank down onto my chair, my gaze still riveted on the spider across the room. I didn't want to look at it but couldn't stop myself either. Did a leg just twitch? The more I stared, the more I thought I detected a slight wiggle. Maybe I'd revived it when I removed the plastic and gave it air.

"No. Impossible." I clenched a ball of paper towels in my fist and stood. My body trembled. My breath came fast, matching the elevated beat of my heart. The shallow gasps made me dizzy and my knees quivered.

"This is stupid." I'm stupid. All I had to do was pick up the magazine and wipe the thing into the trash can with the wad of sweaty paper towels in my hand. Easy. My heart sped up.

Taking a deep breath, I sat down again, started up my laptop and Googled *How to overcome the fear of spiders.* I clicked on a self-help listing that outlined a fifteen-step plan. Start small, it cautioned, and be sure to rate your anxiety level from one to ten during each step. Repeat each step until you no longer feel anxious. Step one, look at pictures and videos of spiders. Step two, hold a toy spider. The last thirteen steps involved various scenarios of observing live spiders and then gradually working your way up to touching and then handling one. At the bottom of the list, the disclaimer read, *if you become too anxious and do not seem to get relief even with prolonged exposure, it could make your fear worse. Be careful and seek consultation with a mental health professional.*

"Freaking great. I don't have time for a shrink." Sweat coated my top lip. More drizzled down my forehead. I did a search for images of spiders. One click, and my screen crawled with dozens of photos.

Some were massive, some tiny. There were thick-legged, fat hairy ones like the one plastered on the comic book and sleek, shiny ones with hair-thin legs. Some hung inside webs. All had eight jointed legs and eight dead-looking eyes. The sight of the treacherous beasts lying in wait, ready to snare unsuspecting prey, repulsed me. Those unfortunate enough to be trapped in the sticky threads would have pieces ripped from their bodies, be mummified in spider silk and then sucked dry of their fluids by hooked fangs.

I had rolled my chair several feet back from the desk. "Anxiety level, eleven." I placed the wireless mouse on my palm and moved the cursor to close the window of images from a safe distance. My heartbeat slowed a bit. I needed help and needed it fast.

Mom had gone through a bout of anxiety attacks about a year ago, right before she retired from nursing. There had been a terrible school bus accident and she was on duty when they brought in the injured children. She had nightmares and panic attacks for weeks following the tragedy. And, she had taken prescription pills to help her deal with anxiety.

I jumped from my chair and ran to the other end of the house to my mom and dad's master suite. Opening their medicine cabinet, I searched though a myriad of toiletries—Band-aids, antiseptic creams, and shaving supplies, but no pills.

I rifled through the drawers in the teak vanity. Tucked away in the back of my mom's makeup drawer an orangey plastic prescription bottle caught my attention. It was labeled Xanax. The directions said to take one pill daily for anxiety. My anxiety was off the charts. To be certain, I shook out four into my palm and tossed them into my mouth, then returned the bottle to the drawer.

"The pills will work. They have to." I went into the kitchen, but my tense stomach had no appetite for the still warm, aromatic quiche cooling on the counter. Instead, I reached for the carton of orange juice in the refrigerator and took a long gulp. Leaning against the cool stainless steel of the refrigerator door, a sense of peacefulness washed over my head and gradually trickled through my entire body. I sat at the kitchen table sipping from the carton and building up my courage while I waited for the pills to take full effect.

The room spun just a teeny bit as I bent and grasped the corner of the comic book in two fingers. The motion made the mangled spider legs wiggle as I carried the book to my bathroom trash can. Eight beady black dots glared at me. I smothered the unnerving sight with the mass of paper towels I clutched in my other hand. Holding the book over the trash, I swiped at the cover. The towels slid on the slick paper until they hit the lump of crusted, stuck-on spider. I bore down harder until a sickening brittle crunch sounded. The lump loosened.

I shoved the wad of paper into the trash can. Something dark twirled in the air and landed on my bare foot. A crooked, spiny leg.

Scrambling to unroll toilet paper, I ripped a handful from the dispenser, bent over and wiped the top of my foot. Due to my profuse sweating, the prickly leg stuck to my damp skin, and my glasses slid down my nose as I leaned and frantically swatted at the spider leg. Without lenses to see, the dark appendage blurred and multiplied.

Adjusting my glasses, I sat on the toilet lid and lifted my bent knee to bring my foot closer. I didn't really need to see it, every nerve in my body pinpointed its location. I squeezed my eyes closed, and using my thumb and forefinger, I plucked the leg from my foot. Its prickly texture stuck to my fingertips. I finally managed to flick it into the trash and then buried it under a wad of toilet paper.

I stood at the sink and scrubbed my foot and then my hands with hot water and soap. The bright overhead lights reflecting off the white tile hurt my eyes. I leaned against the door frame to steady myself before staggering across the bedroom floor and collapsing onto my bed. "I did it."

Bela Lugosi held me in his hypnotic gaze. The corners of his mouth turned upward ever so slightly. He approved.

A loud, steady beeping jarred me from my stupor. Drool covered my bottom lip and left cheek. I rolled onto my side and pushed myself up into a sitting position. After a minute or so my head stopped spinning and my eyes focused outside the window on the source of the noise. A flatbed truck backed up the Fishers' driveway next door. When it stopped, a workman drove a forklift to the open end and began unloading pallets of bundled shingles.

I sat mesmerized by the workmen's organized movements. As I wiped the spittle from my face a thought danced around the edges of my mind of an ant carrying a bull horn. It darted around yelling, but its tiny voice remained just out of earshot. It shouted something urgent—something I needed to do. I stood up. The simple action felt like it would go on forever, each muscle pushing, then pulling my body upward. Would my head hit the ceiling? Reaching up, my hands barely grazed the textured surface above my head. It was absurdly funny. The rough plaster swirls overhead tickled my fingertips. I laughed.

The parchment! Turning, I zigzagged across the room toward my desk. The ant's screams finally broke through my bouts of laughter. "Finish the tasks," it yelled. I stared at the words on the parchment and remembered. I had completed the fear of spiders. Only the fear of heights remained.

My fingers tapped the keyboard on my laptop but the letters in the search field didn't form a word. I sat and forced myself to concentrate as I typed. I needed to find a Ferris wheel. I hit Enter and images of ferrets filled my screen. Their cute, whiskered faces and long, sleek bodies sent me into another wave of giggling.

The persistent ant chastised me, "You're too drugged to drive to an amusement park."

"You're right," I said.

Bela Lugosi nodded in agreement.

I tapped random keys enjoying the rhythmic sound of the faint clicks. Men's shouts outside distracted me. I stood, wobbled over to the window, and opened it. A gust of cool air lifted the sheer curtains. They billowed up over my shoulders. A fine mist of clear droplets formed on my eyeglass lenses. The workmen scurried around the yard next door, covering pallets with bright blue tarps before climbing into their trucks and driving away.

Thick gray clouds drifted in, slowly obliterating the sun. The last of the sun's rays fell on the tall silver and orange ladder leaning against the back of the neighbor's house. It glowed in a surreal light. The shiny silver rungs, each smaller and smaller, led upward toward the last bright spot in the darkening clouds.

Strains of a haunting melody from one of my mother's CDs came to mind . . . I didn't know all the lyrics, only snippets. "There's a lady . . . hmm hmm . . . all that glitters is gold . . . hmm hmm . . . and she's . . . hmm hmm hmm . . . a stairway to heaven."

"You don't need a Ferris wheel," the ant whispered. "The ladder is tall enough for the task."

I glanced up at Bela for confirmation. He winked.

A cool mist blew into my face as I pushed through a narrow opening in the hedge that separated our property from the Fishers' yard. The tall shiny ladder stood feet away, stretching upward toward the swirling gray and purple sky.

I grasped the ladder with both hands and stepped up onto the first rung. Keeping my eyes trained on the smoky lavender clouds overhead, a sense of euphoria enveloped me. I climbed to the second rung. The ant sung bits of the song, substituting *climbing* a stairway to heaven. I didn't argue, just sang along with it, repeating the same verse over and over and as I made my way up the ladder. A tremor ran through me and I stopped. The rungs were cold and wet. My tennis shoe slid forward. The heel tread gripped the etched lines on the rounded aluminum bar. Another voice, more of a low, hoarse whisper spoke, but the ant's shrill singing made it impossible to discern the words.

My fingers stiffened and the tremors continued. I stared upward at the driving rain that hammered my eyeglass lenses and soaked through my shirt and jeans. The wet material tugged against my skin with each step as if unseen hands tried to pull me downward. The low voice sounded again and this time I heard it clearly. "Look down," it said.

I did. An electric shock zipped down my spine. Threading my arms around the ladder, I hugged it with all my might. Three rungs from the top—my head even with the roof line—I remembered I was deathly afraid of heights.

The low voice dominated over the singing ant. "You moron! How are you going to get down?"

"I-I don't know."

A noise distracted me. More voices chimed in my head.

"It's the neighbor's kid, Jim," a gruff voice said.

"His name is Tim," a softer, higher voice said.

The ant's melodic voice stopped. I sang, hoping it would join me. "And I'm climbing the stairway to heaven . . ."

"Good Lord. He's suicidal. Ranting about heaven," the gruff voice said.

The softer voice called out, "Tim? Tim, honey?"

A flash of white below me and to my left caught my eye. Gripping the ladder tighter, I looked down. A pale hand waved a lacy white handkerchief from an open third floor window.

"It's Beatrice, Tim. What are you doing on the ladder?"

The gruff voice answered, "He's gonna jump, that's what, God dammit."

"Shush, George. It's raining, Tim. Why don't you climb down now?"

"I'm not getting sued 'cause some crazy kid probably hopped up on drugs climbs a ladder on my property," the gruff one said. "They can sue the roofers for leaving it up."

"George, please. Go next door and get his parents."

George and Beatrice. The names slowly drilled through the fog in my mind. Our neighbors, the Fishers. Beatrice was a sweet old lady. Baked peanut butter cookies. George was an ass. I hugged the ladder as my right leg shook. All I could do was sing and keep my eyes focused on the sky. The rain stung my cheeks and forehead.

Beatrice talked, but the drumming of the rain on the roof made it difficult to hear her. I unclenched my left hand and waved to her, then grasped the cold wet metal again.

George's gruff voice returned, "Always knew he was a God damned weirdo. No one answered next door. I called the police."

"We have Mindy and Steve's cell numbers. In my notebook by the kitchen phone." Beatrice's voice rose, "Tim, be a good boy now and stay put. I'm going to call your parents."

"And I'm pressing charges. Trespassing. Maybe vandalism. I'll be damned if they think they can sue me cause their son's a damned mental case."

The shaking traveled from my right to my left leg and then up my back. I felt cold, wet, and confused. My arms locked around the sides of the ladder and refused to move.

Voices drifted upward, distorted by the pounding rain and sometimes drowned out completely by rumbles of thunder.

One voice rose above the din and cried out, "Tim!"

"Mom?" I opened my eyes and dared to look down. She looked so small standing on the grass.

"Tim. You hear me son?" Not Mom's voice. Dad's voice.

"Y-Yes, sir," I croaked.

"Listen to me. Stay calm, all right?"

"Yes, Dad."

"Now, you're going to climb down. Same way you climbed up. One step at a time. Understand?"

I ordered my leg to move but it stayed frozen in place.

"C-Can't." I said.

"Yes, you can. Take a deep breath."

I did.

"Lift your right leg and then step down." His tone hardened, his voice amplified. "Don't think. Just do it!"

My right foot jerked off the rung. My leg swung in the air searching for the rung.

"Loosen your arms. The rung is there. Put your right foot on it."

Mom let out a short scream. "Steven, do something!"

"I'm coming up," Dad called. The ladder shook and I grasped it tighter.

The ant screamed, "No! You have to do this yourself. You must conquer your fear of heights."

Heart pounding, I repeated the ant's words. "No, Dad! I have to do this myself. Get over my fear."

The thuds on the lower rungs stopped. "Then do it, Tim. C'mon down. You can do it, son."

I chanced a peek downward. Dad stepped from the bottom rung onto the wet grass.

Sirens sounded in the distance. Then red and blue flashing lights reflected in the shiny glass windows. I turned my head and the strobing array of lights in the driveway made me dizzy. Laying my forehead against the cold metal rung above me I drew in a long breath of cool air and sang as I lowered my right foot to the rung below me.

"Good. Now your left foot." Dad shouted.

The ant sang, this time more softly, sweetly. But no, it wasn't the ant. I looked down. Mom stood beneath the ladder. She sang with me. She knew all the words. I hummed along and only joined in the chorus. ". . . buying a stairway to heaven."

Dad's deep voice carried over the melody. He barked out words like military orders. "Right foot." A pause, then, "Left foot."

I found a rhythm and the euphoric feeling returned. My legs stopped shaking and my feet obeyed. I sang louder as I climbed down the ladder. Near the bottom, I stopped and then raced back upwards. I stood looking around and released my grip on the ladder spreading my arms out to my sides and then above my head.

"I did it!"

"Tim! Get down here now, dammit!" Dad said.

I hurried downward and jumped off the second to last rung into a puddle at the foot of the ladder.

Mom flung her arms around me. Dad clapped a strong hand on my shoulder. Then a young man in a blue jumpsuit stepped forward and draped a gray blanket around my shoulders.

"Thanks." I grinned at him. "I did it."

Beatrice and George watched me from outside their back door, huddled beneath a large red and white striped umbrella. I waved at them. "I did it."

A police officer and two more men in jumpsuits approached. Dad walked toward them.

"Tim, what were you thinking? You've always been deathly afraid of heights," Mom said.

"The ant started singing that stairway song and then the sun lit up the ladder and it looked so shiny and I just—"

"Mindy," Dad interrupted. "The police said they won't arrest him, but only if they take him to the hospital for observation."

Mom's eyes widened and she shook her head. She looped her arm through mine, but the man in the jumpsuit gripped my other arm. A second man asked Mom to release my arm and step back.

"He's not suicidal. There's no need for this," she said. "I'm a nurse. I'll watch him."

"I'm sorry ma'am. You're welcome to ride along."

"Can the ant come, too?" I turned and scanned the wet grass looking for it. "Hey, careful bro, don't step on him."

"Tim, stop talking," Mom said as she hurried along behind me.

My head pounded and my throat felt parched. Squinting up at

the bright lights, the room blurred white. I felt around the mattress for my glasses but found my wrists were secured to steel railings on either side of the bed with white straps. This wasn't my bedroom.

"Hey," I called out, my voice hoarse and barely a whisper. The railings rattled as I pulled against the straps. A loud beep sounded and continued.

A nurse bustled into the room. "Calm down please. Lie still."

She fiddled with something next to the bed and the shrill beeping noise stopped.

"Tim, how are you feeling?" I turned toward the familiar voice. Mom's face hovered over the bedside.

"Thirsty." I squinted to see my surroundings but everything beyond the bed faded into a white blur.

"Here, sweetie." Mom held a paper cup to my mouth. The nurse raised the head of the bed.

The cold water moistened my tongue and dislodged it from the roof of my mouth.

"More, please."

"I'll be at the station if you need anything, Mindy." The nurse left the room and closed the door behind her.

"Mom, is this a hospital? And why are my arms tied down?"

She put down a plastic pitcher and held the cup to my lips again. I gulped the water from the small cup.

Mom pulled a chair close to the bed. She let out a long sigh as she sat. "It's Mercy General. You're on suicide watch, Tim."

"Suicide? What the—? Why?"

"The Fishers thought you climbed their ladder to jump. They heard you singing about heaven."

"Oh." I pushed my head back into the stiff pillow. I remembered it all now. The parchment, the tasks, and overcoming my fear of heights. "I needed to get over my fear of heights."

"They found Xanax in your blood, Tim. Where did you get it? And why would you take it?"

"Shit." I closed my eyes. "I, um, took some of your old pills, Mom. I thought it would help me to not be scared."

Mom rubbed her forehead and then shook her head. "The amount they found, how many did you take?"

"I don't know, three, maybe four. I think."

"Oh, Tim. One pill lasts twelve hours. At that dosage you could have. . ." She hunched forward and cried into her hands.

"I'm okay, Mom. And I'm sorry, I shouldn't have taken your pills. But I wasn't trying to kill myself, I swear."

She took tissues from a box on the nightstand, wiped her eyes and blew her nose. "I believe you," she whispered.

"Then, can we go home now?" Besides desperately wanting to scratch my nose and not being able to reach it, the deadline to complete the tasks ticked away.

"They won't release you until tomorrow. Twenty-four hours is mandatory."

"Tomorrow? What day is it? What time?"

"Wednesday night." She fished her cell phone from her bag at her feet and pressed the screen. "Ten thirty-six."

"Oh, no." Wednesday's gone? I had to go home. Now. "I'm running out of time."

Mom gripped my arm. "Running out of time for what?"

My mind worked slowly, my thoughts murky as I recalled my cover story. My mouth formed clumsy words. "Um, for my new, um job. Getting stuff, uh ready. You know, like packing."

"Sweetheart, maybe now isn't a good time to make a move." She used the balled-up tissues in her hand and dabbed a stray tear rolling down her cheek.

"Mom, I'm fine. Really. Mercy hospital, right? You used to work here. Can't you talk to somebody and get me released?"

"I already did. Originally, they were going to hold you for forty-eight hours. Sharon, Doctor Ghee that is, agreed to interview you tomorrow morning. She's the resident psychiatrist. Your release depends on her recommendations."

"You mean if I fail the interview, they could keep me here?"

Mom nodded and looked down. "Well, not here. A mental facility."

"I made a mistake taking the pills, but I just wanted to get over my fear of heights. That doesn't make me crazy, does it?"

I awoke to an even brighter room with sunlight pouring through

71

the large window. Mom stood by the window pulling the cord to open the mint-green full-length drapes.

An older nurse with short gray hair entered. She held her finger up and told me to stay absolutely still while she removed the restraints on my arms. I waited until she undid both arms before asking permission to rub my nose.

She smiled. "Yes." She turned toward Mom. "He's all yours, Mindy. Breakfast trays will be around in a few minutes. I ordered an extra coffee for you."

"Thanks, Sue." Mom smiled, but her face looked drawn and pale in the sunlight, except for the deep pink ringing her eyes.

"Doctor Ghee will be by at ten." Sue exited, leaving the door open.

I turned to Mom, a petite silhouette against the glaring square of window light. "You stayed here all night?"

"Of course." She smiled and walked to the bed. "Here're your glasses." She slipped them from her purse and handed them to me.

"You shouldn't have stayed. I'm sorry about all this, Mom." With the exception of a constant dull throb in my temples, my mind felt clearer. The eyeglasses brought the rest of the small room into focus. "Thank you."

She nodded and murmured something lost in the clattering of a cart pushed into the room. A tall blond guy in navy-blue scrubs swung a rolling table across the bed and then placed a tray from the stainless-steel cart on it. "Bon appétit." He nodded and then pushed the cart out into the noisy hallway.

I ate one bite of the rubbery scrambled eggs and then moved on to lukewarm toast paired with an icy pat of butter and a plastic cup of molten hot coffee.

Mom sat in the chair and sipped the extra cup of coffee. She shook her head when I offered her some of my breakfast.

The early morning dragged on as I clicked the television remote between news and morning talk shows. Mom excused herself to go stretch her legs, but I noted she clutched her cell phone as she left the room and wondered how ballistic dad would act when, or if, I arrived back home.

Would he search my room and find the parchment? Did I put it

72

in the drawer or leave it out on my desk? Waves of anxiety rolled over me. I pictured Dad burning the parchment and all my vampire posters and comic books in a fit of anger. What if this Doctor Ghee labeled me nuts? They'd lock me up in a psych ward and I'd never get to complete the tasks or see Lorelei on Saturday night. There was only one task left and likely it'd be the most difficult. I needed to find out what it was and instead I was stuck here waiting for a mental evaluation. What if I had blown my only chance to transform my life just by climbing one damn ladder? Shit. Then I would become suicidal.

The door swung open. I expected to see Mom or the nurse, but instead a slim Asian woman in a white coat and black slacks breezed into the room.

"Hello, Tim. I'm Doctor Ghee. I'd like to ask you a few questions." Her smile, though pleasant, didn't change the clinical look in her dark, almond-shaped eyes. Her long black hair slicked back into a ponytail that swung just above her ass as she leaned to reposition the bedside chair.

Under other circumstances, I'd think she was hot.

"So how are you feeling this morning?" She flashed the same practiced smile she'd greeted me with. Her slender fingers held a Bic pen poised over a clipboard she balanced on her crossed knees.

Is that a trick question? I swallowed to moisten my throat and attempted a smile. My upper lip stuck to my dry front teeth. Shit, did I just give her a crazy smile? "Um, fine." I said.

Her long series of questions started out benign, but gradually poked deeper.

"Do you ever think about dying?"

"No. Never." I lied. Once or twice during a beating by a bully in school I welcomed death, but I didn't dare admit that to her.

She paused after each question and wrote on the clipboard. "Tell me why you climbed the ladder, Tim."

My right eye twitched. The lid wouldn't stop quivering. I poked my finger under my glasses and rubbed it, hoping she wouldn't notice. "I wanted to get over my fear of heights."

"Did you?"

I thought a moment. "Yes, I think so."

73

"Do have other fears, Tim?"

Oh, crap. I refused to leap into that rabbit hole. We'd be here for days and she'd commit me for sure. I lied again. "No, not really. Just heights."

"What made you decide to face this fear yesterday?"

"Well, I'm getting ready to start a new job. Move to a new town. I just wanted to, uh, start my new life . . . fearless." I licked my teeth before smiling this time. I hoped I looked sane.

"Tell me about your new job."

Though also a lie, that answer came easy. I rattled on about being a video game designer, my passion genuine. I stopped when she slid the pen into the top of the clipboard. She cocked her head and her smile lit up her eyes this time. Yeah, she was definitely hot.

She stood, still smiling. "I wish you good luck in your new venture." She headed for the door.

"Thanks. Um, Doctor Ghee?"

She turned.

"Can I be released now?"

"Yes. As soon as your paperwork is processed."

"How long will—?"

She hurried off into the hallway without answering.

The nurse returned and administered a fraction of the dosage of Xanax I had originally ingested in order to ease any possible withdrawal symptoms. Mom disagreed with the doctor's order to medicate me further. She said the chances of becoming addicted or experiencing withdrawal after only one dose were practically nil, even though it had been a large dose.

The mild calming effects of the new dose, which the nurse said would stay in my system another twelve hours, did nothing to quell my growing rage at being imprisoned inside a stuffy hospital room. While I did doze off for short naps, when awake, my head ached, and I felt jittery and out of sorts. Allowed to get up, I paced the room and stared at the large clock on the wall, willing its hands with my eyes to stay still. It was nearly one-thirty on Thursday afternoon and my sole concern was to get home and find out what the sixth task was, but the hospital's red tape kept me bound to the small room like a hostage.

Unable to nap in the chair with my fidgeting and complaining, Mom gave up on sleep and went downstairs to the administration office in an effort to speed up my release.

The lunch cart rattled into the room a few minutes after Mom left. When the chubby young woman served my lunch tray, I thought about shoving her into the closet and stealing the food cart to use as a cover to escape from the infuriating hospital situation.

I picked at a nondescript piece of brown meat next to a lump of cool, firm mashed potatoes and a watery pile of corn. If brown had a flavor, then that's how the meat tasted. A small dish of chocolate pudding, cold and sweet, helped smother the growling in my stomach.

Mom finally returned with a stack of papers in hand. "All the insurance is taken care of. You just need to sign these forms." She handed me a packet of papers. "Then we wait for an orderly to bring up a wheelchair and take you downstairs."

"A wheelchair? But I can walk—"

"It's hospital policy, Tim. Now sit, sign, and be quiet. Please."

If her tone didn't indicate she had lost patience with my impatience, the icy glare that accompanied it certainly made her point crystal clear.

At three-seventeen, a white-haired man with a pronounced limp pushed my wheelchair from my room down the hall to the elevators. His snail-like pace made me grip the arms of the chair and dig my fingernails into the dark blue padding, especially when an ancient-looking woman dragging an intravenous stand raced past us as if we were standing still.

Mom walked beside us. Dull thuds replaced her perky footsteps, and she looked like she had aged ten years. I chewed my upper lip to keep from screaming at the old man to push faster.

Finally, on the ground floor, I forced myself to stay seated instead of leaping from the chair and running out the double glass doors.

Mom never drove much above the speed limit and today her exhaustion kept her pinned in the right lane doing ten miles under

75

the speed limit. I gripped the door handle while my right foot pressed an imaginary gas pedal.

"Mom. Mom! You just passed our street." My head swiveled to the right watching the rows of palm trees breeze past.

"I need to pick up a few things for dinner at the supermarket."

I slammed my head back against the head rest and squeezed my eyes shut. Never much of a crier, hot tears of frustration stung the insides of my eyelids and the steady dull throb in my temples kicked into high gear.

"I didn't exactly have time to go grocery shopping last evening like I'd planned." She stared straight ahead at the bottleneck of early rush hour traffic ahead. Her slim fingers showed white knuckles grasping the steering wheel.

I swallowed and forced a deep breath. "I know. Sorry."

The clock on the dash rolled to four forty-six when Mom pulled into our driveway. I opened the passenger door before she shifted into park. Dad walked down the path from the front door to greet us.

"Carry the bags for your mother," he said.

"Yes, sir." I hurried to the open trunk and scooped up all of the plastic bags.

"Careful now, Tim," Mom said.

I rushed past Mom and Dad, into the kitchen, and heaved the unwieldy mass of plastic bags onto the shiny granite counter. A jar of sun-dried tomatoes rolled from one of the bags. I heard the crash of glass shattering on the tile floor.

"Shit. Sorry, Mom."

"Oh, Tim," Mom plunked her keys and purse on the counter. "I'll get the mop."

"Like hell you will. You look exhausted, Mindy." Dad nodded at me. "You know where the mop is."

It was obvious by now that unseen forces of the universe conspired against me. While my father stood, arms crossed and watching me, I cleaned up the broken glass and oily red tomato mess from the floor. The jar held eight ounces of tomatoes, yet the spill somehow spread over a third of the tiled floor. My father's keen eyes supervised while I performed one thorough mopping with soap followed by a rinse with fresh water.

I stood holding the mop and plastic bucket awaiting my father's approval. "Yeah, good enough, I guess." He waved his hand and dismissed me.

"It's fine, Tim," Mom said. "Oh look, it's after five. I need to get dinner started."

Dad wrapped an arm around her shoulders. "I have the grill fired up on the back patio and steaks ready to go." He kissed Mom's forehead. "And a salmon filet for you."

"Oh, that sounds wonderful. I'll make a salad."

I slipped away and returned the mop and bucket to the laundry room. As I passed through the kitchen, Mom sliced tomatoes and Dad stood on the patio tending the gas grill.

Twenty-six hours after climbing the neighbor's ladder I finally returned to my room, locked the door, collapsed into my desk chair and pressed my finger on the number six.

Letters immediately appeared above my fingertip—but under the number five.

You have conquered your fear of heights.

"Yeah, yeah I know. Show me the last task."

Yet you failed to conquer your fear of spiders.

"What? No, I didn't! I scraped that ugly spider off my comic book cover."

A dead spider doesn't count. If you do not conquer your fear, the last task will not be revealed. You will be deemed to be unworthy for transformation.

"What the—? This is bullshit. I did conquer both fears." My body shook with rage as I gripped the parchment and crumpled it in my fist. "Oh, hell." I laid it on the desk and smoothed out the wrinkles. "I can't believe I'm arguing with a damned piece of paper."

This is your last chance to conquer your fear.

The dark ink swirled on the mottled tan surface of the paper until all of the words from tasks one through five snaked into the center of the paper. The letters merged into a large dark ink blot.

"No! No, what's happening? I completed five tasks. You're cheating! It's not fair."

The ink blot pulsed and writhed in the center of the paper. A lump gradually rose upward from the parchment. One by one, eight jointed legs stretched from the lump. Then a head rose upward. Eight shiny, flat eyes glared up at me. The hideous creature crawled toward me. The tips of its hairy legs scratched the paper as it moved.

"Holy crap." The huge spider squatted at the edge of the paper as if poised to jump. The parchment was now blank. My list of completed tasks, obliterated. There was no breeze in my room yet the fine hairs covering its bloated abdomen bristled as if an invisible wind ruffled its fur.

My heartbeat sped up. I understood what I had to do. "Holy mother of crap." I closed my eyes, steeled my shaking hand and held my palm out, inches from the arachnid's head. "I'm not afraid." My teeth clenched together with a loud clack as I willed my hand to stay still. The spider jumped onto my hand. Its weight startled and horrified me. Two of its forward-facing legs lightly scratched my skin, almost a caress. A violent shiver shifted my scalp on my skull and rattled down my spine. The spider crawled toward my wrist. The press of each of its legs sent a cascade of tremors across my skin.

"I can do this. I have to do this." My teeth pressed together so hard I thought they would shatter. Rapid huffs of air flared out my nostrils. The thing crept up my bare arm. I focused on the parchment. I had to conquer my fear in order to be transformed. A dark hairy blur moved slowly in my peripheral vision, then vanished.

I turned my head slightly, feeling its thick legs creeping onto my shoulder before actually seeing it. It sat on my shoulder looking at me, rubbing two hairy fang-like appendages together in front of its mouth. "G-Good boy. Don't bite me."

I drew in a long, jagged breath hoping to activate some of the Xanax in my blood stream. "Stay calm." I closed my eyes and held my left hand out, palm up near my shoulder. "C'mon boy. Jump." Nothing happened. My heart and temples pounded in unison. I suddenly had to pee.

The furry beast walked across the back of my neck. My scalp tingled with each prickly footstep. Every hair on my head lifted. It crawled onto my left shoulder.

"It's just a bug. I'm a thousand times taller, heavier. I could crush it with one hand." The thought of squashing its plump abdomen with my bare hand sent a new ripple of chills through me. The spider reared up and its legs prodded my left cheek.

"No. Not on my face. Oh, nooo." It moved upward using its spiny feet for traction on my cheek and crawled over my glasses. The shadow of its body blocked the vision in my left eye as it scuttled to my forehead and then up on top of my head.

I sucked in deep breaths, feeling its weight and its legs tangling in my hair as it moved around on my head. "I want to be transformed." I repeated the mantra and visualized myself on stage with Lorelei to distract myself from the enormous spider nesting in my hair.

Its legs magnified into thick spiky clubs that stretched across the right lens of my glasses. It took its time moving down my face, then my neck and finally back to my right shoulder where it settled down, its feet clinging to my T-shirt like eight Velcro dots.

I sat as still as possible despite the involuntary tremors which coursed through my body in rhythmic waves. Every cell in my brain screamed at me to knock the disgusting thing off my shoulder and run from the room. I fought back the panic. I sat still and breathed.

In a sudden burst of movement, the spider raced down my right arm and then squatted in my palm, its bulbous body bouncing up and down on bent legs in my open hand.

"O-Ok. Good boy. Go back into the paper now."

Its dead black eyes stared up at me and it bounced again, the hairs tickling my palm and sending chills up my arm. A drop of urine leaked into my underwear.

"Oh. Oh crap." It wants me to touch it. I reached over and swiped my finger across its back. A quick pet, barely grazing its furry body. "There. Good spider. Now go." Its hair felt silkier than it looked. Drawing in a ragged breath, I gave it a longer, gentler pat. It rose up and scuttled from my hand onto the parchment. A second later, it melted into a flattened blob of ink. The ink blot swirled and tiny pieces broke off. They formed into strokes of letters. The fine lines spread across the paper in a dizzying blur. All of the words returned to where they had been before—and now a new line of text appeared under the number five.

You have conquered your fear of spiders.

Tears flowed from my eyes and relief washed over me. My arms and legs quivered and jerked with spasms as the knotted muscles relaxed. "I freaking did it."

I did do it, didn't I?

Not trusting the sadistic nature of the parchment, I placed my finger on the number six and held my breath. Letters formed next to the number six.

You have succeeded in completing five tasks. One final task remains. You must remove the clothing from a corpse and wear it on the night you become a vampire. If you fail to complete this final task, you will never be worthy of transformation.

Chapter 6

Clothes make the man. Naked people have little or no influence on society. —Mark Twain

My first thought was of my deceased grandfather's clothes stored in our attic, but the parchment specifically dictated to *remove the clothing from a corpse*, not from an old trunk in my attic. I knew how literal the damned parchment could be and if I failed this last task, I'd be banned forever from transformation. I had to get this one right.

My mind reeled with grave-robbing scenes from all the old B horror movies I'd watched. It would be dark soon. I could get a shovel from the garage, sneak into a cemetery and then—what? Providing I didn't get arrested, it would take me until dawn or later to dig down six feet and clear away enough dirt to open the coffin lid. I remembered how long it took to dig out a four-foot square garden in the back lawn for my mom, and that was only a few inches deep.

And what if I found nothing but rotted cloth clinging to a skeleton? There was barely enough time to dig up one body, I couldn't keep digging up graves all night until I found a suit I liked. It was a cemetery not a Men's Wearhouse.

"It's impossible. There's no way I can do this in time."

I slumped in my chair and laid my head on my desk. It was over. I failed. My life would continue as before—boring, depressing, and sexless until I eventually died alone—an old, depressed virgin.

I stood up, walked to my closet and pulled out a long cape covered in clear plastic from the dry cleaners. Black wool with a silvery-gray satin lining, the thrift shop owner where I purchased it said it was an authentic Victorian era gentlemen's opera cape. A caplet fell from the shoulders and around the back. Had it a red lining, it would have matched Bela Lugosi's cape. I pictured the original owner as a tall, dark-haired Brit—sporting a black silk top hat, gloves, and holding an ornately-carved walking stick.

Staring into a dusty full-length mirror at the thrift store, I marveled at how the garment changed my entire appearance. The slim tailored cut fit my body perfectly and the extra layer of the caplet added much-needed girth to my shoulders. I had to have it.

Until task six dictated differently, I had planned to wear the cape this Saturday night.

I hung the cape in the dark closet along with my dreams of a new life, walked back to my desk and sank into the chair. The writing on the parchment blurred and I swiped tears from my eyes. I was so close.

When the going gets tough, the tough get going blared in my mind. That was my father's terse reply when I had said digging a garden in the back yard was too hard. He'd either be proud or laugh like hell if he knew how many of his cliché sayings were embedded in my brain.

I turned on my computer and Googled *grave robbery*. Over one million results popped up beginning with tales of ancient Egyptian tomb robbers to present day celebrity souvenir hunters. The articles included gruesome accounts of body snatching for medical dissection, necrophilia, and even cannibalism.

The articles also detailed creative solutions to prevent grave robbery, including Mort safes, coffin collars, and guards hired to watch over the grave until the body sufficiently decomposed. Nowadays, people had burial vaults and grave liners constructed from concrete, metal, and plastic. The practice was so popular in the United States that most cemeteries required a liner to be installed before burial.

Another search confirmed the cemeteries in my immediate area required a vault or liner.

Crap. A simple garden shovel wouldn't penetrate a concrete vault. I'd need a jackhammer or possibly a backhoe—as if I could get my hands on either tonight. Not to mention, jackhammering open a grave at midnight would not go unnoticed. I couldn't afford to be arrested again.

The task was impossible. "I'm screwed." I slammed my mouse down on my desk. The cursor hovered over an ad that expanded and covered my screen. A funeral home advertisement.

A funeral home, of course! No digging required, only nicely dressed embalmed bodies, similar to mannequins in a clothing store except laid out in a coffin instead of propped upright in a department store window. This task might be doable after all. Adrenaline rushed through my body.

I narrowed my search to funeral homes within a fifty-mile radius of my parents' house. The further from home the better, then I wouldn't run into any people who might recognize me. Next, I perused the individual parlors for obituaries of the recently deceased. I finally narrowed it down to three who listed males with viewing hours scheduled for tomorrow.

"Tim, dinner's ready," my Mom called through my closed door.

"Be right there." I shut my laptop and headed to the kitchen, my mind whirling as I formulated my plan. I'd have to wait until Friday evening's viewing hours and then make my move after the funeral home closed. The deadline to complete the last task left no room for screw-ups.

The Decker Memorial Funeral Home stood back from the road behind a wide circular drive and manicured gardens complete with a fountain and stone benches. Behind the modest-sized building, the parking lot backed up against an apartment complex. A row of tall hedges between the two properties provided a convenient natural screen to hide my parked car.

Spotlights positioned in flower beds lit the path as I walked across the back lot and alongside the building. It looked crisp and formal in bright white stucco with black shutters and trim—like a giant square tuxedo. Scanning the exterior as I walked, I didn't see any security cameras or alarm system wires like I had on the first funeral parlor I visited earlier this evening.

I took a deep breath, walked between two white columns at the entrance and pushed open the heavy front door. Inside, a deserted circular lobby greeted me and doors to the viewing rooms lined the circle's border. Only two doors stood open. My sneaker soles squeaked on the polished marble floor as I walked to the nearest open door. On an easel next to the door, a printed cardboard plaque read, D. A. McBriar. The information in the online obituary had been sparse and only stated he died after a long illness.

I took a step into the room, grateful the plush carpeting smothered my noisy feet. I jumped when someone touched my arm.

"Didn't mean to startle you, sir," an old man said, "May I help you find someone?" He stood stooped over and spoke in a polite, hushed tone, reminiscent of a TV golf commentator.

I tried my best to look grief-stricken. Nerves, plus my cottony mouth, added a realistic tremor to my voice. "My uncle, um, is um, McBriar."

"I'm sorry for your loss. This is the McBriar viewing room. Please, go inside." He backed away into the lobby after a slight bow.

The air-conditioned room felt like a chilly vacuum, the heavy silence broken only by soft intermittent sobs. Rows of chairs, mostly empty, sat before a casket. The filled seats were occupied by a handful of elderly people who sat staring forward at the deceased. No one turned or noticed my presence. A quick glimpse of the body laid out in the casket showed wispy gray hair and a pastel pink dress.

Shit! D. A. McBriar was a woman.

I backed out of the parlor as silently as I'd entered.

A hand grasped my shoulder. I spun around and faced the creepy old funeral parlor guy. "Is everything all right, sir?" His rheumy blue eyes studied me from beneath huge brows, gray and fluffy as squirrel tails.

"Uh, my uncle is—was—a man."

The old man frowned. "The only other viewing this evening is a gentleman. Professor James Samples. Are you sure you have the correct funeral home?"

"Yes, um, yes, James Samples. That's my uncle."

The man's left eyebrow formed a bushy arc. "So, now your uncle's name is Samples, not McBriar?"

"Yes." I rubbed my twitching eye. "I'm sorry. I got confused. I'm just so upset."

The creepy guy's head immediately dipped into his practiced

bow. "I understand. This way," he muttered. All he needed was a bigger hump on his back and he would have made a perfect Igor.

I followed him across the lobby, walking on my toes to minimize the squeaking.

He gave me a weird smirk. "Your *uncle* is in this room." He stood to one side of the open double doors, hands clasped in front of him.

Inside, the room buzzed with conversation and soft laughter. When I turned my head, the creepy guy had vanished. I took a few steps into the room and stopped, surprised at the size of the crowd. People stood or sat in small cliques all around the room. The sweet scent of flowers permeated the cool air. Massive floral arrangements on metal stands filled the entire front of the room behind the casket with more in large urns on the floor and smaller vases lined up on a long table near the draped windows.

All of the visitors wore formal clothing. Some of the women had on long dresses and the men wore suits. I felt self-conscious in my black T-shirt and jeans, not to mention I was the only white person in the room. Apparently, James Samples had been a black man.

"Welcome," a soft voice said at the same time a hand grasped my right arm. "Are you one of James' students?"

The woman who spoke had dark brown eyes that peered into mine and straight into my soul. She was older, plump, and her blue silk dress pulled taut across her full chest.

I mentally pulled up the obituary I had memorized. James Tobias Samples, Professor of American History, Alveda Springs University. "Yes. I am, I mean, was."

"Wonderful to meet you. I'm Sarah, James' wife." She entwined her arm around mine and then took my hand in hers and squeezed. She gazed up at me, her eyebrows raised. "What's your name, dear?"

"Um, Jason." Looking into her dewy eyes made me tongue-tied. Shame burned two fires in my cheeks. My body reacted to her warm embrace like a lie detector strap—nervous tremors rippled through me and sweat formed a stripe down the center of my back. Here I was plotting to steal the suit from her dead husband's body and she was hugging me and smiling. Stop being nice to me, lady. "Nice to meet you, Mrs. Samples," I said. "I'm very sorry about the

Professor."

"A group of his students came to this afternoon's viewing. I was moved to see so many young people here to honor James."

"I-uh-couldn't get here this afternoon. I live in Los Angeles," I lied.

The mist in her eyes swelled into plump tears that rolled down her full cheeks. "Oh my, and you drove all this way to pay your respects. Bless you, Jason."

Dryness constricted my throat, muting my voice. I stared down at my hand still encompassed in hers.

She squeezed harder and continued talking. "I miss him so. James touched so many young people's hearts, it brings me such joy to know he lives on in them—and in you, Jason. Thank you for coming." As she spoke, she walked down the center aisle between the array of chairs and tugged me along with her. We waited a few moments while a young couple and two small children stood by the casket, their heads bowed in prayer. As they turned and wandered off to mingle with the other mourners, Sarah slipped her arm around my waist and guided me up to the casket.

"Oh, no!" I clamped my hand over my mouth.

Sarah's arm tightened around me. Her voice soft as warm honey, "It's all right now, son. I know it's a shock to see him like this. James was always so full of life. I can barely believe he's gone myself."

Numb, I nodded. Sarah's murmurs of comfort were lost as my brain silently screamed out at the sight of the deceased professor. His ensemble looked like a bad 1980's prom outfit. James wore a purple suit and lime green shirt. The suit material had a lustre to it that enhanced the bright color and the paisley print bow tie picked up the purple and green and added an additional punch of lemon yellow.

"Are you all right, Jason?"

I looked into Sarah's face, her moist eyes shining with concern. Guilt wouldn't allow me to maintain eye contact. "Yes, thank you." I am a total piece of shit.

"Take your time, dear." Sarah gave me a grandmotherly squeeze on the arm and then shuffled off to join a group of older women sitting in the front row.

I took a breath and composed myself. It's Friday night. I'm out of time. By the time I drive to the next funeral home, it'll be closed. So, it's either James' purple suit or D. A.'s pink dress. If I don't complete the final task, I'll lose my chance for transformation—forever. Facing Chris, the psychopath, spending a night in jail in a dress and then another on suicide watch in the hospital would all be for nothing.

I let out a long sigh and folded my arms across my chest as I gazed down at the casket. James wasn't a bad looking man, old of course, but with a full head of salt and pepper hair and a trim body. Probably much shorter than me. I wondered how his slacks would fit. Not that it mattered, the crayon purple shiny suit and neon shirt would certainly deflect all attention away from my feet.

"Crap. I can't believe this."

A hand gripped my shoulder and for a second I thought Sarah had returned, but the hand felt larger and stronger. I turned and a middle-aged, stocky man smiled at me. He wore a white clerical collar.

"You doing all right, son?" A slight Southern drawl softened his deep baritone voice.

"Yes, uh, Father."

He grinned and stuck his hand out. "I'm Reverend Nathaniel Barrett."

"Reverend." I shook his hand. "I'm Ti . . . oh, ah, Jason."

"Thank you for coming, Tioah Jason." He chuckled. "You young folks have such creative names these days. Is it Native American, by chance?"

Stunned, I nodded.

He smiled. "Sarah said you were one of James' students."

"Um, yes. Yes."

"Poor Sarah was so torn about whether to bury James in this suit or one of his infamous tweed jackets. I'm sure you remember, he had several—brown, tan, blue, and green. He always wore them at the college. All had those leather patches on the elbows."

"Oh, sure, the brown one. Yes, I remember." I shifted my feet and forced a smile. The shocking purple of the suit stabbed into my peripheral vision. I'd have given anything for a subtle tweed jacket.

A young man walked up to the casket. He nodded at me and then stood listening to the Reverend.

"Sarah reluctantly chose this one. Because it was his favorite and he'd worn it on their first date. Later, he saved it for holidays or special occasions. James loved to brag how it still fit him after all these years. His good luck suit, he called it."

"Uncle James was always a colorful dresser," the young man said, winking at me as if we shared a private joke.

I smiled. The joke would be on me—literally. I could hear Lorelei's bodyguards guffawing now. Both the Reverend and the nephew wore suits that looked custom-tailored and expensive, the Reverend's black, the younger man's charcoal gray. Why couldn't one of them be in the box instead of fashion-challenged James?

The creepy-quiet funeral parlor guy tapped the Reverend on the shoulder. Hunched over in his dust-gray colored suit, he looked like an old spider as he stage-whispered, "Pardon me, Reverend, the funeral home will be closing in fifteen minutes."

"Thank you." The Reverend turned to me. "Please excuse me, Tioah. Sarah asked if I'd say a closing prayer tonight. You're welcome to take a seat and join us."

"Thank you, but I uh, have to be going."

Most of the visitors had departed while I had stood near the casket. I headed toward the door as the Reverend began his prayer. His deep voice resonated in the small, floral-scented room. Sarah sat with a small group gathered in front of the casket. Her head bowed, she rocked in her chair and dabbed at her eyes with a pale blue handkerchief.

I hurried out the door and through the lobby. D. A. McBriar's parlor room door was closed, and the creepy funeral director was nowhere in sight. My heartbeat sped up as I slipped into the men's room and flipped off the overhead light switch. I hid inside the end stall, locked the door, and sat cross-legged on the toilet lid to hide my feet from view.

My heart thumped against my rib cage and my stomach coiled into cold knots, the fear of getting caught and the image of Sarah's sad brown eyes haunting me equally. I checked the penlight and latex gloves shoved inside my back jeans pocket. The other pocket held a folded trash bag and a scissors. Hopefully it wouldn't require any other tools to remove the horrid purple suit from the professor's body.

The overhead lights snapped on. I froze, sucked in my breath and held it.

"Hello? Anyone in here? We're closing now. Hello?" The lights flicked off. "All clear, Dave. Ready to go?"

The door closed with a soft bump. I crept from the stall and pressed my ear against it. Men's voices murmured outside in the lobby, then the definite sound of the heavy front door closing and a lock clicking. I waited a few more seconds, pulled on the latex gloves and then under the soft red glow of the emergency exit lights, made my way across the lobby to James Sample's room.

The interior was pitch black. I turned on the penlight. It cut a bright bluish beam through the blackness. The drapes had been drawn across the windows blocking the glow of the outdoor landscape lights. The thick velvet also served to hide my flashlight from being seen from the outside. I propped open the doors allowing the faint red glow from the lobby to spill into the parlor.

The casket had been closed. Holding the thin flashlight in my teeth, I lifted the lid and then placed the light on the corner of the coffin.

"Sorry, Professor." I leaned down and unbuttoned the dreadful jacket.

❧

It took much longer than I anticipated to remove the jacket. There were straight pins everywhere. I removed them and stuck them into the puffy white satin lining inside the casket lid. When I extricated James' arms and pulled the jacket from his body, I saw a neat straight cut up the back. "Oh, great."

The tie came off easily enough, then I wrestled the lime green shirt from his torso. More pins pricked my fingers. Finally, I tugged the second sleeve from his arm. It, too, had a slit up the back.

James wore a bright white T-shirt beneath his dress shirt. I was grateful to find he also wore matching briefs beneath his suit pants. For such a slim, slight man, his body felt like it weighed four hundred pounds. The term "dead weight" made sense to me now.

As I removed the professor's clothes, the odor of formaldehyde became nearly unbearable. It made my eyes water and I saw damp stains where pinkish embalming fluid had seeped into his T-shirt.

The parchment instructed me to remove the clothes, so I slipped his shiny patent leather loafers back on his socked feet. Technically, they weren't clothes and they'd never fit my size thirteen feet.

I crammed the suit, shirt, and tie into the trash bag, then knotted it to contain the chemical smell. The stinging odor reminded me of biology class with a table full of open jars of pickled frogs ready for dissection.

I looked down at James lying in his casket. The bleached white of the underwear made a stark contrast against the mahogany skin on his arms and legs. Even in death, he looked like a nice guy, his expression scholarly with a hint of a smile pulling up the corners of his mouth. Sarah's grieving face flashed in my mind. A lump formed in my throat as I imagined how upset she'd be when she saw her husband tomorrow. I couldn't leave the professor in his underwear. I played the flashlight around the room. Other than the floor length drapes, there wasn't a tablecloth or anything I could use to cover him.

With no other options available, I dragged one of the floral displays over to the coffin. I plucked tall orange gladiolus from the back of the arrangement and laid them over James. The long, bold-colored stalks covered him from his neck to his ankles.

I placed the scrawny remains of the floral piece back where it was and then took a last look at James. The bright orange flowers paled in comparison to his former ensemble. I straightened his gold wire-framed glasses that I had knocked askew while undressing him.

"Sorry, Professor." I lowered the lid.

The large windows had standard latch locks that turned without a sound. I slid open the window and stepped over the low sill into the flower bed. Crouching down behind the shrubs, I reached inside and pulled the drapes closed, then slid the window shut.

I shoved the trash bag with my purple prize under one arm, took a quick look around, and then sprinted across the parking lot, squeezed through the hedge, and climbed into my car.

As I pulled out of the apartment complex's driveway and drove past the funeral home, another flash of Sarah's face filled my mind—mainly her eyes—deep brown and soulfully sad.

I only needed the suit for a few hours tomorrow night. Maybe if I brought the suit back after my transformation, they could still dress the professor in it in time for his burial.

"I'll return the suit when I'm done, Sarah. I promise."

Chapter 7

"If today were the last day of my life, would I want to do what I am about to do today?"
—Steve Jobs, 2005

Saturday morning, I awoke feeling like a five-year-old ready to run to the Christmas tree. I packed my comic collection and computer books into a banana box I had picked up from behind the grocery store on the way home from the funeral parlor last night. It didn't occur to me until now, but I had always avoided these boxes after reading about someone finding a black widow spider in one. Last night I never gave it a thought. Maybe I truly had conquered my fear of spiders.

My underwear, jeans, and T-shirts all fit into one large suitcase. The Victorian cape lay draped over it next to a second box filled with toiletries and odds and ends.

Two boxes, a suitcase, my laptop, and I was good to go. I stood on a chair and carefully pried the push pins from my vampire posters. I rolled them up together into a neat coil, slid them into a cardboard tube for safe keeping and added them to the box. Packing done.

Oddly, I hadn't given any thought as to where I would go or what I would do after tonight. Transformation meant spontaneity. No eight to five job, mowing grass on the weekends, or playing video games alone in my room every night. Tonight, I would choose the hottest woman in the club and go to her place after the Black Swan. Perhaps it would be Lorelei herself. Maybe I'd travel with the band for a while, see the country, party in a new city every night. Once a vampire, everything would fall into place. I just knew it would. I had watched countless vampire movies and spent the last year researching modern vamps online. I was ready. This was my destiny.

Food, if I even needed it, shelter, and money would be provided. Over time, all vampires amassed huge fortunes and traveled the world. I planned to embrace my new life to the fullest and enjoy the journey that lay ahead.

With the packing finished, I walked to my bathroom. James' purple suit hung airing on the shower rod. I gave it another spray of air freshener and closed the door. The formaldehyde odor still lingered. Luckily my mom hadn't picked up on the scent and asked questions.

Though the suit was not my ideal garb for tonight's momentous occasion, I felt a duty to honor James and Sarah. The poor professor was dead. All his lucky suit could do for him now is disintegrate on his bones, whereas I would use the suit to achieve a spectacular new life. Afterward, I'd keep my promise and return it to Sarah.

Mom was making lasagna in honor of my last night of living at home and the savory aroma drifted down the hall from the kitchen. I lay on my stripped mattress as I waited for dinner and stared up at the wall. It felt strange to see an empty space where Bela's poster had hung for so long. Now it's my turn. I'd paint the blank canvas with a lifetime of adventures.

I drifted off into a peaceful twilight picturing the final words on the parchment, *Congratulations. You have completed all six of the tasks and in doing so have proven yourself worthy of transformation.*

The industrial park looked deserted as I pulled into the lot of the warehouse with the Black Swan beneath it. It was nine o'clock and the club didn't open until ten. I placed my cell and wallet in the glove compartment and then stepped outside and hid in the shadow of my car while I changed into James's suit. The hem of the slacks fell about mid-shin and the jacket sleeves ended inches above my wrists. Though I had left the cut in the back of the shirt, I used a stapler to close up the slit in the back of the jacket. The smell of formaldehyde permeated the fabric like an irritating cheap cologne.

I slid the completed parchment into an inner jacket pocket and put my keys and the wad of cash Mom had slipped me into my pants pockets. She had cried and told me at least a half dozen times to call her when I reached my hotel. I had lied and told her the company provided a hotel room free of charge until I found an apartment. Dad even gave me a hug, a slap on the back, and wished me luck. I felt guilty lying to them but telling them I was leaving home to become a vampire wasn't an option.

Every pore in my body tingled in the cool night air. I was *so* ready. The night felt surreal. An invigorating coolness in the breeze, a navy-blue star-studded sky and a bright half-moon above. I wanted to savor every detail of the night I became one of the Night Flock.

I walked to the entrance of the club and stood at the top of the concrete steps leading downward. Without lights, the deep stairwell leading to the door might as well have been an inkwell. The club hadn't opened yet.

Voices and noises came from the side of the building. I walked across the back and turned the corner. An extended-length van stood parked by another stairwell. Shiny black in the moonlight with graphics of a locomotive and electric blue letters that read, *Night Train*. Four men hauled band equipment from the back. I recognized the hulking girth of Seth, Lorelei's main henchman.

I drew in a deep breath, straightened up to my full height and strode towards the men. Seth whirled around. For a split second his eyes glowed amber in the darkness.

The glow faded and he broke into laughter as I approached. "What the hell—?"

The other three put down the instruments they carried and gathered around Seth.

"I'm here to be transformed." I squared my shoulders and stood firm, staring into Seth's scowling face. Though twice my width, I had at least a half inch of height over him.

"What, are you high? Get lost, asshole." He took a step toward me.

I didn't retreat. I had waited too long and worked too hard for this moment. Seth might be twice my weight, but I wasn't giving up. "No, I'm not high. Lorelei told me to come. She promised to transform me. Tonight." I reached into my jacket for the parchment.

Seth's hand moved in a blur as did another of the men's hands. They both aimed guns at me.

"Whoa." My right hand froze inside my jacket and I held up my

94

left. "I just want to show you the parchment."

"Parchment?"

"Lorelei gave me a parchment with six tasks to complete. It's proof she told me to come tonight."

Seth motioned with the barrel of the gun. "Move real slow. Show me."

I slid the parchment from my jacket, unfolded it and held it out toward him.

He snatched it from my hand and studied it, his gun still leveled at my chest.

"What is this shit?"

"I told you, it's—"

"Shut up!" Seth nodded to the other guy holding a gun. Not quite as intimidating as Seth, he moved toward me as Seth turned and walked to the passenger side of the van.

"Hey! Give that back," I yelled.

Seth ignored me and slid open a side door. Extreme high heels attached to long, pale legs emerged. Lorelei stepped from the van and swept her silvery hair back from her face. Seth handed her the parchment.

She strolled toward me, shadowed by her giant bodyguard. In spite of two guns aimed at me, the sight of Lorelei in tiny shorts and a bikini top mesmerized me.

"Lorelei," I called. "I completed the tasks. You promised to transform me tonight. Remember?"

Her eyes stayed focused on the parchment as she moved toward me. She stopped, inches from me. Her eyes glowed bright blue even in the darkness as she looked me over from head to foot and ran her hand over the front of my jacket. Her heels clicked on the asphalt as she circled around me.

In spite of the cool air, sweat formed on my upper lip.

"You actually took that suit from a corpse?" she asked. The men behind her laughed.

"Yes." I swallowed hard, picturing Sarah's face.

Lorelei handed the parchment back to me.

"I did everything you asked. You're going to do it, right?" I asked. "You promised you would."

She whispered something to Seth and then nodded at the other men. Seth tucked his gun into the waistband of his jeans and the other man put his into his vest pocket.

"C'mon," Seth said, motioning to me.

I followed him down the staircase of the side entrance. It led to a dim hallway next to the stage.

"No drinking, understand? Lorelei will not tolerate alcohol in her victim's blood."

I nodded, slightly put off by the word "victim".

"After our second set, make sure you have a seat close to the stage. When Lorelei says—"

"I was here last Saturday. I know the ritual."

"You better." He stared at me for a long moment and then sneered, revealing long pointed canines. "Nice suit, asshole."

I knew the suit looked ridiculous, yet I also knew what I had gone through to get it, not to mention the other tasks. Screw you, Seth. I'm worthy and once I'm a vampire I'll enjoy kicking your giant ass. I gave him a cocky grin and said, "Thanks." Then I strolled into the empty club and took a seat at the same table I had sat at last Saturday night.

The night dragged. Excitement and anticipation made it impossible to sit still. I wandered over to the bar and ordered a Coke, then sipped it as I paced around the perimeter of the dance floor. I ignored the stares and laughter my outfit drew. The bright purple made me stand out in the sea of black-clad patrons. Normally I wore black to blend in, but tonight I wanted to stand out. They can laugh all they want now. No one will be laughing when I'm standing on stage with Lorelei.

I smiled at several young women, secretly checking out who I would choose later. One guy tried to get in my face when I smiled at his girlfriend. I brushed past him, ignoring his jeers, silently vowing I'd beat him up after drinking Lorelei's blood.

I nodded to Lorelei when the band took their break but stood a distance away while she and the men sat together at the bar. She drank the red liquid from the special decanter stored under the bar. As the band walked past to return to the stage, Lorelei gave me a smile, then wrinkled her nose. "That suit stinks," she said.

I couldn't argue. The smell made my eyes water and my back itched. One more hour and I could remove it.

At the end of the second set, the club lights went out and the drumbeat began. My table had been taken by a couple while I paced, so I stood in front of the stage, my heartbeat revving in time to the drum.

The spotlight flashed on and roamed the club, finally settling on me. Tonight, when Lorelei asked my name, I shouted out loud and strong, "Tim!"

Seth and another guitarist stood at the edge of the stage. They didn't pick me up like they had Jane. Instead I struggled to pull myself up. Seth watched, smirking, with his arms crossed. The other guy finally grabbed my arm and helped pull me up.

The crowd gasped behind me. Women tittered and some men hooted and howled as I sprinted across the stage and stood next to Lorelei. She looked like an evil porn queen in her tight black shorts and breasts bulging from her bra top. Tonight, I wasn't a tall skinny geek in a purple suit. I was Lorcan, the vampire character from my video game, standing tall and proud next to sexy Lorelei. I wanted to kiss her, but then Seth appeared, grasped my arm and led me toward the red velvet chair in center stage.

He pushed me down into the chair. "Roll up your left sleeve, douche bag."

I fumbled with the buttons on my shirt sleeve, then pushed it and the purple jacket sleeve up to my elbow. I glared at Seth and sat up tall in the chair.

Lorelei took my hand and entwined her fingers through mine. We held our arms outstretched while Seth did his dramatic sword twirl. For a second I feared he might slit my throat with the long thin blade. The silver blur whipped past my eyes and my arm stung where it had sliced my flesh.

I thought my heart would burst from my chest when Lorelei's cold lips touched my arm. Her tongue flickered across the cut on my skin and then her mouth clamped on my arm. The hardness of her teeth pressed into my skin as she sucked my blood. A hot sensation radiated up my arm, across my chest and down to my groin. My body shuddered. This is it. I am becoming a vampire.

The thud of my heartbeat and panting breath drowned out the beat of the drums and the murmurs of the crowd. I pushed back into the chair and closed my eyes, overwhelmed with ecstasy.

Startled by a voice, I opened my eyes to see Lorelei's pale, bleeding arm in front of my face.

"I said, drink!"

"Yes," I gasped when my lips touched her icy skin and I licked the blood from the open wound. Lorelei's blood didn't taste salty. It was a bittersweet liquid that tasted like dark chocolate laced with wine—the most delicious thing I'd ever tasted. I clutched her arm with both hands and sucked at the sweet fountain that bubbled up from the wound.

"Enough."

I heard her command, but her blood was addictive, intoxicating—I wanted more.

"Stop!" She pulled her arm, but I clung to it with both my hands and my lips, drawing her delectable blood into my mouth. Even as my knees hit the wooden floor of the stage, I still had her arm clasped in my hands and sucked from her wound.

Seth and another man picked me up under the arms, dragged me away from Lorelei, and shoved me back into the chair. I leaned against the velvet cushion chair back licking sweet traces from my lips. A rush like an electric jolt surged through me and left me dizzy, breathless. The stage faded into blackness, the music lost behind the thundering of my heart. The time between each beat took longer and longer. I feared it would stop.

"Wake up, asshole."

My cheek stung. But much worse was the white-hot pain that invaded every pore, every cell of my body. I cried out but had no voice—my mouth wouldn't obey my brain. Raising my eyelids took all of my strength.

A large hand smacked my cheek. "I said wake up. Show's over." Seth loomed over me, a blurry giant. The volume of his voice hurt my ears and echoed in my head.

A flash of silvery white appeared on my left. "He's still out?"

"His eyes are open, but he's really fucked-up."

"He drank too much." Lorelei placed her hand on my forehead, the icy cold sent new waves of pain radiating across my face and up into my scalp.

Something's wrong. Help me. Please, Lorelei. My voice wouldn't work.

"Seth, get him into the van," Lorelei said. "You know what to do. Hurry."

Yes. She heard my thoughts. We must be connected by blood now. Lorelei would get me help.

Seth shoved his hands under my arms and lifted me from the chair. Another man gripped my ankles.

Pain rolled over me in waves, each more ferocious than the last. My efforts to speak only sent drool running down my chin and my own spittle burned my skin.

"Chill. It'll be okay, dude," the man holding my feet said.

The two lugged me up the stairs. The jostling motion was excruciating, as if acid splashed over my internal organs with their every step. My arms hung heavy at my sides. Bolts of pain raced through my body, but my limbs refused to move.

Oh no. No. I'm paralyzed. This isn't supposed to be like this. "Wh hap n to me?" My words came out in a gurgle.

The two men laid me inside the back of the van.

Lorelei appeared in the doorway of the van. "Let's go, Seth. I know where to take him."

The back doors slammed shut, closing me in blackness. A series of muffled sounds as front doors closed, and the engine started up. The van lurched forward.

Were they taking me to a hospital? No. They must have a special place. Someone who knew what to do in this situation. Lorelei knew where to go for help.

Equipment rattled and slid around me. Even in the dark and paralyzed, I sensed the van traveled at a high speed from the screeching tires and rolling motion as it turned corners. Seth may be a huge prick, but he obeyed Lorelei and she had ordered him to hurry. I lay on my back and tried to focus on something besides the pain. The constant motion made me want to puke, but I couldn't turn my head. I'd choke on my vomit.

The van finally jolted to a stop. A door slammed, but the engine still hummed. We arrived. Someone would help me now. Make the pain stop.

Seth and the other guy dragged me out of the van. The scenery blurred, the night sky, a highway. It was dark, no lights. I heard traffic but saw no buildings.

Lorelei stood gazing down at me. I tried to speak, to reach out to her, but nothing worked.

Cold fingers stroked my cheek. "You're not strong, Tim. You were too weak to accept my gift."

She stepped back out of my sight. Power lines above me swayed.

"On three," Seth said.

He and the other goon holding my feet swung me, back and forth.

"So long, asshole."

No! No! Please! You have to help me—I was airborne, if only for a second, then my body crashed onto the ground. I rolled and rolled down a hill. Blades of grass poked at my face and hands like needles. Paper bags and aluminum cans pelted my head and body. I couldn't raise my arms to shield my face. My glasses slid away. Gone.

My body finally settled to a stop at the bottom of the hill. I lay still on my back, looking up at the underside of an overpass. Noises assaulted me. Vibration of the traffic overhead, cars whooshing past on the highway above. The grass poked tiny pins into my palms, but I couldn't move, couldn't yell for help.

The pain welled up inside me and the night sky turned black. Lorelei left me. Threw me away like trash on the side of a road. No one knew where I was. My cell phone was locked in my car. Would they go back to the club and take my car, too?

I thought of my mom, smiling as she pulled the fragrant, piping-hot lasagna from the oven. My father's arms hugging me. I'm so sorry I lied to you. Then, Sarah's brown eyes and tears rolling down her cheeks. I wouldn't be able to return the professor's suit, Sarah. I'm sorry.

My parents would get a call and wonder how I ended up on the side of a road in a purple suit that reeked of embalming fluid. Mom would cry, even more than she cried tonight saying goodbye to me.

Tears streamed from my eyes and ran down the sides of my face. They burned. My whole body burned. I'm all alone and the pain is getting worse.

I'm dying.

Chapter 8

"Nothing is so painful to the human mind as a great and sudden change."

—Mary Shelley, Frankenstein

Noise jarred me awake. I searched the sky for the source but saw nothing but the deep blue above me cluttered with stars, the overpass and a train trestle that loomed overhead.

I'm not dead, at least I don't think so.

To my right, atop the sloping hill, traffic roared. Once the cars passed the night grew quiet. How long had I lain here? The club closed at two in the morning and sometime after that Lorelei's thugs dumped me in this ravine.

My fingers touched dew-covered grass. Cool blades with prickly edges as if recently cut by a dull mower. Wait, my hands moved, my fingers wiggled. With effort, I raised my right arm and aimed my hand toward my face. My arm shook as my hand grazed over my nose and then landed on my chest. The signals my brain sent to my limbs lagged, sometimes glitching or stopping altogether. Clumsy and spastic, still it was movement. I'm not paralyzed.

It took a long while and all of my focus to finally push upward into a sitting position. I guessed it must be around three or four in the morning by the sparse traffic and damp darkness surrounding me.

Trash littered the ravine, fast food papers, cans, and bottles. Even without my glasses I could easily read the labels of a *Monster* energy drink can and a bag labeled *Taco Hut* in bright red letters.

My mind raced, assessing the state of my body: laser sharp vision, hearing amplified and I inhaled so many smells—good and bad—dewy grass, remnants of rotting food and stale beverages. My scalp tingled as I turned my head, sensing a presence before seeing an opossum lumbering in the shadows as it investigated the garbage strewn along the hillside.

My senses clamored for my attention as I scanned my surroundings. One of the more pleasant aromas riding on the breeze induced an intense wave of hunger. More than normal hunger, an urgent growling need for food and a thirst for water overwhelmed me. I breathed in the spicy scent.

Standing took quite a while and when I finally stood upright, my legs paid my mind no attention. Uphill and a short distance down the highway, a yellow glow broke the darkness. The spicy smell of food came from that direction.

I staggered up the hill toward the light, alternately dragging my legs when my knees locked and refused to bend. I tripped and used my arms like two additional legs as I worked my way up the steep bank to the highway. Once on flat ground I forced my feet to keep shuffling forward and stuck my stiffened arms out for balance.

A tiny building sat back from the road. A tilted yellow sombrero formed its roof and the name Taco Hut beckoned in flickering red neon. The place consisted of three glass walls and a solid back wall with enough room for only one or two employees inside to service the drive-through windows.

A white SUV pulled into the drive, passed me, and stopped at the first window. I lurched and stumbled toward the building, afraid if I stopped I would lose momentum and fall on my face in the gravel driveway.

I edged in behind the vehicle, using it and the glass wall of the restaurant for support until I grasped a bright yellow tile ledge beneath the service window.

A child screamed. The shrill sound stabbed my eardrums like glass shards. A little girl's head poked from the rear passenger window, her tiny finger pointing at me. A woman's voice yelled for her to sit down. Strands of the child's long blonde hair stuck out over the top edge of the window as it rolled up. The SUV pulled around the corner to the second window to pick up their order.

I leaned my elbows on the tile ledge of the first window and shuffled along until I stood at the center of the window. Inside, a stocky young Hispanic man stood with his back to me, wrapping tacos in white paper and stuffing them into a red and white bag. He opened the second window and handed the bag to the woman in the SUV, then he turned and gawked open-mouthed at me.

I tapped my fingers on the glass. He shook his head and backed away. The interior left him only a few feet of clearance and his backside was flush against the stainless-steel counter. He pointed at me and shouted, "Get out of here!"

Bright light poured from the glass hut. Lesions showed on my hands. Ugly red blisters that covered the skin. My reflection in the glass, though faint in the harsh light, showed more marks on my face.

I tried to call to him but managed only rasps and gargles.

"Leave, or I'll call the cops," he shouted through the glass.

I fumbled to get my hand into my pants pocket and pulled out the wad of cash Mom had given me.

Pressing my hands together as if in prayer I mouthed, "Please."

He hesitated and took a small step forward. "How many?" He gestured toward a menu board with a numbered list of taco specials.

I had to use my left hand to help my right hand form four fingers and then held them up to indicate the number four special. Four tacos and a large drink for seven dollars and ninety-nine cents.

After considerable fumbling, I picked out a twenty-dollar bill and managed to poke it into the small stainless depression beneath the payment window.

He reached forward, snatched the bill and put in on the cash register. Then he turned and prepared the bag of tacos.

"What drink?"

"Wah ta," I croaked.

"What?" He moved closer to the window.

"W-Wahh tar." The effort caused saliva to foam and bubble in the corners of my mouth.

He pulled a plastic bottle from a cooler and then pointed to the side window.

I staggered around the corner and waited while he rang up the sale and gathered my change.

He motioned for me to step back as he opened the sliding window and placed the bag of tacos and a water bottle on a wide tile ledge.

I waved away the change and grasped the water bottle. My fingers wouldn't cooperate as I tried to twist off the cap.

Hearing a *thunk*, I saw he placed a second water bottle with the cap removed on the outside ledge. He slammed the window and latched it. He motioned and yelled. "Take it. Go!"

Nodding my thanks, I clutched the open bottle and aimed for my mouth. Most of it dumped down my neck and chest, but the icy liquid that did make it down my throat tasted like heaven.

I put the unopened bottle in my jacket pocket, picked up the bag, and stumbled toward an opening in the trees and shrubs that led back down the slope to the ravine.

Moving downhill tested my coordination. It failed. I fell, rolled a few turns and then finally crawled until I reached the bottom. Once settled, I tore into the bag like a ravenous dog, pushing my face inside and eating with my mouth as using my hands proved too much trouble to pick up the food and aim it into my mouth.

The tacos burned my stomach more than they satisfied my hunger. No sooner had I swallowed the last bite when a series of loud, roiling belches exploded in my throat. They ended with a stream of vomit. The chewed remains of the tacos formed a pasty, reddish pile in the grass.

Disgusted and exhausted, I managed to drink the last gulp of water and dropped the plastic bottle. It rolled and joined the rest of the trash at the bottom of the ravine. Still thirsty, I didn't have the strength to battle with the unopened bottle jammed in my jacket pocket.

I sat and tried to wipe my face with my sleeve. Willing my limbs to obey my mental commands proved sporadic. The night sky lightened to a pale gray in the east. Sunrise was coming. I had a general idea where I was, on the side of the main highway leading west toward Los Angeles. The Black Swan, my car and cell phone were approximately ten miles away.

I could never walk that far in my condition. Crossing the highway even in the sparse pre-dawn traffic would most likely end in me getting run over, and even if I crossed the road, I couldn't defend myself if I ran into trouble in the crime-ridden warehouse district. The last thing I needed was to draw attention from law enforcement.

Maybe rest would improve my stamina. The water had helped and the miniscule amount of food that stayed in my system had given me some strength.

The sun poked above the horizon and a faint yellow ray stretched across the grass beneath the overpass. My hand burned. The skin turned pink and a stinging pain stabbed my fingers.

I alternately crawled and scuttled across the grass until I finally settled into the cool shadows next to the concrete abutment between the overpass and the train trestle.

What the hell happened to me? Transformation should have brought strength and power. I had watched that woman, Jane, drink Lorelei's blood last weekend. She had emerged beautiful, strong, and triumphant. Why didn't I? Yet, the sunlight hurt. I stared down at the burn mark on my hand. Vampires couldn't tolerate sunlight. Did this mean I was a vampire?

I wriggled deeper into the shade and sat huddled among the tall weeds and scraggly shrubs. I laid my head back against the cool concrete. Something dark brown fluttered and landed on my arm. I brushed it away and then managed to bring my right hand up to my head to check for bugs. More brown fluff stuck to my hand.

I stared at my open hand. It wasn't a bug. It was my hair. Big tufts of it stuck between my fingers.

I slid sideways into the weeds and laid my cheek down in the dirt. Tears ran from my eyes weaving thin burning trails across my face.

I opened my eyes to darkness and pushed myself up into a sitting position. I assumed it was Sunday evening. I must have slept an entire day. My mind felt sharp and clear, thoughts buzzing like a swarm of bees. I thought I was cured until I attempted to stand up and found I still lacked coordination.

It took some time, but I stood up and took a few halting steps around the ravine to test my legs. Traffic moved overhead and to my left on the highway at the top of the ravine.

I wrestled to remove the water bottle from my pocket and

attempted to grip the cap and unscrew it. I dropped it with each attempt.

Staring down at it lying in the grass I wondered if I could chew through the plastic or beat it against a rock to open it. Thirst and frustration had fueled desperately insane thoughts.

The concrete wall of the overpass rattled, then the air itself vibrated. Something large and noisy approached. I saw a train about a mile away, a dark silhouette hurtling closer on the tracks above me.

Forgetting the water for the moment I stared upward, marveling at how clear my vision was without my eyeglasses. I focused on covering my ears with my hands to shield them from the deafening racket of the train. Now yards away, the engine of the locomotive followed the gentle curve of the elevated tracks overhead. As the middle section of cars followed the curve, I spotted a dark figure on top of the train. No, it couldn't be. Am I losing my mind now, too? I blinked, but the figure only sharpened. A slim woman in dark clothing. She held a surfing stance, arms outstretched, and knees slightly bent. Long strands of golden hair blowing in the wind behind her shone in the moonlight.

She turned her head and looked at me. A millisecond later, the train had passed, yet I had felt her return my gaze and saw the bluish glow of her eyes—and I knew she had seen me. What kind of woman stood on top of a speeding freight train? Was she even human?

Fear trickled though me. I turned and headed for my hiding spot in the deep shadows at the foot of the abutment. I staggered and fell, then remembered the water bottle on the ground. I crawled toward it. As my fingers grazed over its smooth surface, a hand grasped the bottle and jerked it away.

On all fours, I looked up into the face of the woman from the train. She was dazzling up close, blue-green eyes and long waves of golden hair.

"Let me help you," she said and held out her hand.

Her voice sounded familiar. My mind sped back in time. Jane. The woman from the Black Swan. She had said the same thing the night Lorelei's thugs pushed me down the stairs.

Except she no longer looked plain—anything but. Her face shone in the darkness and those eyes, they glowed with an inner aquamarine light.

"N-Naaw," I tried to scurry away on all fours and fell flat on my face.

"Please. I can help you." She took a step closer and extended her hand again. "My name is Jane."

I rolled up on all fours and then sat, too weak to escape.

She crouched down, twisted off the cap of the water bottle and held it to my lips. "Drink. You're dehydrated."

I slurped in gulps of water through my slack lips as she tilted the bottle.

"How did you get here?" she asked.

I shook my head.

"You're a vampire, aren't you?"

"H-Hooww?"

"By the glow in your eyes. But you're very sick. You need help."

She could tell I was a vampire? If I'm a vampire, why am I so weak?

"How did you get here?" she asked again.

"Lurr ahh lie."

Her eyes widened and then her jaw set. The light in her eyes faded. "Lorelei? From *Night Train*?"

I nodded.

"She left you here?"

Again, I nodded.

Jane stood and paced. Then she leaned and extended her hand again. "You need help, or you'll die. I can help you. I'm a vampire, too."

I stared up at her. Beautiful beyond words, but could I trust her? Why would she offer to help? Had Lorelei sent her to finish me off? I shook my head and tried to cross my arms.

She sighed. "At least let me take you home. Where do you live?

"Naww. Naw home."

"You can't stay here."

She was right. If I could get to my car, my phone. "C-Car."

"Car? Where is your car?"

My tongue fought me. Finally, I sputtered, "B-Block Swuun."

"Your car's at the Black Swan?"

I nodded, exhausted from the effort of talking.

"The club is about ten miles away." She studied me for a moment. "You can't walk that far. I'll go get it and drive it back here."

Tears welled in my eyes; the hot liquid burned. Was she working for Lorelei? Would she dispose of my car and then return and kill me? Or just leave me to die. I would die if I stayed here.

But I had no choice, no options. I pulled at the keys in my pants pocket. Jane helped me to extricate them and then she jogged up the steep hill. She stopped at the top and called over her shoulder, "I'll be right back."

I sat and watched until she disappeared from sight.

Shivering, my body listed to one side as I sat on the grassy hill and waited for Jane to return with my car. Thoughts that she wouldn't return haunted me. I had no other plan, though I did have almost two hundred dollars stuffed inside my pants pocket. If she didn't come back, I could stagger to Taco Hut and beg the guy inside to call my parents. Sadly, there was no one else to call. The thought of explaining my condition to my parents made dying alone on the side of a remote highway almost appealing.

Parched, my strength waned by the minute and I stared at the empty water bottle lying next to me. If I didn't get up and try for Taco Hut now, I might not have the energy to walk later. As I struggled to my feet, two bright beams swept along the side of the road above me. A car door slammed, and Jane appeared at the top of the hill.

She reached me before I could take a step and draped a blanket over my shoulders. It smelled of fabric softener—a familiar, comforting scent. It was the extra blanket my mom had stowed in the back seat of my car.

Jane slid her arm around my back and helped me up the steep slope. Her strength amazed and frightened me. She practically carried me the last few steps and lifted me into the passenger seat of my car with ease.

I sat, wrapped in the blanket, while she hurried around the front of the car and slid into the driver's seat. She started the engine and turned on the heater. It let out a welcome blast of warm air. For the first time in two days, I felt hope. I might live.

"Since you say you have no home, I'll let you stay at my place. Just for a few days until you're feeling better." She turned and looked at me. "Understood?"

I nodded. What choice did I have?

She put the car into drive and swung a wide U-turn across the six-lane highway.

My shivering subsided as the car heated up, but a deep chill still gripped my bones. Jane wriggled out of her leather jacket at a red light, revealing tan, toned arms. Every part of her shone with perfection. Even in my near comatose state, I admired her rounded breasts and the sight of her nipples pushing against her black tank top.

I had so many questions I wanted to ask her, yet no energy to voice them. I had put my life in this strange woman's hands and all I could do was hope her intentions were good. I let out a sigh of relief when we sped past the industrial park which housed the Black Swan. At least she didn't take me back there. Perhaps she wasn't in league with Lorelei and her band of thugs.

Jane drove along the main road into a town. The downtown avenue sparkled with lit-up store fronts and a flashing movie marquee. People strolled the wide sidewalks, oblivious to the monster observing them from the passing car. The normality of the scene looked bizarre. She made a quick right turn into the lot of a corner convenience store and parked a few spots away from the glass doors.

"Be right back," she said as she hopped out of the car.

Nodding took the last strength I had. My body had molded into the bucket seat and a corner of the blanket dipped over my head, shielding the right side of my face from view. The bright lights hurt my eyes and I hid my face beneath the shadow of the blanket to avoid curious stares from patrons who passed as they entered and exited the store.

She returned carrying a plastic bag. I watched her long, lean figure approach the car and wished I could sit up straight or act somewhat manly. Even in my normal state, my chances with a woman like Jane were only fantasy.

She sat in the driver's seat and twisted open a water bottle. "Here." She held it for me while I drank. The cold fluid flowed over my sandy tongue and down my dry throat. It revived me from my stupor.

"Thank you." My voice sounded low and ragged, but at least coherent words came out.

Jane busied herself tearing open a cellophane wrapper. She held out a thin brown strip.

The sight of the package on the console made me gasp. I shook my head, no. *Slim Jim.*

Did that psycho Chris Bagwell put her up to this? My mind reeled with thoughts of how Jane and Chris might possibly be connected.

"It's dried meat. You need protein."

Her gleaming blue-green eyes distracted me. I blinked at her intense, yet sincere stare. Maybe she didn't know Chris or the nickname he stuck me with.

"Try to eat a little bit. You'll feel better." She reached over and placed the Slim Jim into my hand.

As she pulled out of the brightly lit lot, I pushed my paranoia aside, raised my hand to my mouth and nibbled on the jerky. I liked Slim Jims, and only avoided them out of my hatred for Chris.

The spicy meat tasted good. Jane unwrapped another stick and handed it to me. I ate the second more confidently. The dry texture didn't make me want to hurl like the tacos had. The last thing I wanted was to vomit all over this gorgeous woman's lap.

I pushed myself up straighter in the seat and focused on the road in front of us. The wide main street and shops had given way to commercial buildings spaced farther apart and the road narrowed from four down to two lanes. I didn't recognize the area.

Jane turned left onto a curvy two-lane road. We zoomed past gated communities and an upscale-looking shopping plaza. She drove on, the traffic thinned, and only woods lined both sides of the road. My paranoia returned. Where the heck was she taking me?

Finally, she slowed and turned into a shadowy opening in the woods. My heartbeat sped up and I managed to grip the door handle, though I knew I wasn't capable of jumping from a moving car and running.

A hard-packed dirt road wound through the wooded area and then opened up into a clearing with a large one-story house perched on a low hill and surrounded by a black iron fence. She slowed the car as she drove up the steep drive, fished a remote from her jacket pocket and aimed it at the double wrought iron gates. The gates slowly opened inward and she pulled up a paved circular driveway and parked by the front entrance. The gates clanged shut behind us.

Jane hopped out and removed something from the back seat. Before I could turn to see what, she appeared at my window and pulled the door open. She held my suitcase in her right hand and reached in with her left to assist me. I left the comfort of the blanket and stepped outside.

I tried not to lean on her as we walked along a stone path and through an archway to the front door. The Spanish-style house was stucco like my parents' home, but the rusty color of it looked older, more authentic.

"My phone." I turned and stumbled. Jane gripped my arm, saving me from falling on my face.

"I'll get it. Let's get you inside first." She unlocked the front door and swung it open. The home's interior glowed with soft amber light. Earth tones and dark wood dominated the decor. I shuffled across the tiled foyer to a wooden straight-backed chair and sat. She set my suitcase down and turned for the door.

"Glove compartment," I said. She moved so quickly I doubted she heard me, my voice barely a whisper. Yet, she returned a moment later holding my cell, laptop, and wallet. She locked the front door.

The door lock, safety chain, and oversized dead bolt overpowered the single wooden door.

"You need to get cleaned up. That suit smells horrible." She walked down a hallway and returned a few moments later. I heard water running. "C'mon, I'll help you to the bathroom."

I accepted her arm and she picked up both my suitcase and the chair in her other hand. Around a corner, an open door revealed a spacious bathroom with steam billowing from a glass shower stall.

She placed the chair in the middle of the room. I sat.

"Are you able to shower by yourself?"

"Y-Yes." The humiliating thought of Jane bathing me like a mangy stray dog provided a shot of adrenaline that broke through my lethargy. "Yes, I can. Thank you."

She pulled two towels from a linen closet and laid them on the sink counter. "I'll get a trash bag for that suit. You do have clothes in your suitcase, right?"

"Yes, but please, don't throw the suit away."

She studied me for a moment. "The suit's awful. Filthy and that stench, is that formaldehyde?"

"I know it's ugly and smells, but it's not mine. I have to return it. I'll get it cleaned."

She shook her head. "Good luck with that. I'll leave a trash bag outside the door. At least it will contain the odor." Jane closed the door behind her.

I managed to strip off my tennis shoes and clothes and then stepped into the shower. I leaned against the tile wall for support as a cascade of hot water flowed over me. The soap stung the sores that covered my head and body. I rinsed under the soothing water until I couldn't stand up any longer.

Dark wet clumps of my hair littered the shower floor and covered the drain. I exited the stall, grasped the chair back to steady myself and wrapped a towel around me. I sat and used the second towel to dry off. Unable to lift the chair, I dragged it closer to the sink counter and wiped the steam from the big oval mirror.

"Oh no. No, no, no." The pasty face staring at me in the mirror was covered in lesions and a few straggly patches of hair stuck out from my bald head.

I slumped onto the chair, buried my face in the towel and sobbed. The tears burned my eyes, but I couldn't stop. Transformation was supposed to have made me handsome. Fierce, powerful, sexy. Instead, it had made me into a monster.

A knock on the door jerked me from my sobs.

"Are you all right?" Jane called.

Swallowing the lump in my throat, I croaked, "Yes." I pulled my suitcase closer and dug inside until I found a long-sleeved T-shirt and a pair of sweatpants. At least the clothes would cover most of me. I struggled to dress, then stood up and opened the door.

Jane stood in the hallway gaping at me, a black plastic trash bag in her hands.

"I have to clean up the hair in the shower. The suit." I bent over to pluck the purple heap from the tile floor. The room spun, then Jane's arms hooked under mine. She held me upright.

"I-I'm sorry . . . dizzy."

"It's all right. C'mon, you need to rest."

She walked me down the hall to a large living room off the foyer. A white sheet covered the sofa she led me to. I lay down, a soft pillow cradled my head, and she covered me with a thick blanket.

I opened my eyes. Jane sat across the room in a red leather chair watching me. Self-conscious, I pulled the blanket up to my nose and folded my arms up to cover my bald head.

She leaned forward in the chair. "How are you feeling?"

I pushed myself up into a sitting position still clutching the blanket under my chin. Jane's startling beauty made me painfully aware of my ugliness.

"Better, I think."

"You should eat more jerky and drink water. It's crucial to stay hydrated." She motioned to a coffee table in front of me. On it were bottles of water, a package of Slim Jims as well as my cell, wallet, the folded parchment, and my wad of cash. An unfamiliar white oblong box sat on the far end.

Seeing the parchment and cash, I remembered I had failed to pick up James's suit. She must have emptied the pockets before bagging it up.

"You didn't throw out the suit, did you?"

"No. It's in a trash bag on the back patio."

"Thank you." I couldn't stop thanking this woman.

"You're welcome. Now, I need to get some blood from you," she said.

Her matter-of-fact tone chilled me to the core. Blood? She wants my blood? Lorelei drank my blood and now I was a horrible freak. Was this Jane-the-vampire's plan all along, take me in and use me as a convenient blood source?

"No. No, please." I tried to stand but Jane crossed the room in a blink, gripped my shoulders and prevented me from rising from the sofa.

"Calm down. I only need a small vial for tests." She picked up the white box and opened it. Inside I glimpsed a hypodermic needle. "I have to analyze your blood to figure out why your transformation went wrong."

I drew in a ragged breath. "A-Are you a doctor?"

Jane smiled. It was the first time I had seen her smile since I met her beneath the train trestle. Her entire face shone. Full lips framed perfect white teeth and her hypnotic eyes sparkled with that amazing inner light. Mesmerized, my fear melted.

"No. I'm a hematologist," she said.

"A what?"

"I study blood, specifically blood disorders and diseases. I work at the university in their medical research center."

Fear returned like an electric shock, a thin cold finger pricking my spine. "You work with blood? That must be um, handy, for a vampire."

Her smile vanished. "I don't use my work for personal gain." She removed an alcohol wipe from the kit on the table. "I have my own lab here at home. I've been researching vampirism for years." She held out her hand and motioned for me to offer my arm.

I clutched the blanket closer to me, wondering if I could muster the strength and coordination to make a run for the front door.

"I can't help you until I can see what is happening to your blood."

"H-How do I know you're not going to drain my blood and . . . and kill me?" I asked.

Jane rolled her eyes. "If I wanted to kill you, I would have left you on the side of the highway. I'm taking a risk too, you know, by allowing you into my home."

"How will looking at my blood help? I'm a mess. And—"

"*And* with hydration and a little bit of protein you're now able to talk and your coordination has improved. I believe you have a chance for recovery, *if* you let me help you."

She stood with her hands on her hips watching me. It's true I could move my limbs and my speech had returned. It was also true if Jane hadn't rescued me, I'd probably be lying dead in the ravine by now. I let the blanket fall to my lap and held out my arm. My body trembled and my arm shook.

"Roll up your sleeve, please." She perched next to me on the sofa and swiped my inner elbow with alcohol. I turned my head as she pushed the needle into my vein. The anticipated pain turned out to be only a quick pinch. When I looked back, she pressed an alcohol-soaked cotton ball over the needle mark and told me to hold it while she unwrapped a Band-aid and secured the cotton to my arm.

"Do you really think I'll get better—my skin, my hair?"

"If you were going to die it would have been in the first twenty-four hours. You survived, so, I'm thinking you're stronger than you appear." She stood up, holding the small vial of blood and the white box. "Drink as much water as you can, and rest. You know where the bathroom is, but please respect my privacy and don't wander around the rest of the house. I'll see you in the morning."

She left the room, her footsteps fading down the tile hallway.

I twisted open a water bottle and drank half of it in one long gulp. I did feel better, yet the sight of my arm covered in sores disgusted me. Worse, the texture of my bare scalp with random tufts of hair poking out sickened me. I rolled down my sleeve to cover my arm, then unwrapped a Slim Jim and ate it.

Jane had placed my suitcase and laptop by the end of the sofa. I found my black wool cap in the case and pulled it over my bald head. I leaned back on the sofa, exhausted from the tiny spurt of activity.

Though lethargic, I wasn't sleepy. I scanned the room wondering about Jane. The furnishings looked older, but well-kept and probably expensive. There were no photographs, just framed oil paintings on the walls. Was this her house or did she rent it? She looked too young to be a homeowner. And how many years did it take to become a hematologist? Was it like medical school? If so, she must have started when she was fourteen. Worse, I wondered if

116

she were married or lived here with her boyfriend. Looking as messed up as I did, I had no business thinking Jane and I might actually hook up. I'm surprised she could stand to touch my arm to draw blood.

Restless, I stood and tested my legs by slowly strolling across the living room. There was a fireplace, bookcases, but no television. I located an unused outlet next to the sofa and plugged my laptop and phone in to charge. I had to piss. A good sign considering it was the first urge I had since guzzling about a gallon of water.

I shuffled down the hall, holding onto the walls for support. After using the bathroom, I stepped into the darkened hall. The main hall leading from the front door and foyer formed a T-shape. I walked down the right side of the T, turned a corner and discovered a library and two bedrooms. The doors were ajar and the rooms dark. I walked down the opposite hall. The doors on that end of the house were all closed, and a faint light shone from under one of them. I assumed it was Jane's bedroom.

A door in the center of the T intrigued me. It stood ajar and I heard splashing noises. I pushed it open and found a tiny hall that led to French doors. Beyond the doors was a courtyard with a huge rectangular swimming pool. The rear courtyard was enclosed by the house on three sides. Tall hedges formed a fourth natural wall and completed the rectangle.

I crept closer to the glass-paned doors. Outside, Jane swam laps in the pool. I huddled in the corner and watched her, thrilled with my sharp night vision. My broken eyeglasses lay somewhere on the side of the highway and I didn't miss them. My enhanced sight was the only advantage I had gained.

Jane emerged naked from the pool, climbing the steps at the far end with her back to me. Silvery rivulets of water reflecting the moonlight streamed down her back, slender waist, and toned butt. I gasped as a sudden pain stabbed my crotch. Though happy my body could still react, my swelling penis hurt, as it too was covered in ugly lesions.

I flattened my back against the wall just as Jane turned and picked up a towel. I sensed her looking toward the doors, so I held my breath and hid in the darkness. A small spider descended on a line of silk in front of my face. I blew it away and peeked through the glass. A faint sound, bare feet on the stone pool deck moved toward a door on the left side of the courtyard. Jane entered her bedroom.

She'd be angry at my snooping around her house. Wishing I could move my limbs as well as I could see, I shuffled into the hall and made my way back to the living room.

I sank onto the sofa. My groin ached and I tried to force the image of Jane's glistening nude body from my mind. I opened my laptop to shift my focus.

Nothing kills a hard-on like computer programming. I clicked on my video game files and scoured the pages of code until I reached the part where I had become stuck. I typed. My fingers fumbled on the keyboard only because I couldn't type fast enough to keep up with the lines of code flowing from my brain.

"Good morning."

Startled, I looked up. Jane stood in the living room doorway. She wore a white lab coat over pale blue scrubs and her long hair was pulled back into a ponytail. Even medical scrubs didn't dull her beauty.

"It's morning?" The heavy drapes over the windows kept out the sun.

"Yes. Did you sleep?"

"Um, no. I started working on some code. Guess I worked all night."

"Insomnia is a vampire's curse. You'll have to learn to fight it or else find yourself a night job." She walked away.

I closed my laptop, yawned, and stood up. My legs didn't shake, and my gait felt steadier. I walked across the foyer and found Jane in the kitchen holding two glasses.

"Here, I think you're ready for this now."

She placed one glass of dark red liquid on the kitchen table and drank from the other.

"Blood?"

Jane sighed. "Pomegranate juice. It's loaded with antioxidants and nutrients."

"Oh." I picked up the glass and sipped. "It's good. Thank you."

"Why don't you just shave your head?"

I ran my hand over the wool cap that covered my baldness.

Jane leaned down and pulled a plastic bin out from a lower cabinet. She removed the cover and held up an object. "It's a dog shearer but works like electric clippers." She laid it on the kitchen table.

I stared at it.

Jane shrugged and returned the bin to the cabinet. "It's here if you want it."

"Will my hair grow back?"

"I'm not sure. I looked at your blood under the microscope last night. The cells are changing, but very slowly. Fascinating, really. I'd like to take another sample tonight for comparison."

I nodded. To smoking-hot Jane, I wasn't a man, just an ugly, bald lab rat to be studied. "Yeah, uh sure." I drank more of the juice, savoring the deep berry flavor.

"I'll be back around four-thirty." She picked up her purse and slung the strap over her shoulder. "Drink water. There's more juice in the refrigerator, if you want it." She donned a pair of dark sunglasses and strode past me.

She stopped by the front door and turned. "Hey, what's your name?"

"Tim."

She nodded. "Don't let anyone in, Tim. I'll see you later."

I walked to the sofa and pulled the warm blanket around me. My dream of being fierce and sexy had turned into a nightmare, one I desperately wanted to awaken from and find myself back in my room, smelling delicious aromas wafting from Mom's kitchen. Instead, here I was a hideous freak hiding under a blanket. What would happen next? Would I crouch in shadows, pluck insects from dank corners and eat them? I wasn't sexy or powerful like Bela, I was ugly and pathetic. I was Renfield.

Chapter 9

"I am here to do Your bidding, Master. I am Your slave, and You will reward me." (8.38)
~*Renfield*, Count Dracula

I slept deeply, more deeply than I ever recall sleeping in my life—at least for a while. Entombed in a bottomless abyss, I floated in liquid blackness where nightmares swam just beyond the periphery of my vision. Strange voices, muted screams, and scratching sounds sent sensations of dread prickling through me even in my sleep. Thankfully most of the creatures stayed hidden in the darkness. Whenever one brushed against me, I forced myself to wake.

As the day went on, I woke myself more and more, though I arose groggy, lethargic, and thirsty—so thirsty. I hauled myself up from the sofa and shuffled across the foyer into the kitchen. The pomegranate juice quenched my thirst and I drained all of the tangy, sweet liquid from the half-gallon bottle. After rummaging through the cellophane packages and devouring the last of the Slim Jims, I turned my attention to the row of water bottles Jane had left on the coffee table.

The urge to urinate also came with each wakening. On one trip to the bathroom, I detoured into the kitchen and picked up the dog shears on the table.

Jane, as usual, was correct. The device worked like electric clippers. I shaved the ridiculous tufts of hair poking from my scalp and then pulled the wool cap back on to cover my baldness. There, it was done. Perhaps it was hopeful thinking, but the sores covering my face and body appeared smaller, darker, more like dried scabs than open lesions. Too tired to inspect my skin more closely, I left the shears on the bathroom counter and staggered back to my lair of blankets in the dim living room. Cradled in the cushions of the leather sofa, I pulled a warm blanket over my face and drifted back into macabre dreams with unseen monsters.

Rustling noises startled me. I flung the blanket off my face expecting to come face to face with a venomous clawed demon but instead saw Jane gathering up pieces of cellophane and empty water bottles from the living room.

"W-What time is it?"

"Five-fifteen." She sprayed the table with an aerosol polish, the lemony scent assaulting my nostrils. I sat up on the sofa and rubbed my eyes to clear the film of sleep.

"I'd appreciate it if you would clean up after yourself."

Jane sounded like my mother. I sat mute, as she rubbed the table with a cloth until the dark wooden surface shone. She headed out of the room carrying the cleaner and a bag filled with my trash.

"Sorry. I meant to clean up."

"Do you know how to grill?" she called over her shoulder.

I stood and followed her into the kitchen. Plastic grocery bags covered the table. She reached into one and drew out a plastic-wrapped package with two thick steaks inside. A drizzle of bright red blood on the white Styrofoam tray mesmerized me.

"Well, do you?"

"Um, yeah. I can grill." My father occasionally relinquished his role of grill master and taught me to grill steaks, burgers, salmon, and chicken.

She handed me the steaks. "There's a gas grill on the back patio."

"Okay." I held the package and hesitated. "Uh, how do you like yours cooked?"

"Do one minute on each side, for mine and for yours."

"Only a minute? These are pretty thick. I like mine well—"

"You won't be able to stomach the meat if it's cooked any longer." She placed a timer and silver tongs onto a large china platter then handed it all to me. "Only one minute per side. Don't ruin them."

I headed down the hall and through the French doors onto the spacious stone patio. The grill sat in the far corner under the shade of a large tree that grew on the other side of the hedges.

121

The pool water glistened in the late afternoon sun and the dappling of light reflecting off the water irritated my eyes. I kept to the shade and turned on the grill.

Terra-cotta pots filled with green plants and flowers dotted the patio. A seating area and a rustic clay chiminea stood in the opposite corner. With the exception of the bright sunlight, the patio was a peaceful retreat hidden within the outer walls of the house and the tall hedge. As I waited for the grill to heat, I entertained myself with the vision of Jane emerging naked from the pool. Arousal still brought pain, so I turned my focus to grilling the steaks, careful to set the timer for one minute on each side.

The steaks still sizzled as I carried the platter into the kitchen. Jane had set the table for two and placed a large bowl of salad greens and a round loaf of crusty bread in the center.

I added the platter of meat to the table. "I'll go clean up outside."

"Let's eat now, you must be starving. You can clean up after." She motioned for me to sit.

I cut into the steak and red juice pooled on my plate. It looked raw inside. I had always preferred meat well-done, yet the quick-seared raw meat tasted delicious. I hadn't realized how hungry I was until I had demolished the entire steak. I fought off the urge to lap the red juice left on the dish.

"Eat some greens." Before I could decline, she heaped a pile of salad onto my plate. Again, Jane reminded me of my mother, pushing vegetables onto my plate.

"Food is fuel and your new metabolism will thrive on specific nutrients."

I shoved a forkful of salad into my mouth. Surprisingly, the crunchy greens tasted almost as good as the steak. Was Jane right about everything? Her authoritative tone reminded me of my father. Between bites of salad I glanced at her across the table, awestruck by her perfection, especially when her tongue flicked across her full bottom lip to capture a drip of red.

After dinner, I cleaned the grill. The sun had sunk close to the horizon and my eyes preferred the dusky purple light. Strangely, the lack of sunlight improved my vision rather than hindering it. I stood for a while gazing up at the intricate details on the undersides of the leaves rustling overhead. Something dropped from the leaves. My body reacted. An instant later I was directly underneath the falling object. I caught a tiny bird in my cupped hands. It looked up and made a small chirping sound. Its miniature body trembled. I spotted the brown, grassy bottom of the nest overhead where two branches joined and formed a deep V. I pulled the iron patio table under the tree and jumped up on it. Another small jump allowed me to grasp one of the thicker branches. I was able to pull myself upward with one hand until I could peer inside the nest. Three baby birds were nestled inside. I carefully tucked the fallen bird in the soft downy interior with its nest mates and then jumped down to the ground. It wasn't until I landed on the patio that the feat I just had performed fully hit me. The branch was high—about twelve feet up—yet I had reached it with ease. Before my transformation I would have had trouble just climbing up on the table, not to mention my fear of heights. I grinned as I watched the mother bird fly into the branches and settle into the nest for the night.

When I returned to the kitchen, Jane had the table cleared and dishes washed.

"You're moving much better this evening. How do you feel?" she asked.

I thought about my bird rescue. "Pretty good. I mean, compared to yesterday."

"I'll get my kit and take another blood sample." She hurried off down the hall.

When she returned, I sat at the kitchen table and rolled up my sleeve. "My skin looks better."

"Yes, you're healing." She drew the blood and then turned to leave.

"Can I see your lab?"

She hesitated in the doorway. "I suppose."

I followed her to the T in the hallway where she turned left, then made a right down the corridor with the two doors. She used a key to unlock the first door and flipped on a light switch as she entered.

The room had the same orangey-colored Saltillo floor tile as the rest of the house, but that's where the similarity ended. The ceiling lights were bright, though not blinding, and long tables with machines, racks of test tubes, and rubber tubing attached to unknown contraptions took up most of the space. A desktop computer station and a closed laptop took up one corner with bookshelves next to it.

She headed for a large microscope, the only thing I recognized from high school biology class.

"Don't touch anything."

Jane's clinical attitude and brusque tone touched off a spark of anger. I was just a lab rat to her, and she even spoke to me like I was a dumb animal.

My anger simmered, but I sat on a stool while she prepared a slide and slid it under the scope.

"Amazing," she murmured.

"What is?"

"Look." She stepped back and motioned for me to look into the eye piece.

It took me a moment to focus, but once I did, I saw a slow-moving video in shades of red. "I see red globs. Darker ones kind of swallowing up the lighter ones." I straightened up and shrugged.

"Those *globs* are your blood cells. The darker are the vampire cells. As you saw, they are slowly consuming the weaker cells."

"Consuming? You mean like a disease?"

"It's a misconception that vampirism is a virus. It's more of a mutation of sorts, though I hate that word, it has a negative connotation."

"A transformation?"

She cocked her head in thought. "Yes. Or, more accurately, an evolution. The weaker cells stay intact but are absorbed and fortified by the stronger ones. Once bonded they become superior in both structure and function."

"So, if I have vampire blood in my veins, that means I *am* a vampire?"

"Technically, you're a hybrid, though it appears your body is still evolving. I've never seen it take this long." The corners of her mouth tweaked. "A late bloomer."

The similarities between gorgeous Jane's words and my mother's were becoming downright annoying.

She picked up a spiral-bound notebook and pen and pulled a second stool closer to mine. "I'd like to ask you some questions, for my research."

An obedient rat, I sat and rested my bare feet on the cold steel rungs. "Yeah, sure."

"When did you first realize you were . . . different?"

"What do you mean?"

"Most hybrids show signs during puberty, for instance enhanced senses, emotional outbursts, increased physical strength."

"I-I, um, no. I always thought vampires were cool. Then I read about vampire cults online. I wanted to be one."

Jane laid her notebook on the counter. "Are you saying you're a mundane and just decided on a whim to become a vampire?"

"A mundane?"

"A human."

"Um, well, yeah, I guess."

Her aquamarine eyes blazed. "You're an idiot."

"Hey, just because I decided to better myself doesn't give you the right to call—"

"Better yourself? What the hell? You think being a vampire is like taking a college course, or joining a gym? You risked dying. By all rights you should be dead." Her voice trembled with barely controlled rage.

I stood and paced the room, the spark of anger ignited. "But I'm *not* dead."

"Only because I found you in time."

"Maybe I wouldn't have died—even without your help." My voice lacked conviction. I turned away from her glaring eyes.

"How did you come to drink Lorelei's blood? You must have lied and told her you were a hybrid. She would never allow a mere mundane to drink her blood."

"I earned the right to drink her blood. And what is all this *mundane* crap?"

"Yeah, you really did your research." Jane huffed and continued to glare at me with her laser-like eyes. She crossed her arms. "How exactly did you earn this right?"

"Just like you, I completed the parchment."

125

"Parchment? What are you talking about?"

"Lorelei gave me the parchment. There were six tasks listed on it and I finished them within the time limit. Don't look at me like that. Lorelei transformed you, so you completed the parchment, too."

"Drinking Lorelei's blood enhanced the hybrid vampire traits I already possessed. And she didn't give me any *parchment*. I think you're lying."

I turned and stalked from the lab down the hall to the living room. Snatching the parchment from the coffee table, I returned to the lab and confronted Jane, shaking the paper in front of her face.

"Here. I'm telling you the truth."

Jane took the paper, unfolded it and studied it for several moments before speaking. "Is this some sort of joke?"

"It's *not* a joke. I nearly died doing those tasks. But I did them. I proved my worthiness and Lorelei rewarded me with transformation."

Jane's eyes narrowed. "Drinking the blood of a virgin and your mortal enemy? How exactly did you accomplish those tasks?"

"I, um—that's none of your business."

"How did you get their blood?" Her upper lip curled in disgust and her nose wrinkled confirming her belief I truly was a vile rodent.

"I didn't hurt anyone." I could never tell her I drank my own virgin blood or wore a dress to trick Chris Bagwell. My anger grew into a rage and the volume of my voice surprised me when I blurted, "You're the one who's lying. I saw you at the Black Swan—before you drank Lorelei's blood. You were mundane and pl—"

"Plain?" Her eyes were dark slits with two beams of green light for pupils. "That's what you were going to say, isn't it?"

The fire inside me cooled. "Um, no, I just—"

"Oh, please. *Plain Jane*. I've heard it all my damn life. Go ahead, say it." Her eyes glinted like rock-hard jewels.

"No. I meant you were . . . normal-looking, not ugly. But after the transformation—now—you're amazing."

Her expression softened. "I admit Lorelei's blood enhanced my skin, my hair, but that wasn't the reason I asked permission to drink it. The physical enhancements were pleasant side effects."

I grunted. "Some side effects. So how come you ended up gorgeous and I look like a freak?"

She tossed the parchment at me and turned back to the microscope. It landed at my feet. "I don't know. I do know Lorelei is a danger, letting mundanes drink her blood. And that parchment is a joke. A cruel one. She most likely gave it to you to get rid of you, believing you would either fail the tasks or die trying."

I bent and picked up the folded paper. "Maybe that would have been better."

Jane turned and looked at me. Her eyes had changed and now gave off a soft bluish glow. "Most mundanes would have failed, or died. You've proven that you're strong, persistent. Hopefully that will work in your favor." She pointed at me and stared, open-mouthed. "The last task. The hideous purple suit . . . that smell— formaldehyde! You stole it from a dead man, didn't you?"

Shame burned my cheeks. "I intend to return it. Well, at least to his wife. I'll get it dry-cleaned."

"How did you get the suit?"

"I hid inside a funeral parlor and after everyone left, I . . . took it."

"What could you have possibly read online about vampires that would possess you to strip the clothes off a dead man? You're either insane or a bigger idiot than I thought."

Her tone fueled a hot raging fire inside me. I yelled at her, "I needed to change my life. And it's none of your damn business why I did what I did!"

"Was your life really so bad before?"

"Was yours? Why did you drink Lorelei's blood if you were already a vampire?"

"None of *your* damn business." She walked past me and snapped off the light switch. I strode into the hallway and she locked the lab door.

"Good night." She walked to the next door, slipped inside and slammed it shut behind her.

Insomnia plagued me. I paced the front part of the house and thought about Jane. Yes, I owed her, maybe she had saved my life, but she had no right treating me like an experiment gone awry.

My insides twisted with frustration and rage. On one hand, every time I looked at her my heart sped up and my mouth turned dust-dry. Then I looked at my own reflection and reality punched me in the gut with an icy fist. I would never have a chance with Jane. Ever.

As much as she awed me with her looks, her personality frustrated me. She hardly ever smiled, except when she showed me pity. Jane treated me like a stray animal she rescued. Diseased, hair falling out, and making a mess in her house. She'd didn't see me as a man, much less a potential lover.

She'd called me a liar and an idiot, looked at me with disgust and talked to me with her condescending, know-it-all tone. Damn her. Who does she think she is? She drank Lorelei's blood the same as I did. She's no better than me.

It was early morning. I had spent the entire night fuming over Jane. I stomped down the hall toward the rear of the house, hell bent on banging on Jane's door until she came out and apologized. I'd kick the damn door in if I had to. I'll show her I'm a man, not some sickly lab rat she can boss around.

I stopped short of crashing into Jane as I rounded the corner. She stared at me and said, "Excuse me." Her tone froze the air between us.

"I'm not moving until you admit you're wrong about me. You owe me an apology!"

"For what?" She squared her shoulders. Even in her white lab coat and pastel pink scrubs she looked formidable.

I straightened my back and shoulders. I stood a head taller than Jane and glared at her. "I'm not a liar or an idiot and definitely not your damn lab rat. You have no right accusing me, judging me and acting so superior all the time."

She clenched her fists. "Move out of my way. Now."

Reason trickled into my fury. What was I going to do? I would never hit a woman. But I had made a stand, I couldn't back down now. "Apologize!" I shouted.

Her fist impacted my left cheek. I found myself sprawled on the floor. The force of her punch left me stunned. I never even saw her arm move. Jane stepped over my legs and headed toward the foyer.

I climbed to my feet and staggered after her. Jane turned into the kitchen.

"I don't need your fucking help. I'm out of here!" Storming into the living room, I gathered up my suitcase, laptop and shoved my wallet and car keys into my sweatpants pockets.

Opening the two front door locks and chain slowed my momentum. I finally flung open the door.

"Tim! Stop! Do *not* go outside," Jane yelled.

"Screw you! I don't take orders fr—" Searing pain cut off my words. Had someone thrown acid in my face? I dropped my things, fell to my knees and clutched my burning face. Hands gripped my arms and dragged me inside the cool house.

"Move your hands away," Jane said.

My fingers trembled as I let my arms drop into my lap. She led me to the sofa. I sat while Jane crouched in front of me and smeared clear liquid over my forehead, nose, and cheeks. My skin tingled with a cool chill everywhere she spread it.

"Aloe Vera will soothe the burn."

Now that the fire on my face as well as the one inside me had been doused, I felt defeated. I slumped back and laid my head against the soft cushions. "What happened?"

"The sun happened." She screwed the cap onto the aloe bottle.

Scenes of movie vampires bursting into flames swirled in my mind. Then the reality hit—but it wasn't cool like in the movies. "I can't ever go out in the sun again?"

Jane left the room without answering me.

Exhaustion sucked me deeper into the sofa. I closed my eyes, touched a finger to my sticky cheek and gasped with pain. The sun had roasted me the moment I stepped out the door. I couldn't sleep at night and could barely stay awake during the day. I was a vampire, but without any of the cool stuff.

Jane's footsteps approached. I opened my eyes. She placed a gallon jug of pomegranate juice and a glass on the table.

"If I go out in the sun, I'll die right? Burst into flames, turn to ashes?"

She rolled her blue-green eyes and blew out a long breath. "No, your skin will sunburn, you'll probably get a painful rash and

129

blisters, and then your skin will peel and eventually heal. Once you're stronger you can go outside, but with your pale complexion, you'll need protection, concealment."

"You mean like a hat or maybe a cape?"

Something hard hit me in the chest. A small plastic bottle Jane had been holding landed in my lap. The label read, Sunscreen SPF 55.

"No, I meant sunscreen, sunglasses, and long sleeves. Photosensitivity is common in vampires." She tapped the bottle of juice. "It's crucial to stay hydrated. You were up all night and didn't drink, did you?"

Last night was an intense blur of emotions. I didn't have the energy to make sense of the rage I had felt. It came out of nowhere and my anger had consumed all reason. I shook my head.

"Drink lots of fluids. I have to go to work."

"Wait. You go outside—and you're tan. How is that possible if you're a vampire?"

"A natural tan is the best protection. I built up the melanin in my skin with gradual sun exposure *before* I drank Lorelei's blood." She left the room and I heard the front door open.

"Jane?"

She poked her head around the doorway. "What?"

"Um, thank you. I should have listened to you, but something came over me last night and I'm sorry."

"Get some rest." She smirked at me. "Of course, only if *you* want to, not because *I* said so."

Though exhausted, my recent humiliation and overall frustration with Jane prevented me from falling into the nightmare-ridden state I now called sleep. I picked up my cell phone from the end table and unplugged it from the charger. I hadn't looked at it since I had entered the Black Swan two days ago.

It displayed three missed calls and eleven texts from my mom and, surprisingly, a text from my former boss wishing me luck at my new job and reminding me to keep in touch.

I blazed through Mom's messages. She was worried because I hadn't called as promised. I stared at the screen through tear-blurred eyes. I wanted to talk to her—hell, a part of me wanted to go home and forget everything that had happened—get my old job back and settle into the safety of my predictable, boring, old life.

The tears burned my eyes and I rubbed them away. I couldn't go back. I'm changed. Whether for better or worse, I don't really know. I only knew I could never explain my appearance and strange new characteristics to my family and coworkers. I imagined telling Dad I could only mow the grass at night, or else risk lighting up like a Roman candle in the sun while straddling a gas-filled mower and blowing up the damn neighborhood. Despite Jane's dismissive comments, my skin had felt like it was about to ignite into flames.

I started to call Mom, then stopped. I didn't trust my voice. Controlling my emotions was becoming increasingly difficult. Bela Lugosi never cried in his movies, he always stayed strong, in control. Texting her would be safer, so I did. *Sorry I haven't called or texted. This hotel has crappy Wi-Fi. Super busy at the new job, lots of late nights. Looks like I'll be heading farther north to work in the company's new offices. I'll call you soon. Don't worry, I'm doing great. Love you, Tim.*

Adding the lie about moving farther north provided an excuse for not going home to visit. New tears welled and overflowed, stinging my sunburned face. I could never go home again. I chugged down half of the bottle of juice on the table, set the alarm on my cell for four o'clock and pulled the blanket over my head. Despite the threat of nightmares, I welcomed the near coma of sleep.

A steady beeping woke me, though it felt like swimming from the ocean floor to the surface just to sit upright and open my eyes. I downed the rest of the juice to quench my nagging thirst.

A new resolve had wormed into my brain while I slept. Until I understood what was happening to me, I was stuck here with Jane. I decided to show her I could be a productive human being—or hybrid—or whatever the hell I was now.

Sniffing at my armpits, I made my way down the hall to the bathroom to take a piss. I hadn't showered in two days, though my skin felt dry and there was no odor of perspiration. Still, a shower might help wash away the cloying web of sleep that clung to me.

Most of the sores on my face and body had vanished, the deepest ones now only small dark scabs. I yanked the wool cap from my head and tossed it on the counter as I stepped into the stall and ducked under the spray of hot water.

My fingertips touched tiny prickles on my scalp. Great, a fresh new hell plagued my body. Holding my breath, I hurried back to the mirror and stood dripping water on the floor as I studied my head. My breath shot out in a gasp. Hair! Though it looked more like a five o'clock shadow, it was definitely hair. I finished showering and dried off, giddy with joy over the new growth on my scalp. Other than my sun-flushed face, I looked almost normal. In a month or so I'd have a full head of hair and all of the scabs should be gone. My eyes not only worked better, they looked different, too, much darker than their former hazel color. An amber glint shone in them as I turned my head and inspected my face in the mirror.

I walked naked to the living room and dug out a pair of jeans and a short-sleeved T-shirt since I didn't have to hide my arms anymore. Once dressed, I retrieved Jane's cleaning supplies from under the kitchen sink, straightened up the living room and then scrubbed down the bathroom. The bright lemony scent filled the house and provided pungent evidence of my cleaning spree. I returned the dog shears to the cabinet where Jane had kept them. The plastic box also held nail clippers and a large red collar. A silvery heart-shaped tag dangled from the collar with "Raven" engraved on it. Jane must have owned a dog at one time. I assumed it had died.

At five o'clock, I opened the refrigerator and removed a package of steaks. I sprinted across the sun-dappled patio to avoid being crisped again in the sunlight and turned on the gas grill, then I went back into the kitchen and prepared a bowl of salad.

At five-fifteen, Jane came through the front door as I entered the house from the rear French doors carrying a platter of barely grilled steaks.

"Dinner's ready." I placed the steaks on the table next to the salad and bread and poured two glasses of pomegranate juice, setting one at her place.

Jane shrugged off her white lab coat, draping it and her purse straps over the chair in the foyer. She sniffed the lemony air and eyed me suspiciously as she took her seat at the table. "This is a surprise."

Her voice held a leery edge. What would it take to impress this woman? I sat and passed Jane the salad bowl. "So, how was your day?" I asked.

"Good." She piled salad on her plate and then handed me the bowl. "Busy, but I prefer to stay busy. How was yours?"

"I cleaned the house. Well, the living room and bathroom." Obviously, I needed to spell out my worth to her. Reaching into my jeans pocket, I took out the cash my mother had given me. "I'd like to contribute some money for the food and all." I pushed the folded bills across the table.

"That's not necessary." Jane slid the cash back toward me. "What kind of work do you—or did you—do, Tim?"

I left the money on the table. "Computer programming, coding. I worked as an IT tech at an insurance company. But I'm hoping to break into video game design."

She nodded. "Have you thought about the future? Getting a job? A place to live?"

"Yes and no. I've been focused on not dying for the past two days. I haven't made a plan—yet—but I will. First, I need to know what to expect, now that I'm a . . . hybrid."

Jane chewed a bite of steak and stared at me.

Apparently, my apology this morning hadn't been enough. "Listen, I really am sorry about this morning. I know I have a lot to learn. And I'm grateful for any knowledge you'll share."

A glimmer of a smile touched her lips and then vanished. "What do you want to know?"

"Everything. Um, so I'm a vampire now, right? I'll need to drink blood, won't I?"

"Yes, when it's time."

"How will I know?"

"Trust me, you'll know. You're still evolving. Once the process is complete, you'll need to find appropriate donors."

The word threw me. I pictured myself lurking behind the Big Red Bus, ready to ambush an unsuspecting victim. "Donors?"

"There are people in our community who aren't vampires, but who choose to donate their blood to sustain us. They have various reasons for doing so and it's important to find reputable, healthy ones. We call them black swans."

"Wow. I had no idea."

"Our community is complicated, Tim. First off, you have the vampires. There are two types, the Sanguine and the Psi. Sanguines require blood, Psi's or psychics, feed off the energy mundanes emit."

"How do I know which I am?"

"Lorelei created you, she's Sanguine, which makes you one as well. Though it's not uncommon for us to be both."

"Are you a Sanguine?"

"Yes."

"And you have donors?"

"Yes."

"Are they men?"

"Your questions are getting rather personal."

"Sorry. I'm just curious."

"Donors are a personal preference. Male or female is irrelevant. Blood is blood."

Jane's curt answer made me pause. Was she a lesbian? Wouldn't that be just my luck. "So, once I find a donor, I'd just, um, what? Bite her?"

She put her fork down and stared at me with eyes that glinted green. In the short time I'd spent with Jane, I'd learned green wasn't her happy eye color.

"Human teeth aren't designed to penetrate skin. Nor would they have the precision necessary to puncture and draw out blood from a vein, no matter what you've seen in movies."

"Then how do you get their blood?"

"A small cut. Usually on the forearm or anywhere the skin is thicker and less likely to scar. We treat our donors with respect. Always clean the skin and the wound before and afterwards with antiseptic. You should also brush your teeth, use mouthwash before you drink their blood to minimize the risk of infection."

"That sounds pretty cold and clinical."

"It is what it is. A practicality. We only require a small amount of blood to survive, to thrive. They supply it willingly."

"So, is it like a . . . sexual thing?"

The green light flashed in her eyes again. "You really should never have been allowed to be transformed."

"Why? Because I'm trying to find the upside to all this? You're young, attractive—with amazing powers—don't you ever let loose and have fun? You make it sound like I'm doomed."

"You really have no clue, do you? You think your new life will be seducing women with your hypnotic eyes, throwing back your silk cape and then biting their throats?"

"You have to admit, that sounds a lot cooler than a surgical cut on the arm—"

"You're an imbecile." She shoved back her chair, stood and stormed out of the kitchen.

My brain screamed to let her walk away even as I chased down the hall after her. "Jane! Wait. How am I supposed to learn about being a vampire if you get pissed off every time I ask something? You're right, all I know is stuff I've seen in movies and read online. Maybe it's not the best information, I admit. But could you cut me a little slack? Please?"

She stopped when she reached her bedroom door and whirled around, eyes blazing green. "There are dangers. People have died—will die—and you act like it's all a stupid Hollywood movie."

"You know, I'm tired of apologizing to you. Do you think this has been easy for me? I was dumped on the side of the road and left to die. Terrified. Paralyzed. Disfigured. Yes, I owe you my life. And I respect what you're telling me, but, c'mon, there must be some perks to being a vampire. Aren't there?"

The inferno in her eyes faded. "You'll live longer, age slower, and have significantly more strength and dexterity."

"Okay, yeah. That's what I mean. Those are all cool perks."

"Yes. But along with those *perks*, comes serious responsibility and danger."

"If I'm stronger than the mundanes, what's the danger?"

"Like I said, it's a complicated hierarchy. There are rival sects among us. The Pure Bloods believe they are superior to hybrids. There've been deadly clashes between the old and new world vampires. And you—a mundane who's been turned—they'll all see you as an abomination."

I leaned against the wall and stared at my feet. "People have seen me as an abomination all my life." I met her gaze. "But I refuse to be treated like one anymore. Especially if I have the power to fight back now."

Jane nodded. "You'll need to fight to defend yourself. And most importantly, learn whom you can trust and whom you can't." She walked from her bedroom to the lab door and unlocked it. "May I get another sample of your blood?"

I let out a long sigh. The evening went nothing like I'd hoped and I was in no mood to play lab rat. "No. I need to clean up the kitchen." I turned and left her standing in her laboratory doorway.

I took my frustration out scrubbing the grill and the dishes. When finished, I went into the living room and opened my laptop. Writing code for my game calmed me. It came so easy now it was like typing the alphabet. By the time Jane reappeared, dressed in pastel green scrubs for work the next morning, I had finished all ten levels of my game. Much of the code was new. I'd invented it on the fly. The sophisticated characters, settings, and actions I'd created went so far beyond anything I had previously imagined that I had impressed myself.

"You looked pleased about something." Jane placed a glass of juice for me on the coffee table.

"Thank you." I took a long sip. "I finished designing my game. All ten levels." Turning the laptop toward her, I showed her the last page of code.

"I don't know what I'm looking at, but this text looks complex."

"It's code. A mix of Java script, C++, and even a little html5 thrown in. Each string denotes a physical characteristic, setting, or an action inside the gaming environment."

"You wrote this page in one night?"

"Nope." I swiped the screen, the scrolling pages blurred past. "I did over one thousand pages last night."

Jane set her glass down and stared at me. "Before you were transformed, how many pages of code could you write in a night's time?"

I sucked on my bottom lip and thought. "I don't know, two on a good night, less if I got stuck." I tapped the screen. "But now I don't get stuck. I see code streaming in my mind. If my fingers typed faster, I could do more."

"So, you had this ability before, and now it's improved, true?"

"Yes."

"What else have you noticed that's improved about yourself?"

My first thought was my eyesight. "I can see now. Not that I was blind before, but my vision was pretty poor. I wore glasses, thick ones, all the time."

"And now?"

"Now I don't, and I can see near and far. I saw the veins on leaves twenty feet away. Ants crawling on tree bark even farther away. Every detail is crystal clear. I see even better in the dark."

Jane had slipped a small notepad from her pocket and scrawled in it as I talked. As I admired the sexy curve of her neck and the way her ponytail cascaded like polished gold silk down her back, she only glanced up at me between scribbling, her expression interested, but neutral.

I sighed, stood, and stretched my arms above my head. My hands knocked the wool cap on my head askew.

"Take off your cap, please," Jane said.

I hated the way she looked at me, evaluating me like some freakish specimen in a glass tube. "I'd rather keep it on." Yet as I straightened it on my head, my fingertips poked under the wool rim. The tiny prickles from yesterday were now short strands. I jogged from the living room to the bathroom mirror.

The new hair on my head was the color of black coffee. Though short, it felt thicker and had a glossy sheen, nothing like my former fine, drab-brown hair.

"Remarkable," Jane said from the doorway.

Even more so to me was the slight bristle covering my upper lip, chin, and jaw line. I would actually need to shave if it grew in any heavier. I studied my reflection. Clear skin, dark eyes, and best of all—hair. For the first time in my life, the face that stared back at me from the mirror didn't disappoint.

"Tim, can we continue this conversation when I get home from work?"

"Sure." Her tone sounded humble and did I imagine it, or had she looked at me differently? I walked her to the front door. "Steak for dinner?"

"Sure."

"Do you eat anything besides steak?" She certainly had a stockpile of it in her freezer.

"Sometimes lamb. They're both meats that can safely be eaten rare."

"Oh, right. I'll see you at dinner."

She smiled at me and left for work.

Seeing Jane smile was an event rarer than how she liked her steak. Her beauty left me weak-kneed even as sleepiness dragged at my eyelids. As I walked toward the sofa, I couldn't resist rubbing the silky hair covering my head.

I lay on the sofa and pictured Jane's dazzling smile. How did she manage to stay up all day and work? Especially at a lab where she would need to stay clear-headed and focused. Though wide awake all night, I felt weak and exhausted by sunrise. I had so many questions and Jane's answers only triggered more.

Jane woke me. "Dinner's ready." Waking up was difficult, but I finally stood and walked to the kitchen. The hazy lavender light streaming in the window signaled sunset. I had forgotten to set my alarm so I could make her dinner. Jane motioned for me to sit. Skewers of rare meat chunks and colorful vegetables adorned our plates.

"This is good, what is it?"

"Lamb."

"Would you like to watch a movie after dinner?"

She shook her head as she chewed and swallowed. "I don't own a TV."

"I have mine in my car. I could set it up or I could stream movies on my laptop. I have a few DVDs, too."

"Thank you, but I have work to do."

We finished our meal in silence, and I helped her clear the table. She washed the few dishes in record time.

I stood in the arched doorway of the kitchen blocking her exit. "You just came home from working all day. Why not take the night off and relax?"

"Thank you, I need to work in the lab. But I would like another blood sample from you." She eyed me for a moment. "You are changing rapidly. It's amazing—unprecedented as far as I know."

An expression of approval flickered across her face. Or had I only imagined it? My clear skin and new hair fueled a new-found cockiness. "If I give you blood, will you agree to watch a movie with me?"

"No."

Her tone deflated me. I sighed. "Fine. You want to take it here or in the lab?"

She slipped past me and started down the hall. "My kit's in the lab. Follow me."

After she drew my blood, I watched her prepare the slide and label it. She wrote in a notebook.

"So, am I a full-blown vampire yet?"

"It would be impossible for a mundane to. . ." She looked up from the microscope, her eyes wide and a deep ocean blue color.

"What is it?"

"Your blood, there are hardly any human cells left." She straightened and studied me.

"Quit staring at me. If you refuse to watch a movie or have any fun, then I guess I'll go work on my game." I walked to the door.

"Tim, you said you finished the game. Could we talk more about your evolution?"

She called me by name and asked rather than ordered. A chance to talk while I mentally fantasized about having sex with Jane was better than nothing.

"Okay, but not here." Away from this science-filled room maybe she'd view me as a man instead of an experiment. "Can we sit on your patio?"

She hesitated and then nodded. "I'm going to change out of my scrubs. I'll meet you out there."

I found wood and matches near the chiminea and started a fire. The smoky scent of burning oak drifted in the balmy air. Jane entered the patio through the French doors leading from her bedroom. She wore a short black robe and her long legs were bare.

My breath caught in my throat. Was she naked under the robe like the other night?

She untied the robe and tossed it onto a chair. Though she wasn't nude, I wasn't disappointed. Jane rocked every millimeter of the modest one-piece bathing suit. "You're welcome to swim if you like." She dove into the pool and arced beneath the surface. Her head emerged and she swam the length of the pool with strong strokes, flipped under the water and then swam back.

"Do you have a suit?" She leaned her chin on folded arms at the side of the pool. Her wet skin and hair shimmered with deep golden tones in the moonlight.

"Um, yeah." I pried my gaze away from her, hurried inside and dug out the one pair of bright tropical-print trunks I owned from my suitcase. Swimming had never been a favorite sport of mine since it involved revealing too much of my puny physique for comfort. While still pale and thin, at least the gruesome sores on my body had vanished. I focused on that positive fact, rather than my skinny legs.

After filling two large wine glasses with pomegranate juice, I made my way back to the patio. Talking to Jane about my evolution into a vampire was the last thing on my mind.

Jane was swimming laps when I placed our drinks on the round metal table. As I turned, she emerged from the pool, dripping wet and drop-dead gorgeous.

"Thanks." She picked up a glass and downed half of the deep red juice in one gulp. "We don't perspire, so it's difficult to know when you're dehydrated. When in doubt," she raised her glass again, "drink." She put the empty glass down and walked toward her bedroom. "I forgot to bring us towels."

Taking advantage of her absence, I stripped off my T-shirt, hurried down the cement steps at the shallow end of the pool and submerged my scrawny torso underwater. Blue lights glowed from the pool's bottom. My strokes weren't as smooth as Jane's and the lights shimmering beneath the undulating water mesmerized me. Ducking my head under, I opened my eyes and saw a pebble and two leaves as clear as day lying on the bottom. I dove and swooped them up. When I emerged, Jane sat on the side of the pool wrapped in a white towel, her legs dangling in the water.

I deposited the debris on the pool side, then swam to the end of the long rectangle and back. Though never athletic, it felt good to stretch my muscles. After swimming three more laps, I noticed a white towel hanging on the railing by the pool stairs. Staying under water as long as I could, I stood, snatched the towel and wrapped it around my upper body. Jane had donned her robe and waited at the table with a new bottle of pomegranate juice and a notepad.

"How did you get so strong?" I settled in a chair across from her and guzzled my juice.

"It's like you and your code writing. I was always athletic. Once I fully evolved, my strength and stamina improved dramatically."

"I always sucked at sports."

Jane smiled. "I sucked at academics, yet I completed four years of college, two years of med school, then switched to hematology and studied it for another six years. Before my awakening, I didn't have the focus necessary for academia."

"Twelve years of school. How is that possible? You aren't old enough."

"How old do you think I am?"

"Um, I don't know. Twenty-two—twenty-four, tops."

She rewarded me with another smile, her glittering blue eyes mirrored the pool water. "I'm thirty-seven."

"No, you can't be." Shit, that made Jane twelve years older than me. Was I too young for her to consider me romantically?

"You said yourself how plain I looked the night you saw me at the Black Swan. Being a hybrid, I've always looked younger than my chronological age. But Lorelei's blood is powerful. Drinking it enhanced my skin and muscle tone. My hair turned from light brown to golden blonde overnight."

"Wow. Now that's a perk." I sipped from my glass. "So, if I work out, my muscles will improve?"

"Absolutely."

"Damn. Maybe I should join a gym."

"You're welcome to use the gym in the house. It's the door around the corner from my lab. The room is small, but it has all the basics for a full body work out. You should lift weights."

I snorted. "You sound like my dad."

"I either swim, run, or weight train in the evenings. Besides keeping in shape, it tires me and helps me sleep. Sleeping at night conflicts with our internal clocks, but since I work during the day, I need to sleep at night. Four or five hours is all we require."

"When did you know you were a vampire?' I asked.

"I was twelve when I started to feel restless and different. My strength and athletic abilities increased. And emotionally, well, I was a hot mess." She laughed. "Extremely more so than the average pre-teen girl."

"I've had trouble controlling my emotions. Sadness, anger. Like yesterday morning, my anger consumed me. That's not like me."

"Maybe this is your belated puberty?"

"Late bloomer." We said it at the same time and laughed. Jane's laughter sounded warm, non-judgmental. The husky tone of it suited her, especially when her eyes shone crystal blue.

"How much of Lorelei's blood did you drink, Tim?"

My cheeks burned as I recalled the two thugs dragging me away from Lorelei's bleeding arm. My tongue flicked across my lips at the memory of the addictive taste. "More than I was supposed to."

"How do you know that?" Jane cocked her head and stared at me. She held a pen and I realized she was taking notes. "The more honest you are, the more I can help you."

My hopes for a romantic evening sipping drinks around the fire evaporated.

I sighed and told her what happened that night. Once I started talking, everything I remembered gushed out like water through a broken dam. Lorelei's rich, delicious blood, being ripped away from her arm, waking up paralyzed, being tossed from the van, rolling down the slope, and finally lying helpless in a ditch on the side of the road.

"Tim, you need to learn to control your anger. It will get you in trouble someday."

I stopped talking and looked down at my balled-up fists. I was standing, pacing between the chair and the chiminea. Unclenching my jaw, I took a deep breath and sat. The anger dissipated but the memory of Lorelei's blood stayed. "When will I be ready to drink blood?"

"Soon. I'll take you to The Haven. So, when it's time, you'll have a donor lined up."

"What's The Haven?"

"It's a private club downtown. I trust the leader and the clan there."

"A private vampire club?" I smirked.

Jane's lips pursed. "Yes, a vampire club. Scoff if you want, there's safety in numbers."

Nothing remotely romantic happened that evening. Jane continued to quiz me, and I answered while she made notes in her pad. When I finished talking, she rose and said good night. I extinguished the remaining embers in the chiminea, picked up our empty glasses, and went into the house. Unable to sleep, I checked out her home gym. As Jane said, it was small but contained a stationary bicycle, an elliptical, and a Nautilus machine. A rack of free weights and a bench with a bar sat near one wall.

I used the gym regularly as a way to work off anger, frustration, and the sexual tension that built up every time I looked at Jane. My father would be proud of my disciplined daily workouts.

Jane and I settled into a platonic pattern over the next few weeks. I fought my body clock and trained myself to fall asleep by two or three in the morning. On her advice, I turned on a small table lamp at night. The soft yellow glow mimicked the morning sunlight and helped induce sleepiness. My nightmares gradually lessened.

I worked out in the gym for hours after Jane left for work, then tidied up the house, worked on my game code, and most evenings had dinner ready when she returned home. Though Jane's standards were higher than mine when it came to cleanliness, I think she appreciated my efforts. Her tone of voice had softened, and she smiled more often.

We usually swam laps and talked after dinner, though she abruptly shut down whenever I asked her any questions about her life. She continued to take samples of my blood and kept meticulous notes. Most importantly she schooled me on what being a vampire entailed. Though I knew I was a curiosity to her, I couldn't convince my mind or my body to stop wanting more out of our strange relationship.

A restlessness grew inside me along with bouts of emotional outbursts. I couldn't live as Jane's man-maid forever. I needed to move on, find a job and figure out how to cope with my new life. Some days those thoughts thrilled me and other days they terrified me.

One morning after she left for work, I slathered on sunscreen, donned long sleeves, a ball cap, and dark glasses. Besides my one impulsive run out the front door and our evenings on the patio, it was the first time I'd ventured outside in the daylight in over a month. The sun felt hotter than I ever remembered, but as long as I drank lots of water and didn't stay in the direct rays for too long, I learned I could tolerate the sun without bursting into flames.

The grass in the front and sides of the house looked shaggy. I opened a small tool shed on the side of the house, found a push mower inside and decided to cut the lawn. Deep down I hoped expanding my services to yard work would extend my usefulness—and my stay—with Jane.

The girth of the grassy swatch of yard extending beyond the hedges in the back of the house surprised me. Between the line of hedges and the woods that ringed the house there was a large, flower-covered mound. An odd place for a flower garden since the tall hedges obstructed the view of it from the back patio. My dad's training kicked in and I concentrated on making straight even tracks with the mower. The end result might even have made him proud.

I greeted Jane that evening with skewers of cubed rare steak and grilled vegetables. Before I could say a word, she blurted, "You cut the lawn? You should have asked me first." Her tone and flashing green eyes indicated her displeasure.

"Hey, it needed cutting, so I—"

She turned on her heel and bolted out the front door. I sprinted after her, bewildered and annoyed by her reaction.

Jane slowed as she approached the flower garden. She let out a long breath. "Oh good. You didn't mow down the flowers."

My annoyance ignited into anger. "What the hell? Do you think I'm an idiot? Why would I mow over your flowers?"

"I'm sorry," she said. "This garden belonged to my . . . . It's very sentimental to me."

Her apology and the deep blue of her eyes squelched my anger before it erupted into full blown rage. I took a deep breath. "Whose garden is it?"

"Was." She stood quiet for a moment. "My adoptive mother's. She left the house to me when she died."

"I'm sorry." Jane was adopted. My curiosity of how she obtained the house was satisfied, but the realization I knew so little about her suddenly saddened me.

She crouched and ran her fingertips through the flower blossoms. Gathering some close to her face, she inhaled and then stood. "Thank you for mowing the lawn." She turned and walked toward the front of the house. I followed her into the house.

Jane stayed quiet and looked deep in thought throughout dinner.

"Feel like swimming tonight?" I picked up our plates and deposited them into the sink.

"No. It's time I took you to The Haven and introduced you to the clan."

"Oh. You mean to find a donor?" Was this her way of telling me it was time for me to leave?

"Yes, that, too. I'm going to change my clothes." She headed into the hall.

"Jane? What should I wear?"

After her pensive mood all through dinner, her unexpected smile dazzled me. "Anything but a red-lined cape." She walked down the hall and called over her shoulder. "Dress casual. Jeans are fine."

I hurried into the living room and dug through my suitcase. I had jeans, though lately my clothes fit oddly. My T-shirts had become uncomfortably snug in the sleeves and across my chest but loose around my waist. The skinny-legged jeans I always preferred didn't fit around my calves.

I finally tugged on a pair of regular-cut blue jeans and stood shirtless while I rummaged through my shirts, searching for one with looser-fitting sleeves.

"You're going to need new clothes to fit your new muscles."

I whirled around. Jane stood in the doorway.

"Give me a minute, would you." I snapped.

She turned and walked off. In spite of my frequent fantasies about Jane, being half naked in front of her made me uncomfortable. At least in the pool I could hide under the water or behind a towel. I glanced down at the taut rows of muscles in my abdomen. Dark hair covered the center portion of my chest now. I never wasted my time before, looking at my body, but Jane's comment made me realize it too had transformed. I had muscles.

I pulled the only large T-shirt I owned over my head, then walked to the bathroom and splashed warm water on my face. My ever-evolving reflection amazed me, and I stared into the mirror. Is this what Jane saw when she looked at me? Or is it only a mirage I conjured in my mind? I had shaved this morning and already a dark shadow of a beard had formed. My hair hung in shiny waves that grazed my shoulders. At the rate it grew, I would have to cut it soon. I ran a comb through it and then hurried to find Jane.

She stood in the opened front doorway jangling her keys. "Mind if I drive?"

"No." I should have felt excited, but instead I felt irritable and nervous. I walked with clenched fists and waited by her red jeep. "So what exactly is going to happen tonight?"

Jane unlocked the doors and slid into the driver's seat while I climbed into the passenger side.

"You have to be officially introduced and accepted into the clan. If you're approved, you can find a safe donor there as well."

"*If*? Shit. You said yourself they'd see me as a freak—an abomination."

Jane sighed as she steered the jeep down the drive and used the remote to unlock the gate. "Some may. But overall the group is fair. Especially Aldon, he's our elder."

"And if they don't approve? Then what—they kill me?"

"Stop being so dramatic, Tim. Do you really think I'd bring you somewhere to be killed? Worse case, they'll shun you."

"Oh, shunned. Yeah, that's freaking great. This is starting to feel like waiting to get picked for a team in gym class."

Jane reached over and squeezed my hand. "Relax. I'm on your team."

Chapter 10

I guess when you turn off the main road, you have to be prepared to see some funny houses.
—Stephen King

The Haven was a two-story stone building tucked between a movie theater and a bookstore in the historic district of downtown San Molina. Though all of the buildings on the street looked historic and impressive, the vampire club stood out. It resembled a genuine gothic castle. Palladian windows on the second floor opened onto wrought-iron-encased balconies. Maybe it really was Dracula's castle.

By the time Jane pulled around the corner and entered the parking lot behind the building, every nerve in my body buzzed with electricity.

"Ready?" She gave me a cheerful, blue-eyed smile.

"No." My stomach churned, and my heart hammered against my rib cage.

"C'mon." Jane slid from her seat and closed the door. She walked around to the passenger side and opened my door. "This is what you wanted, remember?"

I stepped from the safety of the jeep and stood staring up at the balconies overhead. The gray stone fortress with its intricate pattern of iron work looked ancient and forbidding.

Jane strode around the corner, past the book shop, to the front entrance of The Haven while I lagged a few steps behind. Gaslight sconces gave off a soft amber glow on either side of the glossy black front door. A small brass plaque read, *Private Club. Members Only.*

Jane rang the doorbell.

I expected to see a hunchback wielding a torch, but instead a young guy about my age opened the door and broke into a wide smile. "Raina, welcome," he said.

"Good to see you, Wynn. I've brought a guest with me tonight." Jane swept her hand toward me.

The guy eyed me up and down. "Hello." The amber glint in his eyes identified him as a vampire.

"Hey." I shuffled inside behind Jane. The small lobby area led to an arched doorway. In the dim lighting, the place looked like any other upscale bar with rich dark wood tones and shiny brass accents. Round tables and chairs filled with patrons took up most of the room, with an L-shaped bar in one corner. Above, more scrolly iron railing bordered an open second floor and allowed the people seated there a clear view of the ground floor. The patrons upstairs looked down with glowing reddish-amber eyes.

I whispered to Jane. "Why did he call you Raina?"

"Oh, I forgot to tell you, we don't use our real names here. Anonymity adds another level of protection. You'll need to create a name for yourself."

"What? Why didn't you tell me sooner?"

"Sorry, I forgot." Jane wound her way through the maze of patrons to an empty table, nodding and greeting people as she walked. The men and women looked past Jane and focused on me. Everyone in the room stared at me.

Jane motioned for me to sit across from her.

"How the hell could you forget that? This is my initiation. Now I have to think up a name."

"You said you wanted to use the name of your game character, didn't you?"

"Lorcan, yeah, but will they think that sounds stupid? I need more time. Dammit I can't believe you forgot to tell me." I gripped the edge of the table until my knuckles turned white and I thought the wood would splinter in my grasp. Music blared from a juke box, a techno beat that rattled my raw nerves. I glanced around. Dozens of pairs of eyes stared back. The room took on a reddish haze and my heart beat so hard I thought it would shoot out through my chest.

Jane gripped my hands. "Look at me."

I forced myself to focus on Jane's deep blue eyes. "Try to calm yourself. You're vamping out."

148

"H-Huh?" I couldn't speak, my breathing turned fast and heavy.

"It's slang—it means you need blood. Take a deep breath, then walk to the bar and order us some drinks. I need to go upstairs and speak to Aldon." She squeezed my hands. "I'll be right back."

I grasped her hands as she tried to pull away. "D-Don't leave me."

"Focus on getting the drinks. You'll be fine." She stood and headed for the staircase.

Glowing eyes from the shadowy figures on the upper level aimed down at me like laser lights. I stood, legs shaky, and hurried toward the bar. "Get drinks, get drinks," I mumbled. Thinking about the simple task helped. By the time I reached the bar my heart rate and breathing had calmed.

As I leaned on the mahogany bar, I realized I had no idea what to order for Jane. The bartender, an older man dressed in a black suit, greeted me. "What can I get you, sir?"

"Um," I turned and made out Jane's silhouette in the crowd above.

"You're with Raina, yes?"

I swiveled back to the bartender. "Who? Uh, yeah. Yes."

He smiled. "Her usual then?" His expression was pleasant and his eyes a gray-blue color and unmistakably human. A silver name tag pinned to his lapel read, Tristan.

"Um, yes, please."

"And for you, sir?"

"The same."

He poured shots of vodka into two tall glasses, then topped them off with a deep red juice.

I pulled a twenty from my pocket and placed it on the bar.

He slid the money toward me. "Members drink free."

A large brandy snifter stuffed with bills sat on the bar top. I shoved the twenty into it.

"Thank you, sir." His professional smile never wavered on his chiseled face. The gray peppering his dark hair added to his dignified demeanor. He looked like he should be modeling his impeccable suit in a catalogue. "Enjoy." He poked long straws into the glasses.

"Thanks." I picked up the drinks and walked back to the table, keeping my eyes trained on the polished wood floor. I sat and sipped, immediately recognizing the berry sweetness of pomegranate with a much welcome kick from the vodka. I looked up when a young woman with dark blue hair pulled a chair over close to me and sat down. "You're new here," she said. "I'm Velvet. What's your name?"

"Ti—um—Lorcan," Saying the name out loud felt strange, but I hadn't had time to come up with anything better.

"Lorcan. Hmm. I like that." Her smile showed elongated canine teeth, yet her eyes told me she was human. On closer inspection, her canines looked fake. "Are you here looking for a donor, Lorcan?"

"Um, maybe."

Her black-ringed eyes shone with mischief while her lace corset and short skirt promised even more. Velvet tickled her long nails across my forearm. They were painted a shiny midnight-blue that matched her hair. Her slender fingers extended from fingerless gloves which covered her arms in snug black lace to her bare shoulders. "I'm available." She grinned, flashing her teeth. "You're pretty hot."

A sexy young woman called me hot? Was she joking? I stared at her waiting for the punch line, my mouth too dry to speak. She only smiled. Velvet's warm, spicy scent made me wonder if her blood would taste like cinnamon. Jane said each donor had a unique flavor to their blood and I'd eventually find my preference.

"Lorcan."

Startled, I jerked my head around. Jane stood at my side.

"Excuse us." Her eyes glittered with a greenish-blue light as she first glared at Velvet and then turned her gaze to me. "Aldon wishes to meet you."

Velvet slid a card across the table to me, then flipped her long hair over her shoulder and rose from her chair. She winked at me as she sashayed across the room toward the juke box.

The card was black with only her first name and phone number printed in metallic blue. I stood and pocketed the card, then gulped down the remainder of my drink and followed Jane up the stairs.

Jane's cryptic words, *this is what you wanted, remember?* played over and over in my mind as I climbed the stairs behind her. I didn't know what I wanted anymore. Every cell in my body hummed with paranoia. By the time I stepped onto the balcony, my nerves vibrated so hard I feared my body would shatter like glass.

I bumped into Jane's back when she stopped. She bowed her head, moved to one side and motioned to an old man. "This is Aldon, our elder and leader of our clan," she said.

Before me stood a fragile-looking man with perfectly coiffed silver hair. The most impressive thing about him was the ornate gold-handled cane he leaned on. Before I could think of something appropriate to say, he spoke.

"Raina tells me you wish to join our clan. Is this true?" His voice was low, but it reverberated deep inside his chest like a lion's growl.

"Yes." Though old, he had a formidable aura about him. His dark eyes held a fiery amber glint, and the air that surrounded him felt electrified. The hair on the back of my neck stood on end.

"Is it also true you were once a mundane?" he asked.

"Yes." I struggled to utter the single syllable. Intimidation clutched my tongue.

The other vampires rose from their chairs murmuring and gathered around us. Trapped inside their tight circle I felt like the entree for a pride of lions. Dad always told me, don't look like victim and you won't be one. I straightened my shoulders and held my head high. They would most likely slaughter me where I stood, drain my blood and discard my dried-out shell, but at least Jane would see I faced my doom with dignity.

Aldon moved his head slowly as he made eye contact with each member in the circle. Finally, he looked directly at me. A wave of heat emanated from his eyes.

"We have never allowed a former mundane to join our clan. Yet Raina speaks highly of you and has agreed to be your sponsor. Her tests show your blood is nearly pure. I find this incredible—and curious—as do the others. The vote to allow you into our clan is evenly split. Therefore, I must decide."

A tall young man with a shock of platinum hair obscuring one side of his face pushed his way to the front of the circle. He balled up his fists and said, "I say no to this mundane filth." He folded his arms across his wide chest and glowered at me. The murmurs from the circle of vampires grew louder, as did my pounding heart.

Aldon banged the bottom of his cane against the floor. "I said, *I will decide, Braedon.*" He stepped closer to me, the air crackled and super-heated. I fought the urge to shield my face and stood firm.

"What name have you chosen for yourself?"

"Let me guess," Braedon shouted out, "How about Dra-cool? Or maybe Lestat?" He guffawed at his own joke and it started a ripple of laughter that spread through the others like an insidious disease, the volume increasing until my ears pained from it. Sudden rage tinted my vision blood-red and my muscles coiled into tight knots. I looked over at Jane. She nodded.

I glared at Braedon, then turned to Aldon. "Lorcan is the name I've chosen, sir."

"Lorcan. Silent and fierce. A good choice." The old man nodded his approval, yet his piercing eyes showed no emotion. "The question is, can you live up to such a strong name?"

Braedon rushed forward. He stopped an inch from my face. "Fierce my ass. Prove it."

I'd seen that look on other faces many times before, eyes squinted, upper lip curled into a snarl—I'd seen it on every bully who had confronted me all of my life. Their faces flashed before me like a cartoon flip book, all within a fraction of a second. I knew what came next. I braced for the attack.

Braedon didn't disappoint. He planted his meaty hands on my shoulders and shoved. The force sent me flying backwards until I crashed into one of the heavy wooden tables. Glasses clattered and smashed on the floor. This was when I either crawled away to escape the inevitable jeers, or curled up in a defensive ball and begged my attacker not to hurt me.

Tonight, a new instinct took over. I lunged at Braedon. Gripping his leather jacket, I spun him around and then flung him across the room. He landed on top of a table, upending it as he rolled off and then landed in a tangle of toppled chair legs and broken glass. Before he could right himself, I sprang across the room, straddled his prone body and punched him in the face.

Shock and pain registered in his eyes. It empowered me, even as his expression flashed over to rage. He raised his legs and kicked me off him, then leaped to his feet and charged at me.

I grasped a chair as I stumbled and saved myself from falling. I met Braedon head on with my fists ready. Ducking beneath his punches, I sensed the movement in the air before his fist impacted me. We each got in solid body blows before a black stick blurred in front of my face. An unseen force threw me sprawling backward. Braedon's body flew in the opposite direction.

Aldon stood between us with his cane raised. "Enough!" He slammed the tip into the floor. The heavy thud of wood on wood resonated across the balcony. "Get up."

I scrambled to my feet as Braedon did the same. Overturned tables, chairs, and broken glass surrounded us. The circle of vampires hovered around the perimeter of the room, silent and staring.

"Lorcan, I will allow you to join our clan. Raina has agreed to teach you our rules. I warn you, if you break even one, you will never be allowed in our circle again and Raina will be forever shunned as well. Do you understand?"

"Yes, sir."

Aldon walked to one of the few standing tables and sat. He lifted a decanter and poured himself a drink.

Stunned that he granted me membership after my brawl with Braedon, I picked my way to his table, glass crunching under my shoes. "Thank you, sir." I dipped my head as I spoke, just as Jane had when she addressed the elder man.

He pointed his cane at me. The dim lights played off a line of ruby red jewels embedded along the shaft. "Go and find yourself a donor. Blood will help you control your rage."

"Yes, sir."

I turned and spotted Jane coming toward me. She smiled and my breath caught in my throat. Polished gold hair cascaded over her shoulders, her eyes shone brilliant blue, and her body moved in sensuous rhythm with each stride of her long legs. She was, without a doubt, the sexiest, most beautiful woman in the club and best of all she smiled at *me*—walked toward *me*. I stood straighter, puffed out my chest and strode to meet her. Maybe the fight forced her to see me in a different light. The memory of her naked body emerging glistening with water from the pool overwhelmed me. Still pumped from holding my own in a fight, testosterone coursed through my body. I focused on my new goal—having sex with Jane.

A hand gripped my shoulder, the fingertips dug into my flesh. I whirled around and faced Braedon.

"I'm watching you, Lorcan. Real close." He released his grip but stood and stared. Though I was taller, Braedon had a huskier build. Muscles rippled around rope-like veins in his thick neck as he rolled his head from side to side, like a boxer loosening up before a bout. I made a mental note to increase my workouts and double up on my weights.

Jane walked up and stood next to me. Maintaining my eye contact with Braedon, I draped my arm around her shoulders. I remained silent, as my vampire name implied, and concentrated on giving him my fiercest glare. In reality, I had no smart come back to his veiled threat and even if I thought of something cool to say, I had missed my timing.

Jane broke our staring match. "Excuse us, Braedon. I need to speak with Lorcan."

Braedon grunted, smoothed his hair back from his face and ambled away.

"Lorcan, I'd like you to meet someone." Jane took a graceful sidestep away from my embrace. "This is Echo." Next to her stood a girl who looked like an echo of a human being. Stick straight, strawberry-blonde hair framed her pale face and hung to the waist of her wisp of a body.

"Hi, nice to meet you." I had no interest in meeting any of the members tonight. Still high from my first-ever fight and gaining acceptance into the vampire clan, I wanted to add my sexual conquest of Jane to my victories tonight. Her luscious pink lips and exquisite full breasts occupied my full attention.

Oblivious to the fact that in my mind she was arching her naked body in ecstasy under mine, Jane continued to talk, "Echo has agreed to be your donor this evening."

Jane's words paused my fantasy. I studied the girl closer. While she wasn't ugly, her prepubescent waiflike appearance didn't appeal

154

to me. The black sleeveless shirt she wore billowed around her thin torso and the hem skimmed over her bony knees which were covered by black leggings. In contrast to her outfit, her skin appeared as white as paper.

"But you said I could choose—"

Jane's palm thumped against my chest and knocked me back a step. She spoke in a harsh whisper, "Don't be rude. You need blood and I've secured you a safe donor on short notice. It's customary to request an appointment in advance. You should be grateful she's willing." Her eyes flashed with the all too familiar glint of green inner light I'd come to dread.

"Okay, okay. I'm sorry." I forced a smile and nodded at Echo, who stood watching me with washed-out blue eyes, the color so faint they looked more like tinted glass than eyeballs. She pressed her upper teeth into her bottom lip, the bloodless pressure mark blending with the rest of her colorless face.

Jane took my arm. "Let's go to a room for privacy." For a moment I thought she peered into my head where my mental DVD sat paused in mid-sex act. I took a step and stopped, as my sudden erection made walking uncomfortable.

Jane interpreted my halting gait as hesitation. "Don't worry. Echo is one of our most trusted donors. She'll guide you."

The skinny girl offered a tight-lipped grimace that I guessed was her smile. The bulge in my pants deflated as quickly as it had risen. I allowed Jane to lead me through a rear gate in the railing surrounding the balcony and down a narrow corridor that ran the length of the second floor. Dark wooden doors I hadn't noticed before lined a long hallway.

Red satin ribbons dangled from several shiny brass doorknobs. Jane walked to the end of the hall and twisted a knob without a ribbon. She released my arm and stood back as Echo entered the room, the oversized black velvet bag she carried on her shoulder causing her slender body to lean to one side.

I followed Echo inside and stood in the center of the room. Jane stayed outside in the hallway. She plucked a red ribbon from the inside knob, hung it on the outside, and then pulled the door closed and left me inside with Echo.

155

An involuntary trembling began in my knees and worked its way up to my torso. My heartbeat sped up and all saliva in my mouth evaporated. My giddy confidence from minutes before disintegrated into a queasy mixture of fear and anticipation.

I turned and took in the old-fashioned wallpaper and furnishings. The small room held two overstuffed chairs, a green brocade sofa, and a decorative iron door that led to an outdoor balcony.

Echo had settled on the sofa. She dug into her voluminous bag, pulled out a white plastic box similar to Jane's and placed it on a low coffee table supported by carved wooden lion's paws.

"What's your preference, Lorcan?"

My mind blinked back to a porn movie trailer I'd watched as a teenager. A topless brunette sprawled on a bed asked the same question to an audience of one—me. The thirty-second teaser was all I could view for free on the adult website. I had played it over and over, alone and horny in my bedroom.

"Um, I-I don't know." I shuffled across a floral burgundy and green area rug and perched on the edge of the sofa a foot away from Echo. I stared at the rug wondering if the print really was flowers or dried blood from previous trysts.

"I don't participate in any sexual rituals, only blood-letting. Are you okay with that?"

"Uh, yeah. Okay."

"And by preference, I mean some like to drink from flesh while others prefer I draw the blood out with a needle and they drink it from a cup."

My one and only experience drinking blood had been sucking it from Lorelei's arm. "Um, flesh."

"Arm or leg? I also don't allow any cutting above the calf."

Hence the black leggings covering her knobby knees. "Arm. Please."

"Forearm?"

"Sure." Her business-like tone and endless questions fueled my nervousness. I half expected her to ask if I wanted fries with the blood.

Echo picked up a sterile paper-wrapped object from her box. She peeled off the wrapper revealing a thin silver scalpel. With the scalpel poised above her white skin, she paused and glanced up at me. "Raina said you were vamping out. My blood will get you through it. Next time you can choose someone . . . you know . . . someone you like better."

The quiver in her voice struck an old chord. Not being wanted, not being chosen—I knew those feelings all too well. I cupped my hand around her bony wrist. "I'm sorry. I'm just nervous. I've never had a donor before. It has nothing to do with you—really—you're fine."

She lowered the scalpel and the corners of her mouth twitched upward. "It's okay. It's no different here than in the outside world. The cool guys only want the cool girls." She sighed and looked down. Her pale orange eyelashes formed a fluttery fan hovering above her white skin.

"I'm not cool," I said.

She looked up and smiled fully, exposing a mouthful of small, even teeth. "Of course, you are. You kicked Braedon's ass—which by the way was awesome. And you're so good-looking."

"The fight was a tie. And I've never thought of myself as . . . it's only the blood I drank. It transformed me. Made me look a lot better than I really am."

"So, it's true you were a mundane before?"

"Yeah." I leaned back against the sofa. "I guess that's unusual around here."

"Very unusual. I've never met a turned human. Plus, that's Aldon's golden rule. No vampire in this club is allowed to turn a mundane."

"Really? I didn't know that."

"It shocked everyone when he allowed you to join." She cocked her head and studied me. "But, it's because you're with Raina, right?"

"Yeah. Well, not exactly *with* her."

She toyed with the scalpel for a moment. "But you want to be?"

I blew out a long breath. My rattled nerves couldn't handle sexual fantasies about Jane while this pale, skinny girl held a scalpel and stared at me. "Could we just do the blood thing now?"

"Oh. Sure." She rummaged in her bag and pulled out a folded

piece of paper. "Here's my certificate." She shrugged and smiled again. "I forgot. I'm supposed to show it to you first. I guess I was feeling nervous, too."

"Certificate?" I unfolded the paper. It was an official document with a raised seal from the San Molina Health Department.

"Raina's the one who instated the rule. All donors have to be checked out on a regular basis. If anything shows up—STDs or blood disorders—we're banned from the club until we test clean. I don't drink alcohol, so my blood is really clean."

She didn't look old enough to be served alcohol. I folded the paper and handed it back to her. "I trust you." I recalled one of my lessons from Jane. "I brushed my teeth right before I came here."

She nodded and scrubbed a spot on her arm with an alcohol pad.

"So, um, Echo, do you mind if I ask how old you are?"

"Twenty-seven. And, yes, I know I look much younger. Could you scoot a little closer, please?"

I slid closer as she drew the scalpel across her forearm and made a neat slice. Bright red blood immediately oozed from the cut. She stretched her arm out, the bleeding line just below my chin.

I gingerly took her arm in both hands, afraid I'd snap the delicate limb in two if I applied any pressure. Lowering my mouth to her arm, I tasted the blood with my tongue.

Green apples came to mind. Fresh with a hint of tangy sweetness. I hadn't thought about what Echo's blood might taste like, but the light, crisp flavor suited her. I sucked harder.

The room blurred into a swirl of muted colors as I focused on drawing out more blood. The sweet-tart combination was surprisingly addictive and the more I sucked, the more I wanted. A rush of dizziness hit me. I squeezed my eyes shut until the spinning stopped. A warm tingling sensation spread from my head all the way to my ankles. With it came an overwhelming sense of calm.

Dainty fingers tapped my cheek and the slender alabaster fount I drank from pulled away.

"That should be enough to quench you," Echo said.

I raised my head and looked at her. She reclined in a swoon against the sofa's arm, her uncut arm draped across her forehead.

I reluctantly let go of her arm, closed my eyes and ran my tongue over my lips savoring the last smear of blood. When I opened my eyes, the bright red finger marks on her arm made me gasp. "I-I'm sorry—I didn't mean . . . did I hurt you?"

She smiled and shook her head. "No, I'm tougher than I look."

Remembering Jane's teachings, I fumbled in the white medical kit and tore open a small packet containing an alcohol wipe. Echo laid her arm across my knee and I blotted the cut with the wipe. I found a tube of antibacterial ointment, dabbed it on then covered the wound with a large Band-aid.

"Thank you," she said.

"I think I should thank you."

"It's a symbiotic relationship." She sat up, repacked her kit and stuffed it inside her lumpy bag next to a laptop. "Donors derive as much pleasure from giving blood as vampires do drinking it."

"You said something earlier about rituals between vampires and donors. They hook up here?"

"You mean have sex? Yes. Mostly the Psi's—you know, psychic vampires—they require the sexual energy as much as blood."

"Oh, yeah, right. The Psi's."

Echo stood and shouldered her bag. "If you ever need blood and don't have a donor lined up, I'm here every Friday and Saturday night." She held out a scrap of torn notebook paper. "My email address. I'd appreciate a day or two's notice."

My head swam as I took the paper and stood. Echo held my arm until I steadied myself.

"Do you need a few minutes?" she asked.

An intense clarity replaced the wooziness. "No thanks, I'm fine now." More than fine. Renewed energy pulsed through my veins. I felt stronger than I ever had in my life. I opened the door and Echo removed the red ribbon and placed it on the inside knob. Blood tryst etiquette.

"So, that's it?" I wondered if I needed to pay her.

"Uh-huh." Echo looked at me with the same bland expression as when we had first met. She had shrunk back inside her somber, pale shell.

Down the hall, a door opened. A giggling Velvet burst from the room into the hallway, followed by Braedon. She had one arm hooked around his waist as he removed the ribbon on the doorknob and twirled it on one finger in a playful gesture before reaching inside and hanging it on the inside knob. Velvet turned, held up her free hand and wiggled her fingers at me in a coy wave.

Braedon glared at us. His face morphed from anger into a sneer as he directed his gaze from me to Echo and gave her a lewd up and down stare. He turned, pulled Velvet into a tight embrace and planted a kiss on her red glossy lips. His hands groped down the curve of her back and cupped her cute round ass.

Echo hurried ahead of me, head down and face hidden behind her curtain of hair. She darted past the amorous couple and into the balcony area. I lost sight of her pale orange hair as she descended the staircase to the lower floor.

I stood and waited until Braedon and Velvet finally unlocked lips and limbs and walked off arm in arm down the hallway. If my incredible luck continued tonight, that would soon be me and Jane.

Chapter 11

"It's no use going back to yesterday, because I was a different person then."
—Alice in Wonderland

I sensed Jane's presence before I spotted her sitting at the bar talking with the bartender, Tristan. The vampires on the second floor and the humans on the first watched as I descended the staircase, but I detected slight differences from their previous stares. A few of the vampires regarded me with open disgust, especially Braedon and the group of young men sitting around his table, while many of the female vampires and humans greeted me with a nod as I walked past—some even smiled. Their stares, friendly or not, had no effect on me. I felt invincible.

Jane whirled around on her bar stool as I approached. I wondered if she sensed me as well, or maybe that was only my wishful thinking.

"How do you feel?" Her eyes deepened to an indigo blue as she studied my face.

"Excellent."

"Good." She let out a breath and nodded. "So, everything went well with Echo?"

"Yes, it did." At the mention of her name, I searched the downstairs. Echo sat alone at a table in a corner, the light from her laptop screen bathing her pale face and hair in a ghostly blue glow. It suited her.

Jane stood and placed her empty glass on the bar. Tristan reached for it and his hand covered hers. It lingered there longer than I thought appropriate. He leaned across the bar and whispered, "Please be careful." The steely look he shot me acknowledged he knew I heard him—and more importantly, that he didn't care that I had.

I returned Tristan's glare with an equally icy expression until he picked up the glass and walked off behind the bar.

"Ready to go?" Jane asked. She headed for the front entrance.

I fell in step beside her. Feeling cocky, I looped my arm through hers. "Go where?"

"Home."

I waited until Wynn, the smiley front door attendant, said good night and ushered us outside before replying to Jane. "I don't want to go home just yet."

She slowed her brisk stride and unhooked her arm from mine. "I have work to do in the lab."

"You work every day and then in the lab every night. It's Friday, can't you take one night off and have some fun?"

Jane strolled a few more steps and then sighed. "What did you have in mind?"

I stopped at the corner and took in the busy traffic and crowds of people bustling around us. Colors were super-saturated, the downtown lights glittered red, gold, and white. Traffic sounds amplified and I caught snippets of people's conversations from a block away. Most distracting were the scents—perfumes, alcohol, food, and car exhaust mingled with the buttery aroma of popcorn drifting from the movie theater's lobby. Three teenaged girls passed us, their high heels clattering on the sidewalk. Beneath a layer of flowery colognes, their true scents teased my nose—cotton candy, licorice, and citrus. Sampling all of their blood at once would be a vampire buffet.

Jane stood, watching me and waiting for an answer.

"I fought a guy—a big guy—and I didn't get my ass kicked. Aldon granted me membership to The Haven. And I drank blood for the first time since I was transformed." I turned in a circle and ran my hands through my hair, the length and thickness of it still felt wondrously foreign to my fingers. My senses teetered on overload. "I want to celebrate."

"Do you want to go back to The Haven and have another drink?"

"No. I feel way too restless for that—but in a good way." On impulse I reached out and stroked her cheek, my fingers slid downward, caressed the curve of her neck and wandered into her silken hair. "I want to be with you tonight."

Even with my heightened perception I couldn't discern her reaction. For the briefest moment she leaned into my touch, her soft skin pressed against my hand and she laid her hand over mine. My heart thumped, then skipped a beat when she withdrew her hand and stepped back.

"I have an idea," she said. "C'mon." She flashed me a devilish smile, grasped my hand and pulled. We walked toward her jeep. Just holding her hand sent tiny fireworks exploding through my body. I followed her without question. In that moment I realized I'd follow Jane anywhere she led me—into the flames of hell—or into her bed. I so hoped for the latter.

We parked in an empty lot in front of a warehouse. I climbed out and looked around at the barren streets, railroad tracks, and rolling countryside off in the distance. Jane checked her cell phone as she stepped from the jeep, then slipped it back inside her jacket pocket.

"We need to hurry," She sprinted across the two-lane road separating the parking lot from the railroad tracks and climbed up a steep gravel-covered slope that led to a highway overpass.

"What are you doing?" I traversed my way up the slippery rocks as Jane stepped onto a narrow ledge on the exterior side of the overpass bridge.

"You said you were restless and wanted to celebrate, right?"

The ground beneath my feet trembled. In the distance a train horn wailed in the night. I remembered lying helpless in a ditch and seeing Jane silhouetted in the moonlight surfing atop the freight train that had roared by overhead.

"Oh, shit! You're going to ride on top of a train?"

She reached out and grabbed my hand. "No. *We're* going to ride on top of the train. Hurry or we'll miss it."

"But . . . I-I can't."

"Why not?"

My old nemesis, fear, gripped my legs and glued my feet to the ground. "I'll fall off. I'm not as strong or athletic as you."

"Says the guy who held his own in a fight with our strongest guard tonight." Jane smiled. "I won't let you fall. Trust me, you'll love it. It's a rush."

A rush would be holding Jane naked in my arms and making hot, passionate love under the moonlight in her swimming pool, not balancing on a wafer-thin ledge twelve feet above a deserted California back road.

"Tim, you can do this. Didn't you ever surf in the ocean? It's the same idea, easier really."

I had tried surfing once when I was eleven. My cousins came to visit, and we went to the beach. They lent me their surfboard. A lifeguard dragged me out of the water five minutes after I had paddled into the ocean. A wave had knocked me off the board, then it cracked me in the back of the head. I'd nearly drowned.

"Trust your body, your instincts," Jane said. "You're much stronger and more agile now than you think." She moved closer, gripped my right hand, and tugged.

Body numb and mind in a panic, I nodded at her. Whining like a scared little girl would not serve my goal of getting Jane into bed. I willed my feet to abandon solid ground and together we inched our way along the ledge. I pressed my back against the guard rail and gripped the cool dented metal with my left hand, while Jane kept a tight hold on my right. We had no sooner made it to the center of the overpass when she said, "Get ready. Remember to bend your knees."

Bending my knees caused my torso to lean and I started to topple forward. Jane's arm slammed across my chest and steadied me against the railing.

"I *meant* bend your knees when we jump."

The roar of the train's engine grew louder. I dared to glance over my shoulder. About a mile away, white lights pierced the blackness like two evil eyes searing holes in the velvet night. The chugging iron demon sped toward us.

"We'll jump on three." Jane laced her fingers through mine and we raised our arms. "One!"

The engine of the train rumbled past underneath us, the noise thundered in my ears, rattled through my head and further scrambled my chaotic thoughts. All reason fled and left only terror.

"Two, three!"

Jane's body weight yanked me from my precarious perch. Too terrified to scream, my legs pumped, running downhill on air and my left arm flailed in the whoosh of air like a spastic wing.

The sudden thud when we landed stunned me. I stumbled forward and fell to my knees groping with my left hand for something to grasp on the top of the freight car. The death grip Jane held on my hand threw her off balance when I fell, but she quickly recovered and crouched next to me, our hands still clasped.

"Stand up," she shouted over the racket of the train.

Jane helped me to my feet. "Put one foot forward. Loosen up your body."

I teetered from side to side, grasping onto Jane's hand until I found my train legs.

"There! You've got it," Jane said.

We stood side by side on the roof of the freight car with the cool night wind whipping against our faces. Jane let go of my hand. Mimicking her, I stretched my arms out to my sides for balance. Above us, nothing but black sky studded with tiny stars and a wash of wispy purple clouds. A low gray fog rolled down from the hills and settled into the valley on either side of us. The dim twinkling of lights beyond the fog vanished as we left the town behind. Dark hulking mountains loomed in the distance and the wind carried earthy scents of damp grass and pine. The train sliced through the billowing mist and without the ground as a reference point, it felt as though we sped through the clouds in mid-air.

Jane laughed when I threw my head back and gave my best imitation of a wolf's howl.

"This is amazing!" I yelled. The freight car was about ten feet wide and once I had gotten the hang of balancing myself, the flat-topped box felt sturdy under my feet—a giant steel skateboard hurtling on metal rails at fifty miles an hour. The open countryside ahead had no overpasses or people to worry about. A three-quarter moon occasionally peeked from behind the drifting clouds and added a silvery shimmer to the mist-covered ground. The rumble of the locomotive and the adrenalin pulsing through my veins contrasted with the surreal scenery.

"That's where we get off." Jane pointed to a dark silhouette of train trestle with a highway overpass running parallel to it few miles ahead. The trestle arched north, and the highway curved off to the south. "There's a sharp curve up ahead and the train slows down. There's a hill next to the overpass, we can jump off there."

As Jane promised, the train slowed to half its speed as we neared the turn. She took my hand and we jumped together. This time I landed on my feet next to her. She released my hand and we strolled down the hill to a wide ditch and then started to climb up the grassy slope to the highway. My heart thundered with exhilaration and the vibration of the engine still coursed through my limbs.

"Wait." I stopped midway up the hill. The spicy scent of Mexican food drifted in the air. The red and yellow lights of Taco Hut glowed through a tangle of tree branches just over a hill to the west. I looked around the trash-littered ditch and my gaze tracked over to a clump of scraggly bushes by the cement wall of the overpass. They were the same bushes I had taken shelter behind the night Lorelei's thugs had dumped me here to die.

Jane walked down the slope and stood next to me. "This is where I found you," she said.

"Yeah, I know." I walked the length of the ditch and back, randomly kicking at soda cans and plastic bottles on the ground. By all rights my decomposing body should be lying here with the garbage—a putrid-smelling carcass for vultures and maggots to feast upon. My fear and desperation had been so raw that night, a palpable residue of it still haunted the ditch.

"Why did you bring me here?"

"I didn't do it on purpose. It's the last chance to get off the train before it crosses the river and heads up into the mountains."

The clouds parted and long black shadows slithered uphill as silvery moonlight poured into the ditch, highlighting an array of trash. A shiny glint caught my attention. I crouched and swatted away a crumpled, grease-stained paper bag. My old eyeglasses, the right lens smashed, lay in the grass. I picked them up and stood staring at them. When I held the thick lenses up to my eyes, my vision blurred.

Jane squeezed my arm. "I'm so sorry, Tim. I shouldn't have—"

"It's okay." I pocketed the glasses and turned to Jane. "I'm not

166

the same person you found here."

"No, you're not." She smiled and hooked her arm through mine. "He wasn't such a bad guy."

We climbed up the slope together.

The emotions from that dire night dried up and sloughed off of me with each stride I took up the hill. The glasses in my pocket were all that remained of the old me. I don't know why I took them, maybe to keep as reminder, or maybe to finally sever the bond and allow the ghost of me that lingered alone and frightened in the dark ravine to be set free.

"Isn't there a train we can catch to ride back on?" I asked. "I want to do it again."

Jane laughed and shook her head. "The eastbound train doesn't run till after dawn. It's a long walk back to the jeep. We traveled over twenty-five miles on the train. You up for the hike?"

My intense energy from earlier rebounded. "Race you."

Jane grinned at me and then took off running. We ran for miles along deserted sidewalks past warehouses, empty lots, and the sprawling industrial complex where the Black Swan was located.

I had hated running in gym class. I always ended up bent over on the side of the track, winded and holding my knees from the painful stitch in my side while my classmates sprinted past and mocked me. Tonight, I ran without pain, enjoying the feel of my muscles moving like oiled gears, my heart pumping and crisp night air filling my lungs. I chased after Jane, who kept a slight lead, her hair trailing behind her like golden ribbons in the moonlight.

She stopped at an intersection and waited for a lone car to pass. I caught up to her. Both long-legged, we continued walking at a brisk pace.

"This has been the most incredible night of my life." I said. "And I couldn't have done any of it without you. Thank you."

"You were impressive for your first time train surfing."

"Whatever made you think to ride on top of a train?" I asked.

"That restless feeling you talked about tonight. I felt the same way after drinking Lorelei's blood. I went for a run and climbed up on the overpass to take in the view. I saw a train coming and thought it might be fun to jump on it. Now I'm hooked on the thrill of it. "

"So, you do like to have fun."

She rolled her eyes. "Yes."

By the time we reached the outskirts of a town, we had to wait for traffic to pass before crossing some of the larger intersections. I stared at our reflections in a darkened store window and I didn't recognize the tall, muscular guy with long flowing hair standing beside the breathtakingly sexy Jane.

"You should go by Raina all the time. The name suits you better than Jane."

"Raina is the name my adoptive mother gave me."

"So why do you go by Jane?"

"In the state home, I was baby Jane Doe, then later, just Jane Doe."

"I'm sorry. It must have sucked growing up in a state home."

"It made me strong. I keep the name Jane to remind me to stay strong."

"So, you don't know your real parents or if they were vampires?"

"I've tested my own blood and my best theory is my father was a pure blood, my mother a hybrid. Not unusual. Many pure bloods are attracted to hybrids and humans."

"Did you ever try to find your real parents?"

"I thought about it, but, no. Ana adopted me when I was nine. She was a pure blood and she sensed the pureness of the blood in me. She took me into her home, taught me about the Night Flock, guided me, and loved me as if I were her own blood daughter. She was an amazing woman."

"How did she die?"

Jane shook her head and looked away. When she turned back, the deep green color startled me. The color of a forest at night, the leaves shrouded in a dark and profound sadness.

"I don't want to talk about it," she whispered.

"Sorry." I wanted to wrap my arms around her but her brisk stride and the grim set of her jaw kept me at bay. Instead, I walked alongside Jane glancing at myself in the windows we passed to bolster my courage. I arranged words in my mind, adding, deleting, and forming clumsy sentences. When we stopped at a cross street and waited for cars to pass, I dared to say them out loud.

"Do you have a boyfriend, Jane?" The words sounded childish when spoken out loud. I could only imagine how they sounded to Jane, but I needed to know.

"No."

"You're thirty-seven, you must have loved someone—"

"What is it you want to know, Tim?" Her eyes turned a cloudy aquamarine, a perfect mixture of serene blue and heart-stopping green. Like a mood ring stone, they hovered in flux, ready to change.

Following the pattern of my night so far, I dove in and blurted out my thoughts. "I like you. Like being with you. You're smart, strong, and the most beautiful woman I've ever known. I want . . . wondered if you would consider a relationship . . . with me?"

Jane looked away and I couldn't see the color of her eyes. "It's not that I don't like you, Tim, but I have important work to do. I can't be in a relationship right now."

It was the finality in her tone more than her words that crushed me. We had miles to go and now we walked them with a thick blanket of silence between us, Jane staring straight ahead and me processing her response. *Not that I don't like you*, the double negative equaled a positive. So, Jane did like me. I had used the word like only because I feared if I said love it would sound too intense, too soon. But my feelings for her were intense. More than wanting to have sex with her, I wanted her with me forever. I loved Jane. And she *liked* me. Hell, I liked pomegranate juice, but that didn't mean I wanted to sleep with a bottle of it in my arms forever.

"What about Tristan?" I blurted out the question aware of the jealousy in my voice.

"What about him? He's our club bartender and an old friend."

"*Just* a friend?"

Jane shot me a green-eyed glare. "I told you I'm not in a relationship nor do I wish to be."

We walked on. An icy layer of frost covered the blanket of silence.

I finally broke the chill between us as we approached her jeep. "You said Braedon is a guard. What does he guard?"

Jane's shoulders visibly relaxed and she finally looked at me, her

169

eyes a calm sea blue. "He guards The Haven, and Aldon—and all of the members."

"He didn't act very loyal to Aldon. He publicly opposed my joining. Unless that was all an act—to test me, maybe?"

"It wasn't an act or a test. Braedon is young, but his strength places him next in line to lead the clan. Braedon's made it known he thinks Aldon is too old to lead—too soft on important issues. Some believe he might try to force Aldon out and take over leadership."

"But Aldon's not that old, he's what, maybe fifty?"

Jane gave an amused grunt as she unlocked the doors and we climbed into the jeep. "He's one hundred and forty-three."

"What? Seriously?" I settled into the passenger seat as she started up the engine. "Shit, he looks great for his age."

"Aldon is extremely powerful. His blood line is pristine—as in old European pure."

"And let me guess, one of the issues he's gone soft on is allowing former humans—or mundanes as you say—to join the clan?"

Jane sighed and nodded. "It's controversial. It's taken Aldon a long time to accept the idea."

"How do you feel about it?"

"I sponsored you, didn't I?" She turned and looked at me. "But it's not a simple issue. I believe each case is unique and needs to be studied thoroughly."

"Echo implied you had some pull with Aldon. You convinced him to accept me, didn't you?"

"I told Aldon the truth as I always do. Former mundane or not, your blood is nearly pure—purer than the hybrids he's allowed to join. And you have a noble character."

"Noble character?"

She smiled. "A little bird told me."

Jane's statement flattered and humbled me. "Aldon respects you. You risked your place in the clan for me. I was thinking, what if I drank more of Lorelei's blood? Maybe that would turn my blood one hundred percent pure and make everyone happy."

"I would never ask you to do that again. Drinking her blood damn near killed you."

"I'd do it again. I don't ever want you to get hurt because of me.

I'll never let that happen. I swear."

Jane turned to face me. Her eyes shone a new color, a luminous violet.

Chapter 12

"Because what's worse than knowing you want something, besides knowing you can never have it?"
—James Patterson, *The Angel Experiment*

It was after three in the morning when we arrived back at the house. Jane hurried off to the sanctuary of her lab to work, making it a point to tell me she intended to sleep after dawn. More than likely she wanted to escape me and my questions.

Too amped to sleep myself, I fired up my laptop and watched an old Dracula movie I had stored. After riding atop a speeding freight train with Jane, I found the kitschy appeal of Bela whipping his cape around had faded. My new eyesight spied the strings on the rubber bat hovering outside the castle window. I turned off the movie.

On a whim I Googled Create-A-Vision, the video game company I told my parents I now worked for. Ironically, Jane's house put me less than a twenty-minute drive from their corporate headquarters. Clicking on their creative director's contact info, I typed a request for a job interview into the email window. I gave a brief outline of my game's concept, my contact information, copied and pasted a sample of my code into the message and then hit the send button.

Sighing, I closed my laptop and sat on the sofa staring into space, my mind wrestling with the inevitable—I couldn't stay here any longer. Jane had no romantic interest in me, and I was an idiot to think she ever would. Perhaps she did like me but seeing her on a daily basis with no hope of ever having a real relationship would slowly drive me insane.

Getting a job at Create-A-Vision was a long shot, but regardless of whether they granted me an interview or not, I needed to find work so I could afford my own apartment. How naive I'd been to think that vampires didn't have to deal with the drudgery of a holding down a job like the mundanes. I smiled at the memory of the rush of wind in my face and the power of the locomotive rumbling beneath my feet. On the upside, we had way cooler night lives.

My decision to leave stuck like a fish bone in my throat. While I didn't want to swallow it, it forced me to face reality. I turned on the small table lamp and stretched out on the sofa in its soft yellow glow of light. Maybe sleep would smother my chaotic thoughts.

The void of sleep I hoped for evaded me and instead a twilight haze peppered with nightmares of a different sort plagued my mind. Somewhere deep in my subconscious I longed for the return of the clawed, red-eyed demons who usually invaded my dreams.

I ran through a dark tunnel filled with rolling waves of gray fog. Every now and then the rolling grayness would part long enough for me to see Jane running ahead of me. I yelled out her name, but the thick mist seeped inside my open mouth and muffled my voice. I pushed myself to run faster, but the glimpses of her long blonde hair only grew further away.

The fog parted and I stood in front of a door, the knob laden with red ribbons. More ribbons lay piled around my feet. The door was ajar, and I pushed it open. Inside Jane and Tristan lay entwined together on an enormous bed, their bodies covered with a red satin sheet. The room filled with others and in the sea of faces I saw Braedon, Aldon, Velvet, and even the ever-smiling Wynn, though his grin mocked me. They all pointed at me and laughed. The room grew smaller until it disappeared into tiny red dot. I stood alone on a railroad track. The red dot split into two piercing head lamps of a distant freight train barreling toward me. Red ribbons bound my legs and secured my feet to the wooden railroad ties. Echo's ghostly form hovered over me. She wielded a scalpel the size of a machete and deftly sliced through the ribbons binding my legs. As the last ribbon fell away, the front of the train burst through Echo's transparent body.

I awoke with a gasp and bolted upright while patting my torso expecting to feel bloody flesh and mangled bones from the freight train's impact. The persistent ringing of my cell phone broke through my panic. By the time my head cleared, and I fumbled for the phone on the table, it had stopped ringing. The missed call was a number I didn't recognize. I put the phone back on the coffee table and made a mental note to call my mom later today as I stood and walked to the kitchen.

I was glad Jane wasn't in the kitchen. I gulped pomegranate juice straight from the bottle and then threw the empty jug into the trash.

In spite of my poor sleep, my restlessness returned. I walked down the hall to the gym to work off the excess energy. As I opened the door, I was startled to see Jane on the elliptical machine.

"Morning," she said.

Her breasts bounced under her snug blue tank top and taut muscles rippled in her tan legs. I ripped my gaze from her body. "Sorry, I didn't know you were in here." I shuffled backwards, pulling the door closed when she called my name.

I poked my head in the opening. "Yeah?"

"You're welcome to use the other machines or the weights if you want."

Against my better judgment, I chose the weight bench at the opposite end of the room. I added more weights, lay down on the cushioned bench and positioned myself under the bar. As I lifted the barbell, my gaze tracked over to Jane's skin-tight shorts.

My grip slipped and I nearly dropped the heavy bar on my face. "Shit."

"Something wrong?" she asked.

"No." Closing my eyes, I pictured Braedon's taunting face as I pushed through the reps. I counted to one hundred and then eased the barbell up onto the spotter bar. As I sat up, Jane stood mere feet away stretching her arms in the air and then bent and touched her toes. Her shiny Lycra-covered, perfectly proportioned rear pointed straight toward me.

I stood and headed for the door while I could still walk.

"Are you done already?" she asked.

"Yup. All done." I hurried down the hall to the bathroom, locked the door and turned the shower water to full cold.

The spray of icy water on my skin stung like a thousand wasps.

174

"Ouch! Dammit!" My resistance to cold as well as to sunlight had lessened considerably since my transformation.

My cell rang as I sorted through my clothes searching for a shirt and jeans that would fit my new physique. The same phone number from earlier displayed on my screen. "Hello?"

"Is this Tim Gardener?"

"Yes. Who's this?

"Alex Whitbold, Development Director for Create-A-Vision."

"Oh." They called me back! "Yes, I'm Tim. Hello."

"Are you available to come by our office today?"

An interview on a Saturday seemed unusual. "Today?"

"I know it's short notice. But we're excited to meet the man who wrote that superb code."

"Sure, I can meet with you today. I'm about twenty minutes from your building."

"Excellent. How's twelve noon? Lunch is on us."

"Um, yes. I'll be there."

"Super. Looking forward to meeting you, Tim."

I put the phone on the coffee table and plopped down on the sofa. My mind whirled. Holy crap, Create-A-Vision's director is excited to meet *me*. I jumped up and dumped the contents of my suitcase onto the sofa. After pawing through my meager wardrobe, it was evident I'd have to wear the same shirt and pants I wore last night, as nothing else fit. While it had worked for gaining admittance to a vampire club, a T-shirt and blue jeans weren't job interview material.

I checked my phone. It was only nine o'clock. I could stop by a store and buy more appropriate clothes that fit. I hurried and pulled on my jeans and shirt. Jane stood in the doorway, her curves accentuated in a halo of blue Lycra sheen.

"I was thinking of grilling some steaks. You hungry?" she asked.

"I have to go out. I have a job interview."

"On a Saturday? With whom?"

"Create-A-Vision, the video game developer I told you about. I emailed them last night. They said they were excited about my code and wanted to meet today."

"Oh. Great. That's your dream job, right?"

"Yeah, sure is." Jane's tone didn't match her words. If employed, I could afford my own place. Did she care? I shoved my wallet into my back pocket and scooped up my laptop and car keys.

"You'll be back for dinner, right?" Jane asked as I brushed past her in the doorway.

"I think so. Hey, are there any men's clothing stores around here?"

"There're a few. Where's Create-A-Vision located?"

"In Azure Springs, twenty minutes northwest of here."

"Take Sun Glow Boulevard. There's a huge mall on the way. You can't miss it."

"Thanks."

"Tim?"

I squeezed the front doorknob. Would she ask me to stay? "Yeah?"

"It's morning. Sunscreen. Maybe a hat?"

"Oh, right." I hurried into the living room, slathered lotion on my arms and face and snatched a ball cap from the pile of clothes on the sofa. "I'll straighten up this mess when I get back."

"Oh, Tim, don't give out my address." She pulled a pad from the hall table drawer, scrawled on it and handed it to me. "You can use this, if you need."

It was a post office box address. Jane's insistence on privacy bordered on paranoia.

"Okay." I pocketed the paper. "While I'm out. . ." I sprinted down the hallway and out the door leading to the courtyard. James's funeral suit sat secured inside a black trash bag next to a planter where Jane had tossed it. I picked up the bag and then jogged back to the front door. Jane still hovered in the foyer, her teal eyes and neutral expression offered zero insight into what she was thinking.

"See you at dinner. Good luck," she said.

Jane, as usual was correct. The huge shopping plaza on Sun Glow Boulevard couldn't be missed. I found a trendy young men's shop and with the help of a salesclerk who reeked of woodsy cologne, I selected two pairs of jeans and three shirts.

My clothing size had changed. I needed medium-sized dress shirts instead of extra small and they were still snug around my chest and biceps. Perhaps I had grown an inch as well, as I needed longer inseams in my jeans.

I wore the black jeans and a white dress shirt to the cash register. The clerk carefully snipped off the tags dangling from my new clothes. I added two more T-shirts to my purchase and handed him my credit card.

"Um, do you have another card? This one won't go through."

"Why not?" I only had one credit card and hardly ever used it.

"Says it's over the limit," he mumbled.

"It can't be maxed out." The last I used it was months ago to purchase a special edition comic book online—no, wait—I used my card to buy that damn dress and wig to disguise myself when I confronted Chris Bagwell. I knew that old lady at the dress shop looked sketchy. "Shit." I slammed my fist down on the counter.

"Um, if you don't have another card. . ." The salesclerk eyed my outfit and swallowed hard. The guy looked petrified—of *me*. This was a first. I tried not to laugh.

"How much just for the shirt and jeans I'm wearing?" I pulled what was left of the cash my mom had given me from my wallet. Jane had refused to take it. The salesclerk let out a long breath as he focused on the wad of bills. He gave me a nervous smile. "Eighty-two, forty-nine with tax. Shirt's on sale."

I peeled off five twenties and handed the bills to him. He gave me back my useless credit card.

"I'll have to check with the bank."

"There's a Green Leaf Bank on the other side of this plaza," he said. "Do you want me to hold the other clothes for you?"

I glanced at my phone. It was only ten-twenty and I needed clothes that fit me. "Yeah, okay."

The woman at the bank smiled. "You didn't purchase twelve cases of hair barrettes and three gross of women's swimwear?"

"No-o-o, but I bet I know the store owner who did."

"Don't worry, our fraud department will track the purchases back to the shipping address. But I will have to destroy your card.

You'll be issued a new one." She slid a form toward me. "Fill this out and sign, please."

Jane's post office box would have to do for the address.

"Your new card will arrive in about five business days."

While there, I withdrew three hundred dollars, nearly wiping out my debit card account, and then headed back to the clothing store. Create-A-Vision had better hire me, as money was becoming scarce.

With the new clothes in the back seat, I drove around the plaza toward the exit. A dry cleaner on the corner caught my eye. I parked the car, grabbed the trash bag with James's funeral suit and ran inside.

The woman behind the counter gasped as she pulled the suit from the bag. Besides reeking of formaldehyde, and cut up the back, taco sauce and dirt from lying in the ditch stained the shiny purple material.

"I'd like to get it cleaned and the back seam sewn up. Can you do that?"

She shook her head and muttered something in another language as she wrote on a receipt pad. She handed me a copy. "Two weeks, maybe take more time. We call you."

"Thanks. I want it to look as good as new, okay?"

She rolled her eyes at me, reached under the counter and picked up an aerosol can. She sprayed the suit with Lysol as she stuffed it back inside the trash bag, then tied it closed and stapled her copy of the receipt to it. "We do what we can." She tossed the bag onto a pile of clothes on a table behind her.

I arrived at Create-A-Vision at eleven-fifty. The tall ultra-modern white building glittered in the midday sunlight. Rows of tinted windows lined each floor and the iridescent blue glass reminded me of Jane's eyes. With only four other cars in the vast lot, parking wasn't a problem. I chose a spot close to the entrance, shouldered my laptop bag, and sprinted through the treeless lot to avoid the noon sun as much as possible.

My plan worked except the doors were locked when I reached them. The heat progressed from uncomfortable to painful as I stood and peered through the glass doors at the dimly lit, deserted lobby.

"Tim?"

I turned at the sound of my name. A stocky young man in a bright Hawaiian print shirt and tan Dockers hustled toward me. "I'm Alex. I spoke to you this morning." He thrust a thick freckled hand toward me. I shook it, hoping my own hand wouldn't ignite in the sunlight. "Glad you could make it." He swiped a silvery card in a key slot and the door lock clicked.

Though I wanted to shove past him, I stuck my sunburned hands into my jeans pockets to shield them and waited while he pushed open the door. I followed him into the cool lobby.

Shiny black tiles covered the lobby floor and the walls were painted a deep plum color. Low-backed chairs and glass tables accented with chrome dotted the perimeter. Alex headed toward the centerpiece of the space—a cylindrical clear-glass elevator.

He continued his friendly banter as we rode the elevator, remarking on the hot weather and how he planned to take his kids to Disneyland. When the elevator stopped on the eighth floor, the doors slid open with a muted swoosh and we exited the sleek steel and glass tube.

When I saw the group through the glass wall of the conference room awaiting our arrival, I realized I needn't have worried about my clothing. They were all casually dressed in graphic T-shirts, jeans or shorts, and flip flops. Boxes of pizza sat in the middle of the long rectangular table. Alex opened the door for me to enter and the aroma of pepperoni and four pairs of staring eyes greeted me.

As if reading my mind, Alex said, "I called an impromptu meeting. We do dress casually here, but not quite *this* casual." He laughed and then motioned to the four people staring at me. "Tim, I'd like you to meet our lead code writer, Li; my creative assistant, Rudi; and over there are Dennis and Tom, our head programmers."

I nodded to each. "Hello, nice to meet you."

"You don't look like what I expected," Rudi, the only female, said.

Dennis, the oldest of the group at possibly forty snorted. "Nice, Rudi."

She shrugged and adjusted her pointy-edged glasses. "I expected a little geek with glasses, not a hot—"

179

"Do you write your own code?" Li gave Rudi a sideward glare as he cut her off.

"Yes and no," I said, "I've mixed a few languages together."

"It's brilliant—so clean, concise," Li said. "I've never seen anything like it." He focused on his laptop screen and touched the bridge of his nose with his forefinger. A familiar motion. I had pushed my eyeglasses up on my nose countless times. Except Li wasn't wearing glasses. As he turned his head, I caught a glint of light from the edge of his contact lens, probably new.

Alex settled at the table. "Please have a seat, Tim. Let's eat while the pizza's hot and then we'll talk business."

Out of politeness, I picked at a slice of pizza, eating the greasy circles of pepperoni. I hoped the food wouldn't cause my transformed digestive system to react. I passed on the soda and chose a bottle of water instead.

After the crew had their fill of pizza, Tom stacked the empty boxes on one end of the table.

"So, Tim, how long do you project it to take to write the code for the entire game?" Alex asked.

I slid my laptop from the bag and opened it. "Well, I already have the game completed. The first one that is. I'm still working on the sequel."

They waited in silence while my computer booted up and I opened the game file. "Here it is."

Li stood, hurried around the table, and hovered over my shoulder. "Incredible. How long did it take you to do this?"

I hesitated. Technically, I had written over eighty percent of the code in one night at Jane's, though I had started the project over two years ago. "Um, about two years."

The room suddenly hummed with chatter. Tom and Dennis huddled together talking, and Rudi leaned across the table and whispered to Alex.

Li ran his hands through his spiky black hair and said, "Alex?"

Alex nodded and patted my back while the rest gathered behind me checking out my screen.

"Tim, we'd like you to work for us. How do you feel about that?"

I stared into Alex's round, freckled face. "It's always been my dream to work for Create-A-Vision."

"Yes!" Li jumped, both feet leaving the ground, and thrust his fist in the air.

Time had flown once Alex made the job offer. I answered dozens of questions—each member of the team concerned with a different aspect of the game's production. Dennis and Tom assured Alex working with my clean code would make programming it for game play a breeze.

Li traced his finger along the lines of code, stopping often to ask how I thought of this or that. Li's questions were the most difficult to answer. When I concentrated on writing code, it streamed effortlessly from my brain and down into my fingers as I typed. Though I understood what each line did, at times it felt like I channeled the code from a higher intelligence. I worked on autopilot, my thought process a blur, and I couldn't explain to Li how I came up with certain combinations. My lack of details frustrated him. When he pressed, I answered, "I simply knew it would work."

Rudi asked if I had anything in mind for the look of my characters and settings. I had very specific ideas, but my rudimentary marker sketches were less than impressive. Transformation had not given me artistic skills. She promised to gather portfolios from artists they worked with and email them to me so I could see their styles. She assured me I'd be involved in the creative process of the game.

Lorcan the warrior vampire would finally come to life in spectacular high-definition computer-generated imagery.

Alex produced a packet a papers for me to fill out and sign. Create-A-Vision would do all the production work and marketing and I'd pull down a six-figure salary with the option to collect royalties on the game sales.

Best of all, with the exception of mandatory meetings, I could either work at the office or from home on a company-issued laptop loaded with the latest industry software rather than my hacked amateur programs.

I left Create-A-Vision's offices almost as high from the

interview as I had been after drinking Echo's blood last night, though this was a different kind of euphoria. I had accomplished two long-term dreams in a few hours—securing a job with the company of my dreams and having my game produced by them. Though my transformation had certainly enhanced my skills, they were *my* skills.

As I drove, my thoughts waffled. Work from home. Where would my home be? As much as I wanted it to be with Jane, the harsh reality that I had to find my own place deflated my high spirits.

I wanted to hurry to Jane's house and share my incredible luck with her, but the ambiguous way she acted this morning left me confused and fearful. On an impulse, I turned left instead of right when I came to the road that led to Jane's house. Ten minutes later, I pulled into The Haven's parking lot. Maybe vodka and pomegranate juice would give me the courage to tell Jane I was moving out. I needed a drink to handle her reaction. She'd most likely be giddy with relief that I would soon be out of her house and her life.

A solemn-faced young man with shoulders as broad as the doorway admitted me with a grunt, not the cheesy grin and polite banter that the other doorman, Wynn, offered.

At four in the afternoon, only one patron sat at the bar and a few others were scattered around the tables absorbed with their cell phones. One held a book. The upstairs where the vampires sat looked sparsely populated as well. I received only cursory amber-eyed glances as I walked to the bar.

A female bartender greeted me and took my order. I perched on a stool at the end of the bar, eagerly awaiting the tall drink she prepared and set before me.

I downed half of it in one gulp and then swiveled around to check out the room. Velvet teetered toward me in high-heeled black boots that covered her legs to mid-thigh. The red corset and satin shorts she wore did little to cover the rest of her.

"Hey, handsome," she said.

Though still feet away, the odor of rum on her breath overwhelmed me.

She stumbled and I jumped up, catching her before she fell face down at my feet.

Velvet laced her arms around my neck and pressed her body against me. Nuzzling her face into my chest, she mumbled, "You smell good."

"Thanks. You smell like rum." I suppose I could have been more tactful, but I wasn't in the mood to deal with a clingy drunk, even a sexy one. Her hair was still jet black, but the blue streaks were now a blood red that matched her outfit, her lips and her fingernails.

My bluntness had no effect in her inebriated state. She threw her head back and looked up at me with glazed, heavy-lidded eyes. "Wanna go upstairs?"

"No, thanks. I'm good." I held her by her forearms to steady her until she gained her footing.

"How can you be good after drinking Echo's blood? My blood is *hot*. C'mon." She latched onto my arm with both hands and pulled. Her tall heels skidded on the polished wood floor and she started a slow slide downward. I leaned down and gripped her around her waist before the back of her head hit the floor. She wrapped her arms and legs around me and planted a rum-laden kiss on my mouth. Her dead weight nearly toppled me as I struggled to balance myself and lift her upright.

"Velvet, maybe you should head home—"

She clung to me like a Velcro rag doll. "I don't want to go home. I want to do what Jane and Tristan are doing—"

"What?"

"Hey! What the fuck do you think you're doing?"

Still bending to support Velvet's drunken weight, I peered over her head at Braedon storming across the room. Ignoring him, I asked Velvet, "What about Jane and Tristan?'

"Get your hands off her," Braedon bellowed.

He shoved between us, ripping Velvet from my grasp. She fell and lay sprawled on the floor, grinning. I stumbled back a step and then straightened to my full height. "Take it easy. She's too drunk to stand up. I was only helping her."

"Helping her, my ass." He poked my chest, his finger like a steel spike.

On reflex, I swatted his hand away. "Don't poke me. I don't want to fight. I just came in to have a drink."

"You stay away from her, understand?" He slammed his palms against my chest and pushed.

I stood firm.

As he moved to shove me again, I hammered a right jab into his jaw.

Braedon's head jerked sideways from the force of my punch.

I stood with my fists clenched and ready.

Glaring at me and rubbing his jaw, he muttered, "Mundane bastard," then he lowered his head and lunged.

I side-stepped Braedon's charge and he crashed into an empty bar stool.

"Stop this foolishness!" Aldon stood at the foot of the stairs brandishing his bejeweled cane like a sword.

Braedon started to speak then stopped as Aldon approached. For a man over one hundred, he glided across the room at lightning speed. "Braedon, take this girl home. She's in no condition to drive herself. And when she is sober, tell her this is her last warning. One more episode and she will be banned."

Aldon turned his icy gaze at me. "Lorcan, come upstairs. I wish to speak to you."

I hesitated for a moment as Braedon leaned and scooped up Velvet's limp form from the floor. I wanted to question Velvet about Jane and Tristan. Was it only Velvet's drunken ramblings or were they really upstairs together? The thought sent a stinging rage through my veins. I glowered at Braedon, my anger coloring my vision until his face looked as red as Velvet's clothes. For that split second, I wanted to kill him.

"Lorcan?"

I swiveled around and faced Aldon. His expression had softened. He motioned for me to come upstairs. "Bring your drink." He headed up the stairs.

Braedon carried Velvet out the front doors. The bartender waved to me as she set a fresh drink next to my half empty glass. Nodding my thanks, I chugged what remained of my first drink and then picked up the full glass and hurried upstairs.

At the top of the stairs, I stood and scanned the upper floor.

Aldon was nowhere in sight. Had I taken too long and offended him? Would I be banned from the club now, thanks to Braedon?

A woman with long dark hair touched my arm. "This way," she said.

I followed her to the hallway with the red-ribboned doors. She walked to the far end and opened a set of dark wood double doors.

Inside, Aldon sat in deep green leather chair. He motioned for me to take the matching chair across from him. This room was larger and more elaborately furnished than the one I had entered with Echo. Two closed doors on one wall indicated additional rooms, as well as the door to the balcony.

"Your strength is quite impressive for a former mundane. But you must learn to control your impulsive temper."

His tone contained a hint of contempt when he said the word mundane. "Yes, sir." I was exercising all the control I could muster right now to not blurt out that Braedon had started the fight. Plus my mind was occupied with thoughts of running down the hall flinging open all of the beribboned doors to see if Jane and Tristan hid behind one.

"I need someone with your strength, your intelligence. Someone trustworthy."

I stared at him, not sure how to react or if I should react.

Aldon continued, "I see great potential in you, Lorcan. As does Jane. I trust her instincts."

"Potential, sir?"

"Yes. I need a guard I can trust. Braedon is getting too cocky. His judgment is clouded by his feelings for that mundane girl. Utter trash she is. I should ban her from the club."

"Velvet just had too much to drink."

"Her alcohol-tainted blood is fueling my top guard. Do you find that a desirable situation?"

"No, sir, I guess not."

"I'd like you to consider the position."

"Me? A guard?"

Aldon folded his hands. His eyes, soulless and cold, aimed at me like lasers. "Not *a* guard. The leader of the guards and my personal guard."

"But I thought Braedon was the leader? I-I don't know what to say, sir."

"Think about it, Lorcan." He stood and walked to the door. "Of course, first you will have to deal with Braedon, though I'm confident you will prevail."

"You want me to fight Braedon for the lead guard position?"

"I want you to kill him."

He opened the door and left the room before I could answer, not that my open mouth could form an intelligible reply to his final comment. Earlier, in the heat of the moment I had wanted to kill Braedon. Yet, deep down I knew I wouldn't—couldn't. Kicking his ass—yes—but murder was too far across the line.

Aldon's matter-of-fact statement sent a wave of chills arcing across my scalp and racing down my back. My hand shook, sending liquid sloshing over the lip of my glass as I picked up my drink. I walked to the open door and drew in a breath before stepping into the dim hallway, terrified I would come face to face with Aldon and those icy eyes that penetrated to my core.

But Aldon had vanished. Relief washed over me until a flash of golden blonde hair in the dusky hallway made the breath I exhaled catch in my throat. Only a glimpse, yet I recognized Jane's hair, those same silken gold ribbons I chased in my dreams. I pushed the door almost closed and peered through the narrow opening.

Jane had exited a room. Behind her, came Tristan. He pulled Jane close, their heads bowed together, and he whispered. I tried to hear what he said but a cacophony of screams in my own mind made me lose all focus. They stood locked in the embrace for what felt like an eternity to me—their comfort and intimacy in each other's arms unmistakable.

I didn't breathe, only stared at them like a guilty voyeur. A sharp pain grew deep in my gut while at the same time a fiery rage burned in my chest.

Tristan cupped Jane's chin in his hand, pressed his lips to her forehead and held them there for several moments. They finally parted and both headed down the stairs.

As I watched until they disappeared from sight, my stomach felt hollow and bottomless despite a tornado of emotions spinning inside me.

This should have been the best day of my life. For the first time I stood strong, unafraid, successful—I had achieved all of my dreams. Yet with one glimpse down a darkened hall, none of it mattered. I would trade it all for Jane's love.

An hour later I drove through the iron gates of Jane's house, up the drive, and parked near the front door. It didn't matter if my car blocked the entrance. I would stay only long enough to pack.

I used the key she lent me to open the door and tossed it on the foyer table on my way to the living room. The clothes I had left piled on the sofa no longer fit and were useless. I hurried to the kitchen and found a trash bag, then returned and stuffed the clothes into it. That was it. Only a suitcase with some underwear remained and a few toiletries in the bathroom. My new clothes and the rest of my belongings were still packed in my car.

As I headed for the bathroom to gather up my items, I ran into Jane in the foyer as she entered the house carrying grocery bags.

"Hi, how did it go?" she asked.

Her cheeks held a rose-colored flush. She glowed with Tristan's blood. Her lover's blood.

"Fine. Got the job."

"Congratulations. I'm happy for you, Tim. I know landing that job meant a lot to you." She placed her bag on the foyer table and picked up the key. "Here, you left your key on the table."

I held my hand out and nodded dumbly. Words wouldn't come out of my mouth. Jealousy shredded my insides much like the demon claws in my nightmares.

"Would you fire up the grill? I bought lamb. Thought I'd make us shish kabobs tonight."

"I-I can't stay here." I put the key back on the table. "I need to find an apartment."

"Why?" Jane's eyes glimmered to violet then back to deep blue. The color shift would have been missed if I had blinked.

"I've taken advantage of your generosity long enough. I have a job now, so . . ." I shrugged and looked away from her gaze. Was that hurt in her eyes or relief?

Her fingers closed around my hand and she tugged. "Let's go in the kitchen and talk."

Following her like a mute puppy, I focused on the tingling sensations her touch produced.

She placed the grocery bags on the table, pulled out a chair and sat. "You're welcome to stay here. It's close to your new job, isn't it?"

"Yes." Outwardly I stood stiff as a statue while inside my emotions churned and spiraled from my gut to my throat. If I spoke, I would lose control, spew out words I would regret. If I didn't speak, my flesh would crack like plaster and explode.

"Tim, what's wrong?"

Her words pulled the trigger. My body shook as I shouted at her, "What's wrong? I can't stay here because I love you, that's what's wrong. Wrong, because you don't love me, or ever will. You love Tristan. Don't deny it. I saw you two at The Haven tonight. You could have at least told me the truth about him and not lied."

Jane sat silent after my outburst. My heart pounded in my chest and I paced the room wanting to punch the appliances and smash all the dishes. My fingers raked through my hair wanting to rip it from my scalp. Had I actually said out loud that I loved her? Humiliation, cold and overwhelming, flooded the gaping dark hole my spent rage had left. I sank down into a chair and covered my face with my hands. They trembled like the rest of me.

Jane's hands massaged my shoulders. "Tristan is my donor. We're old friends. I knew him from the state home. He's always looked after me."

"But I saw you two in the hallway at The Haven—"

"Saw what? A hug? A kiss on the forehead?" Jane sighed and squeezed my shoulders. "I do love Tristan. I consider him my big brother. If it weren't for him, my time in the orphanage would have been so much worse. He protected me and all the younger kids." Jane walked around me and pulled my hands away from my face. "Do you feel romantically about Echo?"

The question felt off-topic and in my raw state of mind, I couldn't fathom its significance. I mumbled, "No."

"Well, it's the same between Tristan and me. I trust him and that's why he is the only donor I use. But he's not my lover." Jane leaned down and smiled, her radiant face and eyes inches from mine. "Besides, Tristan is gay."

My brain slowly processed her words. "Really?"

"Really." Jane laughed, the sound like the soft pealing of tiny golden bells. "He'd more likely be attracted to you than me."

My mouth twitched into a facsimile of a smile. My emotions so raw and fleeting now that I couldn't decipher what I was feeling at any given moment.

"Tim, I'd like you to stay. In fact, I wanted to offer you a room of your own, rather than the sofa. You can unpack your television and books from your car and be more comfortable there."

Humiliation subsided, drawing away like an icy tide—confusion took its place, then anger spiked. "Separate bedrooms, like roommates?"

Jane took my hands in hers. Tears glistened in her eyes which had taken on the look of tiny planets swirling with blue and violet clouds. Her eyes mesmerized me as they grew larger and then I realized it was because she moved closer. So close, her lips pressed into mine, soft and warm. Her kiss ignited a fire storm that started at my mouth and traveled through my body, my veins the sizzling fuse. I stood and drew her close to me. The feel of her body against me set off electric sparks in mine.

She pulled away and swiped a tear from her cheek. "I-I need time before we. . . There's something I must do. Please, Tim, will you give me time?"

Chapter 13

"I saw that you were perfect, and so I loved you. Then I saw that you were not perfect and I loved you even more." —Angelita Lim

With chaotic thoughts still swirling in my mind after my emotional outburst in the kitchen, I followed Jane down the hall. We each carried boxes and bags of my belongings from my car.

Am I crazy? Why did I agree to wait? But after seeing tears in Jane's eyes, I couldn't say no. In the time I'd known her, I'd never seen her cry, so, of course I agreed to give her time. Hell, I would have grabbed a kitchen knife and cut out my own kidney if she'd asked me to. Yet now new thoughts plagued me. How much time? And what was the mysterious thing she needed to do that prevented her from having a relationship? Despite our time together, she still avoided all personal questions.

We walked past the guest bathroom and turned down the hallway that bordered the pool area on the opposite side of the house from Jane's lab and bedroom. I pushed open the first door and a triangular ray of light from the hallway illuminated a baby's crib and a four-poster bed.

"No, not that room, the next one." Jane continued down the hall to a second room, opened the door and flicked on the overhead light.

The bedroom was spacious with French doors leading outside to the pool. The other three walls housed a bed, a tall bureau, and a desk with a bookcase. The sturdy, dark wood furniture matched the Mission Style furnishings in the rest of the house.

Jane placed the box and bags she carried on the floor. "Let me get a cloth and wipe down everything. I'll be right back."

"No need, it's—" Before I could finish, she had hurried out the door.

A fine layer of gray dust covered the desk and bureau tops—an unusual sight in Jane's spit-polished home. I placed my boxes on the floor and then walked out to my car to retrieve my flat screen television.

When I returned, I found Jane amidst a cloud of lemon-scented furniture polish scrubbing the wood with a white cloth.

She jumped when I came up behind her and laid my hands on her shoulders. "Sorry, I didn't mean to startle you. You're gonna rub the finish off the wood."

"I wanted to make sure the room is clean." She turned and motioned to the bed. "I'll get you fresh sheets."

The bed was piled high with southwestern-patterned throw pillows. I moved them aside, pulled back the comforter and revealed soft, white sheets. "Don't bother. These look fine to me."

She stood in the center of the room, her eyes darting from wall to wall.

"You're sure you don't mind me using this room?" I asked.

"No, not at all." Jane blew out a long breath. "This was my room when Ana first adopted me."

The decor was neutral, certainly not a frilly little girl's bedroom. The comforter had a chevron design in muted rusts and brown tones. The pale bronze stucco walls and dark wood floor adorned with a colorful Indian blanket throw rug created a warm, welcoming feeling. Seemingly immune to its coziness, Jane stood with her arms crossed and her jaw tensed.

"You look uncomfortable in here," I said.

"This room brings back memories." Jane picked up the can of furniture polish and rag. "I'm starving. Would you mind starting up the grill, please? I'll make us a salad." She rushed off to the kitchen.

After dinner I helped Jane clean up, then poured two glasses of pomegranate juice. "There's a full moon and a cool breeze. Want to sit on the patio?"

When we had settled at the patio table, I chose my words carefully. While previously I had regarded Jane as closed and aloof, I now viewed her more like a skittish deer.

"I agreed to give you time, in return I'd appreciate it if you would be more open with me."

She sipped her juice and looked up at the moon, its glow illuminating her amazing blue eyes. "About what?"

"What is it you have to do that keeps you from having a relationship? Is it connected to the work you do in your lab every night?"

"I started out by analyzing my own blood, trying to find answers, comparing it with blood from mundanes—I mean—humans. I even sneaked small samples from work. I wanted to find out exactly what made us different."

"Have you?" I noted she avoided the first part of my question but decided not to press her.

"Yes and no. It's complex. I've isolated plasma, red and white blood cells, and platelets and done dozens of experiments. The plasma and red blood cells contain the most differences."

"Then you've found the answer. Your experiments were a success?"

She sighed and shook her head. "I've isolated the components of the cells that are unique to vampires. But then, when I joined The Haven and Aldon discovered I was a hematologist, he asked me to do further research. More complex experimentation."

An involuntary shiver crawled down my spine at the mention of Aldon. "The work you do every night in your lab is for Aldon?"

"At his request, but not for him personally—it's for the future of the entire Night Flock."

"What exactly did Aldon ask you to do?"

Jane swirled the juice around her glass. "He told me not to discuss it with anyone."

I tried to remain calm, but Jane's reply irked me. Maybe my temper was as impulsive as Aldon said. "So, what? Because I used to be a *mundane,* now I'm *anyone*? Did you tell Tristan?"

"*No* and *no*," Jane's eyes flashed with green. "I'm simply honoring our elder's request."

I took a deep breath to quell my rising anger. "Do you trust Aldon?"

Jane stared at me a moment, her eyes calmed to deep blue. "Of course. I trust him with my life."

"He asked me to consider being a Haven guard today. Actually,

192

lead guard, his personal guard."

Jane's eyes widened and she smiled. "That's a high honor, Tim. What did you say?"

"Nothing, yet. He asked me to think about it. He said my first duty would be to kill Braedon."

"What?"

"You heard me. Aldon wants me to kill Braedon."

Jane stood up shaking her head. "No. That can't be. Aldon would never—you must have misunderstood, Tim."

My anger returned with a vengeance at her dismissive tone. "Like hell I misunderstood. The guy sat in front of me as cold as a damn ice cube and said he wanted me to kill Braedon."

Jane crossed her arms and continued to shake her head no.

"That's what he said. You don't believe me?" I jumped up from my seat, knocking the metal chair over, and paced across the patio, rounded the pool and then faced Jane. "This is great. How can we have a relationship if you don't believe me?"

She stood silent, glaring at me with dots of brilliant green flickering in her eyes.

"Ah, fuck it." I stormed past her and headed for the doors to my room.

"Tim, wait."

I stopped with my hand on the door handle. Jane's footsteps approached.

"My research began when Aldon gave me a sample of his blood. He wanted me to find a way to turn hybrid blood to pure vampire blood."

I whirled around. "Why?"

"He's concerned about the Night Flock dying out. With the exception of him, all of the members of The Haven are varying degrees of hybrids. Some born of Pure Bloods and humans—some more diluted—a mix of two hybrids. He cares about all of us. He wants to keep his race strong."

"Did you find a way?"

Jane looked down at her feet. "When I added a drop of his blood to a hybrid sample, the pure cells destroyed the hybrid cells. It's frustrating, my experiments had been a complete failure until . . ."

"Until what?"

"Until I tested your blood. It's different. I don't know exactly why, but when I your mixed your blood with Aldon's, the results were stronger than Pure blood."

"What do mean by stronger?"

"Each cell is more fortified in every aspect. I'm still working."

"I knew I was only a lab rat to you. Someone you took in for your blood experiments."

"That's not true. I brought you here to save you. What Lorelei did is against all of our rules."

I snorted. "Right, because mundanes are inferior. We aren't worthy to drink a Pure's blood."

"No, because *regular humans* die when they ingest pure vampire blood. That's why I assumed you were a hybrid before you drank her blood. I can't explain how you survived. Not only survived—but thrived and evolved."

"Well I guess that gives you and Aldon lots to talk about." I entered my room and slammed the doors behind me.

Jane called through the closed doors. "I told Aldon about your blood so he would allow you into The Haven. I wanted you to have safe place to go, people who'd support you . . . in case something happened to me."

"I don't need your protection or Aldon's," I shouted.

The doors opened and Jane stood in the doorway silhouetted in the bright moonlight, her hair a shimmering golden veil cascading over her shoulders. Lust stabbed through my anger.

"It's true," she said. "You don't need me or Aldon. You're strong enough on your own now."

Staring at her, my rage drained through me. "I'm sorry. You saved me. I owe you my life."

"You don't owe me anything." She turned and headed across the patio.

I followed her. "Is that why you're holding back from me? Until you finish your experiments for Aldon?"

Jane stopped, with her back to me. She whispered, "No."

"Then what is it?" I gripped her shoulders, turned her around and pulled her close. As I lifted her chin intending to kiss her, the deep indigo color seeping into her irises startled me. The color grew so dark, all light from the moon's rays was sucked into the black abyss of her eyes. Her expression crumpled with my touch and tears streamed down her cheeks. She buried her face in my chest and sobbed. I hugged her tighter.

We stood under the night sky, Jane's muffled sobs, the soft lapping of the pool water and a spattering of cricket calls the only sounds. She tucked her face into the curve of my neck and her tears flowed down my chest and soaked my T-shirt. I rested my chin on the top of her head and breathed in her scent, the smell so sweet, it was indescribable.

I reveled in how perfectly our bodies melded together and the desire to complete the coupling burned in my veins, yet the need to protect Jane from whatever was hurting her overwhelmed me. At a loss for words, I held her and stroked her silken hair.

She drew in a long shuddering breath and then lifted her head. "I'm sorry."

"For what?"

She squirmed from my embrace and grasped my hands. "I believe you. Tomorrow we'll go speak to Aldon, together—find out why he wants Braedon killed—if that's all right with you?"

"I don't give a flying crap about Aldon or Braedon. All I care about is you. What's hurting you?"

"You're strong, but Aldon is extremely powerful, Tim. You don't want him as your enemy. Let's get things settled with him, then I'll tell you anything you want to know about me. Okay?"

Before I could answer, she kissed me. The pressure of her soft lips against mine pushed all thoughts from my mind. Then she was gone, running across the patio and into her bedroom.

After Jane left for work the next morning, the memory of her kiss and holding her close stayed with me as I busied myself waiting for her return. It took less than an hour to unpack and put away my belongings in the new room. I connected my laptop to the television since Jane had no cable in the house. The canned laughter of my Netflix sitcoms did little to distract my thoughts from her.

To pass the time, I cleaned the house, mowed the yard and then worked out in the gym. After a shower, I checked my email and found that Rudi from Create-A-Vision had sent me several artists' portfolios to consider. While all the artwork was well-executed, they looked too cartoonish. I envisioned my characters rendered in a more realistic, gritty style. I hesitated to respond negatively. Although they had treated me like a demigod at the interview, I was the new kid and didn't want to be difficult. Of all the staff, Rudi, though slightly built and mousey-haired, showed the most formidable personality. Plus, she had clout there. It would be best for me to stay on her good side.

I typed a polite email asking if they had any artists with a more realistic, less anime, style. I hit the send button and hoped I didn't offend Rudi.

"Hey."

I looked up from my screen. Dressed in pale blue medical scrubs, Jane stood in the doorway.

Jumping up from the desk chair, I greeted her with a kiss. To my delight, she didn't pull away.

"I thought we could eat out and then go to The Haven and talk to Aldon."

Aldon was the last person I wanted to see, but if I wanted to find out what was bothering Jane, I'd have to face the murderous elder again.

"Um, sure," I mumbled.

"I'll go change." Jane walked down the hallway.

I called after her, "Vampires can eat out?"

She stopped and turned. "Of course. You can eat anything you want, but our metabolism does best on a high protein diet." She smiled. "Don't worry. I know a place."

The small cafe Jane chose had an intimate feel. The dim interior held only candlelit tables for two. The jazz music played softly enough for lovers' conversations. We drank red wine and enjoyed a meal of steak tartare and salad. More than the food, I enjoyed looking across the table at Jane, whose golden glowing complexion made the flickering light from the candles pale in comparison. We were on a date and I didn't want it to ever end.

Jane paid the pricey bill with a platinum credit card. I apologized to her and swore once I received my first paycheck I would reciprocate.

She shrugged. "Ana left me everything in her will. She was quite wealthy."

The statement clarified Jane's nonchalant attitude towards money. Still, I made a mental note to check the post office box to see if my new credit card had arrived, since it would be at least two weeks before I received a paycheck from Create-A-Vision.

Our light conversation and laughter from dinner faded into somber silence as Jane drove to The Haven. Aldon intimidated me and the thought of confronting him with his order to kill Braedon made my nerves hum with dread.

Once inside the club, Jane reminded me to use her club name, Raina. Then she insisted that I get us drinks while she went upstairs and sought out Aldon. "I know how to speak to Aldon and not offend him or challenge his authority."

Nodding, I walked to the bar while she headed upstairs. The place was busy tonight and I recognized some of the regular patrons as I looked around the room waiting for the bartender. Thankfully, neither Braedon nor Velvet was among the crowd. The last thing I needed was another confrontation.

"Will that be two vodka and pomegranates?"

Startled from my thoughts, I whirled around and faced Tristan. With his shiny gelled hair and crisp tailored clothing, he looked like a GQ cover model. He flashed a professional smile.

"Yes. Thanks." I watched him as he poured the drinks, his movements smooth and practiced. Although Jane told me he was gay and merely her friend and trusted donor, I couldn't shake off the prickles of jealousy I felt remembering his and Jane's long embrace the other night.

He placed the drinks on the bar, and I removed my last five-dollar bill from my wallet and dropped it into his tip glass.

"Thank you. Enjoy your evening." He moved on down the bar to take another order.

With drinks in hand, I started up the staircase. Jane appeared at the top of the stairs and waved to me. I followed her to a table tucked into a darkened corner. My heart did an involuntary flip-flop when I saw Aldon sitting at the table.

Though he sat with his shoulders squared and head high, his eyes lacked their usual acid glare.

"Please." He motioned for us to sit.

We'd no sooner settled into our chairs, when he got straight to the point. "Yes Raina, it's true. I did tell Lorcan I wanted him to kill Braedon."

Jane stiffened in her chair. She opened her mouth to speak but stopped when Aldon held up his hand. "It's inexcusable, I know. My anger got the better of me. I had words with Braedon earlier that day when he challenged my authority, yet again, on another matter. Then I witnessed his jealous rage with Lorcan over that drunken whor— girl, Velvet." Tiny crinkles bordered his eyes and his thin lips arced into a smile. "I chastised Lorcan about his impulsive temper, yet I am no better. As leader, I must be better. My sincerest apologies, Lorcan." Aldon paused as he drank a deep red liquid from his wine glass. "I searched for you the other night after we had spoken. I intended to apologize then for my brash words, but you had already left."

"I knew there had to be an explanation," Jane said. "Thank you for clarifying, Aldon."

He nodded at Jane and then turned to me. "Perhaps my words acted as an unintended test. I'm pleased you had the moral fortitude to balk at an order to kill another member. It reinforces my opinion of your fine character. My offer to be my guard still stands."

Aldon sat studying me with his hands folded beneath his chin— a harmless old man—he could be my grandfather, yet a chill ran down my spine. His words weren't blurted in anger the other night, they had been cold and precise.

Jane nudged me.

"Um, thank you," I said.

Out of Aldon's sight, Jane squeezed my hand under the table. "Aldon, would you explain to Lorcan exactly what being a guard entails?"

Again, he smiled at me, his demeanor humble, his eyes benign. "Of course, I forget you are new to our ways. Braedon leads a group of young men who are strong, skilled fighters. They simply stay here during club hours to ensure everyone's safety." He motioned to a table of three men sitting near the balcony railing overlooking the downstairs floor. "Unfortunately, we have had incidents in the past that require such services."

"You mean they're like bouncers in a bar?" I asked.

Jane leaned forward and spoke in a low voice. "There are rival clans of vampires who challenge Aldon. They want to take over his club to add more numbers to theirs and gain power. Occasionally, ignorant humans choose to attack us and then there is a constant threat from the Pure Bloods."

"These Pure Bloods, they want to take over the club, too?" I asked.

"They wish to destroy it, not take it over. The Pures abhor hybrids." Aldon sighed. "And The Haven consists of all hybrids, myself the one exception. They despise me for protecting hybrids."

"Clashes with the Pures are rare, but deadly," Jane added. "There are only a few old family lines left, all European. Most refuse to accept hybrids and shun us—others are hell-bent on murdering us all."

"They come all the way over here to kill us?" I asked.

"Yes, but as Raina said, it's rare. The Pures' beliefs are slowly changing as their elders die off. Most of the vampires left in this world are hybrids. I admit it took me some time to accept hybrids, but they are our future. I've tried to convince the Pures' elders to show tolerance. Jane's tireless work has proven to me that hybrids are strong and resilient. And you, Lorcan, a former human, are still evolving, stronger each time I see you. It's the evolution of a new race for us. A new future."

"What about those ignorant humans you mentioned? What harm could they possibly do to us?"

"More than you'd think. We call them Vans." Jane rolled her eyes. "A slang term after the fictional Van Helsing. They fancy themselves as modern-day vampire hunters. In reality, they're cowards who travel in groups and attack lone vampires. They drive wooden stakes through their victims' hearts. That's another reason we keep our members' identities secret—to protect them from the

Vans."

"They actually drive stakes into people?"

"Yes. It's barbaric. We had a member followed from the club to her home a few years back. They murdered her in her driveway," Jane said.

"The press had a field day." Aldon said. "They soon discovered our previous location in the warehouse district. We've since moved here. We blend into the downtown night life 'hiding in plain sight,' as they say." Aldon drained his glass and set it down. A dark-haired woman carrying a decanter quickly approached and refilled his glass. He waited until she walked away before continuing. "Now do you understand why I need guards, Lorcan? There is danger lurking all around our kind. Braedon is a liability. I can't trust he will stay loyal to me and the Haven. Another clan may offer him money or more power, or that girl he lusts after may lead a group of crazed vigilantes with wooden stakes to our front door. I need someone I can trust to keep him in line."

Though I could no longer sweat, the glass I clutched in my hot hands dripped with condensation. "I have a job. I was just hired yesterday." I felt silly defending my work as a video game developer after the life and death drama Aldon and Jane had described.

"All of my guards lead independent lives outside The Haven. I encourage it. It provides them with a cover of normalcy. They work in shifts. I would welcome you here after your day job," Aldon said.

"If you place me above Braedon, it's only going to cause more problems. What if I joined the guards under Braedon's leadership? I can still keep an eye on him and it might help with the others here who don't like former humans—mundanes. It would give me a chance to prove myself to everyone—maybe even Braedon. He respects strength."

Aldon broke into wide smile showing white, even teeth. He reached across the table and grasped both Jane's and my hands. "You impress me more and more, Lorcan. Though I warn you, it will not be easy. Braedon will be combative."

"I can handle him. If it's okay with you, I'd prefer to earn my place in the guards."

"I'm so proud of you." Jane said as we pulled out of The Haven's parking lot.

In spite of her praise, second thoughts shook my resolve. I had accepted Aldon's offer to become a guard at The Haven mostly to please Jane and now I regretted my rash decision, but I could never let her know that. Braedon didn't scare me. The two confrontations I'd had with him left me confident he posed no real threat. Aldon on the other hand, made me uneasy.

"Do you think Aldon was telling the truth?" I asked.

"Of course. Don't you?"

"I don't know. I guess so."

"Everyone loses his temper. Aldon's a proud man, and as our leader he feels he must always be in control of his emotions. I'm sure it wasn't easy for him to admit his lapse."

"You make him sound human."

"Both humans and vampires have emotions. Ours are more intense." She gave me a sideward look and smirked. "You, of all people, should understand that."

"What's that supposed to mean?"

Jane grinned and patted my knee. "You're proving my point."

I blew out a long breath and crossed my arms. "Very funny."

Her point was valid. I recalled the fleeting moment yesterday when I wanted to kill Braedon. The arrogant son-of-a-bitch had a talent for making people want to murder him. If Jane trusted Aldon so implicitly, who was I to question him? She'd known him for years and I'd only met him three times. Even the head honcho vampire was allowed to screw up now and then. And he did appear to regret his words. Aldon couldn't have been more apologetic and gracious to me than he was tonight.

"Besides," Jane said, "If Aldon really wanted Braedon dead, he'd kill him himself."

Jane's last statement slammed a gavel on my mental debate. As always, she was right. I pushed my concerns about Aldon aside and focused on my real worry. Would Jane keep her promise and tell me why she needed time before entering into a relationship with me? Or was she stalling because she wasn't interested in me? As she pulled into her driveway, I struggled to find the right words to broach the subject—words that wouldn't scare her off or make her eyes turn nuclear green. We walked from her jeep into the house without talking.

I stood in the foyer grappling to find an opening line while Jane secured the three locks on the inside of the front door.

"Does your offer to watch a movie still stand?" she asked.

"Huh?"

"You know, one of those old vampire movies you told me about. I've never seen one."

"Um, yeah, sure, if you want. I have some on my computer and now it's hooked up to my TV."

"Set it up. I'll be right there." We walked down the hallway side by side. Jane turned left toward her room and I turned right to mine. The physical separation of our bedrooms added to my hopelessness. Was watching a movie her way to avoid talking to me?

I queued the movie on the computer and then sat on the edge of the bed and slid off my sneakers. Jane knocked on the open door.

"C'mon in. I have the original nineteen thirty-one Dracula movie ready to go."

Jane gathered an armful of throw pillows from the bed and piled them on the floor. She had changed into shorts and a tank top, and I found my attention drawn to her long tan legs as she lay on her stomach among the soft pillows.

"The movie's slow and a little corny, but it's a classic—the first one based on Bram Stoker's novel." I hit the play button and then sat on the floor and leaned my back against the side of the bed.

Jane stared up at the screen, her chin propped on her folded arms. The old black and white film began with dramatic tinny music that faded into the sounds of a storm and the rattle of a horse-drawn carriage making its way up a winding mountain road on the stormy night. Thunder boomed, wolves howled, and wind thrashed the tree branches in the thick forest that lined both sides of the road. The camera panned up to the top of the mountain and an elongated flash of lightning illuminated a forbidding stone castle just as the movie title *Dracula* filled the screen.

"That's Bran Castle," she said.

"Excuse me?"

"It's a landmark in Romania in the area called Transylvania on the border with Wallachia. Now it's a tourist attraction, although it has nothing to do with Dracula."

I laughed. "How do you know so much about Transylvania?"

Jane pushed herself up into a sitting position and turned toward me. "I've studied all about Romania."

"Why?"

She turned back to the TV screen. "Because I'm going there."

I stared at the back of her head waiting for the punch line, but instead of making a joke, she added, "Day after tomorrow."

"What? You're joking, right?"

She shook her head. "No. I'm leaving in two days to travel to Romania."

On my feet, I hurried to the computer and muted the volume on the movie. "Okay, I get it. You're mocking me—because I like vampire movies and you think it's all Hollywood crap and—"

"I'm not joking or mocking you, Tim." Jane looked down and ran her hand over the pillow next to her. "You asked me what I had to do—why I couldn't have a relationship right now—it's because I have to make this trip."

I crouched down, my face inches from hers. "Why in the world would you go to Transylvania, of all places?"

"There's a tiny bit of truth in these silly movies. Vampires were first documented in that region of the world."

"Okay. You're screwing with me. Real vampires live in Transylvania—"

"I'm going to Zalau, well, actually the outskirts of the city. I have to get my niece and bring her back home."

"I don't understand, you never mentioned a niece. I thought you said you were an orphan?"

Jane sighed and stood up. She walked around the room, absently touching the furniture, lost in her thoughts. "Ana, my adoptive mother, had a daughter named Isabelle, my adoptive sister. She was ten and I was nine when they adopted me. We grew up together—spent hours playing, giggling, borrowing each other's clothes, even fought sometimes, like real sisters. After we had grown, Isabelle gave birth to a daughter—my niece—Emilia."

"So, why do you have to go get your niece? Where's Isabelle?"

"Dead."

"Oh, shit. I'm sorry."

"She and Ana were both killed the same night."

"Damn. Was it a car accident?"

Jane paced the room, her eyes darkened. Tensed, I waited for her to answer.

"No, no accident. The Vasile family—Pure Bloods from the old country—were sent here to murder them."

"Why would they want to kill them?"

"Revenge. Years before, Ana fled from Romania to the U.S. to save Isabelle from their barbaric old-world ways. After several years passed, she believed they had been shunned and forgotten—that she and Isabelle were safe here. But then Isabelle fell in love with a human. A Pure killed him and raped Isabelle . . . their sick way of teaching her a lesson—Pures only mate with Pures. All the Vasiles care about is keeping their bloodlines pure. Ana's family heritage is long—her bloodline pristine. The old-world Pures keep their women enslaved and use them for breeding."

"That's awful. So, your niece, Emilia, she's the baby from the rape?"

"Yes. But in spite of it, Isabelle was determined to keep her, raise her with love, not their hatred."

"If Isabelle was killed, then who has Emilia now?"

Jane ran her hands around the wall next to the small closet. Suddenly a large piece of the wall opened like a doorway next to the closet. "The Vasiles came back after the baby was born. Burst in the front door one night. First, they killed Raven, our German Shepherd. She had tried to protect us."

I nodded, recalling the dog shears and collar under the kitchen cabinet.

Jane pointed to the dark opening in the wall. "Ana pushed me in here. Told me to stay there, no matter what. I hid like a coward listening to the fighting. Their screams. Little Emilia crying and Isabelle begging them not to take her baby. The screaming stopped. And everything turned quiet."

I walked over and peered into the dark, empty space inside the wall. I wrapped my arms around Jane. She trembled all over.

"I can't imagine how awful that must have been. When did this happen?"

"Ten years ago. That's why I have to save Emilia now. The Pures took her because of her bloodline. They'll wait until Emilia's awakening which could start soon. First, they'll brainwash her with their poisonous way of thinking, then they'll use her for breeding."

I hugged Jane closer. "I'll go with you," I said.

"No. You have to stay here. You need to protect the house and The Haven."

"Jane, it's too dangerous for you to go by yourself."

She pushed away from me. Her stance and her eyes, defiant. "Ten years ago I was too weak and afraid to fight the Vasiles. I hid when I should have fought. I need to do this on my own, Tim."

"But how do you know where Emilia is?"

"Ana gave me this." Jane stepped into the dark opening in the wall and then emerged holding a thick leather-bound journal. "Ana was smart. Always prepared. She wrote down everything about her family history and which ones could be trusted in Romania." Jane handed me the book.

I flipped through it, skimming through pages of neat script and a few hand-drawn maps.

"They're hiding Emilia in a small orphanage outside of Zalau, in the Transylvania countryside. A remote area in the mountains."

"And what, you're just going to walk in there and then walk out with her?"

"Basically, yes." Jane sat on the edge of the bed. "Ana's cousin, Cristina, managed to get work at the orphanage so she could keep an eye on Emilia, to make sure she was cared for all this time. We've been in contact for years. She's agreed to help me sneak Emilia out of the orphanage and provide a car. If all goes as planned, we'll drive to Budapest and then get a flight back to L.A."

"This is nuts. Are you sure you can trust this woman? These Vasiles could be waiting and kill you, too. How do you know it's not a setup?"

"I don't know. What I do know is what it's like to grow up in a group home. And I know how much Isabelle loved Emilia, the

205

dreams she had to give her a good life—a real future." Tears flowed down Jane's face and her eyes sparked with fiery green. "I have to save Emilia. Ana and Isabelle were the only family I ever had. I owe it to them."

"I can't let you do this, Jane."

"You can't stop me. I've planned this trip for years. I've studied Romania—studied the route on Google earth. It's the reason I've trained so hard in the gym and why I drank Lorelei's blood, to make myself as strong as possible. I'm ready now."

"But—this is . . . crazy."

"No, crazy was listening to the people I loved being slaughtered—finding them beheaded, dismembered. Their blood on the floor, walls. Everywhere. It took me days to . . . I buried Ana and Isabelle in the flower garden behind the house. Raven, too."

"Did you call the police?"

Jane glared at me. "And tell them what? That a group of vampires murdered my family and kidnapped a pure-bred vampire baby girl?"

"No, I mean tell them men broke in and mur—"

"They wouldn't have believed me. The savage way their bodies were ripped apart, no human could have done that. And the Vasiles are too smart, too strong. The police would never have found them. Even if they had, the Pures would have killed them, too."

The shock of her story hadn't fully settled in my brain. "You're really leaving in two days?" I asked.

"Yes. Cristina told me they are sending more Pures here to attack hybrids. They know about The Haven. How it's grown over the years and has the largest group of hybrids in our community. That's why you have to stay and guard it. This is my best opportunity to sneak in and get Emilia, while most of their guards are here. They won't expect me to come to their homeland."

"But, you're just one person. Does Aldon know anyone in Romania who can help you?"

"He has family there, most of the Pures originated from that area, but," Jane looked down. "Aldon doesn't know I'm going to Romania."

"Why not?"

"Years ago, when I first joined The Haven, I told Aldon what happened to Ana and Isabelle and about my plan to save Emilia. He forbade me to go. Said it was too dangerous and could cause a war with the Pures. He said I would have to let Emilia go for the welfare of The Haven. Better to lose one, than all." Jane shook her head. "But, I can't. I lied to Aldon tonight, told him I'd be out of town for a couple of weeks at a hematologist convention in New York."

"Jane, listen to me, if Aldon thinks it's too dangerous, then—"

"I don't care what he thinks. I'm going, Tim. And you have to promise me you won't tell Aldon—or anyone else—where I am. No matter what happens."

"Shit." I raked my hands through my hair and stared up at the ceiling. Jane's story was as bizarre as the movie playing on my TV screen, but it was real. "Am I the only one who knows you're going?"

Jane looked down. "Tristan is the only other person here. And Ana's cousin in Romania, Cristina, of course."

She stood and grasped my hands, squeezing them so hard I thought my bones would break. "Promise me, Tim. Please."

I stared into her gleaming blue-green eyes. "I-I promise."

She released my hands and flung her arms around my neck. Her soft lips pushed against mine. Tonight, the only longing I felt was to hold her and keep her from leaving on this insane mission.

"And if you succeed and return with Emilia, then what?" I asked. "They'll come after you. They know where you live."

Jane pulled away from me and stood with her hands on her hips. This was the Jane I had first met, strong and confident with defiance blazing a green fire in her eyes. "Not if you and the other guards kill them when they attack The Haven. Aldon is correct. Most of the Pures are content to shun hybrids and stay in the old country. There's only a handful who want to destroy us. You and the other guards have to kill them. That's why you have to stay here. You're the strongest."

It was the second time in as many days I'd been asked to kill. I sat on my bed staring at the hiding place in the wall. The muted Dracula movie flickering on the screen illuminated the black hole with an eerie bluish light.

And Jane, we were so close to starting a relationship and now she tells me she's running off halfway across the world. What if she's killed? I couldn't allow the thought to take hold in my brain, the pain it brought was intolerable.

Yet I couldn't stop her from going, that much was clear to me, and I couldn't convince her to let me go with her. Jane's strength and resolve were undeniable, but how many Pures would she have to fight?

My heart wasn't into defending The Haven. Not that I wished them harm, but I felt no emotional attachment to anyone there—not even pale, scrawny Echo. I'd sacrifice all of them to keep Jane safe.

When I told Jane I'd rather die fighting at her side then live without her, she ran from my room clutching the old leather journal to her heart.

I fought the urge to run after her, since there was nothing I could say to change her mind. I walked over to the opening in the wall. The edges of the doorway were uneven, and when closed, they blended seamlessly into the rough stucco finish on the wall.

Crawling inside the small space, I sat. My arms hugged my bent knees. There was a handle on the inside of the door. I pulled it until the door closed. Total blackness enveloped me. I breathed in dry, stale air. It took only seconds for panic to start to rise inside me and I imagined how Jane must have felt enclosed in this tiny dark space with the added horror of hearing the bloody massacre on the other side of the wall. Her only family, brutally murdered while she hid, wondering if she would be discovered and face the same fate. How terrified she must have been, how helpless and alone she must have felt.

What if it had been my mom and dad and brother who were slaughtered within my earshot? I fumbled with the handle, my panic momentarily escalating to terror until I figured out how to release the mechanism and open the door. I crawled out and slammed the door shut.

As I drew in a deep breath of air, an understanding of Jane's grief trickled over me. If it had been my family, I'd want to save Emilia, too. I'd also want revenge.

Scrambling to my feet, I hurried to the other side of the house. A faint light showed beneath Jane's closed laboratory door. I knocked and waited.

"Come in," Jane called.

I opened the door. Jane sat at her desk in the corner of the lab studying her computer screen.

She didn't turn her head. "Nothing you can say will change my mind."

I stood behind her and rubbed her shoulders. The muscles in her neck and back felt like steel cables beneath her soft skin.

"I know," I whispered. "I hate that you're going, but I understand why you have to."

She looked up at me, her eyes a soft violet and shiny with tears. "Thank you." She swiped at her eyes and sniffed. "Google earth view won't work." She pointed to a map of Romania on her screen.

"Let me see." I leaned over her shoulder and tapped a few keys on her keyboard then guided the cursor to her program files. "Your browser's old. Really old. Your whole operating system needs to be updated."

"Can you do that?"

I snorted. "I'm a geek, that's what I do."

She stood and motioned for me to take the chair.

I sank into it with a long sigh and went to work. In a few minutes, a blue progress bar crawled across the screen.

"It's going to take about an hour to update everything." I leaned back in the chair.

Jane cupped her hands around my face and leaned close. "I know how we can pass the time." She pressed her mouth against mine, her moist lips parted and her tongue licked my lips.

A wave of desire filled the deep hollow of sadness and fear that had opened in me ever since Jane told me she was leaving. Our lips separated for only a second as I stood and wrapped my arms around her. She pushed her body against me, beneath her thin tank top, her nipples poked my chest.

"My room," she murmured.

I thought the zipper on my jeans would burst from the strain before we made our way from the lab to her bedroom next door. Jane reached under my T-shirt; her fingers threaded through my chest hair. I yanked the shirt over my head and tossed it. She raised her arms and I peeled her tank top up and over her head. Cupping her breast in one hand, my other slid down the smooth curve of her back and my fingertips glided under the waistband of her shorts.

We were both breathing hard, our arms and legs tangled by the time we reached the bed and collapsed across it. She rose up on her knees, straddled me and unzipped my jeans while I tugged on her shorts. For a fleeting moment I remembered I was a virgin, then my body took over and shut off all thoughts. Transformation had gifted me with enhanced senses and now a powerful instinct overwhelmed me. I kicked my jeans from my ankles, pulled Jane down onto the bed and rolled on top of her.

My heart beat loud as Jane arched her hips upward and I slid in between her perfect tan thighs. Her heart pounded in her chest and synched with the beat of my own until I couldn't tell which was which. I heard the blood rushing through our veins–a white-hot liquid that increased all sensitivity. My body vibrated with the overload of sensations. Jane's blood scent filled my nostrils with the sweet aromas of roses and smoky chocolate. An aura of light had enveloped us, the same intense violet as Jane's eyes.

Time suspended or so it felt, and our bodies rose from the bed, cradled inside the violet cloud. We hovered above the bed and nothing mattered but the exquisite friction of moving in perfect rhythm. I had found my holy grail and the delicious sensations of sliding in and out of her sent electric ripples through me, each jolt more intense than the last. Her silky legs skimmed the backs of my thighs and her taut calf muscles drew me into her deeper. Jane's fingernails pressed into my back along with the pressure of her teeth on my chest and neck. We hungrily nipped at each, drawing tiny drops of blood. The taste of Jane's, indescribable. The tiny wounds healed instantly, and we nibbled at each other some more.

Jane moaned and shuddered in my arms. I released an instant later. Groaning, I rolled in the air, pulled her on top of me and held her. I never wanted to let her go.

I nuzzled into the soft waves of her hair that flowed over my face and shoulders. Her scent so strong now, it made me dizzy with pleasure. Combing her hair aside with my fingers, I looked into her eyes, deep purple and half shielded by a fringe of long blonde lashes. I savored every inch of her.

I kissed her, slower this time, my tongue sliding over hers as I ran my hands down her slender back, marveling at how she could feel so soft and firm at the same time. Her body spasmed and she gasped sending a puff of warm breath into my open mouth. The thrill of my touch making Jane squirm against me made me smile.

Virgin Tim was gone forever.

We floated over the bed, our arms and legs still entwined. It took several minutes before my body touched the mattress. Once it did, it felt so heavy and exhausted I couldn't move. Jane lay beside me, smiling.

"Sex is a little different when you're a vampire," she said. "You'll get used to it."

It took me several moments to find my voice and then all I could do was whisper, "Yeah."

Jane sat up and I struggled to follow her lead. I swung my legs over the side of the bed and gasped when something sharp bit into my calf. "Ouch! Dammit."

She rounded the bed and picked up a wicked-looking machete. "Oh, sorry."

As I stared at the bleeding gash in my leg, I mentally calculated how many stitches it would need. Yet as I watched, the blood flow slowed, and the flesh sealed together. "Look. It-It healed."

"More proof of the strength of your blood."

I wiped the blood from my leg and then on instinct raised my fingers to my mouth.

"No." Jane leaned and sucked the blood from my finger. "It's bad luck to drink your own blood."

I laughed at her sheepish smile. "So, the scientist is superstitious?"

She shrugged and licked her bottom lip. For a moment I sat hypnotized by her eyes. "Um, why do you keep a machete next to your bed?" Before she could respond, the answer punched me in the gut. "Uh, sorry. Never mind." After Jane's description of the night her adopted mother and sister were slaughtered by the Vasiles, it made perfect sense that she would keep a weapon close by for protection.

She picked up the machete and carefully wiped off the blade with a tissue, then she stood it upright in the slim space between her nightstand and bed.

"Why a machete? Wouldn't a thinner sword or a wooden stake pierce the heart easier?"

"You and your movies." She walked into the adjoining bathroom and emerged carrying two towels. "Let's go for a swim."

I grinned. "Skinny dipping?"

"Would you prefer I put on a swimsuit?"

"Nope." I followed her through the French doors and onto the pool deck.

We swam laps together and steam rose from the water. The intense heat in my veins gradually subsided. After five laps, I felt normal again—or at least, normal for a vampire.

Jane floated on her back, her wet, tan skin glistening in the moonlight. "Driving a sword or a stake through anyone's heart would kill them, human or vampire. But the Vasiles are evolved. They move very quickly. Their flesh is hardened and heals instantaneously. It would be too difficult to aim and plunge a weapon directly into their hearts." Her lips twitched, forming a fleeting but humorless smile. "The most effective way to kill them is to hack off their heads. Their necks are their most vulnerable target. The blood in the jugular keeps the flesh softer there. Hence, the machete."

It saddened me to realize how much thought Jane had put into killing these monsters, though I couldn't blame her. "Makes sense," I said.

We emerged from the pool and Jane handed me a towel. I blotted my face and wrapped it around my waist. She pulled hers around her back and tucked the ends in front, securing it across her breasts.

The water and the cool night breeze had cooled my veins and after hovering in the air making love, I was acutely aware of gravity. Reality had vanished while I made love to Jane, but now her revelations about her niece and her upcoming trip to Romania weighed on my mind like an iron anchor. All of my fears from earlier in the evening returned with a vengeance.

As if she could read my mind, Jane squeezed my hand. "It'll be all right, Tim." She flashed a smile and her eyes lit with an aquamarine light. "C'mon, I want to show you something."

I followed her to the opposite edge of the patio. She pulled out a long wooden kiva ladder that was lying on its side, tucked against the wall. I carried the ladder and she directed me to set it upright at the wall next to the doors leading to my room.

"What's the ladder for?"

She didn't answer and climbed the ladder. Of course, I followed.

When I reached the top of the ladder, I discovered the tiled terra-cotta roof contained a flat section. Jane stood in the moonlight and unwrapped her towel. She spread it on the flat rubbery roof, stretched her arms above her head and then settled down on the towel. I placed my towel next to hers and lay beside her.

She reached over and grasped my hand. "I used to come up here when I was a kid. I tried to coax Isabelle to join me, but she was scared of heights. So, this became my private hideaway. Isn't it beautiful?"

The sky stretched overhead for as far as I could see—an indigo canopy strewn with glittery clusters of stars. My own fear of heights, a far off memory. "Yes, it is."

I turned on my side and propped my head on my elbow. As amazing as the sky looked, my gaze was drawn downward to Jane. I ran my fingers though her silky hair. She moved closer and snuggled her face against my chest. I cherished each warm breath on my skin.

We lay in silence, caressing each other. Though I didn't speak, my thoughts thundered. Please don't go. Stay here with me. Even as the desperate chant repeated in my mind, I knew it was hopeless. Then it changed—let me go with you. I'll keep you safe. How would I survive not knowing if Jane were in danger? Or dead? The helplessness would drive me insane.

"We'd better go check on the computer and then get some rest. I have a lot of preparations to do tomorrow." Jane pulled away from me, her silky hair glided between my fingers as she sat up.

The next day was a blur. Jane had left the house before I awoke. A note in the kitchen said she'd gone to run errands and would be back soon. I wanted to spend every minute with Jane until she left, yet as soon as we had climbed down from the roof last night, Jane acted as if an invisible wall had formed between us. She avoided my embraces and after printing a map from her updated computer, she had excused herself and hurried off to her room. My vision of sleeping with her cradled in my arms evaporated when her bedroom door shut, and the lock clicked.

With Jane gone, I wandered about the house, my insides twisting with growing apprehension. I punched a wall and immediately regretted the action. I'd forgotten my strength, so now I had a hole to repair. I finally showered, dressed, and checked my email to stay busy while I waited for her to return. There were three urgent messages from Rudi at Create-A-Vision. She asked if I had received the latest artwork samples she'd sent and if I had chosen one yet.

My video game was the farthest thing from my mind. I typed a curt reply but stopped myself before hitting the send button. After I paced my room and collected my thoughts, I re-typed a polite message telling Rudi the artwork was great and could I please have a bit more time to decide. The truth—all of the new artwork sucked and all I cared about at the moment was Jane.

I had no sooner sent the email, when I heard the front door open.

I ran down the hall and found Jane in the foyer with an arm load of plastic grocery bags. I gathered them from her and plunked them down on the kitchen table.

"You bought groceries? So, you decided not to go?"

Her eyes flickered green. "I'm still going. I wanted to stock the fridge for you."

"That was stupid. Wasting time food shopping on our last . . . I can take care of myself." I didn't intend to bark at her, but I did.

"I can take care of myself, too." She turned, stomped from the kitchen and down the hall.

"Jane!" I caught up to her before she turned the corner toward her bedroom. Standing in front of her, I gripped her shoulders. "I'm sorry. I wanted to spend today with you. Thanks, um, for the food."

"I also paid the utilities for a month and then stopped at the bank. I withdrew some cash, got my passport from my safety deposit box. And I—."

"Jane. Stop."

". . . had the oil checked and filled the gas tank so I don't have to stop on the way to the airport."

"Stop. Breathe." I pulled her close to me. "I'm driving you to the airport."

"No, I—"

"*Yes*. I am."

She sighed and the tightness in her shoulders relaxed. "Okay."

Though we spent the remainder of the day at the house, tension invaded our time together like an unwanted guest. I sat on the edge of Jane's bed while she packed a pair of jeans, some underwear and a few T-shirts into a worn leather backpack.

"That's all you're taking?" I asked.

"I won't be there long. In and out, that's the plan."

"What about blood? You'll need a donor."

"I'll hide a plastic vial or two on me. It shouldn't set off any alarms going though security."

"Did you pack a gun?"

Jane smirked at me. "That might pose a problem at the airport."

"But how will you defend yourself?"

She picked up the machete and grinned. "I'll carry this on my shoulder and stroll through the security check. Nobody will notice, right?"

I blew out a long breath and glared down at the floor. "I want you to have protection."

"Don't worry. Cristina has weapons, if I even need them." She held the machete in two hands and offered it to me. "I'd like you to have this. Practice using it. Keep it with you, next to your bed at night."

I looked into her eyes. Her blazing blue irises had softened to violet. I took the machete. "I'll hold onto it. Just until you get back."

Later that afternoon, Jane sat at her computer and studied the

Transylvanian landscape on Google Earth. I hovered over her shoulder memorizing every detail of the sparsely populated country road and the fieldstone wall surrounding the modest building that housed the orphanage. Were it not for the dire circumstances, the lush greenery and purplish mountain vista visible in the background would have been beautiful.

She shut down the computer and busied herself tiding up the lab and moving some experimental blood samples from the small refrigerator into the freezer while I paced around the room.

"The red cells will keep in the refrigerator for about forty days. The plasma samples I'll freeze. Should be good for one year," she said.

"A year? What the fuck? You said you'd be gone a week, two at most."

"Calm down. I don't plan on being gone *a year*. The plasma is Aldon's. It's too precious to take any chances with."

I fidgeted with a plastic bag lying next to her purse on one of the tables. An airline pass slid out. "Hey! This is a one-way ticket." I flapped the paper next to Jane's ear as she crouched in front of the refrigerator. She stood and brushed the ticket away. "It's an open-ended reservation. I don't know exactly what day we'll be flying home or which airport for that matter. I didn't want to lose the flight by booking a date and then being delayed."

"What's this?"

Jane took the bag from my hands. "A cheap cell phone. A burner as they say. So, I can call Cristina and not be traced."

"Shit. I hate all this. Please, Jane, you've *got* to let me go with you."

She chewed on her bottom lip a minute, her eye color shielded by half-closed lids and long golden lashes. I expected them to fly open any moment and reveal two green lasers aimed at my head.

"Do you have a current passport?" Her tone was calm, her eyes sea blue.

"Huh?"

"You'll need a passport to travel to Romania."

"Well, no. But . . . I'll get one. Today. Now."

"It takes at least a month for a new application to process." She wrapped her arms around my waist, the first real embrace we'd had since last night. "Tim, I *need* you here. I called Cristina earlier. She confirmed the Vasiles are leaving tomorrow to travel to the States. There should be only one guard at the orphanage. It's very isolated, rural. You saw the place on Google Earth. Whenever a Pure is on guard in the countryside, he'll force Cristina to give him blood. But they never drink enough to kill her, just enough to keep her weak and easy to control. She's going to take sleeping pills.

I can handle one sleepy guard. I'm more worried about you and The Haven. Cristina said they're sending nine of their strongest here. I'm depending on you to lead the Haven guards and destroy all nine Vasiles. If you don't, they'll slaughter everyone at The Haven. And kill you, too. I-I couldn't stand it if anything happened." She swiped at her eyes and cleared her throat. "Then when I return, they'd kill me and take Emilia back. If you don't stay here, my trip to rescue her will all be for nothing."

I held her tight against me. There was nothing to say.

We left for LAX at four the following morning. Jane's flight was at six-thirty.

She babbled non-stop the entire drive, reminding me to get blood from Echo so I don't vamp out again, to work out in the gym, to stay hydrated, to practice with the machete and to take lead of The Haven guards when the Vasiles arrived. "Aim for their necks. Don't hesitate. They won't." she said.

I listened, yet hoped for an epic L.A. traffic jam, or an earthquake, or perhaps a pissed-off Godzilla could pop out of the Pacific and annihilate the airport with his big scaly feet—any apocalyptic event to prevent Jane from leaving would be welcomed.

Instead, the traffic on the freeway sped along at seventy-plus miles per hour. No delays. We made the trip in record time.

I walked her as far as I could before the security checks stopped me from going any farther.

"There's my gate." She bolted toward it.

I ran and caught her in my arms, blocking her from entering the gate. She looked up at me with teary, dark blue eyes. "I-I can't. I hate goodbyes."

I tilted her chin and leaned to kiss her, drawing her to me so tight, she murmured, "You're hurting me."

I loosened my grip. "Sorry."

"It's okay." She touched my cheek and then traced her forefinger over my lips. She smiled, but her indigo eyes remained sad. "I'll be back before you know it."

My heart quaked inside my chest. Jane was scared. I was terrified. But I couldn't let her see my fear. I smiled. "I'll pick you and Emilia up here next week. Call me. Every day. Promise me."

"I will, whenever I can. I promise." Jane wiggled free of my grasp and strode off to her gate. She glanced over her shoulder and waved.

"I love you." My words were obliviated by the bellow of an announcement over the intercom. Jane turned and put her backpack on the conveyor belt, then walked through the metal detector.

In the parking lot, I sat on the hood of my car and watched until the plane took off. I imagined a long rope, one end tied to the plane and the other around my heart. The rope cut into my heart with a burning pain as the plane rose higher, until it ripped my heart clean out of my chest. It dangled in the air, raw and bloody, attached to the silvery speck with blinking lights that vanished into the black sky.

Chapter 14

For every complex problem there is an answer that is clear, simple, and wrong. —H. L. Mencken

The sun rose and even the faint first rays heated my sensitive skin. I climbed into my car and applied the sunscreen lotion I kept in the glove compartment and then donned my polarized sunglasses. My thoughts ran like a flip book through my head as I drove. Jane was ten thousand feet in the air on her way to Romania. That fact hadn't completely sunk into my brain yet. I buried the fear I might never see her again and tried to focus instead on the list of the tasks I needed to do while she was away—take care of the house, work on my video game to perfect it for release, go to The Haven and join the guards—and, oh yeah—behead nine members of the evil Vasile vampire clan. Could I actually bring myself to kill someone? Waving the machete around in the house pretending to attack invisible invaders was one thing, but to slice someone's head from their body . . . What the hell had I gotten myself into?

My focus blurred and I stomped on the brakes to avoid smashing into the van ahead of me that suddenly slowed on the freeway. The epic traffic jam I had wished for earlier had arrived. Vehicles inched along and I felt queasy from the glaring sun and the lurching motion of the car as I hit my brakes every few minutes. I turned off the freeway at the first exit I came to. Though I had no idea where I was, an innate sense of direction guided me northeast along less congested roads. I let my instincts steer the car.

As I made a right turn, a sudden whoop startled me. Red and blue lights flashed in my rearview mirror.

"Shit. Just what I need." I slowed and pulled over on the wide shoulder. The police cruiser parked behind me.

I lowered the window as the cop approached. Trim and blonde, he sported a manicured mustache and dark aviator-style sunglasses.

"Good morning," he said.

"Good morning, Officer." I saw clearly through my own dark lenses and his. His eyes were blue and studied me cautiously, but without malice. He smelled of aftershave and I detected an odor of coffee with coconut undertones on his breath. His uniform shirt looked fresh, creases sharp, as though he had just started his shift.

"You made a right on red at the intersection."

"Yes?"

"There's a sign posted. No right on red allowed."

"Ah, sorry. I didn't see the sign."

He nodded. "May I see your license, insurance, and registration?"

"Sure." I reached overhead to the visor for the registration and then slid my wallet from my back pocket. I removed my license and insurance card and handed it all through the open window.

"You're in a hurry. Late for work?" he asked.

"No, sir. I just dropped my girlfriend off at the airport. I-I was preoccupied."

He smiled and then pushed his sunglasses up and stared at my license. With the sunglasses still on his forehead, he cocked his head and squinted at me. "Please remove your glasses, sir," he said.

I braced for the sun's assault on my eyes, but the cop's body offered shade.

"How old is this picture?" He waved my license at me.

"Um, two years, I think."

"Well, it sure doesn't look like you. I'll be right back. Stay here."

I put my sunglasses back on and waited while he went to his car. I squirmed and sat up to escape the sun beating through my windshield onto my face. The scent of his aftershave preceded his return.

"Well, Timothy, everything checks out, but you need to update your photo."

"Yes, sir. I'll do that."

"I'll forego issuing you a ticket. Consider it a verbal warning about the turn on red, but I'm going to follow you over to the DMV office and make sure you get your license updated. Understood?"

"Yes, officer. Um, thank you."

"Okay then," he handed me back the documents. "Drive two blocks down this road, make a left at the light. The municipal center is half a block down on the right-hand side. I'll follow you."

"Okay." I studied the photo on my driver's license while he strolled back to his patrol car. I looked about fourteen in the picture. The camera flash had washed out all skin tone and the white glare on my eyeglasses partially hid my half-closed eyes. Every photograph of me contained one closed eye, or both eyes lost in lens-glare. I checked myself in the rear-view mirror. The cop was right. I didn't recognize the sickly kid in the photo either. I put the car in drive, made sure to flip on my blinker and slowly pulled out onto the road. I drove five miles under the speed limit until I arrived at the Department of Motor Vehicles. The cop who had tailed me the entire way parked next to me.

I waved and he saluted me with a paper coffee cup as I walked past his car toward the double glass doors.

"Crap." Inside, lines of people stretched from the main counter to the lobby. I turned and peered out the glass doors. The cruiser was still parked next to my Camry. Apparently, he was going to wait.

Sighing, I scanned the overhead signs and stepped into the line marked *Drivers Licenses*. Jane had a fifteen-hour flight and I didn't expect a phone call from her until nine o'clock tonight when she landed. From the looks of the crowded office, I'd still be standing in line when she called.

When I finally got to the window, a middle-aged woman with a perpetual frown looked at my license, reached under the counter and handed me a form.

Her voice sounded gravelly and her breath smelled of cigarettes. "Fill this out. Be sure to include any changes in your address, et cetera. The line for photos is over there." She pointed with one hand and summoned the next person in line with the other.

"Great, another line." The photo area had a number machine and seats. I ripped number thirty-nine from the paper spool and then sat down and filled out the form. I hesitated for a moment but decided to write Jane's address. If I got stopped again, I didn't want anything going to my parent's home in the mail.

A young redheaded woman called my number. She smiled at me as she took the form and my old license.

"Wow, you've really changed," she said.

"Yeah." I sat in front of a blue backdrop while she pressed a button on a digital camera mounted on a tripod. She stood smiling at me while she waited for the photo to emerge from a printer. She held it up for my approval.

Though I knew the pasty geek in the old photo didn't look like me anymore, the contrast with my new photo was startling. The new picture showed long wavy hair, a beard stubble and—the biggest difference—no glaring eyeglasses, just two fully-opened dark brown eyes. No wonder the cop questioned my identity. I questioned it as well.

I looked up at the young girl who stood watching me, biting her bottom lip. "Like it?" she asked.

"Yeah. Looks okay. Thanks." I said.

"Looks *great.*" The clerk giggled and her cheeks flushed deep pink. "Give me a few minutes and I'll have your new license ready. You can pay over there." She handed me the form with a slip of paper stapled to it and motioned to a cashier near a grouping of plastic chairs by a second set of glass exit doors.

Perched in a hard plastic chair, I skimmed my phone for any messages. Seeing none, I searched the internet and found a website that followed airline flights. I tapped in Jane's flight number and waited. A screen popped up with a short message, *in route and on time.*

"Here you go."

I looked up and saw the same blushing redhead holding my new license card.

"Thank you." I reached and took the card. She held onto the other end.

"Um, I noticed your address. I live pretty close to there, on Alto Drive."

"Oh, okay." I didn't understand why she didn't let go of the card and didn't know what to say.

"There's a club near there called Jaspers. I go there most Saturday nights. Maybe I could meet you there this Saturday?"

I stared at her and the pink in her cheeks deepened. She was hitting on me. Though I had no interest in meeting her at a club, I was flattered and didn't want to hurt her feelings. "Um, yeah, sure. Thanks." My new physical appearance hadn't untied my tongue.

"Great." She smiled and released the card. "I'll see you there, then."

"Yeah, right. See you."

As I exited the Motor Vehicles office, the cop stepped out of his cruiser. I stopped and held out my new license.

He took it and studied it. "This is a new address, isn't it?"

"Yes. I moved a couple of months ago."

"Another reason you needed to get your license updated." He handed it back to me. "Drive safely now."

Chapter 15

"Everyone has talent. What's rare is the courage to follow it to the dark places where it leads."
—Erica Jong

My brain churned with disjointed thoughts as I drove. I felt antsy, out-of-sorts. I hadn't slept the night before and the long drive to the airport and saying goodbye to Jane had stressed me, to say the least. The cop and the forced two-hour detour through Motor Vehicles had only added to my stress. I was dehydrated and pissed that I hadn't thought to bring a bottle of water with me. My sunglasses offered minimal relief from the sunlight glaring on the windshield. I hadn't spent this much time in daylight since before my transformation. Though the AC was turned up to max, I felt like a bug roasting under a magnifying glass. I really needed to look into getting my car windows tinted.

My cell phone rang and startled me. Jane? I grabbed the phone and tapped the screen. "Hello?"

"Your suit is ready."

"Excuse me? Who is this?"

"Boulevard Dry Cleaners. Your suit is ready for pick up."

"Oh. Okay. Thank—"

The line went dead. I tossed the phone onto the passenger seat and checked my surroundings as I pulled up to a red light. Unless my new innate sense of direction was mistaken, the dry cleaners should be to the north. I nosed my car into the turn lane. The white SUV I edged in front of honked but allowed me to cut in and make the left turn.

Sure enough, six blocks later I recognized the shopping plaza where I had purchased my new clothes. I parked as close as possible to the cleaners and jogged inside to minimize my sun exposure.

The same woman who had taken the suit stood behind the counter.

"Hi. Name's Tim Gardener. I just got a call that the suit I dropped—"

"Yes. I call you. Wait a minute."

She wound her way through racks of plastic-covered clothing to the back of the store. Moments later, she emerged with the suit draped across her outstretched arms, carrying it like an offering. She laid it on the counter.

I lifted the plastic and inspected it. The yellow shirt and multi-colored tie were neatly arranged on a padded hanger with the suit coat over it. A second hanger held the slacks. Razor-sharp creases accentuated the purple sheen of the material. The combination of the cleaning and my improved vision intensified the colors. The vibrant yellow hurt my eyes. I flipped the hanger over and checked the back of the jacket. Though I could see the stitches that closed the slit up the back, they were minute and uniform. Best of all, the noxious stench of embalming fluid had been replaced by the odor of cleaning chemicals.

"Wow. You did a fantastic job."

The woman smiled, the first I had seen from her. She crossed her arms and nodded. "We do good work. Tell all your friends."

"I will. How much do I owe you?"

"Eighty-nine dollar." She held her hand out.

I paid her and collected the suit.

Despite my need to escape the sun, I felt too weak to run back to the car. The fifty-foot walk in the scorching heat proved torturous. I unlocked the trunk and stowed the box with the suit inside. She had charged me an extra ten dollars to box the suit. The stiff dry-cleaning bill left me short on cash, but it was worth it. They had restored the suit to all of its former gaudy glory. Now all I had to do was figure out a way to discreetly return it to James Samples' widow, Sarah. But that would have to wait until another day. At present, all I could focus on was getting inside the cool car, driving home and drinking vast amounts of water.

I guzzled three bottles of water while I basked in the chill of the open refrigerator door and then reached for a fourth bottle. My throat still felt parched. Carrying the bottle, I made my way to my room and sat on the edge of the bed. Jane's machete lay next to me in its leather sheath along with an envelope. She must have placed it there before we left this morning. Inside, I found a wad of cash and a note. My hands shook as I unfolded the paper. What had she written that she couldn't say to me in person?

Tim, carry the machete with you at all times. Never let your guard down. Use the cash for whatever you need. Make an appointment this Friday with Echo for blood, you need to stay sharp. Eat protein and stay hydrated. Jane

She included her burner cell number and Echo's email address, though I already had both stored in my cell phone.

I had hoped for a declaration of Jane's eternal love, or at least a page of her pining about how much she would miss me. Instead, her note read like a reminder list from my mother. The platonic tone added to my misery. I set the machete on the floor and tossed the cash on the nightstand. The effort made my head spin and I collapsed on the bed, relishing its softness. The heavy drapes on the sliding glass doors and window blocked the rays of the evil fireball in the sky. Dehydrated and weak, I gave in to my exhaustion and closed my eyes.

A noise woke me. I bolted upright and listened. Crickets chirped and then an owl hooted.

"Shit, what time is it?" I slid my phone from my back pocket—seven fifty-four. The fog of sleep addled my brain. I needed to do something tonight, but what? Running my hands through my hair, I closed my eyes and concentrated. Jane's call. Nine o'clock. And The Haven, tonight I was due to report for guard duty under Braedon's leadership.

I drained the remaining water from an open bottle I had left on the nightstand. My heartbeat drummed, slowed and then drummed again. My ears rang and my tongue stuck to the roof of my mouth. Making my way to the kitchen, I grabbed another two bottles of water from the fridge and twisted them open. The more I drank, the more I wanted.

Back in my room, my leg muscles quivered. I sank into my desk chair, turned on my laptop and went to the same website I had used earlier to check on Jane's flight. The notation read: *On schedule. Landing in forty-two minutes.*

I sucked in water and deep breaths. What the hell was wrong with me? If I drank any more water, I'd drown. I checked my email to take my mind off my wobbly legs and pounding heart. My inbox held new messages from Rudi. The attachments offered more sample artwork. Her last email asked if I had chosen an artist from the new batch to draw the characters for my video game.

"No and I don't freaking care." I slammed the lid of the laptop, crossed the room and stretched out on the bed, cell phone in hand. I wasn't sleepy but sitting up proved too strenuous and now all my muscles trembled. How the hell was I supposed to manage guard duty tonight? But I had to—I'd promised Jane.

I rolled on my side and placed the phone next to my face. Waiting for Jane's call frazzled my raw nerves and my heart rate increased with each passing minute. By nine-ten, my heart sounded like a jack hammer. Had Jane been intercepted by the Vasiles at the airport? Was she even alive?

The phone rang and, in my frenzy to answer, it slipped from my shaking hands and hit the floor.

"Jane. Jane!" I dove onto the floor and gripped the phone with both hands. "Hello?"

"Tim, hi. You sound stressed. Are you all right?"

The sound of her voice crashed over me like a wave of relief. I struggled to form a coherent sentence, but my jumbled thoughts rushed out, "Yeah, what you? Late. So worried. You said nine. Everything okay? Where you. Are you?"

"Calm down. I'm fine. I'm in a cab heading for a B and B. Cristina called while I was at the airport. She said the guards are still at the orphanage. I'm going to stay near the city today and contact her tonight."

"But, safe, right?"

"Yes, Tim. I'm safe. You sound—"

"I know. Heart. Racing. All day the sun. Cop stopped—Motor Vehicles, dry cleaners. Have to go to The Haven. Guard duty. So thirsty, I—"

"Tim. Stop talking and listen to me. I think you're vamping out. You need to go to The Haven—for blood. Contact Echo, have her meet you there. I wrote her email in the note I left."

"Not been week since. . ."

"I know, but stress can cause the craving to start sooner. Tell me how you're feeling."

"Heart pounding. Shaky. Ears whistling. So thirsty."

"Are you drinking pomegranate juice?"

"No. Water. Lots."

"Go into the kitchen. Now. Drink some juice."

"B-But I wanted talk you—"

"We can talk while you walk to the kitchen."

"Uh, yeah." I pushed to my knees and gripped the bedpost to pull myself upright. "Y-You talk. I . . . listen." I stumbled toward the kitchen holding the walls for support.

"Stay calm. The juice will help. Then drive to The Haven, carefully. You'll be fine once you get some blood."

"Miss you."

Jane didn't respond. Noises on the other end of the line.

"Jane? What's . . . noises?"

"Hang on a second, Tim. Here you go. Thank you." A car door slammed.

"Jane?"

"I'm fine. I was getting out of the cab. I'm at the bed and breakfast. Are you in the kitchen yet?"

"Yeah. Got juice. Sitting down." I took a long drink. "Drinking."

"You're going to be fine. Remember the last time? Just stay calm and get to The Haven."

I guzzled half the bottle. "I'm sorry."

Jane laughed and I pictured the sparkle in her sea-blue eyes. "Sorry for what?"

"Feel stupid. Should have known I needed blood. I need to be strong. I let you down."

"No, you haven't let me down. Just take care of yourself. Please."

"Where exactly are you? Is it a safe place?"

"Yes, it's safe. I'm about a half an hour from downtown Bucharest. The bed and breakfast is called Villa 11. Very Old World and charming. It's morning here, just after seven, but not very sunny yet. I'm going to check in and get some rest. I couldn't sleep on the plane."

I found a pad and pen in one of the kitchen drawers and scrawled down the name of the place. "As long as you're safe there. Call me. I don't care what time, just call. Promise?"

"I promise. Do you feel any better?"

"Yes, I do. Thanks." My heart rate had calmed, and my thoughts weren't as splintered.

"I'll call you after I talk to Cristina and we have a plan in place. Get to The Haven while you're feeling well enough, don't wait. And don't worry about guard duty if you're not up to it."

"I'll join the guards. I won't disappoint you. Jane, please be careful."

"I will. And you, too. Good night."

Pulling into the The Haven's parking lot felt akin to crossing a twenty-mile marathon finish line. The short drive had demanded every ounce of my energy and focus. My hands shook as I took another long swig from the bottle of pomegranate juice I'd brought along for the ride. The sweet liquid should give me enough strength to walk around the corner to the entrance. I put the bottle on the floor next to the long-bladed machete and gave silent thanks a cop hadn't pulled me over tonight.

Wynn opened The Haven's front door and greeted me with a smile. I nodded and brushed past him searching the downstairs tables for Echo's pale-pinkish hair. I checked my phone. I had emailed her before I left the house, but she hadn't replied. She said she only came on Friday and Saturday nights and tonight was Tuesday.

The sugar kick from the juice was wearing off. I couldn't wait for Echo. I limped toward the nearest table prepared to beg one of the young women sitting there to donate some of their blood.

I was only steps away from the table, when Velvet intercepted me. She reeked of rum and clung to my jacket to steady herself. "Hi, handsome. What are you doing here?"

"Need a donor. Fast. I'm vamping."

The urgency in my voice must have penetrated her drunken stupor. She straightened her shoulders and slid her arm around my waist. "I'll help you," she said.

I followed her to the foot of the stairs and then stopped. "Wait. What about Braedon?" Velvet was his exclusive donor, and probably his lover as well.

Velvet shrugged. "Relax. He won't be here for another hour."

"You sure?"

"Positive. C'mon, you need blood."

Upstairs, I allowed Velvet to lead me down the long hall until she located a vacant room. I staggered inside and sat on the sofa while she placed the red ribbon around the doorknob and closed the door.

"Wow, look at you. You really are dry." She dumped the contents of her small fanny pack onto the coffee table. A black leather pouch concealed alcohol swabs and a cardboard-wrapped razor blade. She wasn't organized or methodical like Echo, but I wasn't in any condition to complain.

She pulled the wide strap of her scarlet tank top down and swabbed her shoulder. "I have to hide the cut from Braedon."

I nodded, mesmerized as the silvery blade nicked her creamy skin and released a precious ruby drizzle. She knelt on the sofa, her knees straddling my legs, and pressed her bleeding shoulder to my mouth.

Her blood tasted of rum and cola, syrupy and sickeningly sweet. I gagged on the first sip, but I needed blood and forced myself to drink.

Velvet snuggled closer in my lap with her head nestled on my shoulder. A vision of Braedon bursting into the room and killing me in a jealous rage came to the forefront of my fractured thoughts, yet the deep urge for blood made me continue to drink.

Velvet didn't pull away or tell me to stop as Echo had and I probably drank too much. Her alcohol-laced blood raced through my body like a hot flame, my veins its wick. I felt instantly intoxicated and dizzy.

I leaned my head back on the sofa and closed my eyes, hoping the sudden drunkenness would dissipate as quickly as it started.

Velvet's voice sounded far away, a whisper. "My turn." The cold steel on my arm broke my blood-glutted haze. My eyelids flew open. Velvet hunched forward, her lips hovering inches above the cut she had made on my forearm.

"No!" I pushed her back and held my bleeding arm away from her reach. "What are you doing?"

"Let me drink!" She wriggled from my grasp and lunged for my arm. "I need it."

I blocked her with my uncut arm. "You can't. It's against the rules."

"Screw the rules. I want to be transformed."

"No." My strength returned, and the alcohol daze faded. I lifted her small frame up as I stood, then turned and deposited her on the sofa.

She jumped up and unzipped her short skirt. The silky black material slid down her legs and pooled around her ankles revealing the lacy red thong she wore beneath. Hugging her arms around my waist, she begged, "I'll let you do whatever you want—if—you let me drink your blood."

She gyrated her hips against me.

"Velvet, stop it. I can't. I won't." I gripped her by her shoulders and pushed her away.

Her face twisted with rage and she screeched at me, "I thought *you* of all people would understand. *You* used to be a mundane. You remember what it's like to want to be a vampire, don't you? Don't you!"

"Shush! You'll have the whole club up here."

She flung herself at me and pummeled my chest with her fists. "If you don't give me some of your blood, I'll . . . I'll tell Braedon you raped me. He'll kill you."

"I won't let you drink my blood."

Her rage deflated, she crumpled to her knees and gripped my legs. "Please, I want to be transformed. Please." Her voice broke into sobs, hot tears soaked through my jeans.

"Velvet, you don't understand. Transformation is dangerous.

231

You could die. I nearly died. I would be dead if Ja—um, Raina hadn't found me."

She gripped my legs tighter, her fingers clawed at my calves, the layer of denim stopping her long nails from gouging my skin. "You've got to help me. My life sucks. I'm begging you. I need this. Transformation is all I've ever wanted. I want the life you have—Braedon has. He won't give me his blood. But I thought you were different. Why are you being so cruel?"

I waited until her sobs subsided and then gently lifted her to her feet and helped her onto the sofa. She sat glaring at me, tears streaming down her face. I tore open an alcohol swab and cleaned the cut on her shoulder, then took a Band-Aid from her leather pouch and covered the wound.

The nick on my forearm had healed and I wiped the dried blood away.

Velvet stood, stepped into her discarded skirt, yanked it up around her waist and zipped it. "I hate you. I should have let you vamp out."

"I'm sorry, Velvet. But I thank you for helping me tonight."

She stomped to the door and flung it open. She ripped the red ribbon from the knob, threw it at me and then ran down the hall. The ribbon fluttered to the floor by my feet.

I waited a few minutes before exiting the room. When I did, I nearly crashed into Aldon in the hallway.

"Ah, Lorcan. I'm glad you're here. I've told Braedon you will be joining the guards tonight."

"I'm sure he's thrilled."

Aldon let out a dry laugh. "I gave him an order. I don't care if he's thrilled or not. I know you'll make an excellent guard." He squeezed my shoulder, his grip incredibly strong for a man his age. "Any man who dares to drink the blood of his archrival's lover must be extremely courageous. Or extremely foolish."

He smiled, though his eyes held a humorless glaze as he walked past me to the balcony and settled into a chair at his usual corner table.

I hurried downstairs, equally grateful and nervous that Velvet was nowhere to be found. I walked to the bar and leaned my back against it while I waited for Tristan to finish serving two female donors. I kept a close watch on the front door in case Velvet made good on her threat. If she had called Braedon, at least I would see him coming.

"I suppose you want the *usual*?"

I turned and faced a scowling Tristan.

"Just pomegranate juice, no vodka."

He poured the juice into a tall glass and slammed it down on the bar. Red liquid sloshed over the sides of the glass and puddled on the bar top.

"Is there a problem?"

The usually cool Tristan glowered at me, his voice trembled with anger, "How could you let Jane go? It's a damned suicide mission."

I swallowed hard. His words hit my gut like a ball of ice. "I couldn't stop her."

He snorted. "If you truly loved her, you would have stopped her."

The chill in my stomach flared into a fiery rage. In a flash, I had Tristan's necktie wound around my fist. His face flushed a fierce red from the pressure on his throat. I leaned across the bar. "You're supposed to be her best friend. Why didn't *you* stop her?"

His eyes closed and his shoulders slumped. He shook his head and sputtered, "I-I tried."

I released my grip and glared into his eyes. "So did I."

He rolled his head from side to side and then straightened his tie. The red slowly drained from his face. "I'm just . . . I'm terrified that she'll be killed."

"I am, too."

He drew in a strained breath and then walked to the other end of the bar.

Someone punched me in my back. I whirled around.

"Ready to start training, O Mighty Lorcan the Mundane?" Braedon chuckled at his lame joke.

I moved toward him so fast that the toes of my boots slammed into his. "Bring it."

For a fleeting instant his eyes widened, then they narrowed to slits. "I will. Follow me."

233

He swaggered toward the stairs.

Chapter 16

The blood of the covenant is thicker than the water of the womb.
—Translation from an ancient Arabic proverb

I refused to trot upstairs like a trained puppy on a command from Braedon, so I turned back to the bar and drank my juice before going upstairs. When I arrived on the balcony, Braedon stood waiting next to a table of eight men. All were clad in long black leather coats identical to Braedon's—the official garb worn by The Haven guards. With Braedon and me, our number was ten. Jane warned that nine Vasile soldiers would be heading to the States. At least we had a slight advantage in our number.

The men gawked at me when I stopped at their table. I straightened my shoulders and held my head high. I sensed it bugged Braedon that I was taller. He puffed his chest out as if the extra girth compensated for the difference in our heights.

"Tonight, we have a pledge who wishes to join our ranks." Braedon paused for effect, though it was obvious he was talking about me. "Lorcan will take the test to see if he has what it takes to become one of us." The men smirked, and one, a wiry guy with a black Mohawk, let out a loud, derisive snort.

Aldon hadn't mentioned any tests. He made it sound like me becoming a guard was a done deal. What had I gotten myself into now?

Braedon gestured to two of the men. "Griffin, you and Vlad stay here, keep an eye on the club. Everyone else, up to the roof."

The six men and I fell in line behind Braedon. We marched down the long hallway, the flapping of leathers and stomping of boots a formidable sound. We exited through a metal door at the end of the hall, next to Aldon's private suite. A dim stairwell with stone stairs led up to the door of the rooftop entrance.

The fresh infusion of Velvet's blood coursed through my veins and warmed my muscles. I felt strong and full of pent-up energy that ached to be released. I was not only ready to fight, I looked forward to it. But if I wanted to succeed as a guard, I had to control my temper and not disrespect Braedon in front of his men. As I watched him swagger across the flat-top roof, it took all of my willpower not to punch the smug sonofabitch in his big mouth. Keeping a rein on my blood-induced cockiness was not going to be easy.

"Line up," Braedon shouted. The six guards scrambled to form a line next to the iron fence that bordered the roof. The scrolly wrought iron matched the building's ornate balconies but the long spiked tips on the upper rail gave me pause. Braedon held up his hand when I approached to join the line.

"Not you," he said.

I stood next to Braedon and faced the other men. The little guy with the Mohawk was first in line, followed by four average-sized men who were fit-looking, but otherwise nondescript. The last man stood at least a foot taller than the rest. His block-shaped body was as wide as a refrigerator and his bald head shone in the moonlight.

Braedon paced in front of his men as he spoke. "We've had attacks in the past by a group of mundanes we call Vans—after the fictional Van Helsing. These mundanes proclaim themselves to be vampire killers. Several of these cowards will stalk a lone vampire and then attack."

He walked over to a metal door on the side of the roof entrance, took a key ring from his pocket and unlocked a storage closet. Reaching inside, he withdrew a wooden spear about four feet long. One end had been chiseled to a sharp point.

"This is a handmade stake we confiscated from a Van. The point is sharp enough to pierce through flesh—and with enough pressure—bone."

The men snickered. I braced myself in case Braedon intended to try and drive the stake into me.

Instead, he held up the point in front of my face for me to inspect. Then he tossed it to Mohawk-guy. The short, wiry guard caught it and stood twirling it in one hand like a baton.

"Demon will play the part of the Van." Braedon motioned to

236

me. "Lorcan, your job is to disarm him. And not get impaled." The men standing in line behind me laughed.

Demon jogged to the middle of the roof and crouched in a fighting stance, stake poised and ready to strike. My senses kicked into overdrive. Smells of car exhaust, fast food, and perfumes wafted up from the street below and mingled with the odors from the men. I'd never noticed how men smelled before, but tonight I detected an earthy scent of worn leather mixed with a musky, animalistic smell.

The other five men heckled from the sidelines, scoffing at me, the mundane turned vampire. From their remarks, none believed I was worthy to join their legion. I blocked out their insults and focused on Demon, his energy so intense, the air around him took on a bluish haze and crackled with static electricity.

I had to prove myself. I charged at him.

The little guy was fast. He circled around and lunged the stake at me. The sharp tip missed impaling my side but snagged on my hoodie and tore a hole in the fabric. From the fierce glint in his dark eyes, I had no doubt Demon intended to jab the stake into me if given the chance. Maybe this was Braedon's plan—to have one of his guards kill me—or at the very least, wound me so I would fail the test.

My plan was to tire Demon out. I let him run at me and then dodged his strikes at the last moment. But I quickly lost count of his attacks and he showed no sign of slowing down. He circled as fast as a greyhound and then leaped at me, the point of stake aimed to pierce my chest. I grabbed the stake just above the pointed end, spun around and yanked.

While I had a firm hold on the sharp end of the spear, I also had Demon still hanging onto the other end. His feet kicked in the air a foot above the ground. The tiny bastard clung to the stick like a rabid pit bull.

Swinging the spear failed to dislodge him. I didn't want to waste my energy hoisting him around the open roof, so I moved toward the railing. I swung the spear up and outward until the blunt end extended over the railing—along with Demon.

He shrieked. His body dangled three stories above the parking lot. The terror on his face and his bloodless, clenched-knuckle hold on the stick told me he was weakening. The musky odor he emitted earlier turned to a sharp, acidic smell. Instinct told me it was the scent of fear. I rested my end of the stake on the railing and waited.

"Braedon, help!" Demon screamed. "I'm slipping."

Before Braedon could react, I whipped the spear upward and back over the roof. The sudden jolt launched Demon's legs higher in the air. His toe tangled in the top rail for an instant and slowed his momentum before he tumbled headfirst onto the rooftop. His somersault flung his long coat over his face and he landed on the roof top on his back.

I stood over him and held the point of stake against his heaving chest.

"Lorcan wins," Braedon shouted.

The smattering of applause from the other men surprised me. Demon glared at me as he climbed to his feet and straightened his clothing. He scurried back to the line.

Braedon took the spear and handed it to the next man, Styx. He had a more defensive fighting style, whipping the tail of his coat around him like a shield to deflect my advances. We grappled for a few minutes before I ripped the spear from his grasp and knocked him to the ground. The next three battles were even less dramatic and all ended quickly. I won them all. The other men's cheers grew louder with each win and blood pumped through my body like a shot of caffeine along with Jane's words, *you are the strongest*. She was right—as usual—and the heady realization empowered me. I was invincible.

Braedon handed the spear to the last guy—refrigerator man.

"Get 'im Bat!" Demon yelled and pumped his clenched fists in the air.

Braedon gave me a wicked grin. "His name's actually Batshit, as in how bat-shit-crazy he gets when he fights."

Bat and I faced off in the center of the roof. We stared at each other, his eyes intent but emotionless, his face a blank mask. My muscles tensed as I readied for his attack, yet my confidence wavered. Bat was an intimidating sight.

I doubted a man so huge and bulky could move very fast, so my strategy was to make him chase me—except he didn't move. He just stood there gripping the spear with two hands, a silent dare as he waited for me to come and take it from him.

The other men jeered me.

"Fight!"

"What are you waiting for?"

"You scared of a bat, Lorcan?"

Throwing my strategy aside, I raced across the distance separating us and gripped the middle section of the spear with both hands. No matter how hard I yanked, it wouldn't budge from Bat's meaty fists. He held the stick out in front of him and used it to plow me backward. An instant later, I lay flat on my back. Bat leaned over me, his eyes shining red and his thick lips curled into a snarl. He aimed the spear at my throat. Fear kicked in and with it a heightened burst of adrenaline. I grabbed the spear's shaft and pushed upward until I created enough space between us to raise my knees. I planted the soles of my boots on Bat's broad chest and pushed with all my might.

He lost his balance and stumbled sideways, just long enough for me to roll away. As I jumped to my feet, my face collided with Bat's fist. My back hit the ground again—hard. His punch, like a clap of thunder, echoed in my ears. This time, Bat pinned me by pressing his massive boot on top of my chest. He drove the stake downward and stopped just as the point pricked the skin on my throat. I held my breath so it wouldn't pierce through.

"Bat wins!" Braedon yelled. The guards broke out into a raucous cheer.

The big man removed his cinder block of a foot from my chest.

I lay still, gasped in air and closed my eyes. Shit. I failed. I was so close. Jane was depending on me. How could I tell her I had failed the test?

"Hey? You all right?"

Opening my eyes, Bat resembled an oak tree looming over me, his arm extended downward like a thick branch and his hand open to help me up.

I grasped his hand and he pulled me to my feet with ease.

He grinned. Two gold-capped eye-teeth glinted in the moonlight.

"You've got good moves."

"Not good enough. I failed."

He frowned. "You won five out of six fights. You only have to win four to pass."

"So, I passed? I'm a guard?"

"Not so fast," Braedon said as he walked up to us. "You passed the first test, but we all agreed in order accept a mundane into our ranks, we needed a second test—to be sure." He grabbed the wooden stake from Bat and then stalked off toward the supply shed.

I turned to Bat. "What's the second test?"

Bat looked at me and shrugged his massive shoulders.

We followed the other men and gathered around Braedon. He handed out wooden practice swords from the storage shed. The swords were weighty, measured nearly three feet long, and had rounded, blunt tips.

When we were all armed, Braedon ordered his six guards to line up across the center of the roof. He and I stood at one end.

"You six are Pure Bloods armed with swords," Braedon shouted. "Lorcan must break through your line. A strike to the heart, neck, or head is fatal and you're out." He sauntered to the side of the mock battleground and leaned against the railing, his arms crossed across his chest. "I'll be the judge."

Great. Six against one—with Braedon as judge. I'm screwed.

"Start on my signal," Braedon said.

The men spread out, formed a semi-circle and brandished their swords. A breeze lifted their coats, the long tails billowing out behind them. The scene triggered a snippet of game code in my mind. I had designed a similar battle sequence in my video game, except with even more attackers. In the game, my protagonist and namesake, Lorcan, rushed through a sword-wielding mob, spinning and striking lethal blows as he went. If only I could . . .

"Go!" Braedon yelled.

The game code played in my head—run, dodge, slash, spin, stab. Visualizing the html code in my mind translated the motions to my body, the same as when applied to a wire-frame animation on a computer screen. My arms and legs automatically performed the actions dictated by the code.

"Styx! You're out," Braedon bellowed from the sidelines.

I spun around after my fatal hit on Styx and slashed two more men across their necks. Though the tip of the blunt wood surely hurt, it didn't draw blood.

"Kain and Crow! Out!" Braedon shouted.

Three more men faced me. Little Demon sprang at me. I ducked and blocked his sword strike with my arm and then swung around and jabbed my blade hard against his chest. The blow knocked the breath from him and he fell to the ground.

"Demon! You're out!"

I faced Bat and one other man. I knew better than to turn my back on Bat, after I had underestimated his agility and strength earlier. The other guy must have realized this and ran behind me, trapping me between the two of them.

I spun in a circle watching both men. Bat stood still but the smaller man lunged. New lines of code flashed through my brain. I jumped higher than I knew I was capable of and spun in mid-air with my sword arm extended. I had leaped over the sword of the man behind me and swiped my blade across both his neck and Bat's in one lightning-fast spin. I landed on my feet, crouched, and ready to attack.

"Renwick, out! Bat, you're out, too."

I straightened up to my full height. The men ambled around the roof mumbling, their arms hung at their sides in defeat with the tips of the wooden blades scraping across the fine layer of black gravel covering the rooftop.

Realization slowly washed over me. The second test was over. I had bested all six guards. Even more amazing, Braedon had been a fair judge.

He strode across the roof toward me.

Pumped from my win, I raised my sword and shouted, "I passed both tests!"

Breaking into a run, Braedon yanked Renwick's sword from his lax grip and charged at me. Of all of the guards, Braedon was the most aggressive and skilled. I stood my ground and blocked his sword strike with mine. The code streamed in my mind again, this time for a one-on-one sword fight. We battled back and forth across the entire rooftop, our wooden blades crashing together with deafening clacks.

Braedon was strong, but I was stronger. My confidence swelled. I could take him. But should I? Should I humiliate him in front of his guards, or let him win to save face? If I lost, I'd forfeit the test. I had come too far tonight to lose. Even more than that, I wanted to beat Braedon.

I grasped my sword with both hands and swung with all my strength. Braedon held his sword two-handed as well and blocked my swing with the long edge of his blade. My blade cracked in two. The longest piece flew over Braedon's head and clattered onto the ground.

Holding only a handle with a splintered shunt of wood, I was forced to turn from offense to defense. I jabbed when I could get close, then spun away and dodged Braedon's vicious counter thrusts.

As I ran past, several of the men held out their swords to me. Not knowing the rules, I hesitated to take one. I refused to give Braedon an excuse to disqualify me.

Then Braedon grabbed a second sword from Crow. So much for rules.

He chased me, the furious swipes of the two wooden blades so fast, air whistled past my ears.

I reached the iron fence and as I doubled back, the tip of Braedon's sword caught the pocket of my hoodie. The material strained against my body until a large swatch ripped away. I twisted free of the shredded cloth, ran and grabbed the sword Bat held out to me. Armed, I turned and raced at Braedon.

My first strike knocked the weapon from his left hand. My second scored a solid hit to the sword in his right. Locked in a test of strength, our two swords formed an X, the upper V of the two blades aligned with our necks. We each pushed toward the other's throat.

For a moment the swords held firm midway between us, then they moved in a slow, shaky arc toward Braedon's neck. His arms shook with his effort to push me away.

Out of earshot of the others, Braedon's voice was strained and hoarse. "Fucking mundane trash. If you win—I'll *never* make you a guard."

I grinned and pushed harder. "*When* I win, I won't be a guard. I'll be the new leader."

Braedon's eyes widened. He tried to knee me in the groin, but I twisted my lower body and his knee glanced off my hip. He wobbled to regain his stance and I pushed the swords to within an inch of trapping his neck between the two blades. The stench of his fear soured the air around us.

His words came out in a whisper, "Stop. I-I'll call a tie."

"And you'll allow me into the guards?"

"Y-Yes."

I pressed harder against Braedon's shaking sword. The veins in his neck and forehead bulged like purple rope beneath his skin as he strained to hold me back. One more push and I'd have him. "If you're lying, I'll crush your neck between these blades—in front of your men."

"I s-swear," he gasped.

"All right. On three, we both step back. Then you call the tie."

He nodded.

"One, two, three."

We each took a step back and lowered our swords.

"T-tie!" Braedon shouted.

In a blink we were swarmed by the other men. They yelled out our names and clapped us both on the back. My body vibrated from the combustive cocktail of fresh blood, adrenaline, and testosterone—the power of it all overwhelmed me. This was what victory felt like.

I relished every second of it.

The rest of the evening passed in a surreal haze. The eight of us clamored down the stairs from the roof and gathered around the big round table on the balcony. No longer the outsider, I took my place at the center of the elite guards. The others, minus Braedon, bought me drinks to celebrate my induction. They raised their glasses and shouted, "To Lorcan!"

Braedon sat hunched forward at Aldon's corner table. They spoke in hushed tones which even my enhanced hearing couldn't decipher, but I was well aware of the glances they threw my way.

Moments later, they both stood. Braedon hurried off down the hallway and Aldon approached our table. The rowdy guards around me fell silent. We all waited for him to speak.

"Lorcan, tonight you have proven yourself worthy to become one of The Haven guards. Stand. Make your vows in front of me and your fellow guards."

The others stood with me.

Aldon's stern eyes focused on mine. "Lorcan, do you vow to protect me, your fellow guards and all other beings under this roof with your life?"

"Yes, sir."

"Do you vow never to disclose your true nature as one of the Night Flock to anyone outside The Haven?"

"Yes."

"Do you vow never to join another circle or betray our clan?"

"Yes, I vow."

"And lastly, do you vow never to give your blood to a mundane?"

"Yes."

Aldon's voice filled the balcony like the low growl of a lion. "Lorcan, you have sworn in front of me and your fellow guards to uphold these rules. If you break any of these vows, you will face the ultimate punishment—death. Do you understand?"

"Yes, sir. I understand."

The old man's gaze never wavered. Did he notice my slight hesitation? I was a former mundane, transformed by blood. Only a few hours earlier Velvet had begged me to transform her. Had I given her my blood, or had she managed to trick me, I'd be facing death now instead of celebration.

Aldon raised his arm and Braedon walked toward us carrying a long black leather coat.

"You are now a Haven guard, Lorcan."

Bat tugged on the sleeve of my shredded gray hoodie and whispered, "Time for a new look, dude."

I shrugged off my tattered jacket and took a step toward Braedon. The amber glint in his eyes betrayed his seething hatred for me, but he dutifully held up the coat as I slid my arms into it.

Aldon presented me with a silver dagger. The long blade, honed razor sharp, shone bright even in the dim light of the club. An *H* was carved in the ornate handle and surrounded by a circle of small rubies. Aldon pointed to a leather sheath hidden inside the coat. Though I wanted to admire it longer, I slid the dagger into the sheath.

He clasped my shoulders, his former stern expression now resembling a kindly old man's with twinkling eyes. "Congratulations, son."

"Thank you, sir. I'm honored." The butter-soft leather of the coat molded to my body perfectly and the hem skimmed my calves. It didn't feel bulky or restrictive. I could picture myself fighting in it.

Aldon returned to his table while the rest of the guards cheered and ordered a fresh round of drinks.

The rounds of drinks finally slowed. The men, now relaxed, talked. Though elite vampire guards, they were also hybrid humans who lived and worked normal jobs in the mundane world.

Ironically, I took an immediate liking to the man I couldn't beat, Bat. Away from battle, he was a soft-spoken giant and a veterinarian. Judging from the plethora of photos on his cell phone that he shared with me, an avid cat lover as well. His eyes shone when he showed me photos of the five strays he had adopted.

Styx and Renwick both worked in retail sales, Vlad was an accountant, and Griffin worked at a bank. Demon owned a small motorcycle repair shop. Crow worked for him. Kain was a musician. He did odd jobs, but his passion was songwriting and playing guitar. He performed at local clubs when he wasn't guarding The Haven.

None of them were married. Demon bragged of his exploits with the *muns*, the term he used for female human donors. He pointed out some of his favorites seated on the first floor.

I learned an unofficial rule among the guards was to avoid each others' preferred donors. Some of their relationships went beyond drinking blood. In spite of this, donors never mingled with vampires on the balcony unless invited, which I also learned, was rare.

I slipped my cell phone from my pocket and checked it as I had about a dozen times before. Still no word from Jane. Worry gnawed deeper into my gut.

On the floor below us, I spotted Velvet as she exited from the rest room and zigzagged her way through a tangle of tables and chairs to the staircase. She stumbled more than once as she climbed the steps, but somehow made her way up to the balcony.

The guards' laughter stopped as she teetered past our table in her high-heeled boots.

My heart hiccupped. She headed straight toward Braedon. Was she going to make good on her threat? She could ruin everything I had fought so hard for tonight with her lie that I raped her. Even if she only told Braedon she had given me her blood, I could be expelled from the guards for my moment of weakness—providing Braedon didn't kill me first.

"Oh, man, that drunken *mun* is gonna get Braedon in deep shit," Demon said. The others nodded but kept their eyes focused downward on their drinks.

Turning to Bat, I asked, "Did Braedon invite her to the balcony?"

"Doubt it. Braedon can't control her. That pisses Aldon off."

I watched as she staggered over to Braedon. My body tensed. Do I run or fight for my life? Would my new-found friends turn on me and kill me?

Bat murmured in my ear. "She wasn't always like this. Velvet's always had a big heart. Worked in a kid's hospital. That's where she and Braedon met."

I choked on the sip I had taken. "Braedon's a doctor?" I couldn't imagine.

"Nah. He's head of maintenance there. Velvet was a nurse's aide."

"Was?"

"According to Braedon she's had a pretty rough life. Dad died when she was a little kid. Her mom became an alcoholic. Then her mom died when Velvet was in her teens. She took care of her mom till the end. She loved working with the kids at the hospital. And they loved her. She wanted to save them all, but some of them were pretty sick. When one died, she just lost it. Started drinking. Lost her job. Braedon let her move in with him."

I watched as Velvet flung her arms around Braedon's neck.

Either a show of affection or her wobbly legs gave out and she grabbed on to him to keep from falling. He stood and lifted her upright with one arm. I tuned out the noise of the guard's conversation and focused on Braedon's voice. "I'm sorry, sir," he said to Aldon.

Aldon didn't reply. He waved his hand for them to leave. Braedon hesitated for a moment while Velvet mumbled gibberish. Aldon stood up so quickly his chair rocked on its legs and nearly tipped. He shot Braedon an icy glare and then stalked off down the hallway and entered his suite.

My eyes met Velvet's for a second, but hers showed no recognition of me. Braedon propped her against the wall, holding her up as he talked quietly to her. I hoped she was too drunk to remember our blood tryst earlier—though I knew she would sober up eventually and possibly make good on her threat.

Braedon told her to never come up to the balcony, especially when he was with Aldon. He gently chastised her for drinking too much. There was no anger in his voice and his soft tone surprised me. I couldn't make any sense of Velvet's slurred responses.

I turned back to the conversation at my table as Braedon slipped his arms under Velvet's back and legs.

Velvet's head rested on his chest, her eyes closed, when he approached our table carrying her. "I'm taking her home." His usual bravado had vanished—he sounded tired, defeated. He cleared his throat. "The club's closing in twenty minutes. Make sure everyone gets to their cars and the place is locked up and secure." He turned to me. "Be here tomorrow night at ten. You'll work until closing." He turned and carried Velvet down the stairs and then out the front door.

"We rotate shifts," Bat explained. "New guys always get late shift." He grinned and patted me on the shoulder. His gesture, though intended as friendly, felt like a grizzly's paw.

Though it was after four in the morning when I arrived home, I wasn't the least bit tired. The early morning air invigorated my lungs. I longed to talk to Jane and tell her I had won my place as a Haven guard, but we had agreed prior to her leaving that it wouldn't be safe for me to call or text her. The sound of her phone at the wrong moment could put her in grave danger. I had no choice but to wait for her to contact me.

Restless, I climbed the wooden kiva ladder up to the roof and stared up at the stars. I felt closer to Jane standing in her favorite childhood spot.

Minutes ticked by. Why hadn't she called? I did the math, it was two in the afternoon in Romania. She was in the heart of enemy territory risking her life to save her niece. My intense need for her approval of my accomplishment disgusted me. It was childish. I decided I would only tell her about becoming a guard if she asked me. Even then, I would try to be as nonchalant as possible.

My mind reeled with the events of the night. Emotions flared and faded and then rose again. I felt overwhelmed by so many things I couldn't quite comprehend. I never had many male friends—or female ones for that matter. I'd never joined sports teams and though I was forced by gym teachers to participate in games, I had never felt part of any team. My dad and brother told stories of the camaraderie they felt with their buddies in the Marines. Their stories never rang true—until tonight. Now I was part of a team, The Haven guards.

I had put myself out there, fought as hard as I could for something and reveled in the competition—the victory. Even Braedon, in his own screwed-up way, accepted me. And I understood his fear to lose a fight in front of his men.

As much as I enjoyed the fight, my new-found aggression also scared me. The adrenaline that flowed through me, enhanced by vampire blood—I honestly didn't know if I would have killed Braedon had he not called our fight a tie. My temper had a will of its own at times, and I merely grasped the reins hoping it wouldn't take off at a full gallop and drag me over a cliff.

Yet, all of the training tonight was fake. I attacked men with a wooden facsimile of a sword while Jane warned a real war was coming—and soon. Am I capable of killing another being? Could I swing my machete and lop a man's head off—even an evil Vasile? Would I let her down when it counted most?

I had created a video game fraught with violence. Hacked off limbs and splattered blood, where my namesake killed with unabridged gusto. But that was only a game.

And then there was Jane—the reason I joined the guards. My body ached to see her ever-changing eyes, smell her sweet scent and touch her silky skin. It was more than sex I missed. Her mere presence made me feel complete, validated in my new existence. I loved Jane—another first for me. Tristan's icy words tonight had pierced my heart. He was right. I should have stopped her from leaving. I couldn't stand to think of something happening to her. My intense need for her terrified me. Maybe it was selfish. If she died, so would I—not physically, but my heart would be dead.

A ring startled me. I checked my phone. Jane!

"Hello?"

"Tim, listen, I don't have much time."

My heart jolted. "What? What's happening?"

"I'm okay. But I'm on the run. I've lost contact with Cristina. I think one of Vasiles spotted me in town."

"Where are you? You've got to get out of the country—get to the airport—"

"No. I've lost him. I'm on my way to the orphanage. I'm on foot. I won't be able to call you for a while. The phone signal here is spotty."

"Jane, you can't—"

"Yes. Yes, I can. I came here to get Emilia. I will get her out."

"But—"

"Tim, please. I'll contact you and let you know the flight number and time."

"Jane. Please don't do this. It's too dangerous."

"Just be ready, Tim. They'll try to get Emilia back. The Vasiles will come for you."

Static blotted out her words. ". . . go now."

"Jane!"

The connection crackled.

"Jane? I-I love you."

The line went dead. I stood staring at the phone, squeezing it until my hand hurt. Transformation had changed my looks and given me physical strength and abilities far beyond anything I had ever imagined. Before I met Jane, that would have been more than enough. Now, I would trade all of it just to bring her home, safe. I wanted to be as strong as Jane, but a frightened, pathetic geek still cowered inside my transformed facade.

He was the first one I needed to kill.

Chapter 17

"...there are no wrong turns, only unexpected paths." —Mark Nepo

A faint gray glow illuminated the eastern horizon. Nearly dawn, I realized I had stood on the roof for over an hour staring at my phone, willing it to ring. But Jane never called me back.

Fear for Jane's safety enveloped me like an icy shroud, though it was the fear of the emerging sun that finally forced my legs to move. I climbed down the ladder, entered my bedroom, and started up my laptop. On Google maps, I alternated between map and street views in an attempt to visualize where Jane might be. A Vasile had spotted her at the bed and breakfast outside of Bucharest and she had shown me where the Romanian orphanage was located. Between those two locations lay vast forests with a few rural roads connecting the sparsely populated villages. If the Vasiles attacked Jane in this desolate area, she would never be found. My stomach tightened. I turned away from the monitor.

Sleep was an impossibility. Instead, I developed a mantra to counter my fearful thoughts and chanted out loud as I worked out in the gym, *Jane is strong. Jane will return to me.* In the meantime, I had to be ready—and would be prepared—no matter what. I slid more weights onto the barbells and tripled my reps. I added a new line to my mantra, *kill the geek.* I needed to destroy the pathetic coward hiding inside me. There was no place for old Tim now. I vowed to harden myself, inside and out, and become the ultimate elite guard. Jane's life depended on me. The weight of that knowledge was far heavier than any I hefted in the gym.

The temptation to text Jane overwhelmed me more than once but I fought back the urge by working out harder. My muscles should be sore, but I felt no physical pain, only a deep, aching void in my gut.

I pumped the bar harder and chanted louder. My transformed physiology responded well to the intense workouts. My muscles grew larger, more defined, and rock-hard.

Between my mental stress and physical fatigue, I would need blood, sooner than later. If the Vasiles were on their way here, I couldn't afford to vamp out again and become vulnerable.

I took a quick shower and then emailed Echo. I asked if she would meet me tonight and donate her blood.

Within minutes she replied with good news, at least for me. She said she could be at the club whenever I needed her, even with short notice. She had been laid off from her job and now collected unemployment while she searched for work.

It was early afternoon when I finally attempted to sleep so I would be rested for guard duty. My physical exhaustion eventually overrode my reeling mind and I drifted off into a twilight daze haunted by visions of Jane's dismembered body strewn across an ancient, mossy forest floor.

I awoke at sunset. It was too early to report to The Haven. Walking to the kitchen, I took a raw steak from the refrigerator and quickly seared it on each side in a frying pan. I paced the room as I ate with my fingers. This wasn't a meal with Jane where we grilled outside, set a table and enjoyed the food, it was simply consuming the protein necessary to keep up my strength.

Once I finished eating, I donned my long leather guard coat and returned to the roof, this time with Jane's machete in hand. For two hours I sparred with imaginary Vasiles. The gaming code I visualized produced deadly strikes—at least in my mind. The lining of the coat contained several hidden pockets and straps to hold weapons. The machete fit securely into one set of straps on my right side.

I arrived an hour early at The Haven. Perhaps it was the black coat, symbolizing I was a guard, but everyone treated me differently. Wynn smiled as usual when he opened the front door, then lowered his eyes and bowed his head. The human donors on the first floor acknowledged me with nods or nervous smiles, then quickly stepped aside to let me pass. No one looked me in the eyes for more than a moment.

The weight of the steel blade against my leg comforted me. I roamed the first floor and spotted Echo alone at a corner table with her laptop. She sat with her back to me. I approached and watched over her shoulder as she colored an illustration of a fantastical woman with huge feathered wings dressed in a leather and lace corset.

"Cool picture," I said.

Echo's thin shoulders jerked. Her head spun toward me as she slammed the laptop lid in one rapid motion. "Lorcan, you scared me."

"Sorry, I got caught up watching you coloring. You're doing an awesome job."

"Thanks." Her palms pressed down on the lid as if she were afraid the computer would spring open by itself. "Do you need a donor?"

"Yes, later on tonight. I'm not in terrible need, but I've been stressed." I pointed to her laptop and changed the subject to avoid any questions. "Is that an online coloring book?"

"Um, no. It's a just drawing I did. I scanned it into my computer. I prefer to add color digitally."

"You drew that? Damn. Could I see it again?"

Two red spots formed on her cheeks, a startling contrast to the rest of her paper-white face.

"I don't show anyone my drawings."

"Why not?"

"They're . . . dumb."

I pulled out a chair, straddled it backwards and sat next to her.

"It's not dumb. You're very talented. Please, let me see it again?"

She hesitated, then opened the lid and turned the screen towards me.

"The details are incredible. Do you have more?"

She nodded.

"Show me."

Echo gave me a tortured look, then minimized her screen and double clicked on a folder. A slide show of illustrations opened on the screen.

"May I?"

She nodded and I slid the laptop closer and clicked the right arrow to flip through the illustrations. A succession of mermaids, vampires, demons, and winged creatures filled the screen. Intricately patterned lace, etched feathers, shiny metallic embellishments—I found incredible details everywhere I looked. The vibrant colors and expert shading made the characters look as though they might jump from the screen any moment. Looking over at Echo, I thought of the story of Dorian Gray. But in her case, the opposite. Her vibrant drawings had sucked all color from her and left her a pale, fragile shell.

"So, you're looking for work as an artist?" I asked.

"Oh, no. Drawing is only a hobby. I do medical transcription work."

"Why? You're an artist."

"My stuff's not good enough. I never went to art school. I don't have a degree."

An idea exploded in my mind. My chair tipped forward as I leaned across the table, my sudden movement and excited expression caused Echo to shrink back in her chair.

"If I described characters to you, could you draw them?"

"I-I don't know."

"Listen, I have a video game in development, and I need an artist to draw the characters. The company sent me sample illustrations from the artists they use, but none of the artwork has the realism I wanted. Your drawings are amazing. You could draw my characters even better than I imagined them."

She frowned at me. "You created a video game?"

"Yeah, I'm a coder by day. I recently signed a contract with Create-A-Vision."

Echo's watery blue eyes widened. "Is this a joke? Are you mocking me?"

"No, I'm serious. I need a warrior vampire character. I, uh, used my club name for him, Lorcan. He's tall, muscular, long dark hair. Dressed in a steam punk-style armor—all black and pewter tones. And a long black leather cape with spikes on the shoulders."

Echo's eyes narrowed. "Sounds like you're describing yourself."

"Hardly." I snorted and shook my head. "The character needs to

254

be handsome, fierce. A real bad-ass. Can you draw something like that?"

"Maybe. I-I can try."

"Please, try." I smiled then reached over and touched her arm. The skin on her bony arm felt cold. She stared down at my hand as if it were a tarantula. I pulled it back. "I'll send your illustration to the creative director at Create-A-Vision. When she sees your work, I'll bet they offer you the project. Maybe even a full-time job. You could get paid for doing what you love."

Echo swallowed hard. "Give me a day or two. I'll email the illustration to you. But, please don't send it to them if you think it's bad."

"Bad? If it turns out half as good as your other drawings, they're going to love it."

After setting a time to meet upstairs for blood later that evening, I left Echo at the table, sketching a rough draft of Lorcan the warrior on a paper napkin. I resumed my patrol of the club.

The few minutes discussing my video game had given me a welcome respite from worrying about Jane. My phone volume was set on high to be heard above the club's music, yet I still checked it for text messages every few minutes.

Griffin and Vlad were the other guards on duty. A young woman tended the bar so I didn't have to endure Tristan's hostile stares or the guilt they brought. Also, to my relief, neither Braedon nor Velvet was at the club. I smiled to myself envisioning Braedon brandishing a broom in his maintenance-man role during the day. It was difficult to picture Velvet as a nurse's aide. I had dismissed her as a sexy, alcoholic vampire groupie.

I paced the club for the next four hours, taking only a short break to drink blood from Echo. Griffin was quiet but personable and showed me the nightly closing routine for the club. We checked all the upstairs donor rooms, walked the roof's perimeter and then checked the restrooms and bar area for any lingering patrons. I escorted three human female donors to the parking lot and waited until they started their cars and drove off. With the club emptied and secured, we bid Aldon good night and then watched as Wynn locked the front door.

Refreshed from Echo's blood, I arrived back at Jane's house after three and proceeded to do my gym workout until dawn. I slept with my cell phone on and charging on the nightstand next to the bed.

The next three nights played out the same. The only difference was Braedon, Velvet, and Tristan returned to the club, though none gave me trouble. Tristan ignored me, as did Braedon for the most part. He barked occasional orders at me and handed me my work schedule for the week. Velvet offered a chilly greeting when we passed each other in the club. I thought about asking her if she had said anything to Braedon, then decided against it. If she had, I had no doubt Braedon would have confronted me by now. She either didn't remember our volatile blood tryst or else she decided against starting trouble. Whichever scenario, I figured it best not to provoke someone as unpredictable as Velvet.

I worked my shifts each night and diligently watched for any suspicious vampires who might be Vasiles. My thoughts were constantly with Jane, wondering if she were safe and waiting for her next call. On one shift, I was asked to remove a drunken man who threatened Tristan when he refused to serve him. As soon as I laid my hand on the unruly man's shoulder, he quieted. I led him out the door without incident. To my surprise, Tristan nodded his thanks and presented me with a glass of pomegranate juice.

On my fourth night at the club, my cell phone rang as I walked the perimeter of the roof at closing time. In the early morning quiet, the loud ring tone startled me.

"Jane? Are you all right? Where are you?"

"Tim! Good news. I freed Emilia. I'm at the Budapest airport now."

My breath gushed out from between my lips as if someone had punched me in the stomach. "Budapest? That's in Hungary, right? I'm so relieved you're out of Romania. When does your flight take off?"

"I've already put Emilia on a flight to L.A. I'll text you her flight number and arrival time."

"But why aren't you with her? What's going—?"

"There were complications. The Vasiles were waiting at the

256

orphanage. They killed Cristina."

My hand squeezed the phone hard. "Oh no. I'm so sorry, Jane."

"She died helping me and Emilia. I avenged her death. I killed two Vasile guards, but more followed us. We hid in the forest at night and traveled into Hungary in daylight. Emilia is safely on the plane and I'm sure the Vasiles believe we're still in Romania."

"I wish I were there to help you."

"I'm fine. Most importantly, Emilia is fine, for now. But I do need your help."

"Anything."

"Emilia refused to leave without another little girl, Angela. Would you pick up both girls at LAX and keep them safe until I get home?"

"Two girls? Is this Angela a Pure also?"

"It's too soon to know, she's only four years old. Emilia wouldn't leave without her. They've formed a bond at the orphanage, like sisters. I'm sorry to burden you with two children, it wasn't what I'd planned. But Emilia insisted and with Cristina gone. . . I had to get both girls out of Romania."

"Yes, of course I'll pick them up, but when are you coming home? I want you on a flight and the hell out of there. It's dangerous."

"I will. A few more days. I'm going back to Bucharest. I'll catch a flight out from there."

"Jane, that doesn't make sense. You're at an airport now—just get on any plane going to the States. I'll drive to whatever airport you land at. Leave, please, before the Vasiles find you."

"I've lost their tail for now. If I travel through Romania, the Vasiles will know. I want them to follow me. It will buy time for the girls to arrive home. Plus, it may give me a chance to kill more of them."

"Jane, don't. You're all alone there. It's too danger—"

"I have to go now. I'll text you the girls' flight information. Keep them safe, Tim, please. The Vasiles will figure out Emilia's gone and come after her. They will slaughter anyone who gets in their way. You must be ready."

"Don't worry. I am. Promise me you won't do anything crazy.

Just come home. We'll fight them together. We'll get justice for what they did to your family."

"Thank you, Tim. That means a lot to me. I'll see you soon."

"Jane, be careful. I love you."

"I love you, too," she whispered. The call ended.

Jane's whisper faded into the silent night. I replayed her whispered words over and over in my mind, not willing to let them disappear into the darkness. Her declaration of love both lifted my heart and deadened it. What if we never got to share our love?

"Lorcan? What's taking so long? Everything all right?" Griffin stood in the open doorway to the roof.

"Yeah. Roof's clear." I waved my phone at him. "Sorry. I had to take a call."

As promised, Jane texted me the girls' flight number and arrival time. She wrote that she listed me as her husband and the girls' adoptive father. I would need to fill out a form and show ID at the airport before the immigration authorities would release the girls to me. Jane took photos of the documents she filled out at the Budapest airport and attached them to her text. I memorized the details.

Of course, I would pick up the girls as I promised. I knew how much Emilia meant to Jane. She risked her life to save the girl. But the more I thought about it, I realized our life together would be changed forever, especially with not one, but two little girls. It would no longer be Jane and I sharing a home, meals—a bed. I knew nothing about raising kids, much less vampire children. Though I tamped it down, my resentment grew. Maybe I wouldn't need to worry about our future. Jane would spend all her time mothering the orphaned girls. I'd become an obsolete member of Jane's household. My mood grew darker. If Jane is killed by the Vasiles for rescuing the girl—child or not—I will blame Emilia forever.

For once, luck was on my side. Braedon scheduled me off from guard duty the next two nights. At least I wouldn't have to ask the obnoxious dick for time off so soon into my new job.

After another restless night, I rose in the early afternoon, showered, ate some meat and then started out for LAX. This time, traffic jams were in full force. The two-hour trip turned into a hellacious four hours of crawling along the jam-packed freeway.

I jogged through the airport and arrived at the gate where I was to meet the girls. There was no one in sight. Frantic, I ran to the nearest counter and interrupted a clerk helping a middle-aged woman.

"Excuse me! I'm supposed to pick up two little girls. My adopted daughters. Traffic was. . . I got to the gate too late. Can you help me find them?"

"Oh, dear. Lost children come before lost baggage." The older woman waved me ahead of her.

"What was their flight number, sir?" the clerk asked.

I double-checked the cell phone text from Jane. "Flight 715 from Budapest."

The clerk made a call and told me to wait. An agonizing sixteen minutes later, a woman in a blue uniform approached me.

"Timothy Gardener?" Her smile looked professional, her eyes suspicious. "I'll need to see ID."

I pulled out my driver's license, suddenly grateful to the coconut-latte-drinking cop who pulled me over last week and forced me to get it updated.

She studied it for several moments. "Follow me, please."

We walked a distance of several city blocks along the polished tile concourse, lightly bumping against luggage-laden travelers heading in the opposite direction. The uniformed woman made a left turn into a narrow hallway. She stopped outside an office with a plate glass window.

Relief flooded over me. Inside on a bench sat a pale-complected girl with hair so black it shone navy blue under the florescent lighting. It had to be Emilia. The resemblance to her mother's photo was obvious. Her bangs hung in a razor-sharp line across her forehead, and beneath them blazed angry, dark eyes. She stared at me, her mouth pressed into a hard line. A smaller, blonde girl lay next to her.

The woman opened the door for me to enter. An older male clerk sitting at a desk stood and walked to the service counter. He adjusted his glasses and looked past me to the woman.

"Mr. Gardener has arrived." She turned on her heel and exited.

The man slid a clipboard with papers across the counter. "I have a few standard questions but first I'll need you to fill out this form." The form had ICE stamped on it.

A half door separated me from the girls in the small waiting area. The smaller one, Angela, lay curled up on the bench, sound asleep. Her head rested in Emilia's lap and her soft blonde curls cascaded over the older girl's knees and fell half-way down her legs. She looked like her name, an angel—the exact opposite of Emilia—with chubby, peach-colored cheeks and a tiny mouth turned up into a smile even as she slept.

Both were dressed in dark bulky coats and black leggings. On a table in front of the bench were two juice cartons and some crumpled chip bags.

My nerves kicked up another notch. What the hell was I supposed to do with two kids until Jane came home? How could I continue my guard work and watch them? And what if the Vasiles came to Jane's house again? Rattled to my core, I focused on the lengthy form. I labored through each page, filled it out and handed the clipboard back to the clerk. He walked a few steps to a copier and ran off copies.

"What is the girls' country of origin?"

"Romania."

"And your wife's name?"

The wife reference made me smile despite my nerves. "Jane."

I wondered why he had me verbally repeat information I had already written. Probably a test since the pen shook in my hand the entire time I wrote. I glanced over at the girls, though I could feel Emilia's brooding stare.

"All righty," the clerk said. "I'll call an ICE supervisor to witness your signature. Just be a minute." He picked up the phone and then smiled at me. "You must be anxious to greet your daughters. Go ahead."

As I opened the swinging half door, Emilia nudged Angela. The little girl rubbed her small fists against her closed eyelids, then sat up and stared up at me with wide-open, sky-blue eyes.

I approached them slowly. "Hello Emilia, Angela. I'm Tim."

Angela scooched closer to Emilia and clutched the older girl's arm with both of hers. Emilia leaned down and spoke to Angela in a language I didn't know. Though I knew they were from Romania, it only now occurred to me the girls wouldn't understand me, or me them. I had no idea how to care for two little girls and a language barrier only added to my frustration. This just gets better and better. I shook off a fleeting pang of anger at Jane for not being here and took a deep breath.

I crouched down so I would be eye-level to the sitting girls. "Jane, um, I mean your mom, told you about me, right? I'm happy you and Angela are safe, Emilia." I added my own spontaneous sign language, hugged my arms together, pointed at the girls and then to the forced smile on my face.

Emilia's hard stare and rigid lips never softened. "My mother is dead. Jane is my adoptive aunt. I speak fluent English, Romanian, Italian, and French. I am tutoring Angela in English."

"Yes, I'm very sorry about your mom." The girl's fiery eyes unnerved me. I cleared my throat. "I didn't know you spoke English. That's, um, great."

Angela whispered to Emilia. The younger girl's shiny blue eyes stayed fixed on me.

Emilia whispered back.

"Papa?" Angela's voice sounded soft and musical, again, befitting of her heavenly name.

I stared at her. My lips moved but no words came out.

"You are Jane's husband, are you not?" Emilia asked. "That makes you our adoptive father."

"Uh, yes." Did Jane tell them we were married? Maybe she did intend to keep me in her future.

The older girl rolled her eyes and motioned to Angela who sat smiling at me.

I shrugged at Angela. "Yeah, that's me, um, your papa."

The tiny girl launched herself from the bench with such force she knocked me backward and I landed on my butt. Her arms tightened around my neck as she giggled and said "Papa" over and over.

The one-minute wait for the supervisor turned into an hour. Once he arrived, we both signed and initialed all sixteen pages of the form. He told me the papers needed to be notarized. I waited again while they located their staff Notary Public.

While I waited, I sat on the bench and attempted to make conversation with the girls. Emilia gave terse one-syllable answers and sat still as a stone on the end of the bench. Yet, much like a creepy painting in a haunted mansion, her eyes followed me wherever I went in the small office.

I had so many questions to ask her about Jane and what had happened at the orphanage. Jane had sounded cavalier when she said she killed two Vasiles. Murdering one would be an awesome feat. Though it was Jane's nature to downplay her accomplishments, I worried she was mortally wounded from the fight and sending the girls home was her last act on earth. But my questions for Emilia would have to wait until we were out of earshot of the ICE staff.

Little Angela crawled into my lap, unashamedly enamored with me. She petted my face and ran her fingers through my hair. Refreshed from her nap, she pointed to the same four objects in the room and repeated their English names, table, chair, drink, and chips. She looked at me for confirmation each time, her face all big blue eyes surrounded by a cloud of pale blonde hair. I had no choice but to nod and smile at her.

As frustrated as I was with the airport red tape and turtle-like pace of its employees, I found it impossible to be annoyed with the little girl. Her smile lit up her entire face, especially her eyes which sparkled every time she pronounced a word. With my tutelage, her English vocabulary expanded to seven words, as she added pen, door, and light to her repertoire.

Angela snuggled into my arms, her drooping eyelids and babbling mouth dueled for a while, then her eyelids won. She was fast asleep in my arms when the clerk finally handed me my copy of the finished documents and told me we were good to go.

Emilia picked up a battered-looking fabric bag with worn leather handles. She struggled to sling it over her thin shoulder.

"I'll carry it for you."

"You are carrying Angela."

"She's light. Here." I held my hand out and Emilia reluctantly handed over the bag.

Though she must have been exhausted, she kept pace with my stride as we made our way through the airport concourse and into the parking garage.

Traffic sped along on the freeway. Angela slumped over the seat belt in the rear, asleep. The foggy smudges from her fingers and lips on the rear passenger window lingered in testament to her rapture with the scenery during the first hour of the drive.

Emilia sat in the front passenger seat. Though she exuded confidence far beyond her age, I caught her staring wide-eyed at the lights of downtown Los Angeles. We were three-quarters of the way home, and now that Angela was asleep, I couldn't wait to ask Emilia about Jane. She startled me and broke her silence first.

"Jane said we must purchase western style clothing so we blend in with American children."

"Huh?"

Emilia repeated herself.

"You want to go clothes shopping? Now?" I glanced at the digital display on the dash. Six forty-five. Most shopping malls should be open another two or three hours.

"Yes. Jane said we should purchase a wardrobe as soon as possible."

"Wardrobe? I don't have that much cash on me."

Emilia rummaged in her coat pocket. She held up a roll of bills secured with a rubber band. "Jane gave me this American money. She said it should be sufficient to buy what Angela and I require."

"Fine. Shopping for kids' clothes, what else would an elite guard be doing?" I mumbled.

"What did you say?"

"I don't know anything about girls' clothes, sizes or—"

"If you will take us to an emporium, I will find the items for Angela and myself."

I sighed and changed lanes to exit the freeway. "You only have about two hours before the stores close."

"Jane provided a list. I shall be most expedient with my choices."

"Right." My only shopping experience with a female was with my mom and expedience never entered into the equation. I took an exit close to the shopping plaza where I had bought my clothes. I hadn't noticed, but with the large number of stores there, at least one had to have kids' clothes. "How is Jane? She told me there was, um, some trouble at the orphanage." I wasn't sure how much Emilia knew.

"Jane is well. She is courageous and strong. We were about to leave the orphanage when two Vasiles arrived. Cristina hid us inside a storage pantry. When the Vasiles discovered I was gone, they interrogated Cristina. She would not answer. They killed her."

Emilia looked straight ahead, her dark eyes solemn.

"I'm so sorry."

"I have seen killing before. The Vasiles often came to the orphanage to drink the children's blood."

"They use child donors?"

Emilia shook her head. "Jane explained how you and she have human donors for your blood needs. The Vasiles are not like you. They never ask humans for their consent. They select a child and bite their neck, wrists, and ankles. Any thin flesh close to large veins. When they are done ingesting the blood, the human is either dead or near to death."

"You witnessed this?"

"Yes. Many times. Cristina took the surviving children to families in nearby villages. Only Angela and I remained at the orphanage. She knew the Vasiles would not kill me and we kept Angela well hidden. With no more innocent blood for them to take, the Vasiles did not come as often."

"That's awful, Emilia. After Cristina was killed, then what happened?"

"The two huddled over her body and gorged on her blood. Jane sneaked behind them with a sword and decapitated one. Then she fought the other."

"Where did Jane get a sword?"

"Cristina had hidden weapons inside the pantry for Jane."

"So, then Jane killed the second Vasile?"

"Jane wounded him. Vasiles are very strong. They are capable of healing their wounds quickly. He still fought. I found a long knife and thrust it into his back. It distracted him. When he turned toward me, Jane cut off his head."

"Holy crap."

"I do not understand your words."

"Never mind." I checked the rearview mirror. Angela still slept. "Did Angela see the killings?"

"Oh, no. No." Emilia shook her head violently. "I made her hide behind the sacks of flour and rice. I warned her not to come out until Jane or I came for her. We covered her eyes with a kerchief when we carried her past the bodies to the outside. Angela saw nothing."

"How did you get to Hungary?"

"Jane drove the automobile Cristina had ready. Another vehicle chased us, but Jane drove faster and hid the automobile in the woods for a time. We waited until sunrise and then drove on to Hungary. The Vasiles rarely come out during the daylight hours."

We drove toward the mall in silence. Emilia sat up straight and stared forward, clutching Jane's list and the money roll in her hands. Though she was a Pure Blood from an ancient and elite bloodline, I reminded myself Emilia was only eleven. Jane described her as exceptionally intelligent and mature for her age. For years, Jane sent money for books, and Cristina had obviously done an excellent job home-schooling the girl. Though Emilia hadn't experienced Awakening yet, her strength and resolve were also far above average. This small glimpse into her life at the orphanage justified her dark persona. My initial resentment morphed into a profound respect. Her brave action probably saved Jane's life and I admired her fierce protectiveness of little Angela.

Emilia struggled to keep hold of Angela's hand as we hurried through the mall searching for a children's clothing store. Distracted by the passing shoppers, colorful window displays, and enticing food court aromas, Angela constantly tugged Emilia in different directions as she scampered to explore.

Emilia stopped in front of a department store and then looked up at me. There were both adult and child mannequins modeling clothing in the display window.

"Let's look inside," I said.

We found the children's section in the rear of the store. Emilia stood amidst racks of clothing, her head turning from side to side.

"I did not think there would be so many clothes," she said.

"Let me see Jane's list."

Emilia handed over the crumpled paper. I scanned through the items, everything from underwear to swimsuits and shoes.

"I am uncertain how your currency works. I do not want to waste Jane's money. I do not know how much this amount will buy. Would you handle the payment?"

I unwrapped the roll and discreetly counted out the fifty one hundred dollar bills. "There's five thousand dollars here. You should have plenty of money for everything on your list."

A young brunette clerk walked up to us. "May I help you?"

"Yes! Um, please."

The salesclerk grinned at my response. I handed her the list and motioned to Emilia and Angela. "My daughters are new here. They need a lot of stuff."

She perused the list and then studied the two girls.

Under the bright lights both looked thin and pale. Their ill-fitting coats showed frayed sleeves and collars, and their pilled woolen leggings bagged around their ankles.

"No problem. I'm happy to help." The clerk rummaged through racks and shelves. She held up some T-shirts and jeans, measuring them against the girls' bodies. "First, let's try these on for sizes." She led the girls to a fitting room a few yards away.

I hovered outside the room, nervous at having my new charges out of my sight for the first time.

The smiling salesclerk approached me. "It's so sweet of you to take your little girls shopping. Is your wife with you?"

"I'm not mar—um—no." I berated myself for my awkward response.

The clerk turned up her smile up a notch and stood close enough for me to smell her underlying blood scent. Buttered popcorn.

The fitting room door flung open and Angela raced out wearing a pink T-shirt and blue jeans with rhinestones on the back pockets. She spun like a kitten chasing its tail in front of a full-length mirror

266

and pointed to her behind. "Papa! Diamonds!"

I didn't recognize Emilia when she stepped out. Without the baggy old clothes weighing her down she stood tall, slender, and her hair which had been tucked under her coat fell to her waist in a sleek black curtain. She studied her reflection for several moments and then turned to me. "Do I look like an American girl?"

I smiled at her perplexed expression. "Yes. You look very nice."

No doubt, Emilia was a budding beauty. In a year or two when she hit puberty, or in her case, Awakening, I would need the machete and a baseball bat to keep the boys away from her.

Armed with both girls' sizes, the salesgirl took Angela's hand and led her to the toddler section. She pointed Emilia to a pre-junior section a few rows over.

"We need to not spend too much money," Emilia told the salesclerk.

Emilia stayed with Angela and helped her choose tops, jeans, and shorts from the sale racks. Angela babbled non-stop, her small arms held out in front of her, piled with bright-colored new clothes.

Emilia's eyebrows knitted together in concern. "Do we need all of this?"

"It's fine," I said. The clerk had shown the girls many discounted specials. I encouraged Emilia to select a few extra items not on Jane's list, including the fluffy pink dress that had Angela mesmerized. She carried the dress during the rest of her shopping and hugged it to her chest so tightly I had to lift her up to the counter so the clerk could scan the tag.

We managed to buy everything on the list and even had time to stop at the food court. The girls devoured a meal of chicken nuggets and fries. The mall was closing when we finally exited. Emilia carried two large shopping bags and I carried three more, plus Angela.

"I believe we have too many things. Did we use all of Jane's money?" Emilia asked as we packed the bags into the trunk.

"No, there's still four thousand, one hundred and change left." I handed the wad of bills to Emilia.

"You may hold the currency, if you prefer."

"No, Jane gave it to you."

Emilia nodded and stashed the money in her voluminous coat pocket.

After I seat-belted a drowsy Angela into the back seat, Emilia and I climbed into the car and I headed toward home.

Emilia stood in the middle of her childhood bedroom and turned in a slow circle taking in every detail. She ran her hand along the railing of the wooden crib.

"This was my bed when I was an infant?"

"Yes."

She walked the perimeter of the space touching all of the furniture, the drapes and the walls. She stopped at the side of the large bed where Angela lay sleeping, exhausted from jumping up and down on the soft mattress for half an hour.

"And this was my mother's bed?" Emilia picked up a pillow and sniffed it. "The smell is sweet." She rubbed her cheek against it. "Soft." Her dark eyes glistened with tears.

Emilia's sudden display of emotion left me uncomfortable. I was just getting used to her dark, hard-ass personality. "You must be exhausted. Try to get some sleep. I'm in the next room down the hall if you need anything."

"Is it the room where you and Jane sleep?"

"Um, no. Jane's bedroom is on the other side of the house."

"Why? She is your wife. Do you not love Jane?"

"Yes, of course I love her. We aren't married, um, yet."

"The woman helping us in the store showed romantic interest in you. Do you love her, too?"

"No. I'm not interested in her or any other woman. I love only Jane." I turned to leave the room.

"That is good. Jane loves you."

I spun around in the doorway. "Did Jane tell you that?"

Emilia shrugged. "No. Her love for you is obvious in her voice and in her eyes whenever she talks about you."

My heartbeat echoed in my throat. I wanted Jane here with me more than anything. "Good night, Emilia."

"Wait!"

Again, I turned toward the girl. Her eyes were wide, and her chin quivered.

"What's wrong?"

"Jane said there is a hiding place. Inside a wall. I need to know where it is so I can hide Angela when the Vasiles come for me."

I reached over and patted Emilia's shoulder. "Don't be afraid. I won't let them take you or hurt Angela. You're both safe now." I hoped my words masked my doubt.

"I must see it."

I sighed. "All right. It's in my room. C'mon, I'll show you."

Emilia practiced opening and closing the door in the wall. She crawled inside and then out and inspected the wall when the door was closed.

"It is a very good place to hide."

"Hopefully you'll never need to use it." She continued to run her hands over the door checking for seams, so I sat at my desk and started up my laptop. My email folder contained over a dozen emails from Rudi at Create-A-Vision. I opened the latest one, time stamped this morning. The tone of her message sounded irritated and stated if she didn't hear from me by end of day tomorrow, she would make the final decision on the artwork for my video game.

"Crap." I hoped Echo would have an illustration ready by tomorrow.

"What is that?"

"What?"

Emilia walked to my desk and pointed at the screen.

"Oh, a laptop computer."

"Jane told me about computers. She said I would like them. I could learn much."

"I guess you didn't have computers at the orphanage?" I regretted my words as soon as I said them. "Sorry."

"There is no technology in the rural mountains. Jane sent cell phones to Cristina. They would not work at the orphanage. She had to travel to a larger town to get a signal and communicate with Jane."

"Of course." I stood and motioned to the machine. "You're welcome to use my laptop. Maybe tomorrow, if you'd like."

"I am used to staying awake all night." Emilia sat and stared at the monitor. "The Vasiles only come when it is dark. I kept watch."

I sighed. "Yeah, I don't sleep much at night either." I clicked on the browser icon and opened a Google search window. I pointed to the letters on the keyboard. "Can you type in English?"

"I know words. I can push the buttons and make words?"

"Yes, exactly. Type and the words will show in the search field." I pointed as I spoke. "Hit the ENTER button. You'll see a list, then use the mouse and click on one. The browser will take you to a website to read about it."

Emilia typed AMERICA into the search window.

She gasped. "It says there are two billion, three hundred and ten million items in this list."

"Yup, that's the internet. You can't trust everything you read here, but there is a lot of valid information out there."

"Do you want to rest now? I will leave your room." Emilia stood.

I smiled. "No, stay. Have fun. I'm going to work out in the gym down the hall."

The following morning, I was awakened by small hands tugging on my T-shirt.

I opened my eyes to Angela, dressed in new pink pajamas with her long curls mussed about her head. She smiled up at me from the side of my bed and proclaimed, "Hungry, Papa."

My cell phone displayed eight-forty in the morning, earlier than I had risen in months.

"Um, okay." I took a deep breath, swung my legs over the edge of the bed and stood. My body balked at being vertical and I sat again. Angela jumped up and down and grasped my hand. I stood slowly, ducked to avoid a ray of sunlight peeking in the window where she had disturbed the drapes, and let her lead me out of the bedroom.

She ran ahead of me down the hallway toward the kitchen. There was nothing in the refrigerator except raw meat, and in the freezer, frozen raw meat.

Still I opened the door and stood staring at the sparse offerings of raw beef and lamb on the shelves.

"Jane said both Angela and I should eat a balanced diet of

carbohydrates and proteins, with some healthy fats included. Once I reach my Awakening, I will need to consume more proteins."

I turned to see Emilia, dressed in her new dark-washed blue jeans and a black T-shirt standing in the kitchen archway. The simple clothing change had transformed her from pitiful orphan into an American pre-teen Goth girl.

"Yeah, well, it seems I'm stocked up on only protein right now," I mumbled.

Angela prodded a plastic-wrapped steak with one finger. The red liquid squished under the plastic. She looked up at me, stuck her tongue out and made a gagging sound.

"We will need to purchase fresh foods for proper nutrition," Emilia said.

I sighed and rubbed my face. "Fine. I'll go change my clothes."

The corners of Angela's mouth drooped as I closed the refrigerator door and headed back toward my bedroom. Emilia wrapped her arm around the little girl's shoulders and spoke to her in what I assumed was Romanian.

I was pulling on my boots when, once again, Angela raced into my room. She wore her bedazzled-pocket jeans and a purple hoodie. She squealed, "Car! Ride!"

Forcing a smile, I considered stopping by a hardware store to buy a latch for my bedroom door.

After I slathered on sun block and secured my wrap-around sunglasses, the three of us ventured outside in the bright morning sun.

The girls already knew the routine and took their designated seats in my Camry. We drove to the supermarket. Two hundred dollars and change later, I hoped I had enough food to satisfy the appetites of my starving child guests for at least a few days.

Emilia, the self-appointed nutritionist, helped prepare eggs, bacon, and toast for both Angela and herself. She was a huge help when it came to taking care of Angela. I left the girls eating in the kitchen and slipped back to my room. My blood felt thick and sluggish from lack of rest and sun exposure.

I checked my phone but found no messages. Worries about Jane plagued me. It wasn't like her not to check and make sure the girls' flight had arrived safely. Plus, she should have contacted me by now with her flight number and arrival time. The only explanation for her silence was that she encountered trouble with the Vasiles. Even in my present state the thought sped up my heart rate.

I wondered if I should text Jane or if my communication might add to her danger. More panic set in when I realized I had to report for guard duty at The Haven tomorrow night and had no idea what to do with Emilia and Angela. I couldn't leave them alone at the house, nor could I bring them to The Haven. If I blew off guard duty until Jane returned, Braedon would surely have me removed from the guards.

The morning excursion in the sunlight left me feeling weak. I pulled the drapes closed and stretched out on my bed. I willed myself to relax. I had to be rested and clear-headed to figure out what to do about Jane, guard duty, and keeping the girls safe.

It felt as though I had no sooner closed my eyes when Emilia's voice woke me.

"Has Aunt Jane contacted you?"

I regretted not stopping at the hardware store. Without opening my eyes, I answered, "No."

"She must have encountered the Vasiles on the way to Bucharest."

"I'm afraid of that also." With rest now impossible, I sat up in the bed. "I want to text her, but we agreed before she left that I wouldn't contact her. If her phone makes a noise at the wrong time, it could put her in danger."

"She is smart and strong, but the Vasiles are also strong and clever. Is there nothing you can do?"

I shook my head. "She's thousands of miles away. I wish she had gotten on the plane with you and Angela."

The sadness in Emilia's eyes made her look much older than her eleven years. "I hope they have not killed her."

I was on my feet and clamped my hands on Emilia's slender shoulders. "Don't ever say that," I growled. I didn't mean to shake her so hard.

She turned and fled the room. I followed her down the hall and into the kitchen.

Angela sat at the table eating apple slices and sipping orange juice. Emilia hurried to the sink and turned on the water to wash their breakfast dishes.

"Emilia, I'm sorry."

"There is no need to apologize."

I stood watching her wash dishes for a few moments. "You're welcome to use my laptop when you're done."

I returned to my room and fired up the laptop. I had a new email, this time from Echo. When I clicked on the attachment, my heart skipped a beat. Her illustration of Lorcan the warrior vampire was breathtaking. I leaned back in my chair and stared at the image on my screen. His dark eyes shone with fierceness and he stood tall and strong, so lifelike. All of the details I had described to Echo, from the long leather cape to the metallic embellishments on his broad shoulders were executed with perfection.

Angela ran into the room clutching a tattered children's story book. She stopped, mouth open, and pointed at the screen. "Papa!"

"Is it a portrait of you?" Emilia asked as she walked in behind the little girl.

"No, it's a character for my video game. A friend of mine drew it."

"What is a video game?"

Rather than try to explain, I opened a game on my computer and showed the girls. "It's like an interactive movie."

The two stood staring at the screen in rapt silence.

Angela pouted when I closed the game and typed an email to Rudi at Create-A-Vision. I apologized for not getting back to her sooner and explained that I'd found an artist who drew a sample rendering of Lorcan. I attached the image and hit send. I couldn't imagine she would reject the artwork—it was stunning.

I stood and removed my phone from the charger. I needed to call Echo and thank her for the incredible image and for doing it so quickly.

As I disconnected the phone from the USB cord, a new text message flashed on my screen. My heart jolted when I read it. Fight 1054. Arriving LAX. Tomorrow. 5:20 A.M. PST. Jane.

"Jane's okay! She's flying in tomorrow morning."

Emilia rushed to my side and peered at the phone screen. I held it out so she could see the text.

"That is good. I am very much relieved," she said.

"Me, too." I sat on the bed and re-read the message several times. It was short but held all the information needed. I hadn't realized I held my breath until it rushed out in a long sigh. Relief washed over me as my fear lifted. I felt a thousand pounds lighter, renewed.

I dialed Echo. She answered on the first ring.

"The illustration isn't good enough, is it?"

"What, are you nuts? It's fantastic. I sent it to Rudi, the art director. She's going to flip when she sees it. Thank you for doing it so fast."

"We'll see what they say."

Echo's lack of confidence in her work befuddled me. But I dismissed it as another thought hit me. "Listen, Echo, can I ask you a huge favor?"

"What is it?"

"I have to pick up a friend at the airport tomorrow morning, early. Would you be able to baby sit two little girls for me? Just until I get back."

"You have children?"

"Um, no. Visiting relatives." I couldn't tell Echo the truth.

"Um, my apartment is pretty small. And I don't know much about baby-sitting kids."

"Yeah, me neither. But they're good kids—well-behaved—and Emilia, the older girl, will take care of Angela, the younger one. I'm sorry for the last-minute imposition. I'll pay you for your time."

"Well . . . I suppose."

I went to my desk, found paper and a pen and scribbled down Echo's address as she told me. "I'll drop them off, about ten o'clock tonight, if that's not too late. That way I won't have to wake you at three in the morning when I leave for the airport? Is that okay?"

"Yes. I'll be home all evening."

I ended the call with Echo and punched the air with the phone still squeezed in my fist. Suddenly life was excellent. All of my dread gone with one short text message. Jane would be home tomorrow morning. Whatever followed afterward with the Vasiles,

I felt confident we could handle together. With Jane by my side, I feared nothing.

Emilia stood with her hands on her hips. Her dark eyes blazed. "Why can we not go to the airport with you and greet Aunt Jane? She said we would be a family." Emilia asked. "We do not need a babysitter. We are not babies."

"It's a slang term. It will be better this way, Emilia. I'll have to leave really early in the morning. Besides, you'll like Echo, she's the artist who drew the picture of Lorcan."

I walked to my laptop and brought up the image. As I stared at it, my email sounded.

Rudi from Create-A-Vision, as predicted, was blown away by the artwork. Her email overflowed with exclamations about the quality of the illustration as well as a series of questions. *Who is this artist? Why haven't we seen their work before? Are they employed by another gaming company? Do they have a contract? We want them to work exclusively for us. Can you get them to come in and sign a contract? When can they start work on the rest of the characters?*

I ignored Emilia who paced and huffed around my desk and Googled the salaries of video game artists. In the Los Angeles area, a tenured artist could make up to ninety thousand a year and the average salary was in the high fifties. That had to beat whatever a medical transcriptionist made. Armed with this information, I called Rudi, prepared to fib a little bit on Echo's behalf.

After Rudi gushed about the artwork for five minutes, I asked her what Create-A-Vision's starting salary for an artist would be.

She hesitated. "It varies. I'll have to talk to Paul. We negotiate a figure, you know, based on experience, demand for their work, how quickly they can turn out artwork."

"Well, she did this drawing as a favor to me. I know this girl has several offers pending." As I spoke, I realized I didn't know Echo's real name. I hoped Rudi wouldn't ask. "She's new to the video game art industry, but the samples she has sent to other companies have caused quite a demand. I know she has at least three other offers." I crossed my fingers. "One is for seventy-five thousand a year."

Rudi's voice never skipped a beat. "We *have* to have her on our team. Let me speak to Paul. I'll call you back."

I put down my phone and grinned as I imagined the shocked look on Echo's face when I told her the good news. My smile faded when I glanced over at Emilia. She still glared at me.

"Emilia, please. It's only for a little while. It will be safer this way. The Vasiles may have followed Jane. Above all, she would want you and Angela to be safe. I promise as soon as I pick up Jane, we'll come directly to Echo's apartment to get you and Angela. Starting tomorrow afternoon, we'll be a real family, exactly like Jane promised."

Angela looked up from the children's book she studied and smiled. "Fam-lee? Mama and Papa."

Emilia's expression softened. "Yes. A family with a mama and papa." She hugged the little girl.

I had Emilia pack the girls' new backpacks with a change of clothes, snacks, and some books for Angela. Angela fell asleep on her bed in the afternoon. To cheer her up, I told Emilia she could take my laptop with her to Echo's house, but she reminded me of the laptop Jane kept in her laboratory. Jane had told her she could have it. Emilia followed me into Jane's laboratory to retrieve it.

"I'll need to update the operating system so it will work better for you. Jane hardly ever used it, she prefers her desk top computer."

Emilia nodded. Though she cooperated, she made it obvious she wasn't one hundred percent on board with spending time at Echo's. She walked around the lab studying the equipment while I disconnected Jane's laptop and rolled up the power cord and charger.

"Hey, stay out of there."

Emilia stood with the door of Jane's refrigerator open.

"Is this blood in these glass vials?"

"Yes. Close the door, it needs to be kept cold."

Emilia complied. "Aunt Jane told me all about her work. A hematologist. It is interesting, all that she has learned about vampires simply by studying their blood. She said your blood is the most fascinating she has encountered. Is it true you were once only human?"

"Yes, it is."

Emilia stood quietly looking at me. "I have heard of hybrids, born from the union of a vampire and a human, but I have never heard of a human who changed into a vampire. Did you drink from a vampire's blood?"

"Yes. Apparently, it's unusual. Most humans don't survive after drinking blood. And the Pures and many of the Hybrids look down on people like me. They call humans Mundanes."

"I am a Pure Blood. My lineage can be traced for centuries. Yet I do not consider you inferior or mundane, as you say."

"Gee, thanks."

Emilia cocked her head. "I am being most sincere. Aunt Jane said you are just as strong as a Pure Blood and have many enhanced vampire traits. She also said your inner character is noble."

"Yeah, well, I try. C'mon. It will take a while to update this laptop. I'll work on it in my room. Plus, I need to get some sleep."

Emilia stayed in her room with Angela. I set up Jane's laptop and started the updates. Too amped to sleep, I worked out in the gym and then showered. I heard the girls in the kitchen and checked on them. Emilia made sure Angela had lunch, which was good, because I had forgotten the need for regular meals since I was transformed.

"You take good care of Angela," I said.

Emilia looked at me with serious eyes. "I tried to protect all of the younger children at the orphanage. I was not always successful."

A darkness crossed her face. I remembered she told of the Vasiles attacking the children for their blood.

"You saved Angela."

Emilia nodded and continued to construct their peanut butter and jelly sandwiches.

"I'm going to get some sleep. Remember, stay inside the house. Wake me if you hear anything unusual."

The sun had set when I awoke. My room was bathed in the pale blue glow from Jane's laptop. *Update completed* showed on the blue screen. Energized, I got up from bed and hurried down the hall. The girls' bedroom door stood ajar. Emilia read aloud to Angela, first in their native language, then she explained what she had read in English.

I knocked on the door and Angela ran to me and threw her arms around my legs. "Hello, Papa."

I leaned down and scooped her up and hugged her. Oddly, only two days ago, the thought of having two kids in my life seemed like a nightmare. Now I wondered what my life what be like without Angela's little arms squeezing my neck, her soft hair tickling my face.

"The laptop is ready, Emilia."

I carried Angela and Emilia hurried behind me to my room. I switched on the light and set Angela down. Then I motioned to Emilia to sit at my desk. I leaned over her shoulder and showed her how to operate the laptop. She caught on in no time.

"Show me how to make a video game."

I downloaded the free software onto her laptop that I had used to construct the rudimentary version of my game. I opened the program on my screen and showed her the code behind the wire frame action scenes.

To my amazement, she showed an aptitude for coding. In minutes she created a scene I recognized. Two figures stooped over a prone body while another sneaked behind and attacked one with a long sword.

"That's Jane at the orphanage, isn't it?"

Emilia nodded. Angela had become bored with the colorless wire-framed figures. She sat on the floor and pulled some of my comic books from the bookshelf.

"I use html code when I fight in real life," I said. "Can you describe how the Vasiles move in a fight scenario?"

Emilia immediately worked her way through another fight scene, pausing here and there for me to help her with the more complex strings of code.

"The Vasiles' movements in battle are very fast. They can leap very high and walk across a ceiling. They use this advantage to surprise their victims," she said.

I crouched next to her and in a little more than an hour we had created three distinct battle scenes. I questioned some of the movements, like walking up walls, but Emilia insisted they were realistic to the Vasiles in battle. I studied the code and committed it to memory.

"I can create other scenarios," Emilia said. "But I think I will need to study this html code more."

I showed her web sites where she could learn code and bookmarked them for her. The girl's capacity for knowledge and her ability to learn the complex code astounded me.

"This will be very helpful to me and Jane, Emilia. The more I know about how the Vasiles move, the better I will be able to fight them."

She smiled for the first time since I had met her.

My cell phone rang, and I ran to check it, wondering if it were Jane. It was Rudi and her words poured out in an excited rush. "I talked to Paul. We are prepared to offer eighty thousand, if—and only if—she signs an exclusive contract with us. And we want to see her rendering of the main female character for your game as soon as possible."

"And if I can convince her to do that, she'll be the exclusive artist for my video game, right?"

"Yes. But you must to get her to agree to sign a contract with us."

I hung up with Rudi and immediately called Echo. I wished I had waited to tell her the news in person as she sounded as if she might pass out on the phone when I told her Create-A-Vision was prepared to pay her eighty thousand dollars.

"Echo, are you there? Echo?"

"Lorcan, you are serious? This isn't a joke?"

"No joke, I swear. But I do need you to draw one more character and then you'll have to meet with Paul and Rudi at Create-A-Vision and sign an exclusive contract."

I could hear Echo gasping for breath on the line.

"Listen, I'll email you a description for the female warrior and Rudi's contact info. Okay?"

I ended the call with Echo and immediately composed the email to her. My description of the female warrior matched Jane to a T. I could hardly wait to see Jane immortalized in a video game.

After I gave Emilia a quick demonstration of how modern

plumbing worked, the girls were showered, packed, and ready to go by eight o'clock. I paced the house making sure all the doors and windows were secured. My excitement to see Jane made it difficult to wait another two hours before leaving, but I didn't want to burden Echo by dropping the girls off too early.

I was shutting down my laptop when a wide-eyed Emilia raced into my room.

"I hear something outside." Her words had barely registered when I heard it also. A car engine running and the shaking of the iron gates at the end of the driveway.

On my feet, I grabbed the machete. "Get Angela. Now! Hide inside the secret wall."

Emilia raced toward her bedroom and as I ran past, I saw her pick up Angela and run back toward my bedroom. My heart beat triple time in my chest as I ripped open the front doors and ran toward the gate.

My transformed vision excelled in darkness. A black sports car engine rumbled, parked outside the gate and a dark hooded figure gripped the iron bars with both hands.

I thrust the machete blade between the iron bars of the gate, ready to strike the intruder's head. The hooded figure cried out, "Lorcan, stop! It's me." Velvet pushed back the hood of her jacket, revealing blue-streaked hair and pale face.

"Velvet!" I pulled the blade back inside the gate. "What are you doing here? How did you know where I lived?"

"I followed you home the other night. Please let me in. I have to talk to you."

Against my better judgment, I lifted the gate latch. "This isn't a good time."

Velvet pushed inside and gripped my arm. "You have to transform me, Lorcan please."

"Velvet, not this again. I've told you I won't do it. You need to go. Now."

Tears streamed down her cheeks. "A little girl died alone because I was weak. Human. I fell asleep when she needed me most. I had promised her I would be there when . . . I need to become a vampire so I can be strong. I don't want to be a useless drunk, I want to

280

help—"

We both turned as heavy footsteps crunched in the leaves on the drive leading from the road up to the front gates. A familiar figure sprinted toward us. Braedon.

Braedon charged me, his fists balled, and his face twisted with rage. I side-stepped his swing and pushed him back. He fell on the drive.

Two more dark figures emerged from woods on the other side of the drive. I didn't recognize either. One jumped atop Velvet's car with the speed of a panther. Dressed in black, the moonlight illuminated his thin, pasty face. He glared down at us with narrowed eyes and open mouth. Curved canines extended over his lower lip. He let out a low hiss as he leaped from the car roof to the hood. In an instant I knew. A Vasile. His legs flexed, ready to jump.

On instinct, I swung the machete with both hands as hard as I could. A long stream of blood flew through the air following the flight of my blade and his decapitated head. The headless body crumpled and fell on the hood of the car. Blood from the dark neck hole leaked over the end of the car hood and slowly coated the shiny grill in a viscous red. The metallic odor of blood mingled with a strong acidic odor that smelled neither human nor like any animal I knew.

The second, another Vasile by his distinctive scent, cleared the sports car in one leap and rushed at us. I swung at him as he dashed past, but he moved so fast I missed. He shoved Velvet from his path, knocking her to the ground, and then ran through the open gates. Braedon had climbed to his feet and hurried to Velvet. The Vasile raced straight for the house. The front doors stood wide open. The girls!

I ran after him swinging the machete, yet the tip only managed to snag the tails of his long coat flying behind him. Once inside the foyer, he spun and faced me, brandishing a long-bladed knife. Then, to my horror, he ran up the wall, flattened his back against the ceiling and somehow hung there, hissing at me. I jumped and lunged at him with the machete. His body slithered along the ceiling, teasing me, just inches beyond my reach. An instant later, he dropped. His weight knocked me onto the floor. He circled so fast, all I could make out was the blur of his pale face and black coat. On my back, I swung my blade wildly. Sparks flew as it clashed against the knife he wielded.

The dizzying swirl of motion stopped. He loomed over me. A glint of silver, then pain, sudden and icy, stunned me. His blade had slashed across my stomach. He crouched low, eyes bulging, and fangs exposed. The stench of his breath made me gag. He gripped my throat with one hand and raised the knife over his head with the other. His fingers tightened around my neck like a steel collar, stopping my breath. My shirt felt wet and heavy with my blood. I tightened my grip on the machete, but my arms lay paralyzed at my sides. His lips twisted into a vicious grin, elongated fangs glistening with saliva. His irises, pitch black, grew until the whites turned black. The two black ovals reflected a double image of my horrified face.

A whirlwind of faces and thoughts flashed in my mind. Emilia. He would kill me and then take Emilia back to spend her life as a breeder for his evil cult. Angela's sweet face. He would drain her blood and leave her to die. And Jane. She trusted me to protect the girls.

I can't let him hurt them.

More images—symbols and letters—formed snippets of code in my mind. I drew up my legs and kicked the Vasile off of me, then jumped to my feet and ran. Emilia's code filtered seamlessly into mine. My feet thundered up the wall. My code initiated another sequence of actions. I flipped backward in mid-air and swung my sword with all my strength. My blade cut deep into one side of the Vasile's neck. Thick white muscle and spurting veins barely held his head on his body. Slowed and with his head flopped to one side, he still lunged at me. I hacked at the open wound. His head thudded against the stucco wall, dropped and then rolled across the floor. It came to a stop next to the convulsing body. The bloody knife still clutched in his hand clattered against the tile until the death throes ended.

I kicked the head away in fear it might somehow reunite with the body. These men had moved so fast, were there only two? Did I miss any? What if others had broken into the rear of the house? I ran

282

down the hall and into my room. The hidden chamber in the wall looked secure, but had the girls made it inside?

"Emilia! Are you in there?"

No answer. Frantic, I ran my hands over the wall until I triggered the mechanism that opened the hidden door.

Crouching, I peered inside the dark space. "Emilia? Angela?"

I ducked as a silver blade stabbed out from the darkness. Emilia's slender hand clutched my Haven dagger.

"Emilia, it's me." Kneeling, I laid my bloody machete on the floor and held out my arms. Still holding the dagger, she crawled out and hugged me.

She sniffed the air. "You killed the Vasiles. I smell their corpses." She pushed away from me and reached back into the dark recess behind her.

Clutching onto Emilia's hand, Angela scrambled from the tiny space, her eyes covered by a pink T-shirt pulled over her face. I stood, removed her blindfold and picked her up. She trembled in my arms, her big blue eyes filled with tears. Burying her tiny face against my cheek, she hugged her arms around my neck and whimpered, "Papa."

Still gripping the dagger, Emilia pointed it at my stomach. "You are wounded."

I felt inside the long rip in my T-shirt. My skin was wet with blood, but my flesh was not cut. It had already healed.

Footsteps pounded in the front foyer. Braedon called out, "Lorcan! Help!"

I sat Angela on my bed, looked at Emilia and held my finger to my lips. Grabbing the machete, I closed the door behind me and sprinted down the hallway. I narrowly missed impaling Braedon as he ran toward me.

"Come quick. That bastard stabbed Velvet."

I followed Braedon as he ran outside to the front gates. My senses prickled on high alert. I listened for footsteps, sniffed the night air like a dog and scanned the yard for more attackers.

Velvet lay on the ground just inside the gates. A dark stain showed on her shirt near her shoulder and blood pooled on the ground next to her head. Braedon dropped to his knees next to her prone body.

Satisfied no other Vasiles waited to attack, I gripped Braedon by his coat collar and dragged him to his feet. "Why did you bring the Vasiles here? Are you working with them?"

He stared at me and his mouth flapped but only made gasping sounds. I loosened my grip so he could talk. "I-I didn't bring anyone. I just followed Velvet here."

"You're not helping the Vasiles?"

"Why would I help that scum? I thought Velvet was cheating on me. Those guys came out of nowhere."

His wide-eyed denial, along with my gut, convinced me he was sincere. I released Braedon, then sprinted to Velvet's car and turned off the ignition so I could listen for approaching footsteps. I grimaced at the headless body draped down the center of the low-slung car hood.

Still paranoid, I locked the gates behind me before joining Braedon to assess Velvet's condition. He knelt and cradled her head against his chest, his mouth twisted in agony. "S-She's dying. I can't let her die."

I crouched next to Braedon to get a closer look at Velvet's wound. Her shoulder had been pierced just under the collar bone. My limited memory of anatomy class told me there were a lot of blood vessels in that area. I recalled how my mother, the nurse, would tsk-tsk whenever we watched movie where the hero suffered *only* a shoulder wound. She'd remark how Hollywood portrayed a shoulder wound as nothing, yet she said it could be a potentially fatal spot.

Velvet's naturally pale face had taken on a grayish cast. Her eyes stared unfocused into the sky and her breath came in erratic, shallow gasps.

"We can't call an ambulance. The bodies. We'll have to drive her to the hospital," I said.

"We'll need to explain the stab wound. A stranger stabbed her?" Braedon asked. "They'll call the police."

"There is no time for a hospital. She will die on the way," Emilia said.

Braedon and I spun around. Emilia stood in the driveway.

"Who's she?" Braedon asked.

"Never mind." I nodded to Emilia. "Go inside. It's not safe out here."

"I do not sense any more Vasiles are near." Emilia pointed to Velvet. "This woman is dying. You must give her your blood. Transforming her is the only way to save her."

"Is that true?" Without waiting for my reply, Braedon fumbled inside the pockets of his leather guard coat and pulled out his Haven dagger, identical to mine. He ran the razor-sharp blade across his wrist. As he held his bleeding wrist above Velvet's lips, his shoulders heaved, and he let out a sob.

"Please work this time, please." Tears leaked from his eyes and joined his blood dripping into her mouth. A gurgling noise escaped Velvet's parted lips which looked purplish beneath her glossy red lipstick. Her eyes closed and her chest no longer rose and fell with breaths.

Braedon gripped my arm, his fingers dug into my flesh. "My blood won't work. I've tried to transform her before and . . . I-I can't." He sobbed harder. "You were human, like her. Maybe yours? Give her your blood. Please. I'm begging you."

He slumped over Velvet's body and cried. The sight, coupled with the anguish in his voice, stunned me. I had never considered Braedon as anything but a selfish, arrogant ass. Now, he looked broken, pitiful. His words stirred in the back of mind. He tried to transform Velvet before? She told me he refused to give her blood. I had believed he only used poor Velvet for blood and sex.

Braedon's hand shook as he held out his dagger to me. My fractured thoughts melded into clarity as his tortured, tear-filled eyes met mine. He truly loved Velvet.

I turned to Emilia who stood watching us. She nodded.

Taking the dagger from Braedon, I swiped the blade across my pants leg to clean his blood from it. Jane would insist on sterilizing it, but there was no time. It may already be too late, if this worked at all. I sliced open the vein in my wrist and pressed the bloody wound to Velvet's cold lips.

"She can't die." Braedon rose to his feet, pulled at his spiky hair and paced in a circle around us.

Emilia leaned down and squeezed Velvet's limp hand. "Continue giving her your blood, Lorcan."

"Who the fuck is this kid? What the hell does she know?" Braedon yelled. He started toward Emilia. I reached out with my free hand and slapped the flat side of my machete against his belly. "Stay away from her."

Velvet made more gurgling sounds, but then she coughed. Her eyelids flew open and her arms flailed at her sides. She moaned. "W-What's happening?"

Braedon dropped to his knees and pushed my arm away. "You're alive!" He gathered her into his arms and gently rocked her body.

"Bring her inside. We need to clean the wound. Give her pomegranate juice," I said.

"Juice? What the fuck will jui—"

Arrogant ass Braedon had returned. "Shut up and do it," I said.

Emilia ran ahead of us into the house. Braedon lifted Velvet in his arms and followed. I checked the yard again and then hurried inside and bolted the front door.

Emilia ran toward us, her arms loaded with sheets and towels. I motioned her into the living room as I flipped on the light switch. She spread a sheet over the sofa.

"Put her on the sofa," I said to Braedon.

I still held Braedon's dagger and used it to cut the strap of Velvet's tank top near the stab wound.

"Hey!" Braedon grabbed my arm "Why'd you cut her shirt?"

"Don't be an ass wipe." I batted his hand away. "We have to clean the wound."

Emilia ran down the hall and returned moments later with alcohol, tape, and gauze she had gathered from the bathroom. She handed them to Braedon.

He stared at the items in his hands, then shoved them at me. "Y-You do it."

I knelt on the floor and saturated a hand towel with alcohol. "This will hurt, but I have to disinfect the wound."

Velvet had quieted, though her eyes were wide and glassy. She nodded.

She gasped when I wiped the blood from around the wound. Her skin was punctured, and the wound looked deep, but the bleeding had stopped. I pressed a folded square of gauze firmly over the wound and taped it in place. Emilia brought in a bowl of warm water and set it on the coffee table. I washed away the smears of blood from around Velvet's mouth.

My cut had healed, and I wiped the dried blood from my wrist revealing unblemished skin. I tossed the towel to Braedon and he cleaned his wrist. A bright red scar remained on his skin.

Velvet stammered, "A-Am I t-transformed?"

"I don't know. But you're alive and the stab wound has stopped bleeding."

"What do you mean *you don't know?*" Braedon asked.

I glared at him. "I've never done this before. I don't know if she's a vampire or what the hell will happen to her."

"How did you get transformed?" he asked.

"I drank a vampire's blood. But then I almost died afterward. My hair fell out. I was sick, covered in sores for weeks. She may go through the same process. I don't know."

Velvet whimpered and tears shone in her eyes. Braedon stroked her hair back and kissed her face. "Don't listen to him. You're going to be fine."

She cleared her throat and drew in a long, ragged breath. "Lorcan's blood saved my life, Braedon. Whatever happens to me now, I'll deal with it. I—we—owe him."

Braedon hung his head, sighed, then thrust his arm out toward me. I instinctively backed up.

He held his palm up. "Velvet's right. Your blood saved her. Mine couldn't. Thank you."

He reached his hand out again and this time I grasped it in mine. We shook.

"I'll get her some juice," I said. "It might sound stupid to you, but it helped me."

On the way to the kitchen, I walked past the head lying in a puddle of blood on the foyer floor. The eyes were wide open but were now veiled by a thick, yellow film.

I took a jug of pomegranate juice from the refrigerator and then retrieved a glass from the cabinet. As I turned to go back to the living room, Emilia entered the kitchen doorway.

"Why did the Vasiles come here tonight?" she asked.

I shrugged. "They've been to this house before, back when—"

"Yes, I know. Eleven years ago, they were here. Murdered my mother and grandmother and kidnapped me. But if Jane is only now on a flight home, how did they arrive here before her?"

"Maybe they left for the States as soon as they found out Jane took you from the orphanage. You said she lost them for almost two days when you all traveled to Hungary. They must have assumed she got a flight out of Romania sooner and came home."

Emilia shook her head. "I do not know. It does not feel right to me."

"I don't know either. What I do know is two more of those murdering bastards are dead, you and Angela are safe, and Jane will be home with us tomorrow. And Velvet's alive. That's all that matters." I patted Emilia's shoulder. "Thank you for your help tonight. I doubted my blood could save Velvet."

"You are very strong. You should never doubt your power."

I scanned the blood on the foyer floor and more spattered up the walls. "I need to clean this mess. Keep Angela in the bedroom until I get rid of the body. And the one outside, too."

"I have told her to stay in our room. She always listens to me. Maybe we should not go to Echo's house and instead all go to the airport together."

"No, Emilia, it's too dangerous. We know the Vasiles are here, but we don't know how many." I checked the clock on the kitchen wall. Nine-thirty. "I'll call Echo and tell her we'll be late."

Velvet was sitting up on the sofa when I returned with the juice. Her bandage was removed and the wound on her shoulder had healed to a thin pink line. Braedon sat next to her, his arm draped protectively around her shoulders.

I poured juice into the glass and handed it to Velvet. "Here, this helped me when I was first transformed. You'll need to avoid solid food for a while, but you must stay hydrated. Keep drinking juice, water." It felt like another lifetime ago when Jane had given me the same advice on this very sofa.

Remembering Velvet's love of drinking herself into a stupor

every night, I added, "And *no* alcohol."

Velvet sipped the juice. "Hmm, this is good. I am really thirsty."

Braedon leaned forward on the sofa. "Aldon can't ever find out about this, Lorcan."

"Don't you think I know that? He'd kill me in a second. I just took a damn vow in front of him that I would never transform a human."

Braedon stood. "He'd kill both of us and Velvet, too." He squared his shoulders and jutted his chin in the air. "I guess we have no choice but to trust each other to keep this secret."

"Look, Braedon, I'm happy Velvet's alive, but I don't want to die. I'm not going to tell anyone."

"What about that kid? Who knows who she'll blab to."

"She won't tell anyone." I said.

"How can you be so sure?"

"Because I am. Now drop it."

Braedon squinted his eyes at me and grunted. "She's a vampire, isn't she?"

"I said drop it. We have bigger worries. The two men who came here tonight are part of the Vasile family. There're more coming. We need to get The Haven guards ready for an attack."

"Why are the Vasiles coming after you?' Braedon asked.

"They're not. I only know they're out to slaughter all the humans or hybrids they can. Anyone who's not a Pure Blood is in danger. And The Haven is full of hybrid vamps and humans."

"Funny, they didn't try to kill me. And that guy had a knife in his hand when he pushed Velvet, it looked more like an accident than him trying to kill her. What the hell have you done, Lorcan? Started a war with the damn Pure Bloods all on your own?" He paced the living room then turned and pointed at me. "Or does this have something to do with that creepy little vampire kid? I picked up a weird vibe from her. She's a Pure, isn't she?"

"You're going to have to trust me. You saw how fast they move, how high they can jump. We all need to be prepared for another attack."

"My guards are all excellent fighters," Braedon said.

"Still, they need to be warned about the Vasiles' fighting tactics."

I doubted most of the guards could fight a Vasile and win. I had beaten all of them, except for Bat, during my test.

"I'll help you fight them. I'm feeling stronger by the minute," Velvet said. Her eyes had taken on an intense midnight-blue color and shone with a luminous inner light. Her hair looked shinier as well, especially the blue streaks which matched her eyes.

I shook my head. "No. You need to stay low until we know if you really are transformed."

"He's right, babe," Braedon said. "You can't come to The Haven anymore. If Aldon sees you, he'll assume I'm the one who turned you. I'd be a dead man."

"You mean I can't hang out at the club with you? What's the point of being a vamp if I can't show it off?"

"Velvet, you can't go back to The Haven—ever. That's final," I said.

Velvet's lower lip, visibly plumper now, jutted out in a pout. "Aldon will notice I'm gone."

"I'll tell him we broke up." Braedon snorted. "That should make the old fucker happy."

Braedon's open disrespect of Aldon surprised me, especially coupled with his earlier admission that he had tried to transform Velvet before. On one hand, Braedon kissed the old man's ass at The Haven. Yet, secretly he defied Aldon's strictest rule and now spoke of him with disgust.

"What if the three of us go to Aldon and tell him the truth?" Velvet asked. "He allowed Lorcan to join The Haven, why wouldn't he allow me? We're both former humans."

Braedon shook his head. "I still can't figure out why he let Lorcan into The Haven. He says he's softened his view on humans after talking with Raina. But he's always looked down on anyone who wasn't a Pure, superior asshole that he is. We can't take the chance. He's old, but strong. He could easily kill all three of us for disobeying his rule."

"We'll figure out how to handle Aldon later. Right now, I have to get rid of two bodies. And then I have an important errand to do. It's not safe for you two to stay here. More Vasiles could be coming."

"So, only your house and The Haven are in danger of being

attacked? And what's this *important errand* you have to do? Cut the bullshit and tell me what the hell's going on, Lorcan," Braedon said.

"That's all I can tell you. I've warned you about the Vasiles so you and the guards will be ready."

Braedon sneered at me. "Or, maybe the Vasiles just want to kill *you*."

"Braedon, stop it," Velvet said. "If it weren't for Lorcan I'd be lying dead in the driveway now. We need to trust each other, help each other. You should start by helping him with the bodies."

The authoritative tone Velvet used with Braedon surprised me, but I was even more surprised when he accompanied me outside to help dispose of the body on Velvet's car.

"I'll get some shovels from the tool shed." I said. "We'll go deep into the woods and bury them."

"You know, they say if you leave the body of a Vasile out in the sun they'll disintegrate. Then all you need is a broom to sweep away the ashes, no digging." Braedon shrugged. "Just saying."

"Except that means leaving two dead bodies lying outside and hoping that's true. What if it's not? I can't have Jane coming home and find—"

Braedon cocked his head. "Who's Jane?"

"She's my, uh, girlfriend." Shit. I couldn't believe I'd blurted out Jane's name. But Braedon only knew Jane by her club name, Raina. Hopefully he wouldn't figure out she's the same woman.

"So, you live with this Jane, huh? I thought you and Raina were. You know." Braedon grinned and repeatedly pounded his fist against his open hand. "That's the rumor around the club, anyway."

I wanted to punch the shit-eating grin from Braedon's face, but now wasn't the time to start a fight. "I keep my private life private," I said.

"Hey, that's cool. Just that I've seen you and Raina at the club together and damn, she's hot." Braedon smiled. "So, is Jane human or vamp?"

"Vamp." Crap. Should I have said human? With everything going on tonight, my mind spun in too many directions to keep track of all the lies. I wished Braedon would shut the hell up and help me with the body instead of flapping his mouth.

"So how come you've never brought Jane to the club?" Braedon paused. A wicked smile twisted his lips. "Oh wait. Now I get it. You don't want Raina to find out about Jane. You're a real dog, aren't you Lorcan?" Braedon slapped me on the back and snickered.

I turned and glared at him with my fists clenched. Braedon held up his hands and stepped back. "Calm down, man. I said, it's cool. I won't tell anybody." The lewd grin painted his face again, belying his words.

"Like I *said*, my private life is none of your fucking business."

"All right. Hey, just one more thing. Now that Velvet's been vamped, is sex different when you're both vamps?" he asked.

As much as I wanted to deck him a second ago, the curious schoolboy look on his face made me laugh in spite of my anger. "Oh yeah. Totally different."

Braedon's eyes and grin widened.

While he snickered and fantasized about vampire sex, I stalked down the driveway and opened the gate. He was no help. I preferred our previous arrangement where we both openly despised each other and didn't speak.

I grabbed the headless body by the legs and dragged it off of Velvet's car.

Braedon's questions angered me, plus he wasn't as dumb as I thought. He had already seen Emilia, deduced she was a Pure Blood and suspected a link between her and the Vasiles. Jane trusted me to protect the girls and to protect her mission in Romania. Now I'd screwed up and revealed Jane's real name. I couldn't wait until she arrived home tomorrow. Together we could handle anything.

Ironically only minutes after Velvet's heart-felt words about trust and helping each other, I reached an obvious epiphany: I couldn't trust Braedon. While his love for Velvet might be sincere, he was still a giant prick in my opinion.

Braedon finally strolled through the gates with his hands in his coat pockets. He watched as I dragged the headless corpse by its ankles into the woods. "Damn. Where's the fucking head?"

I nodded toward the other side of the wooded lane. "Look over there."

Thankfully, acres of dense woods surrounded Jane's property and the nearest neighbors lived miles away. From the main road, the rutted dirt lane leading into the woods appeared to be a forgotten hiking trail. The lane curved and only the section in front of the gates was paved. The full length of it, as well as the house, was obscured by trees from the view of passing drivers.

Dried leaves crunched as I pulled the body through the thick brush. Branches scratched my arms, face, and snagged in my T-shirt. The noise, amplified in the silence of night, spooked an owl. The bird hooted in the darkness and fluttered overhead. Hauling the dead weight over the uneven ground proved more of a slow and tedious chore than I anticipated. Several yards into the woods, I literally stumbled into a small clearing, twisting my ankle in the process. I decided to leave the body there and test Braedon's theory. Hopefully it would turn to ash under the sun's rays tomorrow. After I brought Jane home from the airport, I'd check to be sure. If the corpses hadn't disintegrated, I'd bury them.

As I limped from the woods on my painful ankle, I found Braedon kicking the missing head across the pavement in my direction. Using both his feet, he fielded it like a soccer ball. His last kick sent the head spinning across the lane toward me. It bumped the grassy edge, wobbled and then came to a stop between my feet.

Braedon raised his arms in the air. "Score!"

The severed head's face pointed skyward, one eye closed, the other wide open. The open eye stared through an iridescent yellow film. Bits of leaves and dirt stuck in its long dark hair and to the gray-white, rubbery flesh. Blood oozed from the cut neck and had left a spattered trail on the pavement.

"Great. Now there's more blood to clean up," I said.

Braedon scowled at me. "What the fuck? I wasn't going to pick it up with my hands."

"There's a hose in the tool shed and a spigot near the front door. You can wash the blood off the road and Velvet's car." I stepped over the head and brushed past him to retrieve the other body from inside the house.

I slid a trash bag over the bloody neck end of the body so it wouldn't leak blood when I dragged it outside. The foyer already looked like a slaughterhouse and would take me a while to clean. The black plastic covered most of the torso. I nudged the head toward the bag with the toe of my boot. The open mouth with the upper lip pulled taut over the exposed fangs formed a hideous grin and the furrowed black brows accentuated the eerie yellow-veiled eyes. The same expression as when he tried to kill me.

Outside, Braedon had the hose stretched out to reach Velvet's car. He had also taken a bucket, detergent and a brush from the shed and was busy scrubbing the front grill as I dragged the second body past. The pavement all around the car was wet and puddled with sudsy water. He had listened and hosed away the blood.

The pain in my ankle had vanished. Rapid healing was quickly becoming my favorite vampire perk. I paused at the edge of the road and kicked the one-eyed head into the bag, then dragged the whole bloody mess to the clearing and left it exposed next to the other corpse. I really hoped the sun would finish the job. Alive the Vasiles' scent was unpleasant enough, but death had intensified their foul stench and breathing it in made me queasy. I could only imagine how putrid the odor would be by tomorrow.

When I exited the woods, I found Braedon rolling up the hose as he walked up the driveway toward the shed. I picked up the bucket and brush he'd left behind to wash the foyer floor and walls.

Braedon entered the foyer as I scrubbed on all fours. He stepped over my feet and tracked mud across the portion of the floor I had washed.

"Where's Velvet?" he asked.

I craned my neck and peered around the archway into the living room. "I don't know." The sofa was empty except for a pile of neatly folded sheets and towels stacked on one cushion.

Braedon hurried down the hallway. "Velvet!"

"Hey, hold up." I stood and jogged to catch up with him. If he found the two girls or Jane's laboratory, he'd ask more questions. "Take it easy. She's probably in the bathroom."

"You've got damn Vasiles after you. What if one snuck in while we were outside and—"

"Can't a girl use the bathroom without everyone getting all crazed?" Velvet turned the corner at the end of the hall and sauntered toward us.

We both stopped short and gaped. Though Velvet had been an attractive girl before, she was a striking beauty now. The contrast between her ivory complexion and lustrous blue-black hair was breathtaking.

"You look amazing," Braedon said.

"I felt so different, I just had to find a mirror." She fluttered her lush eyelashes at me. "I figured there must be a bathroom down the hall. Hope you don't mind, Lorcan."

"No, it's fine. How do you feel?"

"Awesome. It's beyond anything I ever imagined. I feel so strong, energized." She smiled and her entire face lit with an ethereal glow, from her perfect white teeth to her luminous, indigo eyes.

She fluffed her hair. "I think my hair's grown about two inches. And my skin, it's so smooth, I can't even see my pores." Velvet giggled like a little girl. "I won't need makeup anymore." She twirled in a circle and then threw her arms around Braedon's neck. "Let's go out and celebrate."

Braedon stood slack-jawed with his arms hanging at his sides.

"You need to take it easy, Velvet. No drinking unless it's juice or water," I said. Not that I wished for Velvet to be bald and covered in pus-filled sores like I was after my transformation, but it somehow didn't seem fair. It took me weeks to fully achieve my physical changes. Yet, for her, only hours. As difficult as the transformation process had been for me, I imagined it would be even harder for a woman, especially one as vain as Velvet.

It was after midnight by the time I'd finished cleaning up all the blood in the foyer. Braedon and Velvet finally decided to leave.

"You saved my life, Lorcan. I'll never forget that." Velvet hugged me and kissed my cheek.

Braedon stood in the open front doorway watching her. "Let's go, babe." Though he tried to sound casual, his white-knuckled grip on the doorknob and clamped jaw betrayed his seething jealousy. Velvet gave him a wicked smile, then turned and kissed me again before joining him.

I locked the gate and front door after they had gone. I was a mess. My shirt, ripped and covered with dried blood, stuck to my torso. I slowly peeled it off as I walked down the hall to check on the girls. Their bedroom door was cracked open a few inches. Emilia played cartoons on Jane's laptop to entertain Angela. The sound of Angela's innocent giggles made me smile. Covered in blood, I hurried past their room into mine so my appearance wouldn't frighten little Angela.

In all the commotion, I had forgotten to call Echo earlier and tell her we'd be later than planned. I picked up my cell, aware my call would probably wake her now, but I had no choice. I needed a safe place to take the girls while I went to the airport to pick up Jane.

She answered on the second ring, and to my relief, sounded wide awake.

"Echo, I'm so sorry to call this late. I, um, got tied up with some stuff. Is it okay if I bring the girls over now?" I had no back-up plan if she refused.

"Oh, sure. Wow, it's after midnight. I lost track of time. I'm working on your female vampire warrior illustration. I'll show you when you get here." Her voice lowered, "I-I think you'll like it."

"I have no doubt."

Echo continued talking. Her chattiness and upbeat tone unusual. "I talked to Paul and Rudi for almost an hour on Skype. Afterwards, they emailed me a contract for eighty thousand, just like you said. Can you believe that?"

"Yes, I can. You're a phenomenal artist, Echo. I'm happy you nailed the job."

"Well, *I* still can't believe it. Thank you, Lorcan. It never would have happened if you hadn't recommended me. I owe you."

"You don't owe me anything. But I appreciate you watching the girls. That's a huge help."

"No problem. Oh, I inflated an air mattress on the living room floor. Is it okay if both girls sleep there? My place is kind of small."

"That's perfect. Thanks again. We'll be there within the hour."

After ending the call with Echo, I stuffed my bloody clothes into a trash bag to deal with later and took a much-needed shower. Red water swirled in the drain for several minutes before it finally turned clear.

After I dressed, I washed the blood from the machete blade. Though I couldn't bring it inside the airport, I planned to hide it in my car. Having it near gave me comfort. Whether it had been luck or skill tonight, I had killed two Vasiles with this blade, lopping off their heads as Jane instructed. The reality that I beheaded two men hadn't quite gelled in my brain. I felt nothing when I decapitated them. My body simply performed the actions the code dictated in my mind. Perhaps the code provided an autonomous barrier to my emotions. Yet, as I scrubbed their dried, foul-smelling blood from the blade, my hands trembled. Though I had killed the two men to protect the girls and myself, the realization I was capable of such heinous acts shook me to my core.

A soft knock on my door startled me. I jumped to my feet, blade ready. A Vasile would break down the door and storm inside, not knock politely. I took a deep breath and called, "Come in."

Emilia entered and held out my Haven dagger. "I saw your long coat hanging in your closet. The Vasiles hide knives in their coats. I searched inside yours. I hope you are not angry that I took it."

"No, Emilia. I'm not angry. You only took it to protect Angela and yourself."

She nodded and walked over to my guard coat and slid the dagger back inside.

On the drive to Echo's apartment, Emilia sat in silence with both hands clasping the laptop. Angela, excited about the car ride, babbled for about ten minutes before the hum of the engine lulled her to sleep. I checked the rear-view mirror constantly to make sure no Vasiles followed us.

Echo lived on the second floor of a modest apartment complex in the suburbs. Before she opened the door, she released a dead bolt and a chain lock. The extra security made me feel better, though it wouldn't stop a Vasile.

The studio had an open living area and a separate bathroom. A kitchenette took up one corner and I imagined the curtained-off area at the other end of the space served as her bedroom. The air mattress on the floor took up most of the main room. The colorful decor surprised me, but not as much as the pink flush in Echo's cheeks and the excitement in her voice when she greeted us.

After brief introductions, Emilia settled on a small sofa and opened her laptop. Angela bounced on the air mattress until Emilia whispered for her to stop. The little girl pouted but then settled down on the soft bed and constructed a fort of pillows around her.

Echo motioned for me to follow as she walked to her computer desk. She tapped the mouse to wake the machine and when the screen saver blinked off, my breath caught in my throat. An image of Jane's face filled the monitor. Her golden hair, moist lips, and honey-colored skin looked so life-like, for an instant I believed it was a photograph. I stared into her intense aquamarine eyes, expecting them to blink.

My eyes stung and Jane's image blurred. I swiped away my tears while Echo's back was turned.

"The description of the character in the email you sent sounded so much like Raina. And since the male warrior looks exactly like you, I thought, well. . . Is this what you wanted?"

Echo mistook my awed silence as disapproval. The corners of her smiling mouth quivered, and her lips compressed into a thin line. "Oh, no. You hate it. I'm so sorry. I-I'll try something different." She wrung her bony hands and then moved the mouse cursor to click the image away.

"Don't." I lifted her hand from the mouse. "Please don't change a thing. She's perfect."

"Are you sure?" She let out a sigh. "You acted like—"

"It just overwhelmed me. Yes, I'm positive. I love her—I mean—the artwork. I love it."

Echo's tenuous smile returned. "Okay, if you're sure." She studied my face. "Are you all right, Lorcan?" She lowered her voice to a whisper. "Do you need blood?"

Blood? Her question made me want to laugh and scream. Hadn't I seen enough blood tonight? I had been drenched in it—the Vasiles', Velvet's, and my own. I shivered at the memory of lying on the floor, my blood leaking from the deep slash in my stomach. I'd almost died.

Then I remembered Echo's blood, clean and crisp like green apples. It gave me physical strength and mental clarity. After the stress I'd been through tonight, maybe I did have a need. The tremor in my hands earlier, and now my sudden tears, could be the first signs of vamping out. I had to stay strong.

I nodded. "Yes, I think I do."

"Give me a few minutes." Echo hurried off into the bathroom and closed the door.

As I walked the few short steps to where the girls were, I wondered how we would manage a blood tryst in the tiny apartment without the girls witnessing it.

Emilia focused on the screen in her lap, immersed in a computer language lesson. Angela snuggled into the pillows and paged through one of her story books. I picked up a tattered stuffed bear next to her. She smiled, dropped the book and reached her hands out. "My bear."

She took the bear from me, pushed its face against my cheek and made kissing noises. She handed the bear to me and I tickled her sides with its faded plastic nose. She squealed with delight.

Echo returned. I gave the bear back to Angela and joined Echo in the kitchenette.

"Here." She handed me a small plastic pill bottle that contained a few ounces of red liquid.

"I thought it would be better like this, you know, with the kids here."

"Yes. Thank you." I slid the precious bottle into my pocket. "I'll be back tomorrow afternoon to get the girls. And Echo, it's important that you keep them inside with the door locked at all times. Don't open the door to anyone. Please, promise me you'll do that."

She looked suspicious and opened her mouth to speak, but then just nodded.

I handed her money and told her to order in food for her and the girls. Echo protested, but I pushed the folded bills into her hand.

As I hugged Angela goodbye, tears welled in her eyes. This would be the first time the girls were out of my care since they arrived. Only three days together yet the depth of my attachment to them shocked me. I felt torn between staying and going, but I had to bring Jane home. Emilia stood, her dark eyes solemn. "We are

299

anxious for Aunt Jane to return to us." She paused and reached for my hand. "And you."

Though I saw no strange vehicles on the drive over, I couldn't quite shake my fear that the Vasiles had followed us to Echo's. I reasoned it was only paranoia and certainly the girls were safer here with Echo than alone at Jane's house, or accompanying me to the airport, especially if the Vasiles had followed Jane.

It was more than a need for blood making me emotional. Seeing Jane's image on Echo's screen triggered an avalanche of raw emotions. The inconsolable void inside me would never be filled until we were reunited. I wanted to hear every detail of her trip and wanted to tell her all about the girls' first days in America. To share with her how intelligent and mature Emilia was and how Angela had flung herself at me and called me papa as soon as we met at the airport.

I would tell her about the Vasile attack and about transforming Velvet to save her life even though I had broken Aldon's golden rule by doing it. Jane would understand. I would never keep secrets from her. Mostly I just wanted to hold her again, breathe in her sweet scent and feel complete again. Ever since she'd left, I'd been only a wireframe outline of myself. Jane brought me to life.

I waited in the car for a while, watching Echo's apartment door, windows, and the surrounding neighborhood to see if any dark figures crept from the shadows. Like a shot of tequila, I downed Echo's blood in one gulp. After the immediate head-rush passed, a calmness washed over me. It still amazed me how a few ounces of blood renewed my body, mind, and spirit. My mind, now clear, laser-focused on my most important task, to bring Jane home. I pulled out of Echo's complex and headed for the airport.

Chapter 18

I know I am in love with you because my reality is finally better than my dreams. —Dr. Seuss

Two and a half hours later, I pulled into a short-term parking lot at LAX. Traffic had been light on the freeway, and I made excellent time, a good omen which buoyed my spirits even higher. It was only four in the morning, so I had an hour and twenty minutes to wait until Jane's flight arrived. I leaned back in the driver's seat and closed my eyes. Between the fresh infusion of blood and my anticipation to see Jane, sleep was an impossibility. My mind drifted to my imminent reunion with Jane. I thought of Braedon and laughed out loud. Now I was the one who grinned and fantasized about vampire sex.

At five o'clock, I locked up the car and walked across the lot to the terminal building. The bright florescent lights inside blinded me for an instant, but unlike sunlight, didn't burn my eyes and skin. I hurried to the computerized display board and scanned through the list for flight number 1054.

The number wasn't on the list. I checked Jane's text message on my phone. 1054 was the correct number. I hurried across the wide concourse to an information desk. The woman behind the desk gave me a smile as crisp and perfect as her blue uniform.

"Good morning." I said. "Flight 1054 is due in twenty minutes, but it's not listed on the board. I need to know which gate it's arriving at?"

"Where is the flight coming from, sir?"

"Bucharest, Romania."

"Oh, this board has domestic flights only. The international board is over there." She smiled again and pointed down the concourse.

"Thank you." I sprinted to the board she indicated and checked the listings. Still no flight 1054. I drew in a deep breath. Jane must have typed the wrong number. Her text message was short as though she had been in a hurry.

I jogged to another counter. A young man looked up at me from behind a computer monitor. Acne spattered his cheeks, chin, and forehead like dots of red ink. An engraved name tag on his jacket read, *Richard*. He pushed his dark-rimmed glasses back in place on his shiny nose. "May I help you, sir?"

"What gate is the flight from Bucharest arriving at this morning?"

"One moment." He tapped keys on his computer for what felt like an eternity and then frowned at the screen. "There are no incoming flights from Bucharest today."

"There's got to be. Check again."

He sighed and typed some more. "Nope. Nada."

"There has to be a mistake. My girlfriend's arriving at five-twenty this morning. She said flight 1054, but she might have the number incorrect."

"Sir, the next flight from Bucharest isn't until two days from now. Flight 1174."

My heart sped up. "There's got to be, unless. . . Would you check for flights from Budapest?"

"As in Budapest, *Hungary*?" Richard arched a bushy eyebrow. "You do know that's in a different country, right?"

I was in no mood for his sarcasm. "Yes. Yes, I do, *Dick*. Just check."

He huffed and then focused on his keyboard. "There was a flight that arrived from Budapest at three twenty-two this morning. Number 1045. It disembarked at gate twenty-six."

"Which way to gate twenty-six?"

He pointed upward to the second level. I bolted up the escalator two steps at a time and then ran through the upper terminal. I dodged past people dragging suitcases and checked the overhead gate number signs as I ran. Maybe Jane had decided to stay in Hungary after all and flew out from Budapest. 1054 and 1045, the numbers were close, two digits transposed. Yet the arrival times were very different. She could have made a mistake in her math when figuring the time difference.

Gate twenty-four, twenty-five, and then finally I arrived at twenty-six. No one sat in the rows of chairs or stood behind the small boarding desk. My heart beat hard inside my chest. I dropped into one of the vinyl chairs. Jane's here somewhere. It's an enormous airport. If her flight arrived at three-twenty, then she's been waiting for almost two hours. Maybe she's in the rest room or the food court. But why hadn't she called me?

Then it hit me. She's not in Romania anymore, I can call her cell.

I scrolled to Jane's name on my phone, hit the call button for her burner cell and waited. "C'mon, answer." But she didn't. I let it ring until a recording told me the party I had called was unavailable with no voicemail activated. She'd disconnected the mailbox before she left as a safety measure.

My heart, now a sledgehammer, pounded against my ribs. What the hell do I do now?

A ding from my cell signaled a new text message from Jane. It read, *Gate 128.*

I jumped up from the chair and ran.

The upper level formed an enormous horseshoe and I ran almost the entire track. Gate 128 was the last gate in the airport. As I neared Gate 126, I slowed to a jog. Orange barricades blocked access to the last two gates. Beyond the barricades, a curtain of dusty construction plastic hung in wide strips from ceiling to floor. A sign attached to the plastic read, *Gates 127 and 128 Closed. Please Pardon Our Dust.*

Why would Jane be at a gate that wasn't even operational? Unless—the Vasiles followed her here and she was hiding. I sniffed the air and scoured the terminal looking for suspicious men dressed in black. I neither smelled nor saw anyone out of the ordinary.

I replied to Jane's text. *Where R U?*

When she didn't respond, I slipped in between the plastic strips. The concourse lights penetrated only a few feet beyond the plastic, then the area turned dark, illuminated by the red glow of emergency lights. My vision preferred the dim lighting. Side-stepping piles of construction materials and debris on the floor, I made my way to the former gate 128. The chairs and counter had been stripped away and it appeared they were preparing to lay new flooring. Only the baggage carousel remained intact. My boots raised dust as I walked, the miniscule particles swirling in the red glow and adding to the stuffiness in the air.

"Jane, where are you? Jane!" My voice echoed in the open space. She's got to be here. I jiggled the handle on a door which led to a detachable corridor for boarding a plane. It was locked. As I turned, a lone, dark shape on the baggage carousel caught my eye. Jane's leather backpack! I rushed to the carrousel and picked it up. "Jane?" I circled the oval conveyor and even reached inside the curtain of rubber strips where the luggage fed from the conveyor belt. An empty, black void greeted my touch.

I hugged her bag close to my chest. Through the worn leather, I smelled Jane's scent.

Opening the bag, I rummaged through the contents. Shirts, a pair of jeans, underwear, and a few toiletries. I lifted the front flap and checked inside the pocket. Empty. The red light illuminated odd marks on the underside of the flap. Though crude, it looked like words written in brown ink, difficult to discern on the aged suede lining. As I ran my fingers over the marks, I smelled a familiar odor. It wasn't ink; it was blood. I brought the bag close to my mouth and touched my tongue to one of the marks. Jane's blood, the taste unmistakable. The bloody letters had matted down the suede and I had to hold the flap directly under the red light to make out the words. *NO TRADE.*

My cell chimed, startling me. I dropped the bag on the carousel and fumbled to retrieve the message. The new text was longer—and not from Jane. *Bring us the Pure girl or we will kill the woman, Jane. We will contact you with a place and time for the exchange.*

A tremor crept down my spine and gained intensity as it traveled. My legs shook and refused to support my weight. I collapsed on my knees. The Vasiles had Jane.

I gathered Jane's backpack into my arms and buried my face in the sweet scent of her clothes. My sobs echoed in the deserted gate.

"Hey, buddy. What are you doing back here?"

I looked up, my eyes blurred with tears. A flashlight beam blinded me. I shielded my eyes with my hand. Two uniformed men stood a few yards away. Security guards. The younger one, tall, with a reddish mustache, placed his hand on his holstered gun, while the other man, older and slighter in build, moved toward me with slow, deliberate steps.

"Put your hands up where I can see 'em," the older guard said.

I held my hands up as my mind shuffled through plausible responses to his question. I can't get arrested. Jane's life depended on me. Only me. The weight of that realization crushed down on me as I slowly rose to my feet.

"What are you doing in here?" the guard asked again.

"I-I wanted to be alone for a few minutes," I said.

The guard stopped a few feet away from me. He ran his flashlight beam from my face down to my feet. "And why's that?"

"My girlfriend . . . she's g-gone."

Mustache guy moved in closer. He snorted and rolled his eyes.

"Sorry for your troubles, buddy," the older one said. "But you can't stay here. This area is off limits to unauthorized personnel."

"I'm sorry. I'll leave."

"Wait a second," Mustache guy said. "What's in the backpack?"

"Her clothes, make-up and stuff," I said.

"Step back. Let me look inside the bag," he said.

I nodded and backed away with my hands in the air while the young guard opened the pack and checked the contents.

"So why do you have your girlfriend's backpack if she broke up with you?" he asked.

My thoughts splintered in opposite directions. I agonized over what to do about Jane but forced myself to stay focused. "She said she had forgotten her pack in my car. Asked me to go get it for her. When I got back, she was boarding a flight with her new boyfriend. She just . . . left me."

The older guard turned to his partner. "Damn, that's cold."

Mustache man patted me down, then asked to see my ID. Once satisfied I wasn't a security threat, the two escorted me from the terminal building. The old guard clamped a hand on my shoulder. "There's plenty of fish out there, buddy. You're young. You'll be all

305

right."

They both stood outside the glass doors and watched as I walked to my car. Dawn had broken in the east, but heavy clouds shielded me from the rising sun. A light mist of rain blended with my tears.

I started the car and drove on autopilot until I exited the airport, then pulled into the first empty parking lot I found—a shopping plaza. It was six-thirty. Jane and I should be together now. Me, holding her hand, taking in her beauty, as we drove home. I had planned to take her back to her house, talk, grill her a steak if she were hungry and then make love before going to pick up the girls. Just a few hours of sweet normalcy.

But any hope of normalcy had been shattered. Shards of images—her smile, her kiss, her incredible, ever-changing eyes—floated in slow motion and sliced through my heart as they fell and smashed into unrecognizable bits.

My initial shock, then devastation, slowly turned to simmering rage. Those filthy murderers had Jane, but where? I had to get her back, but how? I jerked the car into drive and sped out onto the road, headed in the general direction of home.

Give them Emilia.

Sickening. Selfish. Cowardly. The thought disgusted me, and I rejected it the instant it flashed into my mind. I could never hand Emilia over to the Vasiles. She was brilliant, courageous, and above all, only a little girl. After all she had endured, she deserved freedom, happiness, and the chance to choose her own future. In Romania they would keep her locked up. Rape her, breed her like an animal and use her to bring more of their vile kind into the world.

I couldn't let that happen.

Jane knew their plan was to trade Emilia for herself. She'd managed to write a message in her own blood. A message to me. *No Trade.* She'd rather die than sentence Emilia to life with the Vasiles.

I couldn't let Jane die.

But even if I knew where she was, then what? Storm into a Vasile hideout? Me, against a clan of who-knows-how-many blood-thirsty monsters. They'd kill us both. I needed help. But who could I trust?

Braedon was the strongest of the guards, but I didn't trust him. Velvet might offer to help out of some sense of indebtedness she felt

306

toward me. But she weighed ninety pounds tops and had no fighting skills. She'd almost died once at a Vasile's hand. She'd be slaughtered. I doubted any of the other guards would risk their lives to help me.

My mind whirling, I braked hard at a red light. A billboard on the side of the road advertised an exclusive new subdivision. The headline read, *A Luxurious Haven.*

The Haven. Aldon. Jane told me she had confided in Aldon years ago. She'd told him how the Vasiles murdered her adoptive mother and sister and kidnapped Emilia. She'd said Aldon was sympathetic but wouldn't risk starting a war with the ruthless Vasile family. He weighed the hundreds of lives that could be lost against one girl's and ultimately advised Jane to let Emilia go.

But Jane couldn't do that. Instead she'd spent a decade tracking Emilia, communicating with her through Cristina, sending them money—it became her life's mission to rescue her niece. She'd trained herself to fight and then drank Lorelei's blood to forge herself into a hardened warrior.

I couldn't let Jane's life quest end in failure.

Aldon was my only hope. He was powerful and a Pure Blood with a lineage as long as the Vasiles'. He had connections with other influential Pures, both here and overseas. Perhaps he would intervene on Jane's behalf. He admired and respected Jane, or Raina, as he knew her, for both her blood research and the safety measures she implemented at The Haven to keep the vampires and donors free of diseases. She was an asset to Aldon and the entire club. Surely, he wouldn't allow the Vasiles to murder her.

But even if he refused to help me for fear of starting a war, he might at least know the Vasile's hideouts here—where they kept Jane.

Jane had charged into the Vasiles' home country and succeeded in single-handedly rescuing Emilia. I vowed to do the same to save her.

Either way, it meant I would have to betray Jane's trust and tell Aldon the truth. That she'd lied to him about going to the hematologist convention in New York and instead had traveled to Romania to rescue Emilia before she reached her Awakening.

And what if Aldon asked me about Emilia? Do I confess I had her hidden away? I'd sworn to Jane I'd keep Emilia's whereabouts secret from everyone.

I accelerated and zigzagged through lanes to get past the slower traffic. I had to talk to Aldon as quickly as possible. The Vasiles would be contacting me with a time and place for the exchange. My only plan was to destroy the murderous bastards before they set up the trade.

It was nine-forty when I pulled into The Haven parking lot. Dark clouds swirled in the sky and a steady rain fell. The dreary gray morning suited my mood. At least I didn't have to battle sunlight.

The Haven's Gothic spires and ornate wrought iron trim looked at home against the stormy sky. The only vehicles in the parking lot were Aldon's black Cadillac SUV with the dark-tinted windows and next to it, a red Mercedes sports car. I assumed it belonged to his current female companion.

During my guard duty, I'd observed a rotation of about half a dozen women who spent the night with Aldon in his private quarters. I had a difficult time discerning one woman from the other. They were all hybrids with long brunette hair, voluptuous figures, and were much younger than Aldon, though at his age, all of the women at the club were younger. These chosen few he consorted with were off limits to the other vampires at the club. They sat with him at his corner table on the balcony and later accompanied him to his suite. Though the rule was never to stare at Aldon or his female companions, I had sneaked glances on occasion and never witnessed them engaged in conversation. The women sat in silence and only left their seats to fetch Aldon a drink.

My ambitious plan unraveled as I stared up at the building. The club wouldn't open until late afternoon which meant it was locked up tight. The only key holders I was aware of were Wynn, whom I had no way to contact, and Braedon, whom I didn't trust though we had grudgingly exchanged cell numbers when I joined the guards.

I stared up at Aldon's balcony on the second floor. The rain, now heavy, pelted my face and soaked my clothing. I pictured code and it triggered a high jump. My hands gripped the slippery iron and I pulled myself upward. Hands grasped my ankles. The weight attached to them tugged me downward. My fingers slipped off the wet metal. I dropped to the ground and landed on my attacker.

"I knew I couldn't trust you!" Braedon's fist smashed into my jaw. The tamped-down rage inside of me exploded. I shoved Braedon. He flew across the lot and crashed into the side of Aldon's SUV. Eyes dazed, he shook his head, then re-focused and rushed toward me.

I charged across the parking lot to meet him. A flash of black entered my peripheral vision. Velvet stood between us, one slender hand on each of our chests. Her ability to hold us both back stunned me.

"You rotten fucker," Braedon yelled. "I knew you'd try to screw me." He looked at Velvet. "I told you. He wants to be head guard. He's going to tell Aldon I turned you. Get us both killed."

I shouted back, "I don't give a damn about being head guard. I need to talk to Aldon."

Braedon swung at me over Velvet's head. I gripped his fist in one hand and pushed him back. "I swear, if Raina dies because of you . . . I'll rip your fucking heart out."

"Stop it!" Velvet said. "Braedon, at least listen to why he's here."

"I know why he's here. And *you* shouldn't be. I told you not to follow me." He glared at Velvet.

"It's a good thing I did or you two would kill each other." She turned to me. "Please, let's go into the alley out of sight from Aldon's window and talk this through. Calmly."

Braedon grunted. Glowering at each other, we walked to the alleyway between The Haven and the movie theater next door. The narrow space offered some respite from the driving sheets of rain.

"Lorcan, what did you say about Raina dying?" Velvet asked.

I glared at Braedon. "This isn't about you or Velvet. I need Aldon's help. It's personal."

Braedon lunged at me. "Lying sack of—"

My hands tightened around Braedon's throat. I was vaguely aware of Velvet yanking on my arms and yelling. "Stop! You're going to kill him."

As suddenly as it had erupted, my rage evaporated. I released his throat and slumped against the damp brick wall. "The Vasiles have Raina." I mumbled. "I need Aldon's help to save her life."

Braedon huddled against the opposite wall, gasping to catch his breath.

Velvet's deep blue eyes grew wide. "The Vasiles have Raina? Holy crap."

"I don't know where they're holding her. Aldon is my only hope."

Braedon stopped sputtering and leaned back against the wall. His voice came out gruff and strained. "What makes you think Aldon will help you?"

"I don't know if he will. He likes Raina. I think he likes me." Spoken aloud, my words sounded childish, pathetic to my own ears. I slid down the wall and sat with my head in my hands. I had no more tears, but my chest heaved with dry sobs.

"I told you he wasn't here to betray you," Velvet said.

A hand gripped my arm. It was Braedon. "I have a key to the front entrance." He pulled me to my feet. "There's no guarantee the old bastard won't tear you to pieces for knocking on his door and waking him up, but he'll sure as fuck kill you if you break in through his balcony door."

I stood holding onto the brick wall to steady myself.

Braedon turned to Velvet. "Please, go home now. It's too dangerous for you to be here." He leaned down and pressed his lips to her forehead. "Be careful. Love you."

"Love you, too." Velvet pulled her hood over her head and then sprinted through the alley toward the street.

"C'mon." Braedon motioned to me. I followed him to the front of The Haven and he unlocked the entrance doors.

"Thank you," I said.

"Don't thank me yet. I might be cleaning up your bloody body parts in a few minutes."

He turned on a light switch as we entered.

"Why are you here so early?" I asked.

"Liquor delivery. The old man refuses to get his ass up early, so somebody has to let them in." He walked over to the bar, grabbed a handful of cocktail napkins and blotted his wet face.

I continued past him to the stairs and climbed to the second floor. With each step, a new emotion hit me. Fear, despair, anger, self-doubt, all with a pervasive sense of doom that I had failed before I even started.

Rainwater dripped from my hair and clothing, yet my mouth had turned bone-dry. I stood outside the imposing carved wooden door of Aldon's suite, resolved to do whatever was necessary to save Jane.

I knocked.

Soft scuffling footsteps approached. The door opened a few inches. A young brunette woman's face peered up at me. Strands of her mussed hair fell across her eyes. She squinted in annoyance.

"I'm sorry to disturb you. My name's Lorcan. I'm a guard here."

Her dark eyes widened. "Is there a security problem?"

"No, but I must speak with Aldon. It's urgent."

She shook her head. "He's not available until after three." She started to close the door.

I pressed my hand against the door and stopped it from closing. "I can't wait that long."

"I'm not to disturb him unless there is an emergency."

"This is an emergency. Please, wake him."

"One minute." The woman sighed and closed the door. Her rapid footsteps faded off into the interior of the suite.

I gripped the sturdy frame on either side of the door, braced myself and waited.

Heavier footsteps approached the door. This time it swung all the way open. "What is the emergency, Lorcan?" Aldon wore a long, black velvet robe belted at the waist. His silvery-white hair was meticulously combed.

Noises from downstairs distracted us both. A delivery man wheeled a handcart loaded with boxes across the first floor. Braedon followed and instructed the man to unload the liquor near the bar.

Aldon motioned me inside his suite and closed the door. He settled into the same upholstered chair in the sitting room where he had sat weeks ago when he convinced me to join The Haven guards. The woman returned, silent as a ghost, and placed a full wine glass on the table next to him.

311

He pointed to the matching chair across from him. "Take a seat, Lorcan."

Streams of water ran from my body onto the oriental area rug. I stepped back onto the hardwood floor and shook my head. "I'm drenched."

"Sharla, bring some towels for Lorcan," Aldon called.

Moments later Sharla appeared and handed me two thick terry cloth towels.

"Thank you," I said.

She hurried off into an adjacent room and shut the door.

"Now, what is so urgent, Lorcan?"

"It's Raina." I mopped my face and head with one of the towels. "She's been kidnapped."

"Kidnapped? In New York? By whom?"

"No, not in New York." My mind swam. I hated betraying Jane's confidence, but I needed Aldon's help to save her life. "It was either in Romania or at LAX. The Vasiles are holding her."

Aldon was on his feet in an instant. "Vasiles?" The pupils of his dark eyes ignited with an amber fire. "So, Raina lied to me about the hematologist convention in New York. She went after that girl—her niece—in Romania, didn't she? After I explicitly warned her not to."

"She only lied to protect you from any involve—"

"Quiet!" He paced soundlessly on the plush rug. "And now this."

I stared down at the floor. Two puddles had formed around my boots on the polished floorboards.

Aldon spun around. "Why are the Vasiles holding her? What do they want?"

"They want the girl back, in exchange for Raina, but—"

"Raina freed the girl in Romania? By herself?"

"Yes, sir."

"Remarkable." He stopped pacing and appeared to calm. "Where is the girl now?"

I agonized over my answer. Jane's voice pleaded in my head, *Don't ever tell anyone about Emilia. Promise me.* "She's uh, somewhere here, um, in the U.S."

"Do *you* have the girl, Lorcan?"

"I only know that she's safe, hidden away." It wasn't a complete lie. I struggled to maintain eye contact with his penetrating stare for what felt like an eternity.

Finally, Aldon looked away and sat. "Let's hope the child stays safe. The Vasiles are very resourceful and relentless." He sipped the ruby-red liquid in his glass. "If I recall, her name is Emily?"

"Emilia."

"Ah, yes. Emilia."

"Aldon, please, will you help me get Raina back? Or, at least tell me where they're holding her?"

He chuckled, though his eyes stayed hard as granite. "Why? Do you intend to rescue her all by yourself? You are exceptionally strong, Lorcan, but you cannot take on the Vasile clan and win."

"I've already killed two."

His mouth went slack and his eyes widened. "That's impossible—"

"I did. They came to Raina's home last night. I, uh, live there. I guess they thought Emilia might be there. They attacked me and I killed them. I can still smell their foul odor."

"A former human capable of killing two Vasiles? Astounding. Raina was correct, your transformation is like nothing we've seen before."

"I'll kill every last one of the Vasiles if I have to. All I want is Raina back."

"As I told Raina, my interference would incite a war among the Pures. The Vasiles will retaliate. Other Pure families who may be sympathetic may be put at risk as well."

"A war? Over one little girl?"

"Emilia is their future. She has Vasile blood and, in their eyes, she belongs to them."

"She *belonged* to her mother. The Vasiles kidnapped her, kept her locked up in isolation just waiting until she's old enough to use for breeding. It's inhuman."

Aldon let out a dry laugh. "Of course it is. The Vasiles are not human. For that matter neither am I, nor are any of the Pures. The breeding concept, though abhorrent to you, is simply the Vasiles' way of ensuring their future. Their bloodline has become tainted over the years. Many who call themselves Pures are not. Despite their hatred of hybrids, some Pures had indiscretions with hybrids and mundanes as well. They did not consider the consequences—weakened offspring. The foul odor you mentioned is the result. A sign of their impurity. This girl is their best means to rectify these past mistakes and begin to cleanse their future bloodline."

"Why don't they have children with willing Pure women?"

Aldon sighed. "Genetics. All Pure Bloods have predominately male offspring. When a female Pure awakens, there is a huge demand for her . . . services. The males are compelled to impregnate every Pure woman or fear extinction. It's a primal instinct, survival of their bloodline. From what Raina told me, that is how this girl, Emilia, came to be."

"Emilia came to be by violence. The Vasile who raped Emilia's mother also murdered the human man she loved and planned to marry."

"Theirs is an animalistic world view. The strongest survive. Raina told me the girl's mother was of the Adeleian family, a Pure family with a long lineage. The Vasiles despised both the girl's mother and grandmother for abandoning their roots in Romania and moving here. That was insult enough, but they could not allow her to breed with a human. They saw it as their duty to impregnate the woman, in any way possible, to ensure her child would be a Pure."

"So, you agree with their ways?"

Aldon snorted. "None of the other Pure families agree with the Vasiles' ways anymore. A century ago it was the norm, but time has changed loyalties. I still strive to understand my enemies' perspective and because of that I have managed to maintain a tenuous peace with all of the Pure families. It's the only way we can all exist in the same world without complete carnage."

"I only want to save Raina. Please, I'm begging you, sir, tell me where I can find the Vasiles?"

"There are numerous places they could be holding Raina, but I won't send you into a den of Vasiles alone. You are valuable to me and The Haven, Lorcan. I have learned through Raina's research that your unique blood is our kind's hope for a stronger future, a new world vision."

"I have no future without her. What if I asked some of The

314

Haven guards to go with me to fight the Vasiles?"

Aldon shook his head. "The Vasiles send at least nine of their strongest men on an overseas mission. That's equivalent to twenty or more of our hybrid guards."

"Two Vasiles are gone now."

Aldon grunted. "Yes, but seven still makes for poor odds. Though they may be tainted, they are vastly stronger than our guards. And never underestimate their resolve. The Vasiles always get what they want. One way or another."

"Are you saying you won't help me find Raina?"

"No. I'm saying we need a more thought-out plan than foolishly rushing into a Vasile stronghold."

"Do you have a plan, sir?"

Aldon smiled. The amber glint in his dark eyes softened to a warm glow. "The best strategy is to lure your opponent to a place where you can control the outcome of the battle."

"Where would that be?"

"Why, here, of course, at The Haven. I will make a call to the head of the Vasile family and convince him to have Raina brought here. There is an honor among the Pure leaders, the Vasiles included. I believe I can negotiate the time and place for the exchange."

"Exchange? Even if we had Emilia, we can't trade her for Raina."

"Of course not, but we must make the Vasiles believe we will. Otherwise keeping Raina alive provides them no advantage. If she has no value, they will not hesitate to kill her."

Aldon's plan was definitely more thought out than mine, yet all of the unknowns left me nervous. Would these monsters even listen to Aldon? And if they agreed to his terms, once they discovered Emilia wasn't here for the trade, all it would take is one swipe of a blade across Raina's throat.

Aldon sat holding his wine glass and studying me. "Lorcan, I can see how deeply you care for Raina and how much it means to you to save her life."

"She means everything to me, sir."

"Then, some advice, son. Hypothetically, if Raina has confided to you where Emilia is hidden, I strongly advise you bring the girl here."

"But you said there would be no exchange?"

"Not for an exchange, I meant for the girl's safety. I have a fortified basement, our guards, including you, my strongest. This is the only place we can guarantee she will be truly safe. I know how the Vasiles operate. They will not trust us to make an exchange." He drained his glass and placed it on the table. "And it is entirely possible they have tortured Raina and she's revealed the girl's location. They may already have the girl and use the pretense of a trade as an opportunity to slaughter us all."

A new hellish scenario. The thought of those evil bastards hurting Jane fanned a new rage inside me. Except Jane couldn't tell them Emilia's location, because I was the only one who knew where she was hidden. Still, I clung to Aldon's words: Jane had value to the Vasiles, so they wouldn't kill her. Yet.

Aldon stood and grasped my hand in both of his. "I will do everything in my power to resolve this, Lorcan. Now, go downstairs and tell Braedon to wait. After I make the call, I will meet with the two of you to discuss the details. It's imperative we have a solid strategy in place."

Downstairs, I found Braedon slicing open a cardboard carton of liquor with a box cutter and stocking the bottles on shelves behind the bar.

He straightened as I approached, the cutter in his hand. "Well, you're still alive. What did he say?"

"Aldon wants you to hang out here a while. He has plans to discuss with us." I picked up an unopened box from the floor, placed it on the bar and held my hand out. "Borrow your cutter?"

Braedon's shoulders tensed. The knuckles on his hand that clenched the knife whitened.

"What plans? Why does Aldon want to talk to me?"

"Relax. He's agreed to help me get Raina back. We need you and the other guards to fight. Aldon wants to talk to you about a strategy."

"That's it?"

"Listen Braedon, I swear to you, I don't want your job. All I want is Raina back. Aldon's plan is risky, but it's all I've got. And without you and the other guards to help me, I'm screwed."

"You swear you didn't tell him about the other night—Velvet?"

"No, of course not. But I did tell him about the two Vasiles I killed at Raina's house. Me. Alone. I kept my word, Braedon, I swear. I never mentioned you or Velvet. He seemed impressed I killed two Vasiles, so act surprised if he mentions it."

"Wait a second. You said you lived there with Jane? Now you're saying it's Raina's house?"

Shit. I had no clever come back to cover my screw-up this time and my mind was too frazzled to even try. I avoided Braedon's stare, ripped open the box with my hands and then lined up the bottles on the bar for him to stock.

"Here, use this." Braedon tossed the cutter onto the bar. "So, Jane is Raina's real name. Velvet said you weren't the type to play two women. She also said it was obvious you loved only Raina." He sighed. "And, she told me—repeatedly—what a jealous ass I am to think you're trying to steal Velvet from me."

I didn't reply. If I ever saw Jane again, she'd have a whole list of reasons to hate me. First, I told Aldon she'd lied to him. But apparently, I suck at lying because Aldon suspected I knew where Emilia was, hence his hypothetical fatherly advice. And if that weren't enough, now Braedon knew her real name. I stabbed the triangular blade into the center of another box and slit the clear tape securing it.

As I hoisted the box onto the bar, Braedon held out his hand. I handed him the knife, but he put it down on the bar with his left hand and kept his right outstretched.

"Real name's Garrett," he said. "You saved Velvet's life. I'll help you save Raina's."

I made eye contact. His eyes looked sincere. Still, I hesitated to take his hand.

"We're Haven guards, Lorcan. Part of a brotherhood sworn to stand by each other. I give you my word, I'll stand by you. So will the others."

"Thank you. Garrett." I shook his hand. "Mine's Tim."

"Tim?" He grinned. "Seriously, dude? Stick to Lorcan."

I laughed.

Braedon poured us two stiff vodka and pomegranate juice cocktails. We carried the drinks upstairs, sat at a table and waited for Aldon. The alcohol stung my throat as it went down. The strong drink plus my newfound camaraderie with Braedon helped calm my frayed nerves. And the most powerful vampire among us, Aldon, agreed to lead the charge. I wasn't alone in this fight.

"I'm going to have to find a new donor now that Velvet's been vamped." Braedon said. "That's going to be weird. We've been together for over five years. I'll miss her spicy blood."

"Velvet will need a donor now, too," I said.

Braedon scowled. "Yeah, I know. It bugs me thinking of her with another guy, even if it's just for blood." He took a gulp of his drink. "I guess I'm kind of the jealous type."

I gagged on the sip I had just taken. "Kind of? Shit."

Aldon approached the table. We both went silent and stood until he seated himself and motioned for us to do the same.

"I'm pleased to see you two have become friends. This is not the time for petty infighting. We must stay united." His mysterious woman friend appeared, placed a filled wine glass in front of Aldon and then scurried back into his suite.

"It took some persuasion, but the Vasiles have agreed to make the exchange here. They will bring Raina here at ten o'clock tonight."

My heart collided with the vodka running down my throat. "They agreed? And they confirmed Raina is not hurt. She's alive?"

"Yes. They gave me their word she is fine, as I gave mine that we will complete the trade. Of course, in this case, my word is not honorable. They may be brutes, but they do realize keeping Raina alive is their only leverage until the exchange." He sighed and sipped from his glass. "Now we must devise a careful strategy. Once they discover this is a ruse, they will attack. Knowing their history, it will be swift and brutal."

"Exchange?" Braedon asked. "I thought the Vasiles just kidnapped Raina? What do they want in exchange for her?"

"Who, not what. A Pure girl was taken from the Vasiles' clan.

They believe we are harboring this girl," Aldon said.

Braedon shot me a suspicious glance. I sensed his mind churning. He had to know the girl Aldon spoke of was Emilia. I hoped he wouldn't blurt out anything about Emilia.

"But if we don't have this Pure girl, how can we make an exchange?" he asked.

Clearly, Braedon was a better actor than I.

Aldon directed his gaze toward me. "It would be ideal if we had the girl here, for the appearance of a trade and to ensure Raina's safety." He turned to Braedon and sighed. "But since we don't, we are forced to bluff, tell the Vasiles she is hidden here at The Haven until we manage to free Raina. This will be an intense battle. We must be ready.

"Braedon, close the club to patrons tonight. Assemble all of your guards here by seven o'clock. Make ready all weapons and instruct them to be prepared for the fight of their lives. When the Vasiles arrive, all we will have on our side is surprise. It is imperative we kill every one of them. The Vasiles have a telepathic ability among their own kind. If all of them are not destroyed, their thoughts and visions will become shared knowledge with their clan in Romania. Then, we will have an all-out war on our hands." Aldon paused and drank. "The Vasiles are already aware Lorcan killed two of their clan last night. Beheaded them."

"What?" Braedon jerked upright in his chair. "You cut the heads off of two Vasiles?"

I nodded, even more impressed with his performance.

Aldon stood. "Make sure you and the guards are here on time, Braedon. Have them park their vehicles a distance away so as not to warn the Vasiles of our true numbers. I promised only one guard would be here—Lorcan. When the guards arrive this evening, Braedon and I will go over our strategy. Lorcan, you need to arrive by eight o'clock. They will be watching for you."

"The guards will be here at seven sharp and ready to fight, sir."

Braedon's chest puffed when he spoke. He thoroughly embraced his role as captain of the guards. No wonder he became so defensive when he thought I threatened his position. I bet he made a bastard of a head maintenance man as well.

"Good." Aldon stood. "Go now, both of you. Rest and satiate your blood needs. Advise your guards to do the same. You will need all of your strength and then some." Aldon walked toward his suite.

I followed him. "Aldon?"

He stopped and turned.

"Do you believe we can defeat the Vasiles?"

"Yes, though it will be a difficult battle. That is why I want everyone here early to prepare." He smiled. "Of course, I intend to be in the midst of the fray as well. I may be old, but I still have some power."

I smiled at Aldon's humility. "Knowing you're leading this fight gives me confidence. Hope. I understand the risk you took by lying to the Vasiles. I can't tell you how much this means to me."

He placed his hand on my shoulder and smiled. "We will prevail, Lorcan. You and Raina shall be reunited tonight."

Braedon wasn't at the table when I returned, only two watery rings from our glasses remained on the tabletop. I ran down the stairs and found him and Velvet inside the front entrance.

"What are you doing here?" I whispered to her.

"I wanted to hear what Aldon said." She grinned at me. "My hearing is amazing now."

Braedon covered her mouth with one hand and pushed her toward the door. We exited and he locked it. Once outside, he spun Velvet around by her shoulders. "Are you out of your freaking mind? Aldon could have sensed you hiding down there. He might have killed you. And me—when he saw you've been vamped."

Velvet stroked his cheek. "I was careful, baby. I only wanted to know what was happening. I'll help you fight the Vasiles."

"No. You absolutely will not," Braedon said.

"He's right, Velvet," I said. "The Vasiles are superior in strength and speed. You'd be killed."

"And you both could be, too." She threw her arms around Braedon's neck. "I'll go crazy worrying, knowing you're fighting those Romanian creeps. I want to help. That's the reason I wanted to be vamped, to help people."

Braedon smoothed her rain-damp hair away from her face. "The best way you can help is by finding me a new donor. I need to be peaked tonight. Maybe you can call one of the girls from the club?" He frowned and then mumbled, "You're going to need a donor, too."

"I've already found myself a donor."

"Who? Do I know him from the club?" Braedon's eyes narrowed.

"Yes, you do." Velvet crossed her arms and smiled. "*She* is Jasmine, and she's agreed to do a twofer—you and me."

"Oh yeah, Jasmine. She's cute. That's cool." He flashed me a grin and winked.

Velvet smacked the back of Braedon's head. "She only does vials, no flesh contact."

We walked down the street. I stayed a few steps behind the couple, envious of their comfortable banter and the genuine affection they showed each other. I wished Jane were here walking beside me. As we reached the alleyway leading back to The Haven's parking lot, I turned into it to go to my car.

Braedon ran back and followed me into the alley. "Lorcan, the Pure girl Aldon talked about, she's that creepy little girl I saw at your house, isn't she?"

"I can't tell—"

He sighed. "I know, I know, you can't tell me. Listen, if she's part of their clan, then the Vasiles won't hurt her. Why not just give her back? Then they'll return Raina, and everything's cool, right?"

"It's not that simple," I said. "She's just a little girl. I can't hand her over to the Vasiles."

He shook his head. "Right. Just a little girl who's ten going on thirty." He slapped my back. "I'll call the guards and get them stoked for the fight. We're gonna kick Vasile ass tonight."

Velvet walked over and hugged me. "Don't worry. Braedon and the other guards will make sure you get Raina back. And Aldon is on our side. It's going to be all right."

As the effects of the drink wore off, so did my confidence in our plan. Velvet's kind words echoed in my head as I climbed into my car, but my gut wasn't listening.

I sat in the driveway outside Jane's with no desire to enter the empty house. My cell rang. An electric shock of fear raced down my spine. I tapped the phone expecting to hear a Vasile on the other end. Instead, it was Echo.

"Lorcan? Are you coming by to get the girls?"

"I, um, had an emergency come up, Echo. I was about to call you and ask if they could stay with you. Just one more night." What if Jane and I were both killed tonight? What would happen to the girls? Do I ask Echo to keep them forever?

". . . strange."

Drowning in my grim thoughts, I realized Echo was still talking. "I'm sorry, what did you say?"

"Emilia is acting strange. Something's wrong."

"What do you mean? Is she sick?"

"No, not sick. She was so quiet and serious when she first arrived, but now she's having emotional outbursts, crying jags. Then it goes away. She said she needs to be with Raina and you. She's very upset and anxious."

"Can you put her on the phone?"

"Sure. But, Lorcan, I need to know something. Is Emilia a vampire?"

"Why do you ask?"

"I've read a lot about vamps. Emilia said her twelfth birthday is coming up in a couple of months. I wondered if her erratic behavior could be the start of her Awakening."

Shit. The last thing I needed was Emilia freaking out. I knew zero about what to do for a vampire girl going through her Awakening. She needed Jane's expertise. And Angela needed Jane. I needed Jane.

"I'll take that as a yes," Echo replied to my silence.

"Let me talk to her please, Echo."

"Hang on."

"This is Emilia speaking on the cell phone."

Her odd phrasing made me smile. "Emilia, it's Lorcan. Are you all right?"

"I-I do not know. I sometimes feel . . . Is Aunt Jane with you? May I speak with her, please?"

"Emilia, there's been a complication—"

"She is alive, tell me yes?"

"Yes. But it will be at least another day before we can come get you and Angela."

"I see images in my mind." Her voice trembled. "There are fragments of unfamiliar places, people I do not know. And I am feeling strong emotion. It is most confusing to have my mind show me these strange pictures. It frightens me." Her voice rose in volume and her words tumbled out in a rush. "Do not trust the one who grasped your hand in friendship. They are not a friend to you at all. They are a bitter enemy who will hurt you and Aunt Jane."

Did she mean Braedon? We shook hands. He appeared to have finally mellowed and I trusted he would help me tonight. But he also proved to be an excellent actor and liar in front of Aldon. What if he turned on me during the battle, or worse, convinced the other guards to turn on me during the fight tonight?

"Lorcan are you hearing my words?"

"Yes, Emilia. Don't worry. Everything will be fine." I nearly choked on my words.

"The Vasiles have Aunt Jane, do they not? They want me to go back, to bear their children. Is this why you and Aunt Jane are not here? They have threatened to take her life because of me, yes?"

"You won't ever go back there. I promise you—"

"I believe you are not telling me this whole truth to protect me because I am a child to your eyes. But I have their Vasile blood inside my veins. I am changing. I know things. Please tell me, what is the truth?"

I sighed. "Yes, it's true. The Vasiles have Jane. But it's also true our Haven leader and eight other guards will fight the Vasiles with me. We'll get Jane back." I tried my best to filter my fear from my words.

"No. I have decided. You must return me to the Vasile clan. I will travel back to Romania. It is my destiny, I believe. And it is the only way to save Aunt Jane. I cannot stand to think any longer of the danger I have caused you both to be in."

"No. Never. I won't give you to the Vasiles. And neither would Jane." Silence on the other end, interrupted by soft sounds. Emilia was crying. "Please don't cry, sweetie. I need you to stay strong for one more night. Angela needs you to be brave, too. Promise me?"

I took her hiccupping sob as a yes. Listening to her cry wrenched at my gut. The chances she might be left an orphan again grew by the minute. "Emilia, put Echo back on the phone, please."

"Lorcan, what's wrong? Emilia's crying."

"I know, and I'm sorry. She'll be okay. Echo, I hate to ask, but can you spare more blood?" While physically I felt strong, the day's stress had ruined my ability to focus. Tonight, of all nights, I needed to stay sharp.

"Today? But it's hardly been a day since—"

"I know and I have no right to ask you, but it's important I be as strong as possible tonight."

She hesitated, then said, "All right. What time will you be here?"

"Can you meet me at the Sun Coast Mall? Bring the girls with you. It's close to your place."

"I know where it is. You want me to bring the girls? Yesterday you said not—"

"I know what I said, but it's safer than me being followed to your apartment or you leaving them alone. I'll meet you in the food court, at say, six o'clock?"

Distraught with new worries about Echo's and the girls' safety, I wandered into the house, and tried to clear my mind. I had to focus and prepare myself for tonight.

The meat in the refrigerator had spoiled, more evidence of how long Jane had been gone. I tossed it into the trash and removed a steak from the freezer. After thawing it in the microwave, I seared the outside by holding it over the gas burner. The blue flames singed my fingers, but the pain barely registered. I chewed and swallowed the tough, cool meat. I needed protein for strength. I chugged pomegranate juice from the bottle and washed down the tasteless meat. By the time I'd finished drinking, the burns on my fingertips had healed.

I went to my room and took longer than necessary to sharpen the machete. I ran the stone over the blade in long, methodical strokes until it gleamed. When I tested the edge, it cleanly shaved a swatch of hair from my forearm. I secured the machete inside my leather guard coat.

I headed down the hall to the gym to work out and stopped halfway. On an impulse, I tapped my parents' number on my cell and waited for one of them to answer.

"Tim!" It was Mom. "Oh, I'm so glad to finally hear from you. I've texted you, left messages." She gushed on about how much she'd missed me, asked if I were eating well and chided me about how I needed to call more often.

"And how's your job?" she asked, finally taking a breath.

"Great. Keeps me really busy. My game's in development now. I found a fantastic artist to draw the characters." I wished that were all I had on my mind.

"That's wonderful, dear."

I knew the details of my video game work were lost on both my parents, but that was okay. I didn't call to discuss work, I just had an overwhelming need to hear the unconditional love in Mom's voice.

"Have you made friends? You know what they say, all work and—"

"I met a girl, Mom," I blurted. "Her name is Jane and we're in love."

"Oh. Oh, well. I'm so happy for you, Tim. When can we meet Jane?"

"It's actually four of us. Jane adopted two little girls from overseas. They're incredible kids."

"Tim, two children? That's such a huge step. A lot of responsibility and expense."

"I know it is. They're worth it."

My mother called out to my dad. "Steven, pick up the phone. It's Tim."

I pictured Dad, grumbling as he fumbled for the remote to mute the television and then reaching for his glasses so he could find the correct button to push on the phone. For such an intelligent man, simple technology confounded him.

"Tim? How the hell are you? You need to call more. You know how your mother worries."

"Yes, Dad, you're right. But I'm doing great. Job's great. I'm getting ready to go work out in the gym. I just wanted to call and say hi and . . . I miss you guys."

"The gym? Well, good for you. Remember, increase your weights gradually. Do more—"

"Reps. Yes, I remember how you taught me, Dad. Thanks."

"Tim has more news," Mom interjected.

"I'll let Mom fill you in on all that, Dad," I said.

"What news? Does he need money?" Dad asked.

"No, Dad, I'm fine. I really need to get going now."

"Call us again. Soon," Mom said. "We'll set a date for all of you to come over for dinner. Does that sound all right?"

"Yes, I'd really like that. Say hi to Steve-o for me. I love you, Mom. Dad."

"What do you mean by *all* of them, Mindy?" Dad asked.

I ended the call and hurried into the gym.

At five o'clock, I headed out the front door. I had worked out until my muscles bulged so much it was difficult to slide the coat sleeves over my arms. I'd drained the jug of pomegranate juice. All I needed was a fix of Echo's blood and I'd be as ready as I ever was going to be for tonight.

As I opened my driver door, a dark figure ran up to the locked gate and waved at me.

I walked toward the gates, my hand on the handle of the machete.

The figure was petite and slender, definitely not a Vasile, but a young girl. Oh, no. "Emilia?" I quickened my pace. "Where's Echo? How did you get here?" Did she slip away from Echo? Was she acting on her decision to return to the Vasiles in order to save Jane?

Velvet threw back her hood and smiled. "You thought I was Emilia, didn't you?"

The blue streaks in her hair were gone, only shiny, straight back hair cascaded around her shoulders. A line of razor-sharp bangs hung even with her eyebrows—like Emilia's— and her indigo eyes were dark brown, almost black—like Emilia's. The black hoodie and skinny jeans she wore looked identical to the outfit Emilia had worn yesterday.

I opened the gate. "Velvet, what's going on? What are you doing here?"

"I'm going with you to The Haven. I'll keep my hood up and pretend to be a scared kid. They'll think I'm Emilia." She strode past me toward my car.

"No. No, this isn't part of the plan. Does Braedon know you're here?"

"'Course not. Though, he ought to know I'm not about to sit home and binge watch Netflix while the fight of the century is going on at the club."

She shrugged her shoulders and two long pointed knife blades emerged from under the cuffs of her sleeves. "I'm ready to fight."

"This is crazy. I can't let you do this."

"You can't stop me." She repositioned the knives under her sleeves and then gripped my hand in hers. "You know the Vasiles will be watching the club tonight. If you don't show up with a girl to exchange, they'll know the trade is bogus. They'll kill Raina, Lorcan."

She made an excellent point and one that had eaten at my brain ever since I'd spoken to Aldon.

"Braedon will kill me for allowing you to come along," I muttered.

"I'll handle him." She ran to the passenger side of the car and slid inside.

I sat in the driver's seat and started the car. "Um, not to be too personal, but how did you . . .?" I cupped my hands over my chest. Velvet's ample breasts which were usually on full display in a skimpy top now looked non-existent.

"Two sports bras, both two sizes too small, and a hell of a lot of tape." She giggled. "See what I do for you?"

Part of me felt relieved. Velvet was right, without a girl in sight to trade, the probability the Vasiles would kill Jane was all too likely. Still, the reasonable part of me lectured Velvet about the danger she faced as I drove to the mall to meet Echo.

Velvet leaned back in the passenger seat, cool as ice, while I ranted on for miles.

She finally let out a long sigh. "I can handle myself, Lorcan. I finally feel alive. Sober and ready to put my new talents to good use." She pulled down the visor and checked her face in the vanity mirror. "Don't these contacts look real? I found them in a costume shop downtown."

"Yeah." I pulled into the Sun Coast mall lot and parked. "A quick pit stop. Stay here."

I jogged into the mall entrance, then down the wide aisle until I reached the food court. I slowed and then stopped. Angela's shock of platinum blonde hair grabbed my attention first. She sat, chin-height, at a bright orange table eating a chicken nugget. Echo and Emilia sat across from her. The normalcy of the scene gut-punched me. I wished Jane and I could spend the evening at the mall with the girls instead of fighting for our lives against an ancient clan of hell-bent vampires.

Angela jumped off her chair and ran to me as I approached. "Papa! Go home?"

I crouched, gathered her into my arms and hugged her close. "Soon." I buried my face in her cloud of soft hair. It smelled like strawberries.

I picked her up and sat her back in the chair. Echo pointed to a small white bag with a fast food logo sitting on the table. "It's inside." Her voice sounded weak and her complexion made the white bag look colorful.

"I'm so sorry about this, Echo," I said. "Are you all right?"

"I felt a little woozy back at the apartment." She chuckled. "Almost dropped the bottle. Emilia made me lie down and capped it for me." She stroked Emilia's hair and smiled. "She bought me orange juice when we arrived and even thought to ask for a little bag to hide your, um, special order."

I felt terrible as Emilia handed me the bag. Echo was only a thin wisp of a woman to start with and I'd almost drained her dry in two days. My stress depleted the effects of the blood faster than Echo could supply it.

"Do not worry. Echo is doing much better now." Emilia said. "I will get her more juice or a protein food if necessary before we make the return drive to her apartment."

"Okay, good. But please, be careful. Make sure no one follows you. I'm sorry to leave you, but I have to go now." I patted Emilia's back. She surprised me when she jumped up and threw her arms around my neck, Angela-style. "Do not drink the blood now," she whispered in my ear. "Wait until you face the Vasiles for maximum impact."

I nodded, not understanding why she said it. My immediate concern was, if neither Jane nor I survived the night, what would become of the girls? Velvet and Braedon could be killed as well.

I leaned and gave Echo a hug. Her discomfort at my unusual show of affection was obvious by her alarmed expression. I slid a thick envelope filled with the cash Jane had left me into her hand and whispered into her ear, "If anything happens to Raina and me tonight, please, Echo, take care of the girls."

Her pale blue eyes widened, and her mouth fell open. "Lorcan, no, wait—"

I turned and ran toward the exit. Despite the noisy crowd of shoppers and pop music blaring from speakers, Angela's shrill calls of *Papa, come back* filled my ears.

I shoved the white paper bag into a cubby in the console and started the car.

Velvet giggled. "Do you always get a sudden craving for fries before a fight?"

"It's blood," I said.

"Cool. Blood from the mall. Who knew? I'll take a type-O latte with a drizzle of plasma on top."

I sped around the lot to the exit and jammed on the brakes before entering the road. Velvet lurched forward from the motion of the car, her hands braced on the dashboard.

"Is this all a damn joke to you? Raina's life depends on us," I said.

"Hey, chill out. I know exactly what's at stake. Did it ever occur to you some people make jokes when they're nervous?"

I shook my head and pulled out into traffic. We drove the next several miles in silence.

Velvet finally broke the tense quiet. "Emilia would be scared and resist going back to the Vasiles, wouldn't she?"

I snorted and rolled my eyes. "Of course."

Velvet huffed. "The reason I ask is because I want to be in character. I'll act like a frightened girl, maybe even try to run away from you, too. What do you think?"

"You know what I think—this is a really bad idea. I'll drop you off down the street."

"No! You have to show up with a girl to trade or the Vasiles will kill Raina." Velvet reached across the seat and squeezed my forearm. "Have a little faith in me, Lorcan, would you please?"

I blew out a long sigh. "All right. If I had Emilia with me tonight, I would tell her I was only bringing her along to fool the Vasiles into thinking there was going to be a trade—to keep Raina alive. I'd also tell her not to worry, she wouldn't be in any danger from the Vasiles, she'd be protected by Aldon, the guards, and me. She's a brave kid. I think she trusts me. She wouldn't run away from me."

"But the Vasiles don't know all that. From their perspective, you made a choice. You care more about Raina than Emilia. I think I should go with my instincts and play it like a scared kid."

"Shit. What am I thinking? You can't do this, Velvet. Aldon will recognize you. Not only that, he'll see you've been vamped and—"

"*You* didn't recognize me, and Aldon has never even seen Emilia, right? I won't get close to him. I'll keep my hood up and my head down. Besides, Aldon has enough to worry about tonight dealing with the damn Vasiles. He'll only see a shaking kid in a hoodie from a distance."

"Right." My nerves already teetered like a precarious stack of Jenga sticks and now one more nerve got plucked away. "I only hope I get to free Raina before Aldon realizes you've been vamped, or Braedon kills me for letting you do this."

Chapter 19

What's the worst that could happen? —Anonymous

Aldon's black SUV with its dark-tinted windows stood like a lone sentinel in The Haven's parking lot. It resembled a funeral hearse. The thought gave me a chill as I pulled into the lot and parked next to it. Braedon and the guards should already be gathered inside the club. I hoped.

I removed the small pill bottle of blood from the bag. The bottle was full, three times the amount of Echo's last donation. No wonder she looked so pale. I hesitated, tempted to gulp it down to steady my jangling nerves, but instead decided to heed Emilia's advice and wait. It made sense. The Vasiles were not due for three more hours and the rush immediately after drinking blood always provided the most power. I shoved the bottle into my inside coat pocket and climbed out of the car.

Velvet hunched in the front seat. She had her hood pulled forward, covering most of her face. I wondered if she'd lost her nerve. "C'mon, let's go," I said.

"Come around and pull me out of the car."

I slammed my door and jogged to the passenger side. Velvet resisted as I tugged on her arm.

"Make it look real. The Vasiles could be watching us," she whispered.

I reached inside, dragged Velvet out of the car and kicked the door shut. She struggled in my grasp and whimpered, "No, please don't give me to them."

Velvet's fake accent sounded believable enough, but her words weren't right. "*Do not* give." I whispered. "Emilia doesn't use contractions."

We made our way through the dark alley and to the front door. Velvet kept up a convincing act of alternately begging and clinging to me, then tugging to get away from me. As I reached for the front door handle, she bolted. I raced after her, grabbed her around the waist and hoisted her over my shoulder. She pleaded for me to let her go as I carried her inside The Haven.

Though the interior lights were on inside the empty club, the utter silence of the place sent an eerie shiver through me. Instead of the usual raucous music, Velvet's muffled cries and my own pounding heartbeat assaulted my ears. I was about to set Velvet down when Aldon's voice boomed from the second floor, startling me.

"You brought Emilia?"

"Yes." I braced for his angry reaction after I'd lied to him about not knowing her whereabouts.

"Excellent, Lorcan. I'm relieved you were able to locate her in time. She will be safe here. Hurry, come upstairs."

I breathed a sigh of relief that he didn't question how I suddenly found her. Aldon's concern was for Emilia's safety. I decided it better to carry Velvet upstairs so Aldon couldn't get a clear look at her face. I turned as we entered his suite so his only view of the girl over my shoulder was her legs and rear end.

Aldon locked his suite door and lowered his voice. "Let me see you, dear girl." He circled around me toward Velvet's head. My pounding heart bumped up a few more notches.

Velvet squirmed, buried her face in the curve of my neck and made soft sobbing sounds.

"She's terrified of the Vasiles," I said. "I told her she'll be safe here, but she's still frightened."

Aldon patted Velvet's back and spoke in a soft voice, "Don't fret, my child. This is only a temporary hiding place. Rest assured, I will let no harm come to you."

"Where are the guards?" I hoped to divert his attention from Velvet.

"The last arrived an hour ago. Braedon has them assembled in the basement checking weapons and reviewing their strategy. The walls are thick downstairs, so our plans won't be overheard by spies," Aldon whispered. "The Vasiles should arrive with Raina in three hours, though I'm certain they have scouts watching the building." He motioned to me and led the way to one of the interior doors in his suite. "We need to position the guards in the club for our surprise attack."

I set Velvet on her feet. She turned her head and pressed her hooded face against my side.

He swung open the door and motioned for us to enter. "Don't be afraid, child. Watch your step on the steep stairs."

A small landing led to a stone staircase that curved downward into the basement. Aldon shut the door behind us. His ruby-encrusted cane rapped each step as he followed us down the stairs.

The sound calmed me, and my racing heart slowed. With Aldon's power plus eight armed Haven guards on my side, my confidence soared. Physically I felt stronger than ever tonight and knew once I drank Echo's blood my mind would be sharp and focused. I was ready for the battle to begin so I could finally hold Jane in my arms.

The rough-hewn stone ceiling and walls on either side of the staircase looked like they had been built in medieval times. Orangey flames flickered from torches stuck in iron wall sconces. The shifting light and shadow of the fire lit our way down the stairs. The air grew chilly and dank as we descended and the smoke from the torches gave off a strong sage-like fragrance.

Velvet and I stepped from the last step to the stone floor. The room was empty and silent. "Where're Braedon and the guards?"

Something heavy struck the back of my head and sent me sprawling onto the floor. Velvet's hand slipped from mine as I fell.

A silhouette flashed past. Velvet screamed. The dark figure grabbed her around her waist and whisked her across the cave-like room. A putrid odor rose above the burning sage. One I knew all too well. A Vasile.

"Hey! Stop!" My voice sounded hollow in the cavernous room. Thick stone columns obscured my line of vision. I lost sight of the bastard who had run off with Velvet. He turned down a dimly lit corridor that snaked off from the main room.

"Aldon! A Vasile has gotten inside!" On my feet, I whirled around. "Where are the gua—?"

Four Vasiles clad in long black coats faced me. Aldon stood with them, his cane raised in the air.

"Aldon? What—?"

He lowered his cane and smiled.

His icy stare and humorless smile sent a sickening chill through me. "I-I don't understand."

"No? But, you're so astute, Lorcan. The Vasiles are indeed inside. I let them in before The Haven guards arrived. The sage brush masked their scent. But how rude of me, I should formally introduce you to my family."

"Your family? No." My throat strangled the words. "N-No, you can't—y-you're a Vasile?"

"Not *a* Vasile, their sovereign leader. Head of the Vasile family."

The four guards bowed their heads toward Aldon and recited something I didn't understand.

The back of my head throbbed between my stunned thoughts. This can't be happening. I'd trusted Aldon. His plan to save Jane was only a ruse. Terror trickled down my spine. Jane! "Where's Raina? Is she here?"

"Yes, of course. I had her escorted from Bucharest by nine of my best guards." He glowered at me. "Now seven, thanks to you."

The four Vasiles standing at Aldon's side hissed in unison, their lips curling upward to reveal curved, yellowed fangs.

I was paralyzed with disbelief as the four Vasiles swarmed me. Two of them grabbed my arms and the other two moved behind me and gripped my shoulders. Hands tightened on my flesh like steel bands. One reached inside my coat and yanked Jane's machete from its hidden sheath.

My heart thumped like a jackhammer in my dry throat. "What have you done to Raina and the guards?"

"They are alive, well mostly, for the moment," Aldon said.

"Let me see her!"

"Calm yourself, Lorcan. The battle is over. You've lost. However, if you cooperate, I promise Raina's and your comrades' deaths will be quick."

The wavering shadows from the torch light made the dungeon-like room look like a surreal movie set. Panic pressed in on me from all sides. If only this were a movie, or a dream—anything but reality. Aldon had been my only hope to save Jane and I had walked into his trap like a naive child.

A mixture of terror and rage boiled inside me. I fought with the four Vasiles holding me and landed a solid kick into one's knee. As he loosened his grip, I wrenched one arm free. Spinning around I slammed my fist into another's face and then shoved him into the two behind me. Free of their hold, I managed to conjure a basic action code and leaped across the room. The four Vasiles glared, but made no attempt to chase. I was free of their clawing hands, but now what? I crouched next to a stone column. I needed a plan, but my frantic mind only registered shock and anger at Aldon's betrayal.

"Impressive. You have put up a better fight than all of the other guards combined." Aldon's voice echoed across the stone room. "But you will soon learn, as they did, there is no escape."

"Why are you doing this? You've lived here for decades. You opened this club and allowed hybrids and humans to join. Why?"

Aldon's laughter reverberated all around me. "I told you Lorcan, I survive by understanding my enemy. I bided my time, studied your kind's weaknesses. My intent was always to destroy all hybrids. But when Raina had the audacity to take Emilia, I was forced to act sooner."

His cold-blooded tone triggered a full-blown panic. I couldn't fight Aldon and four Vasiles by myself. I had to find Jane and the guards. I turned and ran, dodged past the stone columns and into the dim corridor. I scanned small cave-like rooms with bars that dotted either side. They were dark and silent. Faint noises came from farther down the corridor. I raced toward them. Aldon's and the Vasiles' distant footsteps followed me at a leisurely pace.

Dripping water and muffled groans. The sounds amplified as I neared an opening at the end of the corridor. The entrance, an archway carved from thick rock, had no door but a glow of flickering torch light illuminated the interior. I ran inside and then stopped short, horrified by the sight in front of me.

Jane and the eight Haven guards hung suspended by their ankles with ropes tied to thick metal rings embedded in the stone ceiling. A large steel tub had been placed under each. The dripping sound wasn't water, it was Griffin's blood. His throat had been slashed and the last drops of his blood dripped from the gaping wound and splattered into the blood-filled steel tub below him.

The guards all had their hands bound behind their backs and rags stuffed into their mouths. Braedon's gray eyes burned with rage.

Demon grunted and struggled to free his hands though his efforts proved futile. Bat stared at me, a pleading look in his eyes. Most of the others had their eyes squeezed shut. Some had tears streaming from the corners of their eyes.

Two Vasiles stood guard in front of them. Each held long knives, one's blade coated red. Griffin's blood. A third Vasile, in the corner of the room, guarded Velvet. She cowered on the floor, her hood pulled tight around her face and her knees drawn up to her chin. He pointed a long sword at me but stayed by Velvet.

Forcing my legs to move, I stumbled toward Jane. The Vasiles made no move to stop me.

The sight overwhelmed me. Jane's arms dangled limply alongside her head, her eyes were partially closed showing slits of white. Her clothing was dirty and torn. Bruises and cuts covered her face and arms. They must have deprived her of blood, so she wasn't able to heal herself. My hands shook as I reached out to touch her.

Her skin felt cool. She didn't respond when my fingers grazed her cheek. I laid my hand on her neck and checked for a pulse. Nothing.

I was too late. Jane was gone.

"No, no, no." My breath evaporated and my heart shuddered in my chest. I sank to my knees.

Aldon and the Vasiles entered the room. His guards pulled me to my feet and dragged me away from Jane.

She gasped. My mind so fogged with grief, I thought I'd imagined the sound at first, but then her eyelids fluttered open. Her eyes were dilated, a dull gray color that held no light. She stared without focus. "No . . . trade." Her voice barely a whisper.

She's alive. "Jane, I'm so sorry. I failed you. Failed everyone."

"Bind the mundane. Make certain he is secured." Aldon ordered. "Then, cut the others' throats."

"No! You can't kill them." I writhed, bucked and kicked to free myself from the Vasiles' hold.

"I can and I will. Your precious Raina and pathetic band of so-called guards will provide a blood feast for my men before our journey home." Aldon walked over to me and smiled. "Don't worry, Lorcan. You will not die tonight. I have great plans for you. You will return to Romania as my guest. Your blood will be drained slowly and fed to my family. Then, when the Pure girl Awakens, she will bear the fruit of my clan's enhanced blood." Aldon chuckled. "Eventually, yours will be a noble death. Your blood will ensure our dominance over all others."

The metallic smell of Griffin's blood tainted the stale air and the muffled moans of my fellow guards added a chilling backdrop to Aldon's words. After they slaughtered Jane and the guards, I would live on as a blood-cow for the Vasiles. Aldon had yet to discover the hooded girl in the corner was not Emilia. When he did, would he murder poor Velvet as well, or would the fact my blood flowed in her veins relegate her to the same fate as me?

My grand transformation into a vampire, my new-found strength and fighting skills had only led me to this. I wasn't Lorcan the fierce vampire warrior. He was only a character in a video game. A fantasy. I was Tim. A failure. Jane had depended on me and I failed her in the worst way possible. She was right when she said I didn't deserve to be transformed. She deserved a stronger man. One who could save her.

Braedon had rallied the guards to come here tonight on my behalf. Velvet came to help as well. Now they would all die because of me. Despair smothered me until I could barely draw in a breath. Tears blurred the image of Jane and the guards hanging feet away. Every cell of my body weighted with defeat. What could I possibly do to save them all by myself? It was hopeless.

Aldon signaled and one of the Vasiles stepped toward Jane brandishing a knife. He pressed the blade against her throat. Another guard advanced toward me holding a length of thick rope.

A raw scream rose from deep in my gut. "No! Wait!" I couldn't watch them cut Jane's throat, or the guards. I didn't want to die. I had to act. A kaleidoscope of fragmented thoughts spun in my mind. I couldn't focus. I cursed myself for not drinking Echo's blood earlier.

Blood? Emilia had said to wait. I'm facing the Vasiles now. But four of them had a death hold on my arms. I couldn't reach the bottle of blood inside my coat pocket.

An impossible idea sparked. I didn't know if it would work, or how it might end. But I had no time to think it through.

I turned to Aldon. "Please, at least let me hold Raina. Say goodbye. One last time."

Aldon grunted. "How incredibly *human*. You're physically strong, yet your mundane emotions are your Achilles heel." Aldon swept his hand toward the hanging guards. "Hybrids disgust me— you have weakened our kind. For years I've watched you gather upstairs like it's a costume party. And donors?" He laughed. "You ask permission from a human for a few measly drops of blood? Fools. Humans and hybrids are our food! A pure vampire does not ask, he takes. He rips out throats and gorges until his hunger is satisfied. That is the way it was for thousands of years. And it will be again when I rid the world of abominations like you. The Vasile family will take back our rightful rule."

My heart jolted in my chest when Aldon turned and spoke words I didn't understand to the Vasile with the knife standing next to Jane. But the guard bowed and walked away. As did the man with the rope. The four holding me released their grasp. All six Vasiles moved behind Aldon and formed a line, shoulder to shoulder, blocking the only exit. The seventh maintained his watch over Velvet.

"Go on, Lorcan. Kiss your hybrid lover farewell. Then my guard will cut her throat. Perhaps as you witness her death, you will understand how pathetic and weak your emotions make you."

I ran to Jane, kicked the tub away and knelt, my face close to hers and my back to Aldon and his guards. As I embraced her, I inched my hand inside my coat and flipped the lid off of the pill bottle. With my head bowed as though I was whispering in Jane's ear, I gulped the blood and held it inside my mouth.

Something was wrong. The blood had a strong, berry-like taste, not the usual crisp flavor of Echo's blood. Had her blood been weakened by giving me too much too soon? Desperate, I continued with the only plan I had. I kissed Jane.

Her lips, cold and unresponsive, immediately warmed. As I forced the blood into Jane's mouth, some trickled down my throat. It burned for an instant going down, much like the sting of vodka. Its effect was instantaneous and like nothing I'd experienced before.

Heat spread throughout my body. My veins and muscles pulsed. My senses sharpened. The sage no longer masked the stench of the Vasiles and my nostrils filled with it. The strained breathing of the bound guards sounded like the roar of the ocean and their tears splashing on the stone floor, as loud as rain drops. Jane's body vibrated in my arms. Her wounds faded before my eyes, revealing smooth, golden skin.

My mind focused like a laser.

Jane's lips pushed against mine, she drew her hands up and caressed my face. Her fingertips, dots of fire on my skin. Her hands deftly reached inside my coat. To my surprise, she slid out my Haven dagger. Emilia had placed it in the wrong hidden pocket and the Vasiles missed it when they searched me.

"Can you fight?" I whispered.

Her eyes lit up a fierce lime green. She mouthed, yes, slipped the dagger into my hand and looked upward.

Lines of code streamed effortlessly in my mind. My mental slate filled and my body instantly reacted. I jumped, caught the metal ring that Jane hung suspended from with one hand and slashed the rope binding her ankles with the other.

Aldon shouted, "Kill the woman. Subdue the mundane!" Four of his men drew swords and ran at Jane.

Free of her bonds, Jane flipped in mid-air, landed on her feet, and grasped the steel tub. She wielded it as both a shield and a weapon, deflecting sword strikes and bashing it against the heads of the attacking Vasiles.

Energy electrified my veins, my hands a blur of motion as I swung from ring to ring and sliced the thick ropes that bound the guard's ankles and wrists in one long swipe. Without the benefit of the strange supercharged blood, they fell, crashing into the metal tubs below them. Though stunned, they were freed and, for the moment at least, alive. They scrambled to their feet, took up tubs and charged the attacking Vasiles.

I still held blood in my mouth and feared if I swallowed any more, my heart would burst, and my body would vibrate to pieces. I rushed to Braedon, grabbed him by the collar and pushed my mouth against his.

"What the fu—" He stammered for only a second, then the effects of the blood hit him. I had a few drops left and ran to Bat. His mouth opened in shock as I pulled his head toward my lips and transferred the blood from my mouth into his. His stunned expression faded to a sly smile. He licked his lips, picked up a second steel tub and, with his arms extended, spun like a giant top. The huge man's blows so forceful he tore the head off of one attacking Vasile.

The remaining Vasiles moved as a choreographed fighting force. They leaped, spun, and lunged at us with swords and knives. Keeping track of them proved challenging as they all looked strangely similar—pale, beady-eyed, with prominent noses and oily black hair.

The Vasile guarding Velvet turned to join the battle. As he did, Velvet sprang to her feet and jabbed one of the knives hidden under her sleeves into the guard's back. As he stumbled forward, she ripped the sword from his hand.

"Braedon! Catch." She threw it across the room.

He reached up and caught the sword. His eyes widened. "Vel?" A Vasile jumped into his path. Braedon ducked the man's blade, whirled and swung his sword, slicing right through the man's neck.

As they fell, we plucked weapons from their dead hands and used them to fight the ones still standing. The Vasiles moved slower tonight, or so it appeared to me, while the Haven guards without the benefit of the supercharged blood appeared to stand still. Jane, Braedon, Bat, and I pushed our men back behind us to protect them. They were already bloodied and exhausted from battling the superior Vasiles.

Now armed with a stolen sword, I rammed my dagger through one of the Vasiles' hearts and then whipped the sword across his neck and cut off his head.

The stone beneath our feet puddled with blood and the sickening stench of the dead Vasiles hung in the air. Three Vasiles remained. The lower ceiling of the room offered them no advantage. They couldn't fly above us to avoid our strikes. Instead, they formed a circle of whirling black coats and flashes of steel blades. Braedon, Bat, Jane, and I surrounded them, lunging and swinging our weapons.

Braedon charged into the spinning trio and managed to land several vicious blows to their arms and torsos. He stopped short of cutting off one's head, spun around and faced me and then thrust his sword at me.

"Braedon!" Emilia's warning flashed in my mind.

His blade grazed my leather coat as it pierced through the narrow opening under my arm. A fourth Vasile behind me fell face down on the floor, Velvet's knife still stuck in his back. I jammed the blade deeper into his body and twisted it until it impaled his heart. The metal tip scraped the stone floor. As I stood, I swung my sword over my head. A loud clang rang out as it collided with a Vasile's sword aiming for Braedon's neck. I held back his blade in mid-strike. Braedon grinned at me, swung his blade and lopped off the man's head.

The four of us converged around the remaining two Vasiles. Seconds later, bloody limbs and heads lay scattered across the floor. Jane pried a severed hand from the handle of her machete and reclaimed her weapon.

"Emilia!" Jane screamed.

Aldon stood in the doorway, his arm across Velvet's neck pinning her against his torso. He raised his cane. The line of rubies on the shaft glowed bright red. Jane shielded her face from the intense red light radiating from the cane's tip and stumbled backward.

"Your small victory will not last." Aldon said. "I will return with an army and destroy all of your kind." With his cane raised, he backed toward the door, dragging Velvet with him.

Velvet slid the second blade from beneath her long sleeve. She stabbed the dagger into Aldon's thigh, then broke free of his grasp and ran to Braedon.

Aldon smiled as he yanked the dagger from his leg and dropped it on the floor. No blood showed on his pant leg.

"Come here, girl." He aimed the cane at Velvet. She screamed as the force of it tore her from Braedon's arms and flung her onto the floor. The force dragged her body across the stone floor toward Aldon.

Braedon tried to crawl after her, but the rays proved too intense.

"No!" Jane grabbed a steel tub, held in front of her as a shield and jumped in front of Velvet.

The red stream of light flowing from the cane brightened. The bottom of steel tub bubbled and melted away. I kicked it from Jane's hands and pulled her away from the fiery rays.

Velvet's fingernails scratched at the floor in a futile attempt to stop herself. Aldon reached down, grabbed her by the back of the neck and lifted her. Her feet kicked in the air and she clawed at Aldon's hand on her throat.

Braedon rushed forward. "Let her go, you fucking bastard."

Aldon swiped his cane in the air. Braedon fell and clutched his throat.

Bat and I pulled Braedon to his feet. The red burn mark across his neck had already begun to heal. We held him back from charging at Aldon again.

Aldon released Velvet. She fell onto her knees gasping for breath. He kicked her in her side. She toppled forward onto the discarded knife Aldon had pulled from his leg.

"Get up!" he shouted.

Velvet struggled to rise to her knees, her arms hugged across her chest.

"I said get up! My seed created you. Obey me."

"Your seed?" The green light in Jane's eyes intensified. "*You* raped Isabelle? You're Emilia's father?"

Aldon's laughter bounced off the stone walls and echoed into the corridor behind him. "Rape? I purified her. Saved her from impregnation by a filthy mundane. She and her mother betrayed the Pures. And I thoroughly enjoyed hacking them to pieces." He leered at Jane. "My one regret is I didn't kill you that night, Raina."

Grabbing Velvet by the back of her hood, Aldon yanked her to her feet as he waved the cane. The force shoved us all back. He stepped into the corridor dragging Velvet with him. "The girl belongs to me."

Velvet twisted in his grasp and faced Aldon. Her hood fell back, revealing her face.

"It's you. You're Braedon's drunken whore!" Aldon glared at

Braedon. "Pathetic fool, you turned her. Wasted such power on this chattel. Females can't be trusted. Their only purpose is to breed strong males."

"Screw you." Velvet pulled the knife Aldon had discarded from under her hoodie and jabbed the sharp point through his hand. The cane fell and clattered across the stone floor, the glowing rubies flickered and then turned dark.

Jane and I leaped at the same moment. Her feet thudded against Aldon's chest, knocking him to the ground. I plunged my dagger into his heart at the same instant Jane swung her machete and severed his head from his neck.

I gently pried Jane's fingers from the handle of her machete, took the weapon from her and led her away before the spreading pool of blood from Aldon's severed neck touched her boots. Seconds ago, his angry words had echoed through the stone corridor, now he lay quiet and still on the cold floor. With the tense stand-off ended, the cave-like room took on a surreal silence. The air warm and humid, like a giant breath of relief.

Jane looked up at me, the furious green in her eyes had deepened to blue and a tortured expression haunted them. I put my arm around her and we walked from the blood-spattered room, ripe with the stench of dead Vasiles.

"This was all my fault." Jane said. "I trusted Aldon— encouraged others to trust him. He was my mentor, a father figure."

"It's not your fault, Jane. He had us all fooled."

She stopped partway down the corridor. "Velvet's been vamped? How?"

"Yeah. It's . . . a long story. I'll tell you later."

"Emilia? Angela? Where are they?"

"They're fine. I left them with Echo for the night."

"You're sure they're safe?"

I stopped by the foot of the stairs leading up to Aldon's suite, fished my cell phone from my inside pocket and pressed Echo's number.

She answered on the first ring. "Lorcan? Are you all right? And Raina?"

"We're both fine, Echo. Could you put Emilia on the phone, please?"

I handed the phone to Jane.

Jane's eyes glowed a soft lavender. She gave slight nods and a smile quivered at the corners of her mouth as she listened to Emilia. "I miss you, too. Yes, I promise, we'll see you. Tomorrow morning." She gripped my hand and smiled. "I know it's hard, but everything will be fine. Try to stay calm, Emilia." Jane tucked my phone back inside my pocket, wrapped her arms around my neck and pressed her face against my chest.

I buried my face in her silky hair and breathed in her scent. Her heartbeat vibrated against my chest until I couldn't be certain if it were mine or hers. Everything I had done was all for this moment. I'd never be separated from Jane again.

We both jumped at footsteps approaching.

Velvet, Braedon, and Demon walked toward us. The two men each gripped the handles of a steel tub they carried between them. Inside, Aldon's head lay face down on top of his crumpled body inside the large steel oval. His silvery hair, though barely mussed, was stained red with his blood.

Velvet held up her cell phone. "Weather will be clear and sunny tomorrow."

Jane and I looked at Velvet. "So?" we said in unison.

"So, we're taking the bodies up to the roof." Braedon said. "Let the sun burn these Vasile bastards to ashes."

"And hopefully get rid of their disgusting smell, too," Velvet said.

"I'll help—" I started to reach for the handle Braedon held.

Braedon gripped my shoulder with his free hand. "No way. You're the hero tonight. Saved all of our asses. You and Raina go upstairs to the club and relax. We got this."

Bat carried a tub all by himself, his girth making the tub look more like a bucket. "We cut Griff down. As far as I know, he has no family. We'll make sure he has a proper burial."

Pairs of Haven guards approached. They carried tubs filled with bloodied body parts. Each stopped to thank me or pat me on the back as they walked past and then climbed the stairs with their morbid loads. Their heartfelt expressions of gratitude made me uncomfortable.

"What's wrong?" Jane asked after the last pair ascended the stairs.

I shook my head. "I'm no hero. I never felt so helpless—scared to death. Do you know how close they came to killing all of you?"

"We were all scared, but in spite of your fear, you took action. You are a hero."

I shook my head. "It was a desperate, crazy idea. What if it hadn't worked?"

"It did. That's all that matters. I knew I could depend on you." Jane's slender fingers cupped my face. "I didn't tell you because I feared I might not return, but I should have. I love you, Tim. You know that, don't you?" She kissed me.

Her words lit up my heart and all other thoughts vanished when her lips pressed against mine. "I love you, Jane, more than anything in this world." I hugged her tighter. "Let's get out of this dungeon."

Upstairs in Aldon's suite, we washed the blood from our hands, faces, and clothes as best we could, then we went downstairs to the bar to wait for the others. I poured us both tall glasses of pomegranate juice and placed a bottle of vodka on the bar.

Jane downed the entire glass of juice in one long gulp. She walked around the bar, refilled her glass with more juice and added a healthy dose of vodka. "Whose blood did you pass to us?"

"Echo's. But it tasted different and was much more powerful than usual."

"Strange." Jane shook her head. "But you are a unique vamp, Tim. Perhaps in your heightened state, it changed the properties of her blood?"

"I don't know." I placed my glass on the bar. "This was the second time in two days Echo gave me blood. It left her weak. She said Emilia had to help her cap the bottle. And there was much more in the bottle than usual." I stared at Jane for a moment. "Emilia handed me the blood and whispered not to drink it until I faced the Vasiles. Do you think . . .?"

"She added her blood to Echo's." Jane's eyes grew wide. "Emilia told me she believes her Awakening has started. There is no blood as powerful as that of a Pure girl's first Awakening."

"Then it was Emilia who saved us," I said.

Jane reached up and stroked my cheek. "Her blood gave you extreme power, but you used that power to save us." She smiled. "You'll always be my hero."

I wrapped my arms around her and kissed her. Heat raced through my veins again like a wildfire, this time because my body longed to make love, not fight.

The Haven guards clamored down the stairs and gathered at the tables around us. I reluctantly released Jane and we poured drinks for the men. Braedon raised his glass and made a toast to Griffin. The room fell silent as we held our glasses high in tribute to our fallen friend. Once the somber moment passed, Braedon walked the room and clinked his glass against the others. "Tonight, we remember Griffin but we also celebrate a victory. We avenged his death by killing those filthy Vasiles and Aldon, the traitor. We have taken back The Haven."

"Who's going to run The Haven, now?" Velvet asked.

Braedon nodded his head toward me and raised his voice. "I nominate Lorcan and Raina as the new leaders of The Haven."

I waited until the cheers and foot stomping quieted. "Thank you. I'm honored, but no. I'm happy to be a Haven guard under Braedon's leadership." I slapped Braedon on the back and turned to Velvet. "I think Raina and Velvet should run it. After Aldon revealed his true character, it's only fitting that leadership of The Haven should pass to two strong women."

Velvet's indigo eyes sparkled as she looked around the bar. "I have so many awesome ideas for this place. New decor, music, I can't wait to get started."

"I'll help you run things a bit, Velvet, but I intend to be busy being a mother. I'll keep doing my research and continue to teach safe blood practices." Jane said. "Lorcan, Braedon, and possibly some of the others should be included in any major decisions."

"Agreed." Velvet tipped her glass against Jane's glass.

Chapter 20

"I am not what happened to me, I am what I choose to become."
—C.G. Jung

One month later

Jane floated downward until her body touched the bed. I landed on top of her, not quite as gracefully.

"You're going to be bored by the time we go on our honeymoon."

"Never." I nuzzled my face in the curve of her neck. We had made love every day since Jane returned. "Vampire sex is different. I need practice."

"I think you've figured it out quite well." Jane giggled as she pushed me off her. "We better hurry. Our wedding, remember?"

"We have time." I nibbled on her earlobe and ran my hand down the silky skin of her leg.

She shooed me away and sat up. The bed lay in a shamble of twisted sheets and blankets. "I need to shower and dress. Not to mention getting the girls ready."

I sighed and stood up. "They were all packed last night. Emilia will help Angela get dressed."

Jane bent and picked up pillows from the bedroom floor. "I know, but I don't want to stress Emilia. She's so worried about Angela."

"Since her Awakening, Emilia's been a little overdramatic."

"A little?" Jane laughed. "I warned you a preteen vamp would be a challenge."

I shrugged "I think Angela's fine. Besides, what's the worst that could happen? We'll just raise two vamp daughters."

Jane rolled her eyes and walked off into the shower.

While she was still incredibly smart and mature for her age, Emilia struggled to control the cauldron of emotions bubbling inside her. She had broken down in tears when Jane and I arrived at Echo's to pick up the girls the morning after the battle. When Jane asked, Emilia cried and then finally admitted she added her blood to Echo's. I already knew. I felt the blood bond between us. I hugged her and whispered thank you. Her lips never moved, but I clearly heard, *you are welcome, Papa*. It was the first time she called me Papa.

For days after, Emilia suffered intense crying jags. Finally, through ragged sobs, she confided the true cause of her distress. Angela had seen the cut on her hand before it healed and kissed it, "to make it better." I cringed when Emilia told us, as I had taught Angela the concept by kissing her scraped elbow. Emilia feared the tiny bit of blood Angela tasted would transform the little girl into a vampire.

We knew nothing of Angela's parentage or how she ended up in the remote Romanian orphanage. Jane explained that Angela was too young and therefore immune to the effects of vampire blood. But Emilia wasn't convinced. She said Angela was different and now she had made things worse. No matter how many times we asked, Emilia refused to elaborate on what she meant by "different".

For weeks we all kept a close watch on Angela, but other than a rapidly growing English vocabulary and an overabundance of cuteness, she showed no signs of unusual behavior.

I pulled on a pair of jeans and a T-shirt. My new suit hung on our bedroom closet door next to Jane's lavender dress, both encased in clear plastic. The dress matched her eyes, at least most of the time. She had waffled between the lavender and a blue dress in the store. Every time she looked to me for approval, her eyes turned a luminous shade of violet. I teased that she should buy a green dress as well, in case I pissed her off on our wedding day.

The girls were thrilled when we told them about the upcoming wedding. They both had a deep need for the security of a real family.

Angela pranced around the house and tossed scraps of paper in lieu of rose petals from a beribboned wicker basket in anticipation of her role as flower girl at our wedding.

Emilia, with tears of happiness glistening in her eyes, agreed to be one of Jane's bridesmaids. She chose a deep purple dress, slightly more colorful than her usual black attire. The other two bridesmaids, Velvet and Echo, bought jewel-toned dresses to match.

Emilia wasn't the only emotional vamp. Braedon also teared up when I asked him to be my best man. We had started out like two pit bulls facing off in a ring but had become the best of friends. Though he was the leader of the guards, he treated me as an equal now. He was my first true male friend.

Bat and Demon were my other groomsmen. Polar opposites physically and in their personalities, I considered both close friends as well as fellow guards.

My cell phone rang as I headed down the hall toward the girls' room.

"Hey, Mom."

"Oh, sweetheart, the cake just arrived. I can't wait for you two to see it. It's so elegant. Jane will love it. And the weather looks beautiful for this evening. Now, what time will you all be here?'

"Five o'clock, Mom." I smiled, as this was her fourth phone call in two days to confirm our arrival time.

"Okay, good. Sunset is at six forty-three, so you'll have plenty of time to dress. I think it's so romantic taking your vows by candlelight. Oh, I need to check that all the candles are in place. We have your old room all set up for the girls. So much to think about, but I'm having so much fun."

"We really appreciate all you and Dad have done for our wedding. Plus watching the girls for two weeks."

"It's our pleasure. We can't wait to see all of you again. Your father bought some more flowers. He's going to let Angela plant her own little garden. He mowed the lawn this morning."

I laughed. "I'm sure he did."

"And the minister, Tristan's his name, correct? Does he have directions?"

"Yes, Mom. Tristan, the bridesmaids and groomsmen all have directions." When Jane informed me Tristan was a minster, I readily agreed to have him perform our ceremony. It meant a lot to Jane, he was like an older brother to her. And the fact he was bringing Wynn,

The Haven's doorman, as his date went a long way to quell any leftover jealousy I held toward him.

As we ended the call, I wondered what Mom and Dad would think of Braedon, Velvet, and the other vamps. Hopefully they would take to them as quickly as they had to Jane.

Our first visit to their house had my older brother's jaw on the ground and my dad speechless when they first saw Jane. All Steve-O junior could do was stutter in front of Jane and later babble to me about how gorgeous she was. My dad was also in awe of Jane, but equally stunned by my enhanced appearance. He kept asking me how many times a week I worked out in the gym. I jokingly called Steve-O puny. Dad laughed, but then turned to my older brother and suggested he step up his workouts.

Mom looked surprised when she first saw me, but then only pleased when she determined I was both healthy and happy. "I told you, Steven," she said to Dad with a condescending nod, "Tim is a late bloomer."

Their shock and awe at Jane's incredible beauty and my physical transformation was only overshadowed by their genuine delight with the girls.

Angela had my dad twisted around her tiny pinky in record time. She held his hand and they strolled through the gardens in the back yard while he named the flowers and she repeated after him like a parrot. Later, she curled up next to him on the sofa while he read from one of my old storybooks that Mom had kept.

Emilia charmed my mom with her articulate speech and intelligence. Her thirst for knowledge ranged from asking my mom about her cooking techniques all the way to questions about her career as a nurse. I smiled when my mom told Emilia to take her time and choose a career she loved, the same advice she'd given me when I was Emilia's age.

This would be our third visit in one month and a special one at that. When I called Mom and told her Jane accepted my proposal she had immediately kicked into wedding-planner mode. Jane and I politely declined the huge soiree Mom envisioned at their country club. Instead we decided on a casual ceremony with my family and our close friends. At first, we considered The Haven's rooftop for

350

the venue, but then Mom and Dad offered us their patio and garden. Planning the ceremony at sunset was for our comfort and the other vamps. Mom thought it was romantic.

My parents refused to accept money from us for the wedding, insisting it was their gift to us. So instead, I used my first royalty check from my video game to start college funds for the girls and bought a new truck. The king cab accommodated the girls comfortably and I made sure it was outfitted with the darkest window-tinting legally allowed so sunlight no longer toasted my hands and face. My sequel video game would start production in the fall. Both Echo and I would be well-set financially by winter.

Jane walked outside, her arms loaded with shimmery dresses wrapped in plastic. I laid her gown and the girls' dresses on top of my suit inside the truck bed beside our luggage and other sundries we had packed for our trip.

Emilia followed, toting two cat carriers. Bat had let each girl choose a kitten from a litter of strays he had saved. Angela chose a jet-black kitten while Emilia was immediately drawn to a fluffy gold and white one. It wasn't lost on Jane or me that their choices mirrored their kinship with each other and each quickly formed a bond with her kitten, especially Angela.

Angela ran behind Emilia and pressed her face against the metal grill of her kitten's carrier. She whispered something and the kitten's frightened mews immediately changed to a loud purr.

I slid the two carriers into the middle of the back seat. The girls and their cats would spend the next two weeks at my parents' house while Jane and I honeymooned in Hawaii.

I rearranged the items in the truck bed for the hundredth time to make room for Angela's flower basket which Jane had finally pried from the little girl's hands. Even in the large truck, space was tight for a family of four. I removed the flat cardboard box I had transferred from my Camry's trunk. It contained James Samples' suit. While Jane and the girls ran inside the house to check that they had not forgotten anything, I fiddled with Google maps on my phone under the shade of the portico. I placed the suit box on the front seat and then found a pen in my glove compartment and wrote on the outside of the box.

Several minutes later the girls finally emerged, and Jane locked the front door.

"Let's get going." I lifted Angela into the back seat while Emilia climbed into the other side.

"We're a little early," Jane said as I settled into the driver's seat.

"I know, but I need to make a quick stop on the way to my parents'."

"Where?" Jane asked.

I read from my phone screen, "Sixty-three Sable Drive."

"What's that?"

"Sarah Samples' house." I patted the box between us on the seat. "I need to return James' suit."

Jane smiled as she read the note I had written on the box, her eyes glowed with that amazing amethyst color I loved.

Please forgive me for borrowing the Professor's suit. He knew how special this suit was and now, so do I. It should be kept by his loved ones and cherished always. I want you to know, Sarah, James' suit changed my life forever. Because of it, I found love and happiness beyond my dreams.

"You promised you'd return the suit to her. You do have a noble character." Jane leaned over and kissed my cheek. "Any other stops you plan to make?"

"Well, not today, but one of these days I need to go to the Thrifty Lube in Sago Palm Park and get my oil changed."

"That's hours away. Why drive so far for an oil change?"

"The manager there, Chris Bagwell, gave me a coupon." I punched my fist against my open hand and grinned. "I think it's time I redeemed it."

Jane shook her head. "I think we both need to visit the Black Swan when Lorelei and her group are back in town. She needs to learn the rules of being a vampire." Her eyes flashed green, then returned to their lavender blue.

I started up the truck and glanced in the rear-view mirror as I shifted into reverse. Emilia hunched over the new tablet on her lap engrossed with one of the hundreds of books Jane had downloaded for her to read. Angela looked up and smiled at me. Her eyes glowed a bright yellow green, her pupils thin black lines. She hugged her kitten in her lap, its eyes a startling bright blue in contrast to its pure black fur.

I stomped on the brake pedal.

"What's wrong?" Jane asked. She twisted around in her seat and followed my frozen gaze.

Angela's kitten cuddled its tiny head under her chin.

"Oh, no Sweetie, the cat has to stay in its carrier while we're driving," Jane said. "It's not safe for her to be loose inside the truck."

Jane leaned over the seat, scooped the kitten back into its carrier and secured the latch. "You can take her out when we get to Grandma and Grandpa's house."

Angela sat with her bottom lip stuck out in a pout, her small arms crossed over her chest.

"Did you see that?" I whispered to Jane.

"See what?"

I checked the mirror again. Angela wiggled her small fingers and waved at me. Her wide eyes had returned to their normal crystal blue. The kitten mewed, its eyes now green and wide behind the mesh of the cage.

Had I imagined it?

I blew out a long sigh. "Nothing. Never mind." No point in worrying Jane right before our wedding. Whatever it was, I knew as long as Jane and I were together, we could handle it.

Human, vamp, or otherwise, Angela held my heart and melted it every time she called me Papa. I smiled at my two daughters in the back seat and then reached over and squeezed Jane's hand.

"Let's go get married."

Also by Chris Holmes

Light a Candle, Chase the Devil Away,
Paranormalice Press, LLC

Inky, a short story. Nice neighborhood; bad cat.

Available at Amazon.com